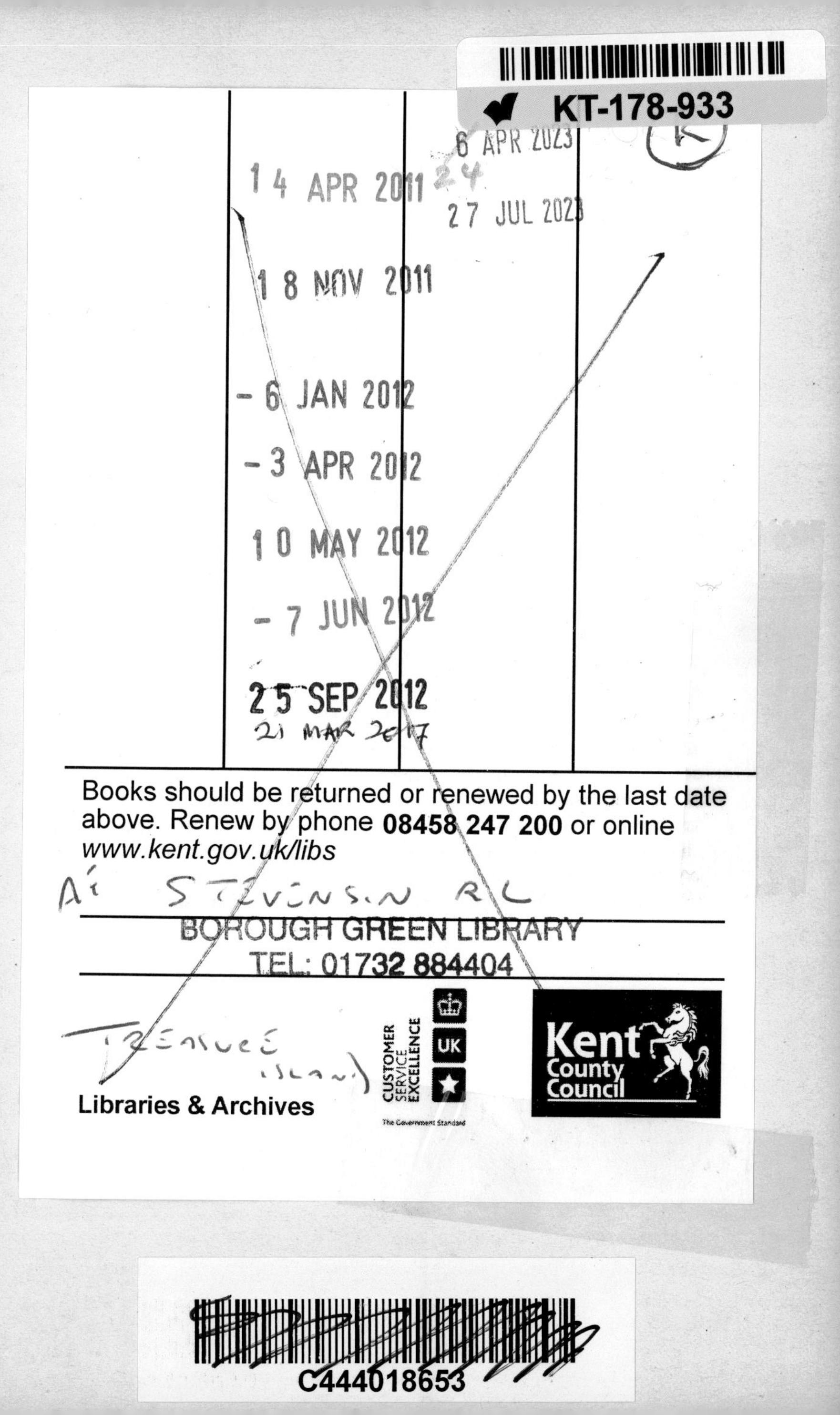

OXFORD WORLD'S CLASSICS

For over 100 years Oxford World's Classics have brought readers closer to the world's great literature. Now with over 700 titles—from the 4,000-year-old myths of Mesopotamia to the twentieth century's greatest novels—the series makes available lesser-known as well as celebrated writing.

The pocket-sized hardbacks of the early years contained introductions by Virginia Woolf, T. S. Eliot, Graham Greene, and other literary figures which enriched the experience of reading. Today the series is recognized for its fine scholarship and reliability in texts that span world literature, drama and poetry, religion, philosophy, and politics. Each edition includes perceptive commentary and essential background information to meet the changing needs of readers.

OXFORD WORLD'S CLASSICS

ROBERT LOUIS STEVENSON

Treasure Island

Edited with an Introduction and Notes by

PETER HUNT

Great Clarendon Street, Oxford ox2 6DP
Oxford University Press is a department of the University of Oxford.
It furthers the University's objective of excellence in research, scholarship,
and education by publishing worldwide in

Oxford New York

Auckland Cape Town Dar es Salaam Hong Kong Karachi
Kuala Lumpur Madrid Melbourne Mexico City Nairobi
New Delhi Shanghai Taipei Toronto

With offices in

Argentina Austria Brazil Chile Czech Republic France Greece
Guatemala Hungary Italy Japan Poland Portugal Singapore
South Korea Switzerland Thailand Turkey Ukraine Vietnam

Oxford is a registered trade mark of Oxford University Press
in the UK and in certain other countries

Published in the United States
by Oxford University Press Inc., New York

First published as a World's Classics paperback 1985
Reissued 1998, 2008.
New edition 2011

British Library Cataloguing in Publication Data
Data available

Library of Congress Cataloging in Publication Data
Data available

Typeset by Glyph International, Bangalore, India
Printed in Great Britain
on acid-free paper by
Clays Ltd, St Ives plc

ISBN 978-0-19-956035-6

CONTENTS

INTRODUCTION

Treasure Island is a rarity: a classic that has high status in both the children's and the adults' canons. George Meredith described it as 'The best of boys' books, and a book to make one feel a boy again', while Henry James thought it was 'unique' in that we see in it the young reader himself: 'we seem to read it over his shoulder, with an arm around his neck'.[1]

In the history of children's literature it is a landmark, a turning point: just as Lewis Carroll's *Alice's Adventures in Wonderland* (1865) redefined the book for girls, siding with its readers against the didactic and moralistic, so *Treasure Island* (1883) challenged, satirized, and subverted the dominant boys' genre that combined adventure, sea, island, and empire-building stories. The story of an expedition 'launched by greed and decorated with murder and treachery, and concluded by luck rather than righteousness',[2] it permanently changed the possibilities of children's literature, and challenged received wisdom about what a book for a child is and what a book for an adult is. It is often assumed that child readers see only an exciting story, while adults detect the ironic anti-romance and the startling ambiguities of character and motive. But it could also be argued, as with other books that are routinely underestimated by adults, such as *The Wind in the Willows*, that the opposite is the case. It seems probable that many adults go to *Treasure Island* to create, rather than recreate, an imaginary childhood reading experience—to read a straightforward, simple adventure of vicarious thrills and uncomplicated morality, where you can kill the pirates with impunity, and take the treasure home to 'play ducks and drakes' with. And it may be that it is the developing reader who is brought up short by (and intellectually nurtured by) the dark and unsettling side of the book which questions accepted attitudes to good and evil. How Stevenson went about playing with the materials of the genre and the idea of the romance, while balancing an ironic mindset, religious and political tensions, and the immediate

[1] *The Letters of George Meredith*, ed. C. L. Cline (Oxford: Clarendon Press, 1970), ii. 730; Henry James, *Partial Portraits* (London: Macmillan, 1894), 68.

[2] F. J. Harvey Darton, *Children's Books in England*, 3rd edn., rev. Brian Alderson (Cambridge: Cambridge University Press, 1982), 295.

exigencies of a very local audience and the need to earn money, is one of the most fascinating tales in literature.

Culturally, *Treasure Island* has come almost to define the adventure story, and its image of pirates and buccaneers resonates in popular culture to this day. As one of Stevenson's biographers puts it: '*Dr Jekyll and Mr Hyde* and *Treasure Island* are so well-known that they hardly require to be read at all. We all understand what "Jekyll-and-Hyde" signifies, and Long John Silver is more real to most people than any historical buccaneer.'[3] Certainly, Long John Silver, '[t]hat formidable seafaring man with one leg' (p. 182) has acquired a mythic status: Sir Arthur Conan Doyle described him as 'not a creation of fiction, but an organic living reality with whom we have come into contact; such is the effect of the fine suggestive strokes with which he is drawn'.[4] *Treasure Island* was the immediate stimulus for H. Rider Haggard's *King Solomon's Mines* (1885)—Haggard's brother bet him a shilling that he couldn't 'write anything half so good'—and directly influenced J. M. Barrie, Rafael Sabatini, and Arthur Ransome. It has inspired writers from Jorge Luis Borges to John Mortimer, and lies behind such twenty-first-century phenomena as *Pirates of the Caribbean*. There are translations into languages across the world, and adaptations for film and television (around fifty versions), musicals, pantomime, graphic novels, and video games. Prequels, sequels, and elaborations (often centring on Long John Silver) range from R. F. Delderfield's *The Adventures of Ben Gunn* (1956) and Robert Leeson's *Silver's Revenge* (1978) to the surreal *Pussy, King of the Pirates* (1996) by experimental novelist Kathy Acker.

But despite, or perhaps because of, its popularity, *Treasure Island* has until recently been neglected by the critics: not only was it for children, a fact that almost axiomatically removed it from the critical radar—but it was (at least at first glance) a 'romance'. As Stevenson wryly observed in 'A Gossip on Romance' (*Longman's Magazine*, November 1882): 'English people of the present day are apt, I know not why, to look somewhat down on incident, and reserve their admiration for the clink of teaspoons and the accents of the curate.

[3] Claire Harman, *Robert Louis Stevenson: A Biography* (London: HarperCollins, 2005), xvi.

[4] Sir Arthur Conan Doyle, 'Mr Stevenson's Methods in Fiction' (*National Review*, Jan. 1890), in Lance Salway (ed.), *A Peculiar Gift: Nineteenth Century Writings on Books for Children* (Harmondsworth: Kestrel, 1976), 396.

It is thought clever to write a novel with no story at all, or at least with a very dull one.'[5]

The contemporary reviewers could not square this circle. A review, probably by Andrew Lang, in the *Pall Mall Gazette* (15 December 1883), described *Treasure Island* as 'a book for boys which can keep hardened and elderly reviewers in a state of pleasing excitement and attention', but concluded that 'after this romance for boys he must give us a novel for men and women'. On the same day, a review in the *Graphic* agreed on the book's excellence, but added: 'Yet we want no more boys' books from Mr Stevenson. We want him to employ his unique gifts in the highest department of literature now open to him—contemporary fiction.'[6] Even J. M. Barrie had his reservations. In his portrait of his mother, *Margaret Ogilvy*, he reported: 'I remember how she read "Treasure Island", holding it close to the ribs of the fire (because she could not spare a moment to rise and light the gas) and how, when bedtime came, and we coaxed, remonstrated, scolded, she said quite fiercely, clinging to the book, "I dinna lay my head on a pillow this night till I see how that laddie got out of the barrel." ' He admitted himself that 'Over "Treasure Island" I let my fire die in winter without knowing I was freezing'; but his verdict on Stevenson was that 'it is so much easier to finish the little works than to begin the great one . . . He experiments too long; he is still a boy wondering what he is going to be.'[7]

Stevenson's reputation suffered through much of the twentieth century: he was seen as an empty stylist, a lightweight in inferior genres: 'because he chose to work in kinds thought low, he has been fired from the canon'.[8] His fame rested on two boys' books, *Treasure Island* and *Kidnapped* (1886), and a literary curiosity, *Strange Case of Dr Jekyll and Mr Hyde* (1886) which (equally curiously) often appears on publishers' children's lists. There are some parallels

[5] Robert Louis Stevenson, *Memories and Portraits*, in *The Works of Robert Louis Stevenson*, Tusitala Edition (London: Heinemann in association with Chatto and Windus, Cassell, and Longmans Green, 1924), xxix. 124.

[6] Paul Maixner (ed.), *Robert Louis Stevenson: The Critical Heritage* (London: Routledge and Kegan Paul, 1981), 139, 141.

[7] J. M. Barrie, *Margaret Ogilvy* (New York: Scribner, 1896), 145; *An Edinburgh Eleven: Pencil Portraits from College Life* (1889) (London: Hodder and Stoughton, 1897), 98, 99.

[8] Alastair Fowler, 'Parables of Adventure: The Debatable Novels of Robert Louis Stevenson', in Ian Campbell (ed.), *Nineteenth-Century Scottish Fiction* (Manchester: Carcanet New Press, 1979), 107.

between Stevenson's recent critical reinstatement and the admission of children's literature to serious literary study, and critics have come to appreciate Northrop Frye's dictum that 'romance is older than the novel, a fact which has developed the historical illusion that it is something to be outgrown, a juvenile and undeveloped form'.[9] It is no longer tenable to suggest that *Treasure Island* is valuable only in proportion to the extent that it transcended and transformed its generic origins and that it can only be genuinely valuable in so far as it appeals to 'sophisticated' adults. Equally, to regard it as a children's book is no longer to denigrate it, or to denigrate the acuity of child readers. *Treasure Island* transcends the boundaries between children's books and adults' books just as it transcends the boundaries between the novel and the romance. It may be a *jeu d'esprit*, but at no point is the author's critical and personal intelligence asleep; as one biographer argues: 'Louis brought so much of himself to *Treasure Island* that it is hard to speak of the book except in terms of his life . . . It was the world as Stevenson's imagination understood it.'[10]

Biography and Background

In an article, 'My First Book', written at the request of Jerome K. Jerome for his magazine *The Idler* (August 1894; reprinted here as Appendix 1), Stevenson described his situation when he began to write *Treasure Island*: 'I was thirty-one; I was the head of a family; I had lost my health; I had never yet paid my way, never yet made £200 a year . . . I was indeed very close on despair' (p. 189). *Treasure Island* was both the distillation of and the turning point of his career.

Stevenson was born in 1850, into a famous family: his grandfather was the engineer and lighthouse builder Robert Stevenson, and his father Thomas, and his uncles Alan and David followed that profession. Robert Louis (christened Lewis) was a sickly child, and his upbringing was sheltered. It was (notoriously) governed by his nanny, Alison Cunningham ('Cummy'), whose extreme Free Church views had a lasting (and morbid) effect on Stevenson's imagination, and which may have sown the seeds of his lifelong

[9] Northrop Frye, *Anatomy of Criticism: Four Essays* (Princeton: Princeton University Press, 1957), 306.

[10] Ian Bell, *Robert Louis Stevenson: Dreams of Exile, A Biography* (Edinburgh: Mainstream, 1992), 165.

religious rebelliousness. His stepson, Lloyd Osbourne (although not always the most reliable biographer), reported on Stevenson's consequent views on child-rearing:

A child should early gain some perception of what the world really is like—its baseness, its treacheries, its thinly veneered brutalities; he should learn to judge people, and discount human frailty and weakness, and be in some degree prepared and armed for taking his part later in the battle of life. I have no patience with this fairy-tale training that makes ignorance a virtue. That was how I was brought up, and no one will ever know except myself the bitter misery it cost me.[11]

There was another long-lasting childhood influence, which certainly surfaces in *Treasure Island*: the cardboard toy theatre. Stevenson, who shared an enthusiasm for these with the likes of Charles Dickens, Aubrey Beardsley, and Ellen Terry, wrote enthusiastically in 'A Penny Plain and Twopence Coloured' (*The Magazine of Art*, April 1884) about the 'stagey and piratic Skelt', publisher of 'Skelt's Juvenile Drama'. 'Every sheet we fingered was another lightning glance into obscure, delicious story; it was like wallowing in the raw stuff of story-books . . . here is the inn (the drama must be nautical, I foresee Captain Luff and Bold Bob Bowsprit) with the red curtains, pipes, spittoons and eight-day clock.' G. K. Chesterton felt that for many years Skelt's 'peepshow' remained for Stevenson 'the true window of the world'.[12]

A third major factor in Stevenson's life was his complex relationship with his father; he was at once rebellious, unwillingly dependent, and affectionate. Several critics have seen *Treasure Island*, and Jim Hawkins's tortuous relationship with Long John Silver, as an extended meditation on this. For example, the scene in which Jim is surrounded by the pirates, and shows the kind of pluck so conspicuous in his fictional forebears in facing down Long John, has been read as part of a classic Freudian scenario: 'the representation of the adolescent confronted by a castrating father-figure who, however, already bears the marks of a son's desire to turn the tables on him by being himself maimed, that is symbolically emasculated'.[13]

[11] Lloyd Osbourne, 'Stevenson at Thirty-Two', *Works* (1923), vol. ii, pp. xv–xvi.

[12] *Memories and Portraits*, xxix. 104, 107, 108; 18. G. K. Chesterton, *Robert Louis Stevenson* (London: Hodder and Stoughton, 1927), 95. See also George Speaight, *The History of the English Toy Theatre*, 2nd edn. (London: Studio Vista, 1969).

[13] Alan Sandison, *Robert Louis Stevenson and the Appearance of Modernism: A Future Feeling* (Basingstoke: Macmillan, 1996), 52.

Be that as it may, Thomas Stevenson tried to persuade his son to become an engineer, and when that failed, to become an advocate. Stevenson, however, chose to train himself as a writer, acquiring a reputation as an essayist, notably in the *Cornhill Magazine*; its editor, Leslie Stephen, introduced him to W. E. Henley. A collection, *Virginibus Puerisque*, was published in 1881. Such was Stevenson's reputation for this lightly philosophical kind of writing that when, in 1893, Kenneth Grahame published a not dissimilar collection of essays, *Pagan Papers* (many of which had first appeared in Henley's *National Observer*), a reviewer noted that he was 'only one in a crowd, only one in a generation who turns out a "Stevensonette" as easily and as lightly as it rolls a cigarette'.[14] Despite the *succès d'estime* of two travel books, *An Inland Voyage* (1878) and *Travels with a Donkey* (1879), Stevenson remained reliant on his father for money.

The Writing and Publication of Treasure Island

In 1879, despite very poor health, Stevenson travelled to California, where he married Fanny Osbourne; August 1881 found them, with Fanny's son Samuel Lloyd Osbourne (then known as Sam) and Stevenson's parents, staying at a cottage in Braemar. It was here that *Treasure Island* (and the myth of *Treasure Island*) was begun. Just as *Alice's Adventures in Wonderland* and *The Wind in the Willows* have accumulated a certain romance about their beginnings, so *Treasure Island*'s beginnings have been embroidered. It certainly seems to have begun with a map, but whether it was one drawn by Lloyd (as Lloyd claimed) or by Stevenson (as Stevenson claimed) has been debated. What is clear is that the book was under way by 25 August, when Stevenson wrote to Henley (using some phrases that have become bywords in the study of children's books):

> I am now on another lay for the moment, purely owing to Sam; but I do believe there is more coin in it than in any amount of crawlers [horror stories]: now, see here
>
> The Sea Cook
> Or Treasure Island:
> A Story for Boys.

[14] Patrick R. Chalmers, *Kenneth Grahame: Life, Letters and Unpublished Work* (London: Methuen, 1933), 48.

If this don't fetch the kids, why, they have gone rotten since my day. Will you be surprised to learn that it is about Buccaneers, that it begins in the Admiral Benbow public house on [the] Devon coast, that it's all about a map and a treasure and a mutiny and a derelict ship and a current and a fine old Squire Trelawney . . . and a doctor and another doctor, and a Sea Cook with one leg, and a sea song with the chorus 'Yo-ho-ho and a bottle of Rum'. . . . No women in the story: Sam's orders and who so blythe to obey? It's awful fun boy's stories; you just indulge the pleasure of your heart; that's all. No trouble. No stress. No writing, just drive along as the words come and the pen will scratch! The only stiff thing is to get it ended; that I don't see, but I look to a volcano . . . It's quite silly and horrid fun—and what I want is the *best* book about Buccaneers that can be had—the later B's above all, Blackbeard and sich.[15]

Henley seems to have obliged by sending Captain Charles Johnson's *A General History of the Robberies and Murders of the Most Notorious Pyrates, and also their Policies, Discipline and Government, from their First Rise and Settlement in the Island of Providence, in 1717, to the Present Year 1724*. For many years attributed to Daniel Defoe, this book lies behind many of the ideas about pirates that exist today; it provided Stevenson with not only names for characters (Morgan, Israel Hands), but references to real pirates (Blackbeard, Edwards) and incidents ('the fishing up of the wrecked plate ships') which lend his book an air of authenticity. Perhaps most importantly, Stevenson found the material on the 'Articles' or codes of behaviour of the pirates, the curiously inverted set of 'laws' and customs that chime so well with the ironies of the novel. They appear to provide a subcultural parody of the normative middle-class codes of behaviour, and yet those middle-class codes are slowly revealed as both self-serving and selective. Silver says to the pirates: 'I know the rules, I do; I won't hurt a depytation' (p. 152), but Captain Smollett and his respectable followers won't help Silver to get up when he comes to them under the flag of truce, and let him crawl (p. 108).

At Braemar, Stevenson wrote the first nineteen chapters (according to a letter to Henley in September[16]) or fifteen (according to 'My First Book') at great speed, if not actually a chapter a day. He confessed to Henley: 'I have all my work cut out to write my daily

[15] *The Letters of Robert Louis Stevenson*, ed. Bradford A. Booth and Ernest Mehew (New Haven: Yale University Press, 1994–5), iii. 225.

[16] *Ibid.* 231.

chapter of *The Sea Cook*. We are away at sea now, which vilely bores me.'[17] His wife, Fanny, did not like it: she wrote to Mrs Edmund Gosse: 'I'm glad Mr Gosse liked "Treasure Island" . . . I don't. I liked the beginning but after that the life seemed to go out of it and it became tedious.'[18] The manuscript was taken away by a visitor, Alexander Japp, who showed it to James Henderson, publisher of the magazine *Young Folks*, which had begun life in 1871 as *Our Young Folks' Weekly Budget*, and sold at ½*d*. When Stevenson saw a copy of it he was not impressed: 'What bosh the stories are—I mean the two I have looked at! 'cré nom! Surely mine should do in such company.' Henderson bought the serial rights, and Stevenson, despite his habit of not finishing books that he was writing, optimistically allowed the serial to begin publication before the book was complete. He wrote to Japp on 6 September: 'I do not think there will be any difficulty in letting him go ahead whenever he likes.'[19]

Inspiration, or concentration, lapsed (Stevenson much preferred to paint a toy theatre for Sam), and it was not until the family arrived at Davros in Switzerland, where they were staying for the winter for Stevenson's health, that the book was finished. Even then, as Fanny remarked, 'the work was taken up, but intermittently. Had it not been appearing as a serial, I doubt if it would have been finished.'[20] Stevenson was paid £34 7*s*. 6*d*., and the serial, under the title *Treasure Island* (by Captain George North), duly appeared, with moderate success. (A Captain Nathaniel North appears in *The History of the Pyrates*: son of a sawyer, he was first a ship's cook, then buccaneer.[21]) Stevenson, although in need of money, made no attempt to publish it in book form, and it was W. E. Henley, then editor of Cassell's *The Magazine of Art*, who (according to Sir Newman Flower, later director of Cassell) 'entered the room of the chief editor, threw the cuttings of "The Sea Cook" . . . on to his desk, and exclaimed in his

[17] *Letters*, 226.

[18] Quoted by James Pope Hennessey, *Robert Louis Stevenson* (London: Cape, 1974), 154; and see Frank McLynn, *Robert Louis Stevenson: A Biography* (London: Hutchinson, 1993), 197.

[19] *Letters*, iii. 228.

[20] 'Prefatory Note [to *Treasure Island*] by Mrs R. L. Stevenson', *Works* (1923), vol. ii, p. xxi; and compare Stevenson's account, p. 189.

[21] [Daniel Defoe], *A General History of the Pyrates*, ed. Manuel Schonhorn (Mineola, NY: Dover, 1999), 511.

usual abrupt manner, "There's a book for you!" '[22] Henley negotiated a fee of £100 plus royalties of £20 per thousand copies sold (which were paid until 1944) and Stevenson wrote in delight to his parents on 5 May 1883: 'A hundred pounds, all alive, oh! A hundred jingling, tingling, golden, minted quid. Is this not wonderful?'[23]

On 26 January 1882, he wrote to his father, 'You may be pleased to hear that I mean to re-write *Treasure Island* in the whole latter part, lightening and *siccating* throughout . . . I mean to cut down like a fiend.'[24] He made some effort to revise the novel for book publication (see Note on the Text), but generally resisted his father's suggestions that a little more piety would be in order. Stevenson's ambivalent feelings about his father, and his rebellion against his religious upbringing, are deeply embedded in the book; he wanted to please his father, but could only compromise so far on his own beliefs.

Treasure Island was well, if occasionally patronizingly, received, although the Chicago *Dial* observed that 'the effort to recover a pirate's buried treasure . . . is neither dignified nor edifying. It will be relished by adventure-loving boys, but whether it will be wholesome reading for them is more than doubtful'.[25] An early biographer noted that 'Statesmen and judges and all sorts of staid and sober men became boys once more, sitting up long after bedtime to read their new book'. These included Gladstone, of whom Stevenson did not approve, and he wrote to his mother in December 1884: 'It appears Gladstone talks all the time about *Treasure Island*; he would do better to attend to the imperial affairs of England.' W. B. Yeats wrote that his seafaring grandfather read *Treasure Island* 'upon his death-bed with infinite satisfaction'.[26]

Treasure Island sold only 5,600 copies in the first year and averaged around 4,500 a year until 1897[27] but it was Stevenson's first step

[22] Quoted in Roger G. Swearingen, *The Prose Writings of Robert Louis Stevenson: A Guide* (London: Macmillan, 1980), 67.

[23] *Letters*, iv. 119–20.

[24] *Ibid.* iii. 276.

[25] Maixner (ed.), *Critical Heritage*, 42.

[26] Graham Balfour, *The Life of Robert Louis Stevenson* (London: Methuen, 1913), 211; *Letters*, v. 33 n. 2; 49; J. C. Furnas, *Voyage to Windward: The Life of Robert Louis Stevenson* (London: Faber and Faber, 1952), 181.

[27] Stephen Gwynn, *Robert Louis Stevenson* (London: Macmillan, 1939), 105; Christopher Harvie, 'The Politics of Stevenson', in Jenni Calder (ed.), *Stevenson and Victorian Scotland* (Edinburgh: Edinburgh University Press, 1981), 108.

towards financial independence and genuine literary fame, and when *Strange Case of Dr Jekyll and Mr Hyde* was published his reputation and financial stability were assured.

Treasure Island *and the History of Children's Literature*

In the introductory verse to *Treasure Island*, 'To the Hesitating Purchaser', Stevenson claims that his is a traditional sea story, 'all the old romance, retold | Exactly in the ancient way', placing himself in the tradition of Kingston, Ballantyne, and Cooper. In 'My First Book' he admits to plagiarizing Defoe, Poe, Marryat, and Washington Irving (although, as with almost all Stevenson's pronouncements on the book, both of these statements need to be approached with some care). *Treasure Island* is clearly a source-hunter's paradise, a densely layered texture of borrowings and echoes, but the genre Stevenson was working with was not as monolithic as is often supposed. To claim that he 'jettisoned, without a thought, all the moral attitudes which previous writers for children had thought it proper to maintain . . . blurring . . . the usual black-and-white of right and wrong' is to over-simplify.[28]

The history of children's literature in the nineteenth century was characterized by two overlapping trends. The first was the move away from didacticism and religion towards fantasy and secularism; the second was the development of the distinction between books for girls and books for boys (given that both were widely read by adults). Broadly speaking, girls' books looked inwards, either to social benevolence or the life of the imagination, embracing folk- and fairy-tales; boys' books looked outward to conquest and active adventure, developing a symbiotic relationship with nationalism, capitalism, and codes of behaviour rooted in a combination of religion and commercialism.

One of the earliest genres to be adopted by writers for boys was the island story, which from Shakespeare's *The Tempest* to Defoe's *Robinson Crusoe* (1719) had crossed the exotic and the adventurous with strong mercantile, religious, and racial ideologies; merging with the travel book and the sea story, this was ideal material for the literature of empire. *Robinson Crusoe*, much imitated and soon adapted for

[28] John Rowe Townsend, *Written for Children* (Harmondsworth: Kestrel, 1974), 65–6.

children, transmuted into Johann Wyss's *The Swiss Family Robinson* (English translation by William Godwin 1816), and thence, via Captain Marryat, into a new genre. In the 'Preface' to his *Masterman Ready* (1841) Marryat objected to the inaccuracies in Wyss's book:

I pass over the seamanship, or want of it . . . as that is not a matter of any consequence: as in the comedy, where, when people did not understand Greek, Irish did just as well, so it is with a large portion of the seamanship displayed in naval writing. But what compelled me to abandon the task [of writing a sequel, as his children had asked] was that much ignorance, or carelessness had been displayed in describing the vegetable and animal productions of the island on which the family had been wrecked. The island is supposed to be far to the southward, near to Van Dieman's land; yet in these temperate latitudes we have not only plants, but animals introduced, which could only be found in the interior of Africa or the torrid zone, mixed up with those really indigenous to the climate. This was an error that I could not persuade myself to follow up. It is true that it is a child's book; but I consider, for that very reason, it is necessary that the author should be particular in what may appear to be trifles, but which really are not, when it is remembered how strong the impressions are upon the juvenile mind. Fiction, when written for young children should, at all events, be *based* on truth.

He would not have approved of Stevenson's approach to the flora and fauna, which was at best anachronistic, and at worst (in Marryat's terms) cavalier. The vegetation of Treasure Island is not Caribbean (as it should be, to judge from clues about the island's whereabouts) but is loosely based on the Monterey peninsula: as Stevenson noted, 'the scenery is Californian in part, and part chic'.[29] But, bearing in mind Stevenson's playfulness, it may equally be a parody of the writing of Captain Mayne Reid, who said of his *The Boy Hunters* (1853) that it was written 'so as to create a taste for that most refining study, the study of nature'.[30] Stevenson *did* respect (so far as he was able) the necessity for accurate descriptions of seamanship that Marryat so despairs of—although, as he admits in 'My First Book': 'I was unable to handle a brig (which the *Hispaniola* should have been), but thought I could make shift to sail her as a schooner'. However, as he wrote to Henley (mid-December 1883): 'Of course my seamanship is Jimmy . . .

[29] *Letters*, iv. 300.
[30] Edward Salmon, *Juvenile Literature as It Is* (London: Henry J. Drane, 1888), 35.

I make these paper people to please myself, and Skelt, and God Almighty, and with no ulterior purpose.'[31]

Novels which deal with the sea (together with the terms 'swab' and 'lubber') have been traced back to Tobias Smollett's *The Adventures of Roderick Random* (1748) although only thirteen of its sixty-nine chapters are set at sea. (The first mate of the ship that Random sails in, *Thunder*, is Mr Morgan, and they visit Hispaniola.) As Stevenson said in his essay 'The English Admirals': 'No reader can forget the description of the *Thunder* . . .: the disorderly tyranny; the cruelty and dirt of officers and men; deck after deck, each with some new object of offence . . . There are portions of this business on board the *Thunder* over which the reader passes lightly, and hurriedly, like a traveller in a malarious country.'[32] Not, perhaps, the stuff of romance, and so a more convincing candidate for the founder of the genre might be James Fenimore Cooper (who pointed out that he had taken a different course from Smollett). His *The Pilot* (1824) was based upon his own naval experiences—and features an old seaman called Long Tom Coffin. (Another candidate for the first sea story is Eugène Sue's 'Kernok, the Corsair', which appeared in *La Mode* in 1830, and in *Plik et Plok* in 1858.)

The island-sea-adventure genre was picked up by the producers of the 'penny dreadfuls': from the 1840s publishers like Edward Lloyd found that there was a 'spasmodic demand for tales of smugglers or buccaneers'. However, as E. S. Turner observes, 'There was precious little ozone or salt spray in the earlier stories . . . One of Lloyd's titles was *The Death Ship, or The Pirate's Bride and the Maniac of the Deep.* The seas were cluttered with spectral barks and gallows ships.'[33]

Religion was central to the work of writers in the genre at the respectable end of the market, such as W. H. G. Kingston and R. M. Ballantyne. However, as early as *Masterman Ready*, there was a move away from strict moralizing: Tommy, the spoiled little boy in Marryat's book who causes Ready's death because of his laziness at the fight at the stockade, is not made to feel guilty about it. This was not a steady progression—Kingston's later books reverted to an evangelical tone—and attitudes towards religion and empire were generally more

[31] *Letters*, iv. 217.
[32] *Virginibus Puerisque* (1881), *Works* (1924), xxv. 87–8.
[33] E. S. Turner, *Boys Will Be Boys* (Harmondsworth: Penguin, 1976), 25.

subtle and more variable than is often thought. Ballantyne, for example, was far from being a jingoist; his books are generally opposed to militarism, and his use of irony and masquerade have been seen as a starting point for Stevenson's writing, rather than as a convention to be challenged.[34] The one consistent trend in the genre was the move from adult to boy heroes, as the idea of the noble British Boy—with its ramifications of class and masculinity—became one of the central pillars of colonial ideology.[35]

It is clear that Stevenson was often very close to his predecessors, but almost always in matters—liberality, and freedom of thought, for example—with which they are *not* commonly credited, and further away from his predecessors in matters with which they *are* credited. In *Treasure Island*, Stevenson's efforts at piratical history (in the mode of G. A. Henty) or natural history (as in Mayne Reid) were cheerfully spurious. Perhaps most of all, his use of violence has been misread: Jan Needle suggests that *Treasure Island* deploys 'the classic ingredients of the adventure yarn [with] unremitting intensity', that it is 'the story of a child in a world not just of adults, but of totally ruthless, indeed mentally crippled adults', and that it is distinguished by the fact that Stevenson was 'prepared to stare this fact in the face'.[36] The idea, often repeated, that Stevenson's violence is more graphic than that of his predecessors is quite wrong. In a study of boys' periodicals Kirsten Drotner suggests that the 'new adulation of the victor marked an important ideological change from the earlier ideals of religious submission . . . Unlike the martyr or the missionary, the manly adventurer embodied a contemporary male norm, while performing norm-breaking actions such as manslaughter or rape.'[37] If this seems unlikely, a single page of chapter 9 of Marryat's *The Pirate* (1836)

[34] See Stuart Hannabus, 'Ballantyne's Message of Empire', in Jeffrey Richards (ed.), *Imperialism and Juvenile Literature* (Manchester: Manchester University Press, 1989), 53–71; Fiona McCulloch, *The Fictional Role of Childhood in Victorian and Early Twentieth Century Children's Literature* (Lampeter: The Edwin Mellen Press, 2004), 70.

[35] See Kelly Boyd, *Manliness and the Boys' Story Paper in Britain: A Cultural History, 1855–1940* (Basingstoke: Palgrave, 2003), 47, 51; C. C. Eldridge, *The Imperial Experience: From Carlyle to Forster* (London: Macmillan, 1996), 68–9; Graham Dawson, *Soldier Heroes, British Adventure, Empire and the Imagining of Masculinities* (London: Routledge, 1994), 55.

[36] Jan Needle, 'Needle on Treasure Island', in Chris Powling (ed.), *The Best of* Books for Keeps (London: The Bodley Head, 1994), 3–7.

[37] Kirsten Drotner, *English Children and Their Magazines 1751–1945* (New Haven and London: Yale University Press, 1988), 100; and see Kevin Carpenter, *Desert Isles and*

sees Captain Cain break the wrist of his captive, and then throw him and his betrothed overboard; then the Bishop's daughter throws herself to the sharks, rather than be 'turned over to the crew'—and things were worse down among the 'penny dreadfuls'. One problem, as F. J. Harvey Darton has pointed out, was that 'lawless adventure was the feat that haunted the advocates of manliness. As Satan was sometimes considered the hero of *Paradise Lost*, so the Pirate King might almost be given a romantic halo.'[38]

The pervasiveness of the genre can be seen in Lieut.-Col. Robin Redforth (aged 9) in Charles Dickens's *A Holiday Romance* (1868), or the children of the 1860s at play, cutting down the pirate captain in 'A Saga of the Seas' as portrayed in Kenneth Grahame's *Dream Days* (1898). But times were changing, and the faltering of confidence of the high Victorian era, and the liberalization of attitudes to childhood meant that the established genres were becoming ripe for overhaul. In an increasingly godless universe, issues of faith and doubt, and fantasy and realism became part of the matrix of the children's book, notably with writers such as Lewis Carroll, Richard Jefferies—and Robert Louis Stevenson.

How Treasure Island *Reimagined the Genre*

'I know of no more striking example', wrote one of Stevenson's biographers, 'of an artist's taking a cheap, artificial set of commercialised values—which is fair enough to the Victorian "boys' story"—and doing work of everlasting quality by changing nothing, transmuting everything, as if Jane Austen had ennobled soap-opera.'[39] Stevenson's relationship with his models was, as we have seen, far from straightforwardly oppositional; but in his hands a genre that was largely self-righteous and self-confident, politically and religiously conservative, artificial and brutal became ambiguous and questioning, subversive of conventional politics and religion, and authentic and thoughtful about its violence. The great achievement (or paradox) is that this was carried off with such a zestful adherence to the surface characteristics of the genre that *Treasure Island*'s true character has been masked

Pirate Islands: The Island Theme in Nineteenth-Century English Juvenile Fiction, A Survey and Bibliography (Frankfurt am Main: Peter Lang, 1984), 89.

[38] Darton, *Children's Books*, 294.

[39] Furnas, *Voyage to Windward*, 182.

from the outset. A review in the *Daily News* admired it as one of 'the stirring, wholesome narratives of adventure' which helped to 'make boys manly, inventive and independent' and encouraged 'the spirit of enterprise which drives our race all over the world'.[40]

At first sight, *Treasure Island* might seem to be the apotheosis of generic convention. What happens? A treasure map comes into the hands of our young hero; he becomes part of an expedition to recover the treasure from an exotic island; he encounters a devious villain and a marooned seaman; by good luck he saves his colleagues from treachery; there is a pitched battle with pirates; the treasure is recovered, and our hero arrives home safely.

From Ballantyne through G. A. Henty, and into the 1920s with writers like Percy F. Westerman, the archetypal island-sea-adventure story is a circular quest, closely related to folk-tale patterns and based on individual and cultural wish-fulfilment. The hero, generally middle class, is often the narrator: he is frank, upstanding, straightforward, and unreflective. Jack Martin, of Ballantyne's *The Coral Island,* is characteristic:

> Jack Martin was a tall, strapping, broad-shouldered youth of eighteen, with a handsome, good-humoured, firm face. He had had a good education, was clever and hearty and lion-like in his actions, but mild and quiet in disposition. Jack was a general favourite. (chapter 2)

The hero, sometimes in straitened circumstances, has a father (or the memory of a father) he can look up to, and a mother of whom he can think fondly—otherwise, female characters are rare. He often has special skills, and/or acquires a talisman to help him on his quest.

Jim Hawkins, as the admirable Captain Smollett—possibly the only genuinely grown-up character in the book—observes, is not someone he would wish to sail with again (p. 178). He is a 'real' boy, with boyish impulses (on which the plot turns) and weaknesses (such as bullying the boy who takes his place at the inn). As a narrator, his sense of disillusionment can make him an uneasy companion for the reader. Jim's father is weak and no match even for such a broken-down pirate as Billy Bones. His attitude to his mother is ambiguous: 'how I blamed my poor mother for her honesty and her greed, for her past foolhardiness and present weakness!' (p. 29). She is not mentioned on his return. Nor is Jim an upstanding British boy: he is no fighter,

[40] *Letters*, iv. 216.

and rather than growing into a man through his experiences, he remains boyish—even when being pursued around the deck of the *Hispaniola* by a homicidal pirate, he sees it as 'such a game as I had often played at home about the rocks of Black Hill Cove' (p. 137). Nor does he take responsibility for his actions: when he shoots Israel Hands, he does not even claim self-defence: 'I scarce can say it was by my own volition, and I am sure it was without a conscious aim' (p. 139). And even the talisman, the map, is stolen.

Our hero now sets out on his adventure, and the genre usually equips him with reliable friends (like himself), and/or an older guide or mentor whom he can respect. After a bracing voyage (complete with extensive, if perhaps bewildering sailing instructions) he arrives in exciting foreign parts, whose flora and fauna are meticulously described.

Stevenson, approaching his task with considerable enthusiasm ('gleeful' crops up quite often in critical commentaries), consciously or unconsciously demolished most of these conventions. Jim's 'friends', the Squire and the Doctor, are as driven by greed as the pirates; and his 'mentor' is that master of duplicity, Long John Silver: and Silver and Jim become, by a great irony, like father and son. Trelawney, Smollett, and the Doctor, the 'good' characters and the more obvious father-figures, are simply inadequate. Perhaps only the unbending Captain Smollett, or Grey, the reformed mutineer, can be described as virtuous: Trelawney is, at least initially, portrayed as a buffoon, and the Doctor's veneer of honesty and competence is not without its cracks (as Smollett says to him: 'If that was how you served at Fontenoy, sir, you'd have been better in your berth'). But it is Long John, the antithesis of Masterman Ready and his stolid and trustworthy successors, who is at the heart of Stevenson's subversion. Reflected through the unreliable prism of Jim the narrator, he epitomizes the frisson generated by the romance, of realistic evil made safe by existing, as Sir Walter Scott put it, in a world of 'marvellous and uncommon incidents'.[41] In Stevenson's surreal, not to say postmodern fable, 'The Persons of the Tale' (reprinted here as Appendix 2), Silver, taking a break with Captain Smollett from the plot, reveals the secret:

'What I know is this: if there is sich a thing as a Author, I'm his favourite chara'ter. He does me fathoms better'n he does you—fathoms, he does.

[41] Sir Walter Scott, 'Essay on Romance' (1824), in Miriam Allott, *Novelists on the Novel* (London: Routledge, 1965), 49.

And he likes doing me. He keeps me on deck mostly all the time, crutch and all . . . he's on my side, and you may lay to it!' (pp. 192–3)

Silver, quick-witted and quick-tongued (as his name suggests), moves between the two worlds of the gentry and the seamen relying on his linguistic dexterity: as Israel Hands says, 'He had good schooling in his young days, and can speak like a book when so minded' (p. 58). He can, of course, also speak like a sailor, and when he first encounters Jim, as the caricature of a sailor: 'When I was an A B master mariner I'd have come up alongside of him, hand over hand, and broached him to in a brace of old shakes, I would' (pp. 48–9). Stevenson's success in making such scenes plausible hinges simultaneously on the flawed character of Jim, and on the fact that, as narrator, Jim has a dual identity—the boy in the story, and the older boy (or man) telling the story. The storyteller is analytic enough to maintain the interest of the readers—he describes Silver as 'too deep, and too ready, and too clever for me' (p. 48)—while carefully and unanalytically showing his younger self in a good light. Thus, when Jim takes 'French leave' from the stockade, the narrator observes 'that was so bad a way of doing it as made the thing itself wrong. But I was only a boy, and I had made my mind up' (p. 117). We are not simply watching a story; we are watching the narrator watching the story. And so, when Jim interacts with John Silver, he can at one moment wish to kill him through the barrel (p. 59), call him 'John' throughout the scene when Tom is murdered (pp. 78–9), describe Silver's abject fear of the gallows (p. 160), and casually note, as he stands with him beside the excavation, 'He was brave, and no mistake' (p. 175). It is not only Silver who shifts his character, and not only the boy who responds, but Jim the narrator who colludes or judges. The Silver–Jim relationship is not one of an obvious villain playing with a gullible boy; it is one of a complex human contemplated by a confused human: the narrator-Jim does not, for all his piousness, know how to judge Silver. Thus, the reader is often left to make a judgement on both Jim the boy and Jim the narrator, as when, surrounded by pirates, Jim appeals to Silver:

'I believe you're the best man here, and if things go to the worst, I'll take it kind of you to let the doctor know the way I took it.'

'I'll bear it in mind,' said Silver, with an accent so curious that I could not, for the life of me, decide whether he were laughing at my request, or had been favourably affected by my courage. (p. 148)

The mechanics of the voyage itself are dismissed in two sentences: 'It was fairly prosperous. The ship proved to be a good ship, the crew were capable seamen, and the captain thoroughly understood his business' (p. 56). But if the sailing does not seem to interest Stevenson, the language of the sea does: the speeches of Long John Silver and Israel Hands, especially, are so densely spattered with sea terms, and the sailing of the schooner described without a glossary (although one is provided in this edition) that it is tempting to see the arcane language as an elaborate joke. This perhaps reaches its peak with Silver's challenge: 'Have I lived this many years, and a son of a rum puncheon cock his hat athwart my hawse at the latter end of it?' (pp. 148–9).

But despite these touches, and the verve of the telling, *Treasure Island* is not a light-hearted or optimistic book. The contrast with R. M. Ballantyne's *The Coral Island* (1858) could not be more stark. For example, when Ballantyne's boys are surveying the island on which they have been wrecked, Ralph Rover rhapsodizes on what he sees:

I cast my eyes about, and truly my heart glowed within me and my spirits rose at the beautiful prospect which I beheld on every side . . . A sandy beach of dazzling whiteness lined this bright green shore, and upon it there fell a gentle ripple of the sea . . . My heart was filled with more delight than I can express at sight of so many glorious objects, and my thoughts turned suddenly to the contemplation of the Creator of them all. (chapter 4)

And here is the seasick Jim, contemplating Treasure Island for the first time:

Perhaps it was this—perhaps it was the look of the island, with its grey, melancholy woods, and wild stone spires, and the surf that we could both see and hear foaming and thundering on the steep beach . . . and from that first look onward, I hated the very thought of Treasure Island. (p. 71)

As Stevenson wrote to J. M. Barrie (1 November 1892), 'If you are going to make a book end badly, it must end badly from the beginning', and he certainly applies his rule to the episodes on Treasure Island itself.[42]

Once on the island, our conventional hero would battle natives and pirates, but always honourably, with British pluck, and with an innate knowledge of his own superiority. The villains come to a bloody, or wet, end. There are occasional homilies, based upon a moral code

[42] *Letters*, vii. 413.

directed at boys by men. Finally, our hero returns home to his family, covered with glory and/or wealth, validated by the conservative values of a stable society.

From the fanciful flora to Jim's progress, which is ruled by luck rather than pluck, and Silver's final escape, things on Treasure Island do not go by the book—or by the old books. The chess game of greed is not played between the good and the bad, but between two classes, the more-or-less disciplined gentry, and the undisciplined pirates ('I never in my life saw men so careless of the morrow', p. 163), one group with knowledge and one without ('We're all foc's'le hands . . . We can steer a course, but who's to set one?' p. 63). Long John Silver is caught between the two: as the Doctor says: 'Camp in a bog, would you? Silver, I'm surprised at you. You're less of a fool than many, take you all round; but you don't appear to me to have the rudiments of a notion of the rules of health' (p. 158). But even here Stevenson subverts obvious contrasts: it is only Captain Smollett who can maintain the necessary discipline in the stockade, and it is only Israel Hands, 'a careful, wily, old, experienced seaman, who could be trusted at a pinch with almost anything' (p. 57), who can instruct Jim how to sail the *Hispaniola*. And if the gentry feel their superiority over the sailors, it cannot be in terms of purity of motive, or wisdom of action, or any attempt to transcend class prejudices: Captain Smollett's belief is 'Spoil foc's'le hands, make devils' (p. 59) and of the £700,000 of treasure, Ben Gunn's 'ample share' is £1,000.

If there is a conspicuous lack of principle on the island, there is also a conspicuous lack of religion, a point not missed by Stevenson's otherwise supportive father, who particularly disapproved of the second half of the novel. His comments on what might be added when Ben Gunn is introduced to the tale sum up the conventional moralizing of the genre so comprehensively that they are worth quoting at length.

> I would interject a long passage . . . of a religious character. I would have him ask if Jim had ever been at some little . . . village say Mousehole . . . & whether he had ever heard of his father or mother. The want of such an enquiry strikes me as unnatural. Then I would have him regret the fatal day on which he had run away from his home and some pathetic passage should follow as to what he had lost and what troubles he had passed through and something about his misspending of Sundays and something about the Minister of the place and the sayings of his father or his mother and so forth. So far as I can see this is the only way of harking back to something

higher than incident. Perhaps some story of his going with a companion and netting or nutting in the woods on Sunday and his mother's objections. In short you might have here a striking and pathetic passage to relieve the more bloody work which goes after. . . . I want you to make a real point of his breaking away from home and this should be a kind of religious tract and should be fully done but all in the Defoe style. (Letter dated 26 February 1882)

Stevenson, the ambivalent rebel, initially seemed to agree—'I had meant to dwell on Benjamin later on, and never had room for him; but, as you say, we'll put a whole religious tract in that very place'[43]—but in fact he added only ten lines about Gunn's pious mother and (a device of great antiquity) the cause of his downfall: 'and it begun with chuck-farthen on the blessed grave-stones!' (p. 83). He stood firm, however, on the question of Long John Silver: 'I own I do not agree with you about the later chapters of *Treasure Island*. I think John Silver in his later developments about as good as anything in it. I should say about the best of it' (March 1882).[44]

Jim's grim departure from Treasure Island, with the cries of the marooned men in his ears ('to take them home for the gibbet would have been a cruel sort of kindness', p. 181), is diametrically opposed to the departure of Ralph Rover and his friends from the Coral Island:

It was a bright, clear morning when we hoisted the snow-white sails of the pirate schooner and . . . glided quickly over the lagoon under a cloud of canvas. Just as we passed through the channel in the reef the natives gave us a loud cheer; and as the missionary waved his hat, while he stood on a coral rock with his grey hairs floating in the wind, we heard the single word 'Farewell' borne faintly over the sea. (chapter 35)

Finally, there is no happy homecoming in *Treasure Island*, and scant joy in the treasure. We used it, the narrator reports wearily, 'wisely or foolishly, according to our natures' (p. 182). The point of the story is the adventure, the romance, not the rewards. Nor is there any spiritual resolution: 'Unlike Crusoe, Jim Hawkins is not justified by his works; material success does not resolve moral uncertainty.'[45] The ending spirals around to a grim rejection of the very place that

[43] Maixner (ed.), *Critical Heritage*, 127.

[44] *Letters*, iii. 294.

[45] William Blackburn, 'Mirror in the Sea: *Treasure Island* and the Internationalization of Juvenile Romance', *Children's Literature Association Quarterly*, 8/3 (1983), 11.

at the beginning of the book seemed to hold out a vision of excitement and reward.

Stevenson and the Romance

In short, in Stevenson's hands the ambiguities inherent in the genre shift uneasily into the foreground. The fact that Stevenson could sustain the illusion of writing a hearty adventure was partly due to his chameleon-like nature as a writer (so detrimental to his reputation) which allowed him to produce so skilful and affectionate a pastiche of the adventure-thriller writer's mode. From the first paragraph, with its 'treasure not yet lifted', Stevenson provides the grace notes of hints and foreshadowings: 'but in all my fancies nothing occurred to me so strange and tragic as our actual adventures' (p. 41); 'But good did come of the apple barrel, as you shall hear' (p. 59). Tension is built slowly, as when Jim and his mother are searching the pirate's chest, and there are sudden shocks, as when Jim finds himself among the pirates in the stockade. Stevenson (perhaps notoriously) uses the maimed and the grotesque as villains—Black Dog, Billy Bones, Pew, the wounded Israel Hands (seen as the AntiChrist by one critic)[46]—and trims out any details which do not contribute directly to the action or the image.

These are the techniques of the romance, of stories that exist in a parallel universe, where emotions and reactions give a satisfying illusion of reality. As Stevenson observed:

> Character to the boy is a sealed book; for him, a pirate is a beard, a pair of wide trousers and a liberal complement of pistols. The author, for the sake of circumstantiation and because he was himself more or less grown up, admitted character, within certain limits, into his design; but only within certain limits . . . Danger is the matter with which this class of novel deals; fear, the passion with which it idly trifles . . . To add more traits, to be too clever, to start the hare of moral or intellectual interest while we are running the fox of material interest, is not to enrich but to stultify your tale.[47]

Those sentiments are from 'A Humble Remonstrance', written in

[46] Edwin M. Eigner, *Robert Louis Stevenson and Romantic Tradition* (Princeton: Princeton University Press, 1966), 119–20.

[47] Robert Louis Stevenson, 'A Humble Remonstrance', *Memories and Portraits*, xxix. 138.

response to Henry James's 'The Art of Fiction', in which James (who later became a very close friend of the Stevensons) deplored the 'clumsy separation' of novel and romance because it does not 'answer . . . to any reality'.[48] Stevenson argued that there is a useful distinction to be made between the novel of adventure (or romance) with its sensual appeal, the novel of character, with intellectual appeal, and the dramatic novel, with emotional and moral appeal, and he passionately refuted James's idea that the novel competes with life. 'No art . . . can successfully compete with life . . . Life goes before us, infinite in complication.'[49]

For James, the art of the romancer was 'insidiously to cut the cable' that ties 'the balloon of experience' to the earth, 'to cut it without our detecting him'.[50] One result of this is that as Northrop Frye observed: 'Certain elements of character are released in the romance which make it naturally a more revolutionary form than the novel.'[51] Perhaps unsurprisingly, given Stevenson's quicksilver intellect, *Treasure Island*, which James so admired, largely contradicts Stevenson's own theorizing: the book 'not only enacts the delights of romance, but also meditates on some of its dangers . . . hesitancy about romance is at the heart of *Treasure Island*'.[52] Stevenson *does* 'start the hare' of intellectual interest, and his prediction that the 'clever reader' would 'lose the scent' has proved groundless;[53] as he said in 'A Gossip on Romance', 'True romantic art . . . makes a romance of all things. It reaches into the highest abstraction of the ideal; it does not refuse the most pedestrian realism.'[54] There is a paradox here, as Edward Salmon complained:

> The only objection which can honestly be argued against this sort of romance is that it contains none of the higher attributes and aspirations of which mankind is capable. It is romance pure and simple. There is little

[48] Henry James, 'The Art of Fiction', in *The Art of Criticism: Henry James on the Theory and Practice of Criticism*, ed. William Veeder and Susan M. Griffin (Chicago: University of Chicago Press, 1986), 174–5.

[49] Stevenson, 'A Humble Remonstrance', xxix. 137, 134.

[50] James, 'Preface to *The American*' (1907), in *The Art of Criticism*, 281.

[51] Frye, *Anatomy of Criticism*, 394–5.

[52] Julia Reid, *Robert Louis Stevenson, Science and the Fin de Siècle* (Basingstoke: Palgrave Macmillan, 2006), 33, 37.

[53] Stevenson, 'A Humble Remonstrance', xxix. 139.

[54] Robert Louis Stevenson, 'A Gossip on Romance', *Works* (Tusitala Edition), xxix. 127.

poetry, little humanity. It is desperately realistic, and desperately earnest; and regards nothing but the circumstances attending the strife for lucre and life.[55]

And so on the one hand, in *Treasure Island* Stevenson uses the conventions of its genre, essentially a type of romance, to absorb and stimulate the reader: as he observed in 'The English Admirals', 'It is not over the virtues of a-curate-and-tea-party novel, that people are abashed into high resolutions. . . . to stir them properly they must have men entering into glory with some pomp and circumstance.'[56] On the other, he uses the genre as a stalking horse for an exploration of some of the 'infinite complications' of life.

All of this is reflected in two of Stevenson's preoccupations as a writer, which come to fruition in *Treasure Island* and which are developed through many of his other works: self-reflexiveness and dualism. There is a sense of shared play in *Treasure Island*: author and readers know the rules; the narrator himself certainly does; in his imagination, 'Sometimes the isle was thick with savages, with whom we fought; sometimes full of dangerous animals that hunted us' (p. 41). There is, therefore, a positive collusion when these rules are broken. Equally, Stevenson's fascination with the double nature of people—*Strange Case of Dr Jekyll and Mr Hyde* is the most obvious example—is particularly effective in *Treasure Island*. Nobody is quite what he seems: the Squire can be 'sometimes proud he [Captain Flint] was an Englishman' (p. 36), and even the irredeemable Billy Bones can sing 'a kind of country love-song' (p. 22).

Consequently, *Treasure Island*'s themes of power are disguised by the idea, as Stevenson put it, that 'romance is the poetry of circumstance . . . where interest turns, not upon what a man shall choose to do, but on how he manages to do it; not in the passionate slips and hesitations of the conscience, but in the problems of the body and of the practical intelligence'.[57] Several critics have seen *Treasure Island* 'as a sort of social parable . . . an embattled microcosm of civil society—squire, doctor, captain and retainers—being menaced by the lower orders under brutal and materialistic leadership . . . Silver ends up in the position of some teetotal Jacobin, trying (unsuccessfully) to

[55] Salmon, *Juvenile Literature*, 107.

[56] Robert Louis Stevenson, 'The English Admirals', *Virginibus Puerisque*, xxiv. 94.

[57] Stevenson, 'A Gossip on Romance', xxix. 120, 121.

get his mob out of the pubs and on to the streets'.[58] The gentry are the law, exercising power as of right, even if their motives can hardly be distinguished from those of their opponents, and while Stevenson seems to be endorsing his conservative models, modern critics have seen this as a demonstration of his straight-faced irony. We only see the pirates through the eyes of their opponents, and whereas, for example, Silver's murder of Tom is described in horrific detail, the Squire can 'pick off' a distant pirate almost casually.[59] Similarly, *Treasure Island*'s critique of empire is masked by the symbolism of money that pervades the book. Much has been made of the driving force of the lust for gold displayed by almost all the characters, of the packing of the gold coins into breadbags (normally the repositories of the wholesome 'element of community'), of the connotation of corruption and debasement attached to silver in a world moving to the gold standard[60] and of the way in which the real meaning of the gold is blurred until Jim's bitter reflections on what it had cost, when he is sorting the treasure: 'what blood and sorrow . . . what shame and lies and cruelty' . . . (p. 178). But even then, Jim casts the blame on Silver, Morgan, and Ben Gunn—'who had each taken his share in these crimes'. Modern readers are perhaps less myopic:

> The treasure in *Treasure Island* is actually blood-money which has been laundered by time. It is money severed from social relations, morally neutral, the treasure of a child's world of finders-keepers. The slaves who mined and minted it, the pirates who murdered to get it, the real price of Flint's treasure no longer matter when the righteous get their hands on it.[61]

No romance can entirely float away from reality, and critics have suggested several other possible ways of reading the undergrowth of *Treasure Island*. It has not been immune to psychological interpretations (John Silver's crutch has been particularly tempting) and we have seen that a case can be made for a biographical reading. Alastair

[58] Harvie, 'Politics of Stevenson', 121; and see Nicholas Rankin, *Dead Man's Chest: Travels after Robert Louis Stevenson* (London: Faber and Faber, 1987), 203.

[59] See Marjorie Hourihan, *Deconstructing the Hero* (London: Routledge, 1997), 148–9; Troy Boone, *Youth of Darkest England: Working-Class Children at the Heart of Victorian Empire* (London and New York: Routledge, 2005), 81.

[60] Fowler, 'Parables of Adventure', 115; Naomi J. Wood, 'Gold Standards and Silver Subversions: *Treasure Island* and the Romance of Money', *Children's Literature*, 26 (1998), 62–6.

[61] Rankin, *Dead Man's Chest*, 159.

Fowler suggests that there may be a metaphor for Stevenson's career in who gets the treasure: 'Not the pirates; not Dr. Livesey; not even Captain Smollett; but Ben Gunn the maroon. The solitary, that is to say; one who has achieved independence and survived rejection by a society tired of the quest'.[62] Several critics have also pointed out that Stevenson's Scottishness should not be overlooked. Alan Riach suggests that Scottish writers, notably Grahame, Buchan, Doyle, Barrie, and Stevenson, 'bear witness to a peculiarly ambiguous relation between imperial authority and the aspirations of childhood' and that the power struggles in *Treasure Island* reflect this.[63]

Novel or romance, or something of both, *Treasure Island* has proved to be a durable source of both intellectual and sensuous excitement to children and to adults. It is a sustained literary juggling act, exciting and dazzling, concealing and revealing the deeply ambiguous nature of the adventure story. It is, like the smooth John Silver, not what it seems, at once flamboyant and morally serious, liberating and pessimistic—but, most of all, and like much great literature, dangerous.

[62] Fowler, 'Parables of Adventure', 111.

[63] Alan Riach, '*Treasure Island* and Time', *Children's Literature in Education*, 27/3 (1996), 181–93 at 186; also in Alan Riach, *Representing Scotland in Literature, Popular Culture and Iconography: The Masks of the Modern Nation* (Basingstoke: Palgrave Macmillan, 2005), 88–100 at 93.

NOTE ON THE TEXT

Treasure Island; or The Mutiny of the Hispaniola by Captain George North was published in *Young Folks* in eighteen parts from 1 October 1881 to 28 January 1882. The text used here is that of the first edition in book form (Cassell, 1883), which was set from Stevenson's revised original manuscript (Roger G. Swearingen, *Prose Writings of Robert Louis Stevenson—A Guide* (London: Macmillan, 1980), 63).

Stevenson made around six hundred minor changes, additions, and deletions to the serial version. Some critics suggest that they make Jim Hawkins less brash, Long John Silver more subtly threatening, and Dr Livesey less pompous.

More substantial additions are:

11 now the leg . . . abominable fancies.
18 die, and go to your own place . . . Bible.
41 I brooded by the hour . . . actual adventures.
44 One of my last thoughts . . . old brass telescope.
48 Here I have this confounded son of a Dutchman . . . Now, here it is:
83 Now, for instance . . . the pious woman!
170 Dick had his Bible out . . . bad companions.
171–2 Dick alone still held his Bible . . . on his crutch.

The most notable changes and deletions include:

78 John seized the branch of a tree . . . poor Tom] *Young Folks* reads: John whipped the crutch out of his armpit, and, bereft of his support rolled face-forward on the ground; but, at the same instant, that uncouth missile, hurtling through the air, struck poor Tom

82 Of all the beggar-men . . . accoutrement] *Young Folks* reads: His dress, if it could be called a dress, was a kilt of goatskin, bound about his waist with an old brass-buckled leather belt, a case or waistcoat of the same about his body, and a round, pointed cap upon his head, with the long hair hanging over his eyes. He had no weapon, and, except the belt, no mark of civilization.

88 when I reached the stockade] *Young Folks* reads: when I came plump on the stockade. That same moment I knew it had been laid out by

a man with a head on his shoulders. I will own that this surprised me, as, from all I had known of pirates, I had conceived them to be mostly fools, Silver alone excepted. However, it was, perhaps, Silver who designed the fort.

89 with half a dozen muskets . . . back to the Hispaniola] *Young Folks* reads: with a dozen muskets; and, in two minutes more, Hunter was hurrying back again to join him, loaded like a cow, and I was breaking my medical wind in the jolly-boat, rowing like a fellow in a race.

97 little enough powder already, my lads] *Young Folks* continues:

'Hard to be sure of that, captain', I replied. 'They have pistols, as you see.'

'Oh, and muskets too, I make no doubt,' he added. 'We'll see the muskets as soon as they've had time to grapple for them. All stowed away among the cargo. Mr John Trelawney is a good owner to me, sir, and a cool head and a good shot, which is better; but you'll, perhaps, excuse me for saying that he's a most egregious ass.'

97 doing no further damage] *Young Folks* continues: Hunter, Joyce, and the squire were all pretty white about the gills. Cannon shot, when you're not used to it, is telling on the nerve. But the captain and I had seen these bowls running before now, and Gray was as steady as a rock.

148 The laugh's on my side . . . gallows] *Young Folks* reads: And if you ask me how I did it, tortures wouldn't drive me, in the first place; and, in the second, much good would it do you, now the harm's done, and you ruined. And now you can kill me, if you please. The laugh's on my side. I've as good as hanged you, every man, and I'm not fifteen till my next birthday.

148 I believe you're the best man here . . . by my courage] *Young Folks* reads: I hate you, but I believe you're the best man here, and I'll take it kind of you to let the doctor know the way I took the thing and even if I get frightened after this, you'll tell him I outfaced you at first . . . by my pluck.

RECOMMENDED READING

David D. Mann and William H. Hardesty III, 'Stevenson's Revisions of *Treasure Island*: "Writing Down the Whole Particulars"', *Text: Transactions of the Society for Textual Scholarship* 3, ed. David D. Mann and W. Speed Hill (New York: AMS, 1987), 377–92.

Patricia Whaley Hardesty, William H. Hardesty III, and David Mann,

'Doctoring the Doctor: How Stevenson Altered the Second Narrator of *Treasure Island*', in *Studies in Scottish Literature*, 21 (1986), 1–22.
David Angus, 'Youth on the Prow: The First Publication of *Treasure Island*', in *Studies in Scottish Literature*, 25 (1990), 83–99.

SELECT BIBLIOGRAPHY

Website

Robert Louis Stevenson Website: <http://www.robert-louis-stevenson.org>

Editions

Collected editions of the works of Stevenson include the Tusitala Edition (London: William Heinemann in association with Chatto and Windus, Cassell, and Longmans, Green, 1923–4), and the Centenary Edition (Edinburgh: Edinburgh University Press, 1995–2003). The Centenary Edition includes *Treasure Island*, ed. Wendy R. Katz (1998).

Letters

The Letters of Robert Louis Stevenson, 8 vols., ed. Bradford A. Booth and Ernest Mehew (New Haven: Yale University Press, 1994–5).

Henry James and Robert Louis Stevenson: A Record of Friendship and Criticism, ed. Janet Adam Smith (London: Rupert Hart-Davies, 1948).

Biography and Background

Graham Balfour, *The Life of Robert Louis Stevenson* (London: Methuen, 1913).

Ian Bell, *Robert Louis Stevenson: Dreams of Exile, A Biography* (Edinburgh: Mainstream, 1992).

Dennis Butts, *R. L. Stevenson* (London: Bodley Head, 1956).

David Daiches, *Robert Louis Stevenson and His World* (London: Thames and Hudson, 1973).

J. C. Furnas, *Voyage to Windward: The Life of Robert Louis Stevenson* (London: Faber and Faber, 1952).

Stephen Gwynn, *Robert Louis Stevenson* (London: Macmillan, 1939).

Claire Harman, *Robert Louis Stevenson: A Biography* (London: HarperCollins, 2005).

Frank McLynn, *Robert Louis Stevenson: A Biography* (London: Hutchinson, 1993).

James Pope Hennessey, *Robert Louis Stevenson* (London: Cape, 1974).

Nicholas Rankin, *Dead Man's Chest: Travels after Robert Louis Stevenson* (London: Faber and Faber, 1987).

Harold F. Watson, *Coasts of Treasure Island: A Study of the Backgrounds and Sources for Robert Louis Stevenson's Romance of the Sea* (San Antonio, Tex.: Naylor, 1969).

Criticism

William Blackburn, 'Mirror in the Sea: *Treasure Island* and the Internationalization of Juvenile Romance', *Children's Literature Association Quarterly*, 8/3 (1983), 7–12.

Troy Boone, *Youth of Darkest England: Working-Class Children at the Heart of Victorian Empire* (London and New York: Routledge, 2005).

G. K. Chesterton, *Robert Louis Stevenson* (London: Hodder and Stoughton, 1927).

Linda Dryden, *The Modern Gothic and Literary Doubles: Stevenson, Wilde, and Wells* (Basingstoke: Palgrave Macmillan, 2003).

Edwin M. Eigner, *Robert Louis Stevenson and Romantic Tradition* (Princeton: Princeton University Press, 1966).

Leslie Fiedler, *No! in Thunder: Essays on Myth and Literature* (Boston: Beacon, 1960).

Alastair Fowler, 'Parables of Adventure: The Debatable Novels of Robert Louis Stevenson', in Ian Campbell (ed.), *Nineteenth-Century Scottish Fiction* (Manchester: Carcanet New Press, 1979), 105–29.

Robert Fraser, 'The Divided Self, Robert Louis Stevenson', in Corinne Saunders (ed.), *A Companion to Romance* (Oxford: Blackwell, 2004), 389–405.

Susan Gannon, 'Robert Louis Stevenson's *Treasure Island:* The Ideal Fable', in Perry Nodelman (ed.), *Touchstones: Reflections on the Best in Children's Literature* (West Lafayette, Ind.: Children's Literature Association), i. 242–52.

—— 'The Illustrator as Interpreter: N. C. Wyeth's Illustrations for the Adventure Novels of Robert Louis Stevenson', *Children's Literature*, 19 (1991), 90–106.

Christopher Harvie, 'The Politics of Stevenson', in Jenni Calder (ed.), *Stevenson and Victorian Scotland* (Edinburgh: Edinburgh University Press, 1981), 107–25.

Nathalie Jaëck, 'Pip and Jim Hawkins: The Spontaneous Generation of Two Mistakes in Fiction', in Rosie Findlay and Sébastien Salbayre (eds.), *Stories for Children, Histories of Childhood* (Tours: Presses Universitaires François Rabelais, 2007), 189–200.

Robert Kiely, *Robert Louis Stevenson and the Fiction of Adventure* (Cambridge, Mass.: Harvard University Press, 1964).

Ann Lawson-Lucas, 'The Pirate Chief in Salagari, Stevenson and Calvino', in Richard Ambrosini and Richard Dury (eds.), *R.L. Stevenson:*

Writer of Boundaries (Madison: University of Wisconsin Press, 2006), 338–47.

Diana Loxley, *Problematic Shores: The Literature of Islands* (New York: St Martin's, 1990).

Fiona McCulloch, *The Fictional Role of Childhood in Victorian and Early Twentieth Century Children's Literature* (Lampeter: The Edwin Mellen Press, 2004).

Paul Maixner (ed.), *Robert Louis Stevenson: The Critical Heritage* (London: Routledge and Kegan Paul, 1981).

Andrew Noble (ed.), *Robert Louis Stevenson* (London: Vision Press; Totowa, NJ: Barnes and Noble, 1983).

Glenda Norquay, 'Trading Texts: Negotiations of the Professional and the Popular in the Case of *Treasure Island*', in Richard Ambrosini and Richard Dury (eds.), *R. L. Stevenson: Writer of Boundaries* (Madison: University of Wisconsin Press, 2006), 60–9.

Christopher Parkes, '*Treasure Island* and the Romance of the British Civil Service', *Children's Literature Association Quarterly*, 31/4 (2007), 332–45.

Julia Reid, *Robert Louis Stevenson, Science and the Fin de Siècle* (Basingstoke: Palgrave Macmillan, 2006).

Alan Riach, '*Treasure Island* and Time', *Children's Literature in Education*, 27/3 (1996), 181–93; also in Alan Riach, *Representing Scotland in Literature, Popular Culture and Iconography: The Masks of the Modern Nation* (Basingstoke: Palgrave Macmillan, 2005), 88–100.

W. W. Robson, *The Definition of Literature and Other Essays* (Cambridge: Cambridge University Press, 1982).

Edward Salmon, *Juvenile Literature as It Is* (London: Henry J. Drane, 1888).

Alan Sandison, *Robert Louis Stevenson and the Appearance of Modernism: A Future Feeling* (Basingstoke: Macmillan, 1996).

Roger G. Swearingen, *The Prose Writings of Robert Louis Stevenson: A Guide* (London: Macmillan, 1980).

Naomi J. Wood, 'Gold Standards and Silver Subversions: *Treasure Island* and the Romance of Money', *Children's Literature*, 26 (1998), 61–85.

Related Topics

Joseph Bristow, *Empire Boys: Adventures in a Man's World* (London: HarperCollins Academic, 1991).

Kevin Carpenter, *Desert Isles and Pirate Islands: The Island Theme in Nineteenth-Century English Juvenile Fiction, A Survey and Bibliography* (Frankfurt am Main: Peter Lang, 1984).

[Daniel Defoe], *A General History of the Pyrates*, ed. Manuel Schonhorn (Mineola, NY: Dover, 1999).

Liz Farr, 'Paper Dreams and Romantic Projections: The Nineteenth-Century Toy Theater, Boyhood and Aesthetic Play', in Dennis Denisoff (ed.), *The Nineteenth-Century Child and Consumer Culture* (London: Ashgate, 2008), 43–61.

Margery Fisher, *The Bright Face of Danger: An Exploration of the Adventure Story* (London: Hodder and Stoughton, 1986).

Claudia Nelson, *Boys Will Be Girls: The Feminine Ethic and British Children's Fiction 1857–1917* (New Brunswick and London: Rutgers University Press, 1991).

Barbara Wall, *The Narrator's Voice: The Dilemma of Children's Fiction* (Basingstoke: Macmillan, 1991).

Further Reading in Oxford World's Classics

H. Rider Haggard, *King Solomon's Mines*, ed. Dennis Butts.

Robert Louis Stevenson, *South Sea Tales*, ed. Roslyn Jolly.

—— *Strange Case of Dr Jekyll and Mr Hyde and Other Tales*, ed. Roger Luckhurst.

A CHRONOLOGY OF ROBERT LOUIS STEVENSON

1850 (13 November) Robert Lewis Balfour Stevenson born in Edinburgh, the only child of Margaret Isabella Balfour and Thomas Stevenson.

1851 W. H. G. Kingston, *Peter the Whaler*.

1852 (May) Alison Cunningham employed as Stevenson's nurse (with family until November 1872).

1855 Charles Kingsley, *Westward Ho!*

1856 R. M. Ballantyne, *The Young Fur Traders*.

1857 Joseph Conrad born.

1858–67 Privately educated because of ill health.

1860 J. M. Barrie born.

1863 Charles Kingsley, *The Water Babies*. Arthur Quiller-Couch born.

1864 Lewis Carroll, *Alice's Adventures in Wonderland*.

1866 *Pentland Rising* published at his father's expense. *Boys of England* (–1906).

1867–71 Studies engineering at Edinburgh University.

1868 Charles Dickens, *A Holiday Romance*. Gladstone prime minister for first term.

1869 Tours Orkney and Shetland islands with the Commissioners of Northern Lights.

1871–2 Studies for the Scottish Bar. G. A. Henty, *Out on the Pampas*.

1873 Friendship with Sidney Colvin. Travels to the south of France because of ill health. First paid publication, 'Roads' in *Portfolio*.

1874 Continues to study for the Bar. Contributes to *Macmillan's Magazine*, and the *Cornhill Magazine*.

1875 Meets W. E. Henley in Edinburgh. Called to the Bar but does not work as an advocate. Contributes to *Vanity Fair* and *The Academy*.

1876 Takes a trip around the canals of northern France by canoe; meets Fanny Osbourne. Mark Twain, *The Adventures of Tom Sawyer*.

1878 Fanny returns to her husband in California. Stevenson travels with his donkey, Modestine, in the Cévennes. *An Inland Voyage*; *Edinburgh: Picturesque Notes*.

1879 Despite serious chest infection travels to California. (December) Fanny is divorced. *Travels with a Donkey*. *Boy's Own Paper* (–1967).

1880 (May) Marries Fanny in San Francisco. They stay at Silverado, and return to Scotland. Stevenson collaborates with W. E. Henley on a play, *Deacon Brodie*.

1881 At Braemar, begins *Treasure Island*; completed in Davos in Switzerland, and serialized in *Young Folks*, October 1881–January 1882. *Virginibus Puerisque*.

1882 Moves to Hyères, France. *Familiar Studies of Men and Books*; *New Arabian Nights*. Richard Jefferies, *Bevis*.

1883 (14 November) *Treasure Island* in book form. (June–October) Serialization of *The Black Arrow* in *Young Folks*.

1884 (January) *The Silverado Squatters*. (September) Moves to Bournemouth (–August 1887). Henry James, 'The Art of Fiction'. (December) 'A Humble Remonstrance', Stevenson's response to James's 'Art of Fiction'. *Austin Guinea* and *Beau Austin* (with W. E. Henley).

1885 Moves to 'Skerryvore', a house bought by Thomas Stevenson for Fanny; visits by Henry James. *A Child's Garden of Verses*; *Prince Otto*; *More New Arabian Nights*; *The Dynamiter* (with Fanny Stevenson); *Macaire* (with W. E. Henley).

1886 *Strange Case of Dr Jekyll and Mr Hyde*; *Kidnapped* (serialized in *Young Folks*, May–July). H. Rider Haggard, *King Solomon's Mines*.

1887 (May) Thomas Stevenson dies. (August) Stevenson moves to Saranac Lake in the Adirondacks, for health reasons. *The Merry Men*; *Underwoods*; *Memories and Portraits*.

1888 Voyage in the South Seas, Tahiti, and Hawaii. *The Black Arrow*; *A Memoir of Fleeming Jenkin*.

1889 Voyage to the Gilbert Islands and Samoa. *The Wrong Box* (with Lloyd Osbourne); *The Master of Ballantrae*.

1890 Buys Vailima, on Samoa. Further voyages and ill health. (September); Goes to live at Vailima. *In the South Seas*; *Ballads*. Issues privately printed broadside in support of Father Damien, the 'leper priest'.

1892 Involved in Samoan politics. *A Footnote to History*; *Across the Plains*; *The Wrecker* (with Lloyd Osbourne).

1893 *Island Nights' Entertainments*; *Catriona*.

1894 The tribe of Mataafa build 'The Road of Loving Hearts' to Stevenson's house as a gesture of thanks for his political help. *The Ebb-Tide* (with Lloyd Osbourne). (3 December) Dies of cerebral haemorrhage.

1896 *Weir of Hermiston.*

1897 *St Ives* (completed by Sir Arthur Quiller-Couch, 1898).

TREASURE ISLAND

TO

THE HESITATING PURCHASER

If sailor tales to sailor tunes,
    Storm and adventure, heat and cold,
If schooners, islands, and maroons*
    And Buccaneers* and buried Gold,
And all the old romance, retold
    Exactly in the ancient way,
Can please, as me they pleased of old,
    The wiser youngsters of to-day:

—So be it, and fall on! If not,
    If studious youth no longer crave,
His ancient appetites forgot,
    Kingston, or Ballantyne the brave,
Or Cooper* of the wood and wave:
    So be it, also! And may I
And all my pirates share the grave
    Where these and their creations lie!

To

S. L. O.,*

AN AMERICAN GENTLEMAN,

IN ACCORDANCE WITH WHOSE CLASSIC TASTE

THE FOLLOWING NARRATIVE HAS BEEN DESIGNED,

IT IS NOW, IN RETURN FOR NUMEROUS DELIGHTFUL HOURS,

AND WITH THE KINDEST WISHES,

Dedicated

BY HIS AFFECTIONATE FRIEND,

THE AUTHOR.

CONTENTS

PART I

THE OLD BUCCANEER

PART II

THE SEA COOK

PART III

MY SHORE ADVENTURE

PART IV

THE STOCKADE

PART V

MY SEA ADVENTURE

PART VI

CAPTAIN SILVER

A Scale of 3 English Miles.

Foremast Hill

North Inlet

Spye glasse open ✕ clears banks

Spye glass Hill

Strong tide here

Cape of ye Woods

Mizzen mast Hill

Haulbowline Head

Spring

Cavern

Swamp

Graves

Bulk of Treasure here

Skeleton Island

White Rock

Foul ground

Treasure Island
Augt 1750. J. F.

Given by above J. F. & Mr W. Bones Maite of ye Walrus
Savannah this twenty July 1754 W. B.

Facsimile of Chart; latitude and
longitude struck out by J. Hawkins

PART I
THE OLD BUCCANEER

CHAPTER I
THE OLD SEA-DOG AT THE 'ADMIRAL BENBOW'

SQUIRE TRELAWNEY,* Dr Livesey, and the rest of these gentlemen having asked me to write down the whole particulars about Treasure Island, from the beginning to the end, keeping nothing back but the bearings of the island, and that only because there is still treasure not yet lifted, I take up my pen in the year of grace 17—, and go back to the time when my father kept the 'Admiral Benbow'* inn, and the brown old seaman, with the sabre cut, first took up his lodging under our roof.*

I remember him as if it were yesterday, as he came plodding to the inn door, his sea-chest following behind him in a handbarrow; a tall, strong, heavy, nut-brown man; his tarry pigtail* falling over the shoulders of his soiled blue coat; his hands ragged and scarred, with black, broken nails; and the sabre cut across one cheek, a dirty, livid white.* I remember him looking round the cove and whistling to himself as he did so, and then breaking out in that old sea-song that he sang so often afterwards:—

> 'Fifteen men on the dead man's chest*—
> Yo-ho-ho, and a bottle of rum!'

in the high, old tottering voice that seemed to have been tuned and broken at the capstan bars. Then he rapped on the door with a bit of stick like a handspike that he carried, and when my father appeared, called roughly for a glass of rum. This, when it was brought to him, he drank slowly, like a connoisseur, lingering on the taste, and still looking about him at the cliffs and up at our signboard.

'This is a handy cove,' says he, at length; 'and a pleasant sittyated grog-shop.* Much company, mate?'

My father told him no, very little company, the more was the pity.

'Well, then,' said he, 'this is the berth for me. Here you, matey,' he cried to the man who trundled the barrow; 'bring up alongside and help up my chest. I'll stay here a bit,' he continued. 'I'm a plain man; rum and bacon and eggs is what I want, and that head up there for to watch ships off. What you mought call me? You mought call me captain. Oh, I see what you're at—there;' and he threw down three or four gold pieces on the threshold. 'You can tell me when I've worked through that,' says he, looking as fierce as a commander.

And, indeed, bad as his clothes were, and coarsely as he spoke, he had none of the appearance of a man who sailed before the mast; but seemed like a mate or skipper, accustomed to be obeyed or to strike. The man who came with the barrow told us the mail had set him down the morning before at the 'Royal George;' that he had inquired what inns there were along the coast, and hearing ours well spoken of, I suppose, and described as lonely, had chosen it from the others for his place of residence. And that was all we could learn of our guest.

He was a very silent man by custom. All day he hung round the cove, or upon the cliffs, with a brass telescope; all evening he sat in a corner of the parlour next the fire, and drank rum and water very strong. Mostly he would not speak when spoken to; only look up sudden and fierce, and blow through his nose like a fog-horn; and we and the people who came about our house soon learned to let him be. Every day, when he came back from his stroll, he would ask if any seafaring men had gone by along the road. At first we thought it was the want of company of his own kind that made him ask this question; but at last we began to see he was desirous to avoid them. When a seaman put up at the 'Admiral Benbow' (as now and then some did, making by the coast road for Bristol), he would look in at him through the curtained door before he entered the parlour; and he was always sure to be as silent as a mouse when any such was present. For me, at least, there was no secret about the matter; for I was, in a way, a sharer in his alarms. He had taken me aside one day, and promised me a silver fourpenny* on the first of every month if I would only keep my 'weather-eye open for a seafaring man with one leg,' and let him know the moment he appeared. Often enough, when the first of the month came round, and I applied to him for my wage, he would only blow through his nose at me, and stare me down; but before the week was out he was sure to think better of it, bring me my fourpenny piece, and repeat his orders to look out for 'the seafaring man with one leg.'

How that personage haunted my dreams, I need scarcely tell you. On stormy nights, when the wind shook the four corners of the house, and the surf roared along the cove and up the cliffs, I would see him in a thousand forms, and with a thousand diabolical expressions. Now the leg would be cut off at the knee, now at the hip; now he was a monstrous kind of a creature who had never had but the one leg, and that in the middle of his body. To see him leap and run and pursue me over hedge and ditch was the worst of nightmares. And altogether I paid pretty dear for my monthly fourpenny piece, in the shape of these abominable fancies.

But though I was so terrified by the idea of the seafaring man with one leg, I was far less afraid of the captain himself than anybody else who knew him. There were nights when he took a deal more rum and water than his head would carry; and then he would sometimes sit and sing his wicked, old, wild sea-songs, minding nobody; but sometimes he would call for glasses round, and force all the trembling company to listen to his stories or bear a chorus to his singing. Often I have heard the house shaking with 'Yo-ho-ho, and a bottle of rum;' all the neighbours joining in for dear life, with the fear of death upon them, and each singing louder than the other, to avoid remark. For in these fits he was the most overriding companion ever known; he would slap his hand on the table for silence all round; he would fly up in a passion of anger at a question, or sometimes because none was put, and so he judged the company was not following his story. Nor would he allow anyone to leave the inn till he had drunk himself sleepy and reeled off to bed.

His stories were what frightened people worst of all. Dreadful stories they were; about hanging, and walking the plank, and storms at sea, and the Dry Tortugas,* and wild deeds and places on the Spanish Main.* By his own account he must have lived his life among some of the wickedest men that God ever allowed upon the sea; and the language in which he told these stories shocked our plain country people almost as much as the crimes that he described. My father was always saying the inn would be ruined, for people would soon cease coming there to be tyrannised over and put down, and sent shivering to their beds; but I really believe his presence did us good. People were frightened at the time, but on looking back they rather liked it; it was a fine excitement in a quiet country life; and there was even a party of the younger men who pretended to admire him, calling him a 'true sea-dog,' and a 'real old salt,' and suchlike names, and saying there was the sort of man that made England terrible at sea.

In one way, indeed, he bade fair to ruin us; for he kept on staying week after week, and at last month after month, so that all the money had been long exhausted, and still my father never plucked up the heart to insist on having more. If ever he mentioned it, the captain blew through his nose so loudly, that you might say he roared, and stared my poor father out of the room. I have seen him wringing his hands after such a rebuff, and I am sure the annoyance and the terror he lived in must have greatly hastened his early and unhappy death.

All the time he lived with us the captain made no change whatever in his dress but to buy some stockings from a hawker. One of the cocks of his hat having fallen down,* he let it hang from that day forth, though it was a great annoyance when it blew. I remember the appearance of his coat, which he patched himself upstairs in his room, and which, before the end, was nothing but patches. He never wrote or received a letter, and he never spoke with any but the neighbours, and with these, for the most part, only when drunk on rum. The great sea-chest none of us had ever seen open.

He was only once crossed, and that was towards the end, when my poor father was far gone in a decline that took him off. Dr Livesey came late one afternoon to see the patient, took a bit of dinner from my mother, and went into the parlour to smoke a pipe until his horse should come down from the hamlet, for we had no stabling at the old 'Benbow.' I followed him in, and I remember observing the contrast the neat, bright doctor, with his powder* as white as snow, and his bright, black eyes and pleasant manners, made with the coltish country folk, and above all, with that filthy, heavy, bleared scarecrow of a pirate of ours, sitting, far gone in rum, with his arms on the table. Suddenly he—the captain, that is—began to pipe up his eternal song:—

'Fifteen men on the dead man's chest
  Yo-ho-ho, and a bottle of rum!
Drink and the devil had done for the rest—
  Yo-ho-ho, and a bottle of rum!'

At first I had supposed 'the dead man's chest' to be that identical big box of his upstairs in the front room, and the thought had been mingled in my nightmares with that of the one-legged seafaring man.

But by this time we had all long ceased to pay any particular notice to the song; it was new, that night, to nobody but Dr Livesey, and on him I observed it did not produce an agreeable effect, for he looked up for a moment quite angrily before he went on with his talk to old Taylor, the gardener, on a new cure for the rheumatics. In the meantime, the captain gradually brightened up at his own music, and at last flapped his hand upon the table before him in a way we all knew to mean—silence. The voices stopped at once, all but Dr Livesey's; he went on as before, speaking clear and kind, and drawing briskly at his pipe between every word or two. The captain glared at him for a while, flapped his hand again, glared still harder, and at last broke out with a villainous, low oath:* 'Silence, there, between decks!'

'Were you addressing me, sir?' says the doctor; and when the ruffian had told him, with another oath, that this was so, 'I have only one thing to say to you, sir,' replies the doctor, 'that if you keep on drinking rum, the world will soon be quit of a very dirty scoundrel!'

The old fellow's fury was awful. He sprang to his feet, drew and opened a sailor's clasp-knife,* and, balancing it open on the palm of his hand, threatened to pin the doctor to the wall.

The doctor never so much as moved. He spoke to him, as before, over his shoulder, and in the same tone of voice; rather high, so that all the room might hear, but perfectly calm and steady:—

'If you do not put that knife this instant in your pocket, I promise, upon my honour, you shall hang at the next assizes.'*

Then followed a battle of looks between them; but the captain soon knuckled under, put up his weapon, and resumed his seat, grumbling like a beaten dog.

'And now, sir,' continued the doctor, 'since I now know there's such a fellow in my district, you may count I'll have an eye upon you day and night. I'm not a doctor only; I'm a magistrate; and if I catch a breath of complaint against you, if its only for a piece of incivility like to-night's, I'll take effectual means to have you hunted down and routed out of this. Let that suffice.'

Soon after Dr Livesey's horse came to the door, and he rode away; but the captain held his peace that evening, and for many evenings to come.

CHAPTER II

BLACK DOG APPEARS AND DISAPPEARS

It was not very long after this that there occurred the first of the mysterious events that rid us at last of the captain, though not, as you will see, of his affairs. It was a bitter cold winter, with long, hard frosts and heavy gales; and it was plain from the first that my poor father was little likely to see the spring. He sank daily, and my mother and I had all the inn upon our hands; and were kept busy enough, without paying much regard to our unpleasant guest.

It was one January morning, very early—a pinching, frosty morning—the cove all grey with hoar-frost, the ripple lapping softly on the stones, the sun still low and only touching the hilltops and shining far to seaward. The captain had risen earlier than usual, and set out down the beach, his cutlass* swinging under the broad skirts of the old blue coat, his brass telescope under his arm, his hat tilted back upon his head. I remember his breath hanging like smoke in his wake as he strode off, and the last sound I heard of him, as he turned the big rock, was a loud snort of indignation, as though his mind was still running upon Dr Livesey.

Well, mother was upstairs with father; and I was laying the breakfast table against the captain's return, when the parlour door opened, and a man stepped in on whom I had never set my eyes before. He was a pale, tallowy creature, wanting two fingers of the left hand; and, though he wore a cutlass, he did not look much like a fighter. I had always my eye open for seafaring men, with one leg or two, and I remember this one puzzled me. He was not sailorly, and yet he had a smack of the sea about him too.

I asked him what was for his service, and he said he would take rum; but as I was going out of the room to fetch it he sat down upon a table, and motioned me to draw near. I paused where I was with my napkin in my hand.

'Come here, sonny,' says he. 'Come nearer here.'

I took a step nearer.

'Is this here table for my mate, Bill?' he asked, with a kind of leer.

I told him I did not know his mate Bill; and this was for a person who stayed in our house, whom we called the captain.

'Well,' said he, 'my mate Bill would be called the captain, as like as not. He has a cut on one cheek, and a mighty pleasant way with him, particularly in drink, has my mate, Bill. We'll put it, for argument like, that your captain has a cut on one cheek—and we'll put it, if you like, that that cheek's the right one. Ah, well! I told you. Now, is my mate Bill in this here house?'

I told him he was out walking.

'Which way, sonny? Which way is he gone?'

And when I had pointed out the rock and told him how the captain was likely to return, and how soon, and answered a few other questions, 'Ah,' said he, 'this'll be as good as drink to my mate Bill.'

The expression of his face as he said these words was not at all pleasant, and I had my own reasons for thinking that the stranger was mistaken, even supposing he meant what he said. But it was no affair of mine, I thought; and, besides, it was difficult to know what to do. The stranger kept hanging about just inside the inn door, peering round the corner like a cat waiting for a mouse. Once I stepped out myself into the road, but he immediately called me back, and, as I did not obey quick enough for his fancy, a most horrible change came over his tallowy face, and he ordered me in, with an oath that made me jump. As soon as I was back again he returned to his former manner, half fawning, half sneering, patted me on the shoulder, told me I was a good boy, and he had taken quite a fancy to me. 'I have a son of my own,' said he, 'as like you as two blocks, and he's all the pride of my 'art. But the great thing for boys is discipline, sonny—discipline. Now, if you had sailed along of Bill, you wouldn't have stood there to be spoke to twice—not you. That was never Bill's way, nor the way of sich as sailed with him. And here, sure enough, is my mate Bill, with a spy-glass under his arm, bless his old 'art to be sure. You and me'll just go back into the parlour, sonny, and get behind the door, and we'll give Bill a little surprise—bless his 'art, I say again.'

So saying, the stranger backed along with me into the parlour, and put me behind him in the corner, so that we were both hidden by the open door. I was very uneasy and alarmed, as you may fancy, and it rather added to my fears to observe that the stranger was certainly frightened himself. He cleared the hilt of his cutlass and loosened the blade in the sheath; and all the time we were waiting there he kept swallowing as if he felt what we used to call a lump in the throat.

At last in strode the captain, slammed the door behind him, without looking to the right or left, and marched straight across the room to where his breakfast awaited him.

'Bill,' said the stranger, in a voice that I thought he had tried to make bold and big.

The captain spun round on his heel and fronted us; all the brown had gone out of his face, and even his nose was blue; he had the look of a man who sees a ghost, or the evil one, or something worse, if anything can be; and, upon my word, I felt sorry to see him, all in a moment, turn so old and sick.

'Come, Bill, you know me; you know an old shipmate, Bill, surely,' said the stranger.

The captain made a sort of gasp.

'Black Dog!' said he.

'And who else?' returned the other, getting more at his ease. 'Black Dog as ever was, come for to see his old shipmate Billy, at the "Admiral Benbow" inn. Ah, Bill, Bill, we have seen a sight of times, us two, since I lost them two talons,' holding up his mutilated hand.

'Now, look here,' said the captain; 'you've run me down; here I am; well, then, speak up: what is it?'

'That's you, Bill,' returned Black Dog, 'you're in the right of it, Billy. I'll have a glass of rum from this dear child here, as I've took such a liking to; and we'll sit down, if you please, and talk square, like old shipmates.'

When I returned with the rum, they were already seated on either side of the captain's breakfast table—Black Dog next to the door, and sitting sideways, so as to have one eye on his old shipmate, and one, as I thought, on his retreat.

He bade me go, and leave the door wide open. 'None of your keyholes for me, sonny,' he said; and I left them together, and retired into the bar.

For a long time, though I certainly did my best to listen, I could hear nothing but a low gabbling; but at last the voices began to grow higher, and I could pick up a word or two, mostly oaths, from the captain.

'No, no, no, no; and an end of it!' he cried once. And again, 'If it comes to swinging, swing all, say I.'

Then all of a sudden there was a tremendous explosion of oaths and other noises—the chair and table went over in a lump, a clash of steel followed, and then a cry of pain, and the next instant I saw Black Dog in full flight, and the captain hotly pursuing, both with drawn cutlasses, and the former streaming blood from the left shoulder. Just at the door, the captain aimed at the fugitive one last tremendous cut, which would certainly have split him to the chine* had it not been intercepted by our big signboard of Admiral Benbow. You may see the notch on the lower side of the frame to this day.

That blow was the last of the battle. Once out upon the road, Black Dog, in spite of his wound, showed a wonderful clean pair of heels, and disappeared over the edge of the hill in half a minute. The captain, for his part, stood staring at the signboard like a bewildered man. Then he passed his hand over his eyes several times, and at last turned back into the house.

'Jim,' says he, 'rum;' and as he spoke, he reeled a little, and caught himself with one hand against the wall.

'Are you hurt?' cried I.

'Rum,' he repeated. 'I must get away from here. Rum! rum!'

I ran to fetch it; but I was quite unsteadied by all that had fallen out, and I broke one glass and fouled the tap, and while I was still getting in my own way, I heard a loud fall in the parlour, and, running in, beheld the captain lying full length upon the floor. At the same instant my mother, alarmed by the cries and fighting, came running downstairs to help me. Between us we raised his head. He was breathing very loud and hard; but his eyes were closed, and his face a horrible colour.

'Dear, deary me,' cried my mother, 'what a disgrace upon the house! And your poor father sick!'

In the meantime, we had no idea what to do to help the captain, nor any other thought but that he had got his death-hurt in the scuffle with the stranger. I got the rum, to be sure, and tried to put it down his throat; but his teeth were tightly shut, and his jaws as strong as iron. It was a happy relief for us when the door opened and Doctor Livesey came in, on his visit to my father.

'Oh, doctor,' we cried, 'what shall we do? Where is he wounded?'

'Wounded? A fiddle-stick's end!' said the doctor. 'No more wounded than you or I. The man has had a stroke, as I warned him. Now, Mrs Hawkins, just you run upstairs to your husband, and tell him, if possible, nothing about it. For my part, I must do my best to save this fellow's trebly worthless life; and Jim, you get me a basin.'

When I got back with the basin, the doctor had already ripped up the captain's sleeve, and exposed his great sinewy arm. It was tattooed in several places. 'Here's luck,' 'A fair wind,' and 'Billy Bones* his fancy,' were very neatly and clearly executed on the forearm; and up near the shoulder there was a sketch of a gallows and a man hanging from it—done, as I thought, with great spirit.

'Prophetic,' said the doctor, touching this picture with his finger. 'And now, Master Billy Bones, if that be your name, we'll have a look at the colour of your blood. Jim,' he said, 'are you afraid of blood?'

'No, sir,' said I.

'Well, then,' said he, 'you hold the basin;' and with that he took his lancet and opened a vein.*

A great deal of blood was taken before the captain opened his eyes and looked mistily about him. First he recognised the doctor with an unmistakable frown; then his glance fell upon me, and he looked relieved. But suddenly his colour changed, and he tried to raise himself, crying:—

'Where's Black Dog?'*

'There is no Black Dog here,' said the doctor, 'except what you have on your own back. You have been drinking rum; you have had a stroke, precisely as I told you; and I have just, very much against my own will, dragged you headforemost out of the grave. Now, Mr Bones—'

'That's not my name,' he interrupted.

'Much I care,' returned the doctor, 'It's the name of a buccaneer of my acquaintance; and I call you by it for the sake of shortness, and what I have to say to you is this: one glass of rum won't kill you, but if you take one you'll take another and another, and I stake my wig if you don't break off short, you'll die—do you understand that?—die, and go to your own place, like the man in the Bible.* Come, now, make an effort. I'll help you to your bed for once.'

Between us, with much trouble, we managed to hoist him upstairs, and laid him on his bed, where his head fell back on the pillow, as if he were almost fainting.

'Now, mind you,' said the doctor, 'I clear my conscience—the name of rum for you is death.'

And with that he went off to see my father, taking me with him by the arm.

'This is nothing,' he said, as soon as he had closed the door. 'I have drawn blood enough to keep him quiet a while; he should lie for a week where he is—that is the best thing for him and you; but another stroke would settle him.'

CHAPTER III

THE BLACK SPOT

ABOUT noon I stopped at the captain's door with some cooling drinks and medicines. He was lying very much as we had left him, only a little higher, and he seemed both weak and excited.

'Jim,' he said, 'you're the only one here that's worth anything; and you know I've been always good to you. Never a month but I've given you a silver fourpenny for yourself. And now you see, mate, I'm pretty low, and deserted by all; and Jim, you'll bring me one noggin of rum, now, won't you, matey?'

'The doctor—' I began.

But he broke in cursing the doctor, in a feeble voice, but heartily. 'Doctors is all swabs,' he said; 'and that doctor there, why, what do he know about seafaring men? I been in places hot as pitch, and mates dropping round with Yellow Jack,* and the blessed land a-heaving like the sea with earthquakes—what do the doctor know of lands like that?—and I lived on rum, I tell you. It's been meat and drink, and man and wife, to me; and if I'm not to have my rum now I'm a poor old hulk on a lee shore,* my blood'll be on you, Jim, and that Doctor swab;' and he ran on again for a while with curses. 'Look, Jim, how my fingers fidges,' he continued, in the pleading tone. 'I can't keep 'em still, not I. I haven't had a drop this blessed day. That doctor's a fool, I tell you. If I don't have a drain o' rum, Jim. I'll have the horrors,* I seen some on 'em already. I seen old Flint in the corner there, behind you, as plain as print, I seen him; and if I get the horrors, I'm a man that has lived rough, and I'll raise Cain. Your doctor hisself said one glass wouldn't hurt me. I'll give you a golden guinea for a noggin,* Jim.'

He was growing more and more excited, and this alarmed me for my father, who was very low that day, and needed quiet; besides, I was reassured by the doctor's words, now quoted to me, and rather offended by the offer of a bribe.

'I want none of your money,' said I, 'but what you owe my father. I'll get you one glass, and no more.'

When I brought it to him, he seized it greedily, and drank it out.

'Ay, ay,' said he, 'that's some better, sure enough. And now, matey, did that doctor say how long I was to lie here in this old berth?'

'A week at least,' said I.

'Thunder!' he cried. 'A week! I can't do that: they'd have the black spot* on me by then. The lubbers is going about to get the wind of me* this blessed moment; lubbers as couldn't keep what they got, and want to nail what is another's. Is that seamanly behaviour, now, I want to know? But I'm a saving soul. I never wasted good money of mine, nor lost it neither; and I'll trick 'em again. I'm not afraid on 'em. I'll shake out another reef, matey, and daddle 'em again.'

As he was thus speaking, he had risen from bed with great difficulty, holding to my shoulder with a grip that almost made me cry out, and moving his legs like so much dead weight. His words, spirited as they were in meaning, contrasted sadly with the weakness of the voice in which they were uttered. He paused when he had got into a sitting position on the edge.

'That doctor's done me,' he murmured. 'My ears is singing. Lay me back.'

Before I could do much to help him he had fallen back again to his former place, where he lay for a while silent.

'Jim,' he said, at length, 'you saw that seafaring man today?'

'Black Dog?' I asked.

'Ah! Black Dog,' says he. '*He's* a bad 'un; but there's worse that put him on. Now, if I can't get away nohow, and they tip me the black spot, mind you, it's my old sea-chest they're after; you get on a horse—you can, can't you? Well, then, you get on a horse, and go to—well, yes, I will!—to that eternal doctor swab, and tell him to pipe all hands—magistrates and sich—and he'll lay 'em aboard at the "Admiral Benbow"—all old Flint's crew, man and boy, all on 'em that's left. I was first mate, I was, old Flint's first mate, and I'm the on'y one as knows the place. He gave it me at Savannah,* when he lay a-dying, like as if I was to now, you see. But you won't peach* unless they get the black spot on me, or unless you see that Black Dog again, or a seafaring man with one leg, Jim—him above all.'

'But what is the black spot, Captain?' I asked.

'That's a summons, mate. I'll tell you if they get that. But you keep your weather-eye open, Jim, and I'll share with you equals, upon my honour.'

He wandered a little longer, his voice growing weaker; but soon after I had given him his medicine, which he took like a child, with the remark, 'If ever a seaman wanted drugs, it's me,' he fell at last into a heavy, swoon-like sleep, in which I left him. What I should have done had all gone well I do not know. Probably I should have told the whole story to the doctor; for I was in mortal fear lest the captain should repent of his confessions and make an end of me. But as things fell out, my poor father died quite suddenly that evening, which put all other matters on one side. Our natural distress, the visits of the neighbours, the arranging of the funeral, and all the work of the inn to be carried on in the meanwhile, kept me so busy that I had scarcely time to think of the captain, far less to be afraid of him.

He got downstairs next morning, to be sure, and had his meals as usual, though he ate little, and had more, I am afraid, than his usual supply of rum, for he helped himself out of the bar, scowling and blowing through his nose, and no one dared to cross him. On the night before the funeral he was as drunk as ever; and it was shocking, in that house of mourning, to hear him singing away at his ugly old sea-song; but, weak as he was, we were all in the fear of death for him, and the doctor was suddenly taken up with a case many miles away, and was never near the house after my father's death. I have said the captain was weak; and indeed he seemed rather to grow weaker than regain his strength. He clambered up and downstairs, and went from the parlour to the bar and back again, and sometimes put his nose out of doors to smell the sea, holding on to the walls as he went for support, and breathing hard and fast like a man on a steep mountain. He never particularly addressed me, and it is my belief he had as good as forgotten his confidences; but his temper was more flighty, and, allowing for his bodily weakness, more violent than ever. He had an alarming way now when he was drunk of drawing his cutlass and laying it bare before him on the table. But, with all that, he minded people less, and seemed shut up in his own thoughts and rather wandering. Once, for instance, to our extreme wonder, he piped up to a different air, a kind of country love-song, that he must have learned in his youth before he had begun to follow the sea.

So things passed until, the day after the funeral, and about three o'clock of a bitter, foggy, frosty afternoon, I was standing at the door for a moment full of sad thoughts about my father, when I saw someone drawing slowly near along the road. He was plainly blind, for he tapped before him with a stick, and wore a great green shade over his eyes and nose; and he was hunched, as if with age or weakness, and wore a huge old tattered sea-cloak with a hood, that made him appear positively deformed. I never saw in my life a more dreadful looking figure.* He stopped a little from the inn, and, raising his voice in an odd sing-song, addressed the air in front of him:—

'Will any kind friend inform a poor blind man, who has lost the precious sight of his eyes in the gracious defence of his native country, England, and God bless King George!—where or in what part of this country he may now be?'

'You are at the "Admiral Benbow," Black Hill Cove, my good man,' said I.

'I hear a voice,' said he—'a young voice. Will you give me your hand, my kind, young friend, and lead me in?'

I held out my hand, and the horrible, soft-spoken, eyeless creature gripped it in a moment like a vice. I was so much startled that I struggled to withdraw; but the blind man pulled me close up to him with a single action of his arm.

'Now, boy,' he said, 'take me in to the captain.'

'Sir,' said I, 'upon my word I dare not.'

'Oh,' he sneered, 'that's it! Take me in straight, or I'll break your arm.'

And he gave it, as he spoke, a wrench that made me cry out.

'Sir,' said I, 'it is for yourself I mean. The captain is not what he used to be. He sits with a drawn cutlass. Another gentleman—'

'Come, now, march,' interrupted he; and I never heard a voice so cruel, and cold, and ugly as that blind man's. It cowed me more than the pain; and I began to obey him at once, walking straight in at the door and towards the parlour, where our sick old buccaneer was sitting, dazed with rum. The blind man clung close to me, holding me in one iron fist, and leaning almost more of his weight on me than I could carry. 'Lead me straight up to him, and when I'm in view, cry out, "Here's a friend for you, Bill." If you don't, I'll do this;' and with that he gave me a twitch that I thought would have made me faint. Between this and that, I was so utterly terrified of the blind beggar that I forgot my terror of the captain, and as I opened the parlour door, cried out the words he had ordered in a trembling voice.

The poor captain raised his eyes, and at one look the rum went out of him, and left him staring sober. The expression of his face was not so much of terror as of mortal sickness. He made a movement to rise, but I do not believe he had enough force left in his body.

'Now, Bill, sit where you are,' said the beggar. 'If I can't see, I can hear a finger stirring. Business is business. Hold out your left hand. Boy, take his left hand by the wrist, and bring it near to my right.'

We both obeyed him to the letter, and I saw him pass something from the hollow of the hand that held his stick into the palm of the captain's, which closed upon it instantly.

'And now that's done,' said the blind man; and at the words he suddenly left hold of me, and, with incredible accuracy and nimbleness, skipped out of the parlour and into the road, where, as I still stood motionless, I could hear his stick go tap-tap-tapping into the distance.

It was some time before either I or the captain seemed to gather our senses; but at length, and about at the same moment, I released his wrist, which I was still holding, and he drew in his hand and looked sharply into the palm.

'Ten o'clock!' he cried. "Six hours. We'll do them yet;' and he sprang to his feet.

Even as he did so, he reeled, put his hand to his throat, stood swaying for a moment, and then, with a peculiar sound, fell from his whole height face foremost to the floor.

I ran to him at once, calling to my mother. But haste was all in vain. The captain had been struck dead by thundering apoplexy.* It is a curious thing to understand, for I had certainly never liked the man, though of late I had begun to pity him, but as soon as I saw that he was dead, I burst into a flood of tears. It was the second death I had known, and the sorrow of the first was still fresh in my heart.

CHAPTER IV

THE SEA CHEST

I LOST no time, of course, in telling my mother all that I knew, and perhaps should have told her long before, and we saw ourselves at once in a difficult and dangerous position. Some of the man's money—if he had any—was certainly due to us; but it was not likely that our captain's shipmates, above all the two specimens seen by me, Black Dog and the blind beggar, would be inclined to give up their booty in payment of the dead man's debts. The captain's order to mount at once and ride for Doctor Livesey would have left my mother alone and unprotected, which was not to be thought of. Indeed, it seemed impossible for either of us to remain much longer in the house: the fall of coals in the kitchen grate, the very ticking of the clock, filled us with alarms. The neighbourhood, to our ears, seemed haunted by approaching footsteps; and what between the dead body of the captain on the parlour floor, and the thought of that detestable blind beggar hovering near at hand, and ready to return, there were moments when, as the saying goes, I jumped in my skin for terror. Something must speedily be resolved upon; and it occurred to us at last to go forth together and seek help in the neighbouring hamlet. No sooner said than done. Bare-headed as we were, we ran out at once in the gathering evening and the frosty fog.

The hamlet lay not many hundred yards away though out of view, on the other side of the next cove; and what greatly encouraged me, it was in an opposite direction from that whence the blind man had made his appearance, and whither he had presumably returned. We were not many minutes on the road, though we sometimes stopped to lay hold of each other and hearken. But there was no unusual sound—nothing but the low wash of the ripple and the croaking of the inmates of the wood.

It was already candle-light when we reached the hamlet, and I shall never forget how much I was cheered to see the yellow shine in doors and windows; but that, as it proved, was the best of the help we were likely to get in that quarter. For—you would have thought men would have been ashamed of themselves—no soul would consent to return with us to the 'Admiral Benbow.' The more we told of our troubles, the more—man, woman, and child—they clung to the shelter of their houses. The name of Captain Flint, though it was strange to me, was well enough known to some there, and carried a great weight of terror. Some of the men who had been to field-work on the far side of the 'Admiral Benbow' remembered, besides, to have seen several strangers on the road, and, taking them to be smugglers, to have bolted away; and one at least had seen a little lugger in what we called Kitt's Hole. For that matter, anyone who was a comrade of the captain's was enough to frighten them to death. And the short and the long of the matter was, that while we could get several who were willing enough to ride to Dr Livesey's which lay in another direction, not one would help us to defend the inn.

They say cowardice is infectious; but then argument is, on the other hand, a great emboldener; and so when each had said his say, my mother made them a speech. She would not, she declared, lose money that belonged to her fatherless boy; 'if none of the rest of you dare,' she said, 'Jim and I dare. Back we will go, the way we came, and small thanks to you big, hulking, chicken-hearted men. We'll have that chest open, if we die for it. And I'll thank you for that bag, Mrs Crossley, to bring back our lawful money in.'

Of course, I said I would go with my mother; and of course they all cried out at our foolhardiness; but even then not a man would go along with us. All they would do was to give me a loaded pistol, lest we were attacked; and to promise to have horses ready saddled, in case we were pursued on our return; while one lad was to ride forward to the doctor's in search of armed assistance.

My heart was beating finely when we two set forth in the cold night upon this dangerous venture. A full moon was beginning to rise and peered redly through the upper edges of the fog, and this increased our haste, for it was plain, before we came forth again, that all would be as bright as day, and our departure exposed to the eyes of any watchers. We slipped along the hedges, noiseless and swift, nor did we see or hear anything to increase our terrors, till, to our relief, the door of the 'Admiral Benbow' had closed behind us.

I slipped the bolt at once, and we stood and panted for a moment in the dark, alone in the house with the dead captain's body. Then my mother got a candle in the bar, and, holding each other's hands, we advanced into the parlour. He lay as we had left him, on his back, with his eyes open, and one arm stretched out.

'Draw down the blind, Jim,' whispered my mother; 'they might come and watch outside. And now,' said she, when I had done so, 'we have to get the key off *that*; and who's to touch it, I should like to know!' and she gave a kind of sob as she said the words.

I went down on my knees at once. On the floor close to his hand there was a little round of paper, blackened on the one side. I could not doubt that this was the *black spot*; and taking it up, I found written on the other side, in a very good, clear hand, this short message: 'You have till ten to-night.'

'He had till ten, mother,' said I; and just as I said it, our old clock began striking. This sudden noise startled us shockingly; but the news was good, for it was only six.

'Now, Jim,' she said, 'that key.'

I felt in his pockets, one after another. A few small coins, a thimble, and some thread and big needles, a piece of pigtail tobacco* bitten away at the end, his gully* with the crooked handle, a pocket compass, and a tinder box, were all that they contained, and I began to despair.

'Perhaps it's round his neck,' suggested my mother.

Overcoming a strong repugnance, I tore open his shirt at the neck, and there, sure enough, hanging to a bit of tarry string, which I cut with his own gully, we found the key. At this triumph we were filled with hope, and hurried upstairs, without delay, to the little room where he had slept so long, and where his box had stood since the day of his arrival.

It was like any other seaman's chest on the outside, the initial 'B.' burned on the top of it with a hot iron, and the corners somewhat smashed and broken as by long, rough usage.

'Give me the key,' said my mother; and though the lock was very stiff, she had turned it and thrown back the lid in a twinkling.

A strong smell of tobacco and tar rose from the interior, but nothing was to be seen on the top except a suit of very good clothes, carefully brushed and folded. They had never been worn, my mother said. Under that, the miscellany began—a quadrant, a tin canikin,* several sticks of tobacco, two brace of very handsome pistols, a piece of bar silver, an old Spanish watch and some other trinkets of little value and mostly of foreign make, a pair of compasses mounted with brass, and five or six curious West Indian shells. I have often wondered since why he should have carried about these shells with him in his wandering, guilty, and hunted life.

In the meantime, we had found nothing of any value but the silver and the trinkets, and neither of these were in our way. Underneath there was an old boat-cloak, whitened with sea-salt on many a harbour-bar. My mother pulled it up with impatience, and there lay before us, the last things in the chest, a bundle tied up in oilcloth, and looking like papers, and a canvas bag, that gave forth, at a touch, the jingle of gold.

'I'll show these rogues that I'm an honest woman,' said my mother. 'I'll have my dues, and not a farthing over. Hold Mrs Crossley's bag.' And she began to count over the amount of the captain's score from the sailor's bag into the one that I was holding.

It was a long, difficult business, for the coins were of all countries and sizes—doubloons, and louis-d'ors, and guineas, and pieces of eight,* and I know not what besides, all shaken together at random. The guineas, too, were about the scarcest, and it was with these only that my mother knew how to make her count.

When we were about half-way through, I suddenly put my hand upon her arm; for I had heard in the silent, frosty air, a sound that brought my heart into my mouth—the tap-tapping of the blind man's stick upon the frozen road. It drew nearer and nearer, while we sat holding our breath. Then it struck sharp on the inn door, and then we could hear the handle being turned, and the bolt rattling as the wretched being tried to enter; and then there was a long time of silence both within and without. At last the tapping recommenced, and, to our indescribable joy and gratitude, died slowly away again until it ceased to be heard.

'Mother,' said I, 'take the whole and let's be going;' for I was sure the bolted door must have seemed suspicious, and would bring the whole hornet's nest about our ears; though how thankful I was that I had bolted it, none could tell who had never met that terrible blind man.

But my mother, frightened as she was, would not consent to take a fraction more than was due to her, and was obstinately unwilling to be content with less. It was not yet seven, she said, by a long way; she knew her rights and she would have them; and she was still arguing with me, when a little low whistle sounded a good way off upon the hill. That was enough, and more than enough, for both of us.

'I'll take what I have,' she said, jumping to her feet.

'And I'll take this to square the count,' said I, picking up the oilskin packet.

Next moment we were both groping downstairs, leaving the candle by the empty chest; and the next we had opened the door and were in full retreat. We had not started a moment too soon. The fog was rapidly dispersing; already the moon shone quite clear on the high ground on either side; and it was only in the exact bottom of the dell and round the tavern door that a thin veil still hung unbroken to conceal the first steps of our escape. Far less than half-way to the hamlet, very little beyond the bottom of the hill, we must come forth into the moonlight. Nor was this all; for the sound of several footsteps running came already to our ears, and as we looked back in their direction, a light tossing to and fro and still rapidly advancing, showed that one of the new-comers carried a lantern.

'My dear,' said my mother suddenly, 'take the money and run on. I am going to faint.'

This was certainly the end for both of us, I thought. How I cursed the cowardice of the neighbours; how I blamed my poor mother for her honesty and her greed, for her past foolhardiness and present weakness! We were just at the little bridge, by good fortune; and I helped her, tottering as she was, to the edge of the bank, where, sure enough, she gave a sigh and fell on my shoulder. I do not know how I found the strength to do it at all, and I am afraid it was roughly done; but I managed to drag her down the bank and a little way under the arch. Farther I could not move her, for the bridge was too low to let me do more than crawl below it. So there we had to stay—my mother almost entirely exposed, and both of us within earshot of the inn.

CHAPTER V

THE LAST OF THE BLIND MAN

My curiosity, in a sense, was stronger than my fear; for I could not remain where I was, but crept back to the bank again, whence, sheltering my head behind a bush of broom, I might command the road before our door. I was scarcely in position ere my enemies began to arrive, seven or eight of them, running hard, their feet beating out of time along the road, and the man with the lantern some paces in front. Three men ran together, hand in hand; and I made out, even through the mist, that the middle man of this trio was the blind beggar. The next moment his voice showed me that I was right.

'Down with the door!' he cried.

'Ay, ay, sir!' answered two or three; and a rush was made upon the 'Admiral Benbow,' the lantern-bearer following; and then I could see them pause, and hear speeches passed in a lower key, as if they were surprised to find the door open. But the pause was brief, for the blind man again issued his commands. His voice sounded louder and higher, as if he were afire with eagerness and rage.

'In, in, in!' he shouted, and cursed them for their delay.

Four or five of them obeyed at once, two remaining on the road with the formidable beggar. There was a pause, then a cry of surprise, and then a voice shouting from the house:—

'Bill's dead!'

But the blind man swore at them again for their delay.

'Search him, some of you shirking lubbers, and the rest of you aloft and get the chest,' he cried.

I could hear their feet rattling up our old stairs, so that the house must have shook with it. Promptly afterwards, fresh sounds of astonishment arose; the window of the captain's room was thrown open with a slam and a jingle of broken glass; and a man leaned out into the moonlight, head and shoulders, and addressed the blind beggar on the road below him.

'Pew,' he cried, 'they've been before us. Someone's turned the chest out alow and aloft.'

'Is it there?' roared Pew.

'The money's there.'

The blind man cursed the money.

'Flint's fist,* I mean,' he cried.

'We don't see it here nohow,' returned the man.

'Here, you below there, is it on Bill?' cried the blind man again.

At that, another fellow, probably him who had remained below to search the captain's body, came to the door of the inn. 'Bill's been overhauled a'ready,' said he, 'nothin' left.'

'It's these people of the inn—it's that boy. I wish I had put his eyes out!' cried the blind man, Pew. 'They were here no time ago—they had the door bolted when I tried it. Scatter, lads, and find 'em.'

'Sure enough, they left their glim* here,' said the fellow from the window.

'Scatter and find 'em! Rout the house out!' reiterated Pew, striking with his stick upon the road.

Then there followed a great to-do through all our old inn, heavy feet pounding to and fro, furniture thrown over, doors kicked in, until the very rocks re-echoed, and the men came out again, one after another, on the road, and declared that we were nowhere to be found. And just then the same whistle that had alarmed my mother and myself over the dead captain's money was once more clearly audible through the night, but this time twice repeated. I had thought it to be the blind man's trumpet, so to speak, summoning his crew to the assault; but I now found that it was a signal from the hillside towards the hamlet, and, from its effect upon the buccaneers, a signal to warn them of approaching danger.

'There's Dirk again,' said one. 'Twice! We'll have to budge, mates.'

'Budge, you skulk!' cried Pew. 'Dirk was a fool and a coward from the first—you wouldn't mind him. They must be close by; they can't be far; you have your hands on it. Scatter and look for them, dogs! Oh, shiver my soul,' he cried, 'if I had eyes!'

This appeal seemed to produce some effect, for two of the fellows began to look here and there among the lumber, but half-heartedly, I thought, and with half an eye to their own danger all the time, while the rest stood irresolute on the road.

'You have your hands on thousands, you fools, and you hang a leg!* You'd be as rich as kings if you could find it, and you know it's here, and you stand there skulking. There wasn't one of you dared face Bill, and I did it—a blind man! And I'm to lose my chance for you! I'm to be a poor, crawling beggar, sponging for rum, when I might be rolling in a coach! If you had the pluck of a weevil in a biscuit you would catch them still.'

'Hang it, Pew, we've got the doubloons!' grumbled one.

'They might have hid the blessed thing,' said another. 'Take the Georges,* Pew, and don't stand here squalling.'

Squalling was the word for it, Pew's anger rose so high at these objections; till at last, his passion completely taking the upper hand, he struck at them right and left in his blindness, and his stick sounded heavily on more than one.

These, in their turn, cursed back at the blind miscreant, threatened him in horrid terms, and tried in vain to catch the stick and wrest it from his grasp.

This quarrel was the saving of us; for while it was still raging, another sound came from the top of the hill on the side of the hamlet—the tramp of horses galloping. Almost at the same time a pistol-shot, flash and report, came from the hedge-side. And that was plainly the last signal of danger; for the buccaneers turned at once and ran, separating in every direction, one seaward along the cove, one slant across the hill, and so on, so that in half a minute not a sign of them remained but Pew. Him they had deserted, whether in sheer panic or out of revenge for his ill words and blows, I know not; but there he remained behind, tapping up and down the road in a frenzy, and groping and calling for his comrades. Finally he took the wrong turn, and ran a few steps past me, towards the hamlet, crying:—

'Johnny, Black Dog, Dirk,' and other names, 'you won't leave old Pew, mates—not old Pew!'

Just then the noise of horses topped the rise, and four or five riders came in sight in the moonlight, and swept at full gallop down the slope.

At this Pew saw his error, turned with a scream, and ran straight for the ditch, into which he rolled. But he was on his feet again in a second, and made another dash, now utterly bewildered, right under the nearest of the coming horses.

The rider tried to save him, but in vain. Down went Pew with a cry that rang high into the night; and the four hoofs trampled and spurned him and passed by. He fell on his side, then gently collapsed upon his face, and moved no more.

I leaped to my feet and hailed the riders. They were pulling up, at any rate, horrified at the accident; and I soon saw what they were. One, tailing out behind the rest, was a lad that had gone from the hamlet to Dr Livesey's; the rest were revenue officers, whom he had met by the way, and with whom he had had the intelligence to return at once. Some news of the lugger in Kitt's Hole had found its way to Supervisor Dance, and set him forth that night in our direction, and to that circumstance my mother and I owed our preservation from death.

Pew was dead, stone dead. As for my mother, when we had carried her up to the hamlet, a little cold water and salts and that soon brought her back again, and she was none the worse for her terror, though she still continued to deplore the balance of the money. In the meantime the supervisor rode on, as fast as he could, to Kitt's Hole; but his men had to dismount and grope down the dingle, leading, and sometimes supporting, their horses, and in continual fear of ambushes; so it was no great matter for surprise that when they got down to the Hole the lugger was already under way, though still close in. He hailed her. A voice replied, telling him to keep out of the moonlight, or he would get some lead in him, and at the same time a bullet whistled close by his arm. Soon after, the lugger doubled the point and disappeared. Mr Dance stood there, as he said, 'like a fish out of water,' and all he could do was to despatch a man to B—— to warn the cutter. 'And that,' said he, 'is just about as good as nothing. They've got off clean, and there's an end. Only,' he added, 'I'm glad I trod on Master Pew's corns;' for by this time he had heard my story.

I went back with him to the 'Admiral Benbow,' and you cannot imagine a house in such a state of smash; the very clock had been thrown down by these fellows in their furious hunt after my mother and myself; and though nothing had actually been taken away except the captain's money-bag and a little silver from the till. I could see at once that we were ruined. Mr Dance could make nothing of the scene.

'They got the money, you say? Well, then, Hawkins, what in fortune were they after? More money, I suppose?'

'No, sir; not money, I think,' replied I. 'In fact, sir, I believe I have the thing in my breast-pocket; and, to tell you the truth, I should like to get it put in safety.'

'To be sure, boy; quite right,' said he. 'I'll take it, if you like.'

'I thought, perhaps, Dr Livesey—' I began.

'Perfectly right,' he interrupted, very cheerily, 'perfectly right—a gentleman and a magistrate. And, now I come to think of it, I might as well ride round there myself and report to him or squire. Master Pew's dead, when all's done; not that I regret it, but he's dead, you see, and people will make it out against an officer of his Majesty's revenue, if make it out they can. Now, I'll tell you, Hawkins: if you like, I'll take you along.'

I thanked him heartily for the offer, and we walked back to the hamlet where the horses were. By the time I had told mother of my purpose they were all in the saddle.

'Dogger,' said Mr Dance, 'you have a good horse; take up this lad behind you.'

As soon as I was mounted, holding on to Dogger's belt, the supervisor gave the word, and the party struck out at a bouncing trot on the road to Dr Livesey's house.

CHAPTER VI

THE CAPTAIN'S PAPERS

We rode hard all the way, till we drew up before Dr Livesey's door. The house was all dark to the front.

Mr Dance told me to jump down and knock, and Dogger gave me a stirrup to descend by. The door was opened almost at once by the maid.

'Is Dr Livesey in?' I asked.

No, she said; he had come home in the afternoon, but had gone up to the Hall to dine and pass the evening with the squire.

'So there we go, boys,' said Mr Dance.

This time, as the distance was short, I did not mount, but ran with Dogger's stirrup-leather to the lodge gates, and up the long, leafless, moonlit avenue to where the white line of the Hall buildings looked on either hand on great old gardens. Here Mr Dance dismounted, and, taking me along with him, was admitted at a word into the house.

The servant led us down a matted passage, and showed us at the end into a great library, all lined with bookcases and busts upon the top of them, where the squire and Dr Livesey sat, pipe in hand, on either side of a bright fire.

I had never seen the squire so near at hand. He was a tall man, over six feet high, and broad in proportion, and he had a bluff, rough-and-ready face, all roughened and reddened and lined in his long travels. His eyebrows were very black, and moved readily, and this gave him a look of some temper, not bad, you would say, but quick and high.

'Come in, Mr Dance,' says he, very stately and condescending.

'Good-evening, Dance,' says the doctor, with a nod. 'And good-evening to you, friend Jim. What good wind brings you here?'

The supervisor stood up straight and stiff, and told his story like a lesson; and you should have seen how the two gentlemen leaned forward and looked at each other, and forgot to smoke in their surprise and interest. When they heard how my mother went back to the inn, Dr Livesey fairly slapped his thigh, and the squire cried 'Bravo!' and broke his long pipe against the grate. Long before it was done, Mr Trelawney (that, you will remember, was the squire's name) had got up from his seat, and was striding about the room, and the doctor, as if to hear the better, had taken off his powdered wig, and sat there, looking very strange indeed with his own close-cropped, black poll.

At last Mr Dance finished the story.

'Mr Dance,' said the squire, 'you are a very noble fellow. And as for riding down that black, atrocious miscreant, I regard it as an act of virtue, sir, like stamping on a cockroach. This lad Hawkins is a trump, I perceive. Hawkins, will you ring that bell? Mr Dance must have some ale.'

'And so, Jim,' said the doctor, 'you have the thing that they were after, have you?'

'Here it is, sir,' said I, and gave him the oilskin packet.

The doctor looked it all over, as if his fingers were itching to open it; but, instead of doing that, he put it quietly in the pocket of his coat.

'Squire,' said he, 'when Dance has had his ale he must, of course, be off on his Majesty's service; but I mean to keep Jim Hawkins* here to sleep at my house, and, with your permission, I propose we should have up the cold pie, and let him sup.'

'As you will, Livesey,' said the squire; 'Hawkins has earned better than cold pie.'

So a big pigeon pie was brought in and put on a side-table, and I made a hearty supper, for I was as hungry as a hawk, while Mr Dance was further complimented, and at last dismissed.

'And now, squire,' said the doctor.

'And now, Livesey,' said the squire, in the same breath.

'One at a time, one at a time,' laughed Dr Livesey. 'You have heard of this Flint, I suppose?'

'Heard of him!' cried the squire. 'Heard of him, you say! He was the bloodthirstiest buccaneer that sailed. Blackbeard* was a child to Flint. The Spaniards were so prodigiously afraid of him, that, I tell you, sir, I was sometimes proud he was an Englishman. I've seen his top-sails with these eyes, off Trinidad, and the cowardly son of a rum-puncheon* that I sailed with put back—put back, sir, into Port of Spain.'*

'Well, I've heard of him myself, in England,' said the doctor. 'But the point is, had he money?'

'Money!' cried the squire. 'Have you heard the story? What were these villains after but money? What do they care for but money? For what would they risk their rascal carcases but money?'

'That we shall soon know,' replied the doctor. 'But you are so confoundedly hot-headed and exclamatory that I cannot get a word in. What I want to know is this: Supposing that I have here in my pocket some clue to where Flint buried his treasure, will that treasure amount to much?'

'Amount, sir!' cried the squire. 'It will amount to this; if we have the clue you talk about, I fit out a ship in Bristol dock, and take you and Hawkins here along, and I'll have that treasure if I search a year.'

'Very well,' said the doctor. 'Now, men, if Jim is agreeable, we'll open the packet;' and he laid it before him on the table.

The bundle was sewn together, and the doctor had to get out his instrument-case, and cut the stitches with his medical scissors. It contained two things—a book and a sealed paper.

'First of all we'll try the book,' observed the doctor.

The squire and I were both peering over his shoulder as he opened it, for Dr Livesey had kindly motioned me to come round from the side-table, where I had been eating, to enjoy the sport of the search. On the first page there were only some scraps of writing, such as a man with a pen in his hand might make for idleness or practice. One was the same as the tattoo mark. 'Billy Bones his fancy;' then there was 'Mr W. Bones, mate.' 'No more rum.' 'Off Palm Key he got itt;' and some other snatches, mostly single words and unintelligible. I could not help wondering who it was that had 'got itt,' and what 'itt' was that he got. A knife in his back as like as not.

'Not much instruction there,' said Dr Livesey, as he passed on.

The next ten or twelve pages were filled with a curious series of entries. There was a date at one end of the line and at the other a sum of money, as in common account-books; but instead of explanatory writing, only a varying number of crosses between the two. On the 12th of June, 1745, for instance, a sum of seventy pounds had plainly become due to someone, and there was nothing but six crosses to explain the cause. In a few cases, to be sure, the name of a place would be added, as 'Offe Caraccas;' or a mere entry of latitude and longitude, as '62° 17′ 20″, 19° 2′ 40″.'

The record lasted over nearly twenty years, the amount of the separate entries growing larger as time went on, and at the end a grand total had been made out after five or six wrong additions, and these words appended, 'Bones, his pile.'

'I can't make head or tail of this,' said Dr Livesey.

'The thing is as clear as noonday,' cried the squire. 'This is the black-hearted hound's account-book.* These crosses stand for the names of ships or towns that they sank or plundered. The sums are the scoundrel's share, and where he feared an ambiguity, you see he added something clearer. "Offe Caraccas," now; you see, here was some unhappy vessel boarded off that coast. God help the poor souls that manned her—coral long ago.'

'Right!' said the doctor. 'See what it is to be a traveller. Right! And the amounts increase, you see, as he rose in rank.'

There was little else in the volume but a few bearings of places noted in the blank leaves towards the end, and a table for reducing French, English, and Spanish moneys to a common value.

'Thrifty man!' cried the doctor. 'He wasn't the one to be cheated.'

'And now,' said the squire, 'for the other.'

The paper had been sealed in several places with a thimble by way of seal; the very thimble, perhaps, that I had found in the captain's pocket. The doctor opened the seals with great care, and there fell out the map of an island, with latitude and longitude, soundings, names of hills, and bays and inlets, and every particular that would be needed to bring a ship to a safe anchorage upon its shores. It was about nine miles long and five across, shaped, you might say, like a fat dragon standing up,* and had two fine land-locked harbours, and a hill in the centre part marked 'The Spy-glass.' There were several additions of a later date; but, above all, three crosses of red ink—two on the north part of the island, one in the south-west, and, beside this last, in the same red ink, and in a small, neat hand, very different from the captain's tottery characters, these words:—'Bulk of treasure here.'

Over on the back the same hand had written this further information:—

'Tall tree, Spy-glass shoulder, bearing a point to the N. of N.N.E.

'Skeleton Island E.S.E. and by E.

'Ten feet.

'The bar silver is in the north cache; you can find it by the trend of the east hummock, ten fathoms south of the black crag with the face on it.

'The arms are easy found, in the sand hill, N. point of north inlet cape, bearing E. and a quarter N.

'J. F.'

That was all; but brief as it was, and, to me, incomprehensible, it filled the squire and Dr Livesey with delight.

'Livesey,' said the squire, 'you will give up this wretched practice at once. To-morrow I start for Bristol. In three weeks' time—three weeks!—two weeks—ten days—we'll have the best ship, sir, and the choicest crew in England. Hawkins shall come as cabin-boy. You'll make a famous cabin-boy, Hawkins. You, Livesey, are ship's doctor; I am admiral. We'll take Redruth, Joyce, and Hunter. We'll have favourable winds, a quick passage, and not the least difficulty in finding the spot, and money to eat—to roll in—to play duck and drake with* ever after.'

'Trelawney,' said the doctor, 'I'll go with you; and, I'll go bail for it, so will Jim, and be a credit to the undertaking. There's only one man I'm afraid of.'

'And who's that?' cried the squire. 'Name the dog, sir!'

'You,' replied the doctor; 'for you cannot hold your tongue. We are not the only men who know of this paper. These fellows who attacked the inn to-night—bold, desperate blades, for sure—and the rest who stayed aboard that lugger, and more, I dare say, not far off, are, one and all, through thick and thin, bound that they'll get that money. We must none of us go alone till we get to sea. Jim and I shall stick together in the meanwhile; you'll take Joyce and Hunter when you ride to Bristol, and, from first to last, not one of us must breathe a word of what we've found.'

'Livesey,' returned the squire, 'you are always in the right of it. I'll be as silent as the grave.'

PART II
THE SEA COOK

CHAPTER VII
I GO TO BRISTOL

It was longer than the squire imagined ere we were ready for the sea, and none of our first plans—not even Dr Livesey's, of keeping me beside him—could be carried out as we intended. The doctor had to go to London for a physician to take charge of his practice; the squire was hard at work at Bristol; and I lived on at the Hall under the charge of old Redruth, the gamekeeper, almost a prisoner, but full of sea-dreams and the most charming anticipations of strange islands and adventures. I brooded by the hour together over the map, all the details of which I well remembered. Sitting by the fire in the housekeeper's room, I approached that island in my fancy, from every possible direction; I explored every acre of its surface; I climbed a thousand times to that tall hill they call the Spy-glass, and from the top enjoyed the most wonderful and changing prospects. Sometimes the isle was thick with savages, with whom we fought; sometimes full of dangerous animals that hunted us; but in all my fancies nothing occurred to me so strange and tragic as our actual adventures.

So the weeks passed on, till one fine day there came a letter addressed to Dr Livesey, with this addition, 'To be opened, in the case of his absence, by Tom Redruth, or young Hawkins.' Obeying this order, we found, or rather, I found—for the gamekeeper was a poor hand at reading anything but print—the following important news:—

'Old Anchor Inn, Bristol,
'March 1, 17—.

'Dear Livesey,—As I do not know whether you are at the Hall or still in London, I send this in double to both places.

'The ship is bought and fitted. She lies at anchor, ready for sea. You never imagined a sweeter schooner—a child might sail her—two hundred tons; name, *Hispaniola*.*

'I got her through my old friend, Blandly, who has proved himself throughout the most surprising trump. The admirable fellow literally slaved in my interest, and so, I may say, did everyone in Bristol, as soon as they got wind of the port we sailed for—treasure, I mean.'

'Redruth,' said I, interrupting the letter, 'Doctor Livesey will not like that. The squire has been talking, after all.'

'Well, who's a better right?' growled the gamekeeper. 'A pretty rum go if squire ain't to talk for Doctor Livesey, I should think.'

At that I gave up all attempt at commentary, and read straight on:—

'Blandly himself found the *Hispaniola*, and by the most admirable management got her for the merest trifle. There is a class of men in Bristol monstrously prejudiced against Blandly. They go the length of declaring that this honest creature would do anything for money, that the *Hispaniola* belonged to him, and that he sold it me absurdly high—the most transparent calumnies. None of them dare, however, to deny the merits of the ship.

'So far there was not a hitch. The workpeople, to be sure—riggers and what not—were most annoyingly slow; but time cured that. It was the crew that troubled me.

'I wished a round score of men—in case of natives, buccaneers, or the odious French*—and I had the worry of the deuce itself to find so much as half a dozen, till the most remarkable stroke of fortune brought me the very man that I required.

'I was standing on the dock, when, by the merest accident, I fell in talk with him. I found he was an old sailor, kept a public-house, knew all the seafaring men in Bristol, had lost his health ashore, and wanted a good berth as cook to get to sea again. He had hobbled down there that morning, he said, to get a smell of the salt.

'I was monstrously touched—so would you have been—and, out of pure pity, I engaged him on the spot to be ship's cook. Long John Silver,* he is called, and has lost a leg; but that I regarded as a recommendation, since he lost it in his country's service, under the immortal Hawke.* He has no pension, Livesey. Imagine the abominable age we live in!

'Well, sir, I thought I had only found a cook, but it was a crew I had discovered. Between Silver and myself we got together in a few days a company of the toughest old salts imaginable—not pretty to look at, but fellows, by their faces, of the most indomitable spirit. I declare we could fight a frigate.

'Long John even got rid of two out of the six or seven I had already engaged. He showed me in a moment that they were just the sort of fresh-water swabs we had to fear in an adventure of importance.

'I am in the most magnificent health and spirits, eating like a bull, sleeping like a tree, yet I shall not enjoy a moment till I hear my old tarpaulins tramping round the capstan. Seaward ho! Hang the treasure! It's the glory of the sea that has turned my head. So now, Livesey, come post;* do not lose an hour, if you respect me.

'Let young Hawkins go at once to see his mother, with Redruth for a guard; and then both come full speed to Bristol.

'JOHN TRELAWNEY.

'*Postscript.*—I did not tell you that Blandly, who, by the way, is to send a consort after us if we don't turn up by the end of August, had found an admirable fellow for sailing master—a stiff man, which I regret, but, in all other respects, a treasure. Long John Silver unearthed a very competent man for a mate, a man named Arrow. I have a boatswain who pipes, Livesey; so things shall go man-o'-war fashion on board the good ship *Hispaniola.*

'I forgot to tell you that Silver is a man of substance; I know of my own knowledge that he has a banker's account, which has never been overdrawn. He leaves his wife to manage the inn; and as she is a woman of colour, a pair of old bachelors like you and I may be excused for guessing that it is the wife, quite as much as the health, that sends him back to roving.

'J. T.

'P.P.S.—Hawkins may stay one night with his mother.

'J. T.'

You can fancy the excitement into which that letter put me. I was half beside myself with glee; and if ever I despised a man, it was old Tom Redruth, who could do nothing but grumble and lament. Any of the under-gamekeepers would gladly have changed places with him; but such was not the squire's pleasure, and the squire's pleasure was like law among them all. Nobody but old Redruth would have dared so much as even to grumble.

The next morning he and I set out on foot for the 'Admiral Benbow,' and there I found my mother in good health and spirits. The captain, who had so long been a cause of so much discomfort, was gone where the wicked cease from troubling. The squire had had everything repaired, and the public rooms and the sign repainted, and had added some furniture—above all a beautiful arm-chair for mother in the bar. He had found her a boy as an apprentice also, so that she should not want help while I was gone.

It was on seeing that boy that I understood, for the first time, my situation. I had thought up to that moment of the adventures before me, not at all of the home that I was leaving; and now, at the sight of this clumsy stranger, who was to stay here in my place beside my mother, I had my first attack of tears. I am afraid I led that boy a dog's life; for as he was new to the work, I had a hundred opportunities of setting him right and putting him down, and I was not slow to profit by them.

The night passed, and the next day, after dinner, Redruth and I were afoot again, and on the road. I said good-bye to mother and the cove where I had lived since I was born, and the dear old 'Admiral Benbow'—since he was repainted, no longer quite so dear. One of my last thoughts was of the captain, who had so often strode along the beach with his cocked hat, his sabre-cut cheek, and his old brass telescope. Next moment we had turned the corner, and my home was out of sight.

The mail picked us up about dusk at the 'Royal George' on the heath. I was wedged in between Redruth and a stout old gentleman, and in spite of the swift motion and the cold night air, I must have dozed a great deal from the very first, and then slept like a log up hill and down dale through stage after stage; for when I was awakened, at last, it was by a punch in the ribs, and I opened my eyes, to find that we were standing still before a large building in a city street, and that the day had already broken a long time.

'Where are we?' I asked.

'Bristol,' said Tom. 'Get down.'

Mr Trelawney had taken up his residence at an inn far down the docks, to superintend the work upon the schooner. Thither we had now to walk, and our way, to my great delight, lay along the quays and beside the great multitude of ships of all sizes and rigs and nations. In one, sailors were singing at their work; in another, there were men aloft, high over my head, hanging to threads that seemed no thicker than a spider's. Though I had lived by the shore all my life, I seemed never to have been near the sea till then. The smell of tar and salt was something new. I saw the most wonderful figureheads, that had all been far over the ocean. I saw, besides, many old sailors, with rings in their ears, and whiskers curled in ringlets, and tarry pigtails, and their swaggering, clumsy sea-walk; and if I had seen as many kings or archbishops I could not have been more delighted.

And I was going to sea myself; to sea in a schooner, with a piping boatswain, and pig-tailed singing seamen; to sea, bound for an unknown island, and to seek for buried treasures!

While I was still in this delightful dream, we came suddenly in front of a large inn, and met Squire Trelawney, all dressed out like a sea-officer, in stout blue cloth, coming out of the door with a smile on his face, and a capital imitation of a sailor's walk.

'Here you are,' he cried, 'and the doctor came last night from London. Bravo! the ship's company complete!'

'Oh, sir,' cried I, 'when do we sail?'

'Sail!' says he. 'We sail to-morrow!'

CHAPTER VIII

AT THE SIGN OF THE 'SPY-GLASS'

WHEN I had done breakfasting the squire gave me a note addressed to John Silver, at the sign of the 'Spy-glass,' and told me I should easily find the place by following the line of the docks, and keeping a bright look-out for a little tavern with a large brass telescope for sign. I set off, overjoyed at this opportunity to see some more of the ships and seamen, and picked my way among a great crowd of people and carts and bales, for the dock was now at its busiest, until I found the tavern in question.

It was a bright enough little place of entertainment. The sign was newly painted; the windows had neat red curtains; the floor was cleanly sanded. There was a street on each side, and an open door on both, which made the large, low room pretty clear to see in, in spite of clouds of tobacco smoke.

The customers were mostly seafaring men; and they talked so loudly that I hung at the door, almost afraid to enter.

As I was waiting, a man came out of a side room, and, at a glance, I was sure he must be Long John. His left leg was cut off close by the hip, and under the left shoulder he carried a crutch, which he managed with wonderful dexterity, hopping about upon it like a bird. He was very tall and strong, with a face as big as a ham—plain and pale, but intelligent and smiling. Indeed, he seemed in the most cheerful spirits, whistling as he moved about among the tables, with a merry word or a slap on the shoulder for the more favoured of his guests.

Now, to tell you the truth, from the very first mention of Long John in Squire Trelawney's letter, I had taken a fear in my mind that he might prove to be the very one-legged sailor whom I had watched for so long at the old 'Benbow.' But one look at the man before me was enough. I had seen the captain, and Black Dog, and the blind man Pew, and I thought I knew what a buccaneer was like—a very different creature, according to me, from this clean and pleasant-tempered landlord.

I plucked up courage at once, crossed the threshold, and walked right up to the man where he stood, propped on his crutch, talking to a customer.

'Mr Silver, sir?' I asked, holding out the note.

'Yes, my lad,' said he; 'such is my name, to be sure. And who may you be?' And then as he saw the squire's letter, he seemed to me to give something almost like a start.

'Oh!' said he, quite loud, and offering his hand, 'I see. You are our new cabin-boy; pleased I am to see you.'

And he took my hand in his large firm grasp.

Just then one of the customers at the far side rose suddenly and made for the door. It was close by him, and he was out in the street in a moment. But his hurry had attracted my notice, and I recognised him at a glance. It was the tallow-faced man, wanting two fingers, who had come first to the 'Admiral Benbow.'

'Oh,' I cried, 'stop him! it's Black Dog!'

'I don't care two coppers who he is,' cried Silver. 'But he hasn't paid his score. Harry, run and catch him.'

One of the others who was nearest the door leaped up, and started in pursuit.

'If he were Admiral Hawke he shall pay his score,' cried Silver; and then, relinquishing my hand—'Who did you say he was?' he asked. 'Black what?'

'Dog, sir,' said I. 'Has Mr Trelawney not told you of the buccaneers? He was one of them.'

'So?' cried Silver. 'In my house! Ben, run and help Harry. One of those swabs, was he? Was that you drinking with him, Morgan?* Step up here.'

The man whom he called Morgan—an old, grey-haired, mahogany-faced sailor—came forward pretty sheepishly, rolling his quid.*

'Now, Morgan,' said Long John, very sternly; 'you never clapped your eyes on that Black—Black Dog before, did you, now?'

'Not I, sir,' said Morgan, with a salute.

'You didn't know his name, did you?'

'No, sir.'

'By the powers, Tom Morgan, it's as good for you!' exclaimed the landlord. 'If you had been mixed up with the like of that, you would never have put another foot in my house, you may lay to that. And what was he saying to you?'

'I don't rightly know, sir,' answered Morgan.

'Do you call that a head on your shoulders, or a blessed dead-eye?' cried Long John. 'Don't rightly know, don't you! Perhaps you don't happen to rightly know who you was speaking to, perhaps? Come, now, what was he jawing—v'yages, cap'ns, ships? Pipe up! What was it?'

'We was a-talkin' of keel-hauling,' answered Morgan.

'Keel-hauling, was you? and a mighty suitable thing, too, and you may lay to that. Get back to your place for a lubber, Tom.'

And then, as Morgan rolled back to his seat. Silver added to me in a confidential whisper, that was very flattering, as I thought:—

'He's quite an honest man, Tom Morgan, on'y stupid. And now,' he ran on again, aloud, 'let's see—Black Dog? No, I don't know the name, not I. Yet I kind of think I've—yes, I've seen the swab. He used to come here with a blind beggar, he used.'

'That he did, you may be sure,' said I. 'I knew that blind man, too. His name was Pew.'

'It was!' cried Silver, now quite excited. 'Pew! That were his name for certain. Ah, he looked a shark, he did! If we run down this Black Dog, now, there'll be news for Cap'n Trelawney! Ben's a good runner; few seamen run better than Ben. He should run him down, hand over hand, by the powers! He talked o' keel-hauling, did he? *I'll* keel-haul him!'

All the time he was jerking out these phrases he was stumping up and down the tavern on his crutch, slapping tables with his hand, and giving such a show of excitement as would have convinced an Old Bailey judge or a Bow Street runner. My suspicions had been thoroughly re-awakened on finding Black Dog at the 'Spy-glass,' and I watched the cook narrowly. But he was too deep, and too ready, and too clever for me, and by the time the two men had come back out of breath, and confessed that they had lost the track in a crowd, and been scolded like thieves, I would have gone bail for the innocence of Long John Silver.

'See here, now, Hawkins,' said he, 'here's a blessed hard thing on a man like me, now, aint it? There's Cap'n Trelawney—what's he to think? Here I have this confounded son of a Dutchman* sitting in my own house, drinking of my own rum! Here you comes and tells me of it plain; and here I let him give us all the slip before my blessed dead-lights! Now, Hawkins, you do me justice with the cap'n. You're a lad, you are, but you're as smart as paint. I see that when you first came in. Now, here it is: What could I do, with this old timber I hobble on? When I was an A B master mariner I'd have come up alongside of him, hand over hand, and broached him to in a brace of old shakes, I would; but now—'

And then, all of a sudden, he stopped, and his jaw dropped as though he had remembered something.

'The score!' he burst out. 'Three goes o' rum! Why, shiver my timbers,* if I hadn't forgotten my score!'

And, falling on a bench, he laughed until the tears ran down his cheeks. I could not help joining; and we laughed together, peal after peal, until the tavern rang again.

'Why, what a precious old sea-calf I am!' he said, at last, wiping his cheeks. 'You and me should get on well, Hawkins, for I'll take my davy* I should be rated ship's boy. But, come, now, stand by to go about. This won't do. Dooty is dooty, messmates. I'll put on my old cocked hat, and step along of you to Cap'n Trelawney, and report this here affair. For, mind you, it's serious, young Hawkins; and neither you nor me's come out of it with what I should make so bold as to call credit. Nor you neither, says you; not smart—none of the pair of us smart. But dash my buttons! that was a good 'un about my score.'

And he began to laugh again, and that so heartily, that though I did not see the joke as he did, I was again obliged to join him in his mirth.

On our little walk along the quays, he made himself the most interesting companion, telling me about the different ships that we passed by, their rig, tonnage, and nationality, explaining the work that was going forward—how one was discharging, another taking in cargo, and a third making ready for sea; and every now and then telling me some little anecdote of ships or seamen, or repeating a nautical phrase till I had learned it perfectly. I began to see that here was one of the best of possible shipmates.

When we got to the inn, the squire and Dr Livesey were seated together, finishing a quart of ale with a toast in it,* before they should go aboard the schooner on a visit of inspection.

Long John told the story from first to last, with a great deal of spirit and the most perfect truth. 'That was how it were, now, weren't it, Hawkins?' he would say, now and again, and I could always bear him entirely out.

The two gentlemen regretted that Black Dog had got away; but we all agreed there was nothing to be done, and after he had been complimented, Long John took up his crutch and departed.

'All hands aboard by four this afternoon,' shouted the squire, after him.

'Ay, ay, sir,' cried the cook, in the passage.

'Well, squire,' said Dr Livesey, 'I don't put much faith in your discoveries, as a general thing; but I will say this, John Silver suits me.'

'The man's a perfect trump,' declared the squire.

'And now,' added the doctor, 'Jim may come on board with us, may he not?'

'To be sure he may,' says squire. 'Take your hat, Hawkins, and we'll see the ship.'

CHAPTER IX

POWDER AND ARMS

THE *Hispaniola* lay some way out, and we went under the figureheads and round the sterns of many other ships, and their cables sometimes grated underneath our keel, and sometimes swung above us. At last, however, we got alongside, and were met and saluted as we stepped aboard by the mate, Mr Arrow, a brown old sailor, with earrings in his ears and a squint. He and the squire were very thick and friendly, but I soon observed that things were not the same between Mr Trelawney and the captain.

This last was a sharp-looking man, who seemed angry with everything on board, and was soon to tell us why, for we had hardly got down into the cabin when a sailor followed us.

'Captain Smollett,* sir, axing to speak with you,' said he.

'I am always at the captain's order. Show him in,' said the squire.

The captain, who was close behind his messenger, entered at once, and shut the door behind him.

'Well, Captain Smollett, what have you to say? All well, I hope; all shipshape and seaworthy?'

'Well, sir,' said the captain, 'better speak plain, I believe, even at the risk of offence. I don't like this cruise; I don't like the men; and I don't like my officer. That's short and sweet.'

'Perhaps, sir, you don't like the ship?' inquired the squire, very angry, as I could see.

'I can't speak as to that, sir, not having seen her tried,' said the captain. 'She seems a clever craft; more I can't say.'

'Possibly, sir, you may not like your employer, either?' says the squire.

But here Dr Livesey cut in.

'Stay a bit,' said he, 'stay a bit. No use of such questions as that but to produce ill-feeling. The captain has said too much or he has said too little, and I'm bound to say that I require an explanation of his words. You don't, you say, like this cruise. Now, why?'

'I was engaged, sir, on what we call sealed orders, to sail this ship for that gentleman where he should bid me,' said the captain. 'So far so good. But now I find that every man before the mast knows more than I do. I don't call that fair, now, do you?'

'No,' said Dr Livesey, 'I don't.'

'Next,' said the captain, 'I learn we are going after treasure—hear it from my own hands, mind you. Now, treasure is ticklish work; I don't like treasure voyages on any account; and I don't like them, above all, when they are secret, and when (begging your pardon, Mr Trelawney) the secret has been told to the parrot.'

'Silver's parrot?' asked the squire.

'It's a way of speaking,' said the captain. 'Blabbed, I mean. It's my belief neither of you gentlemen know what you are about; but I'll tell you my way of it—life or death, and a close run.'

'That is all clear, and, I daresay, true enough,' replied Dr Livesey. 'We take the risk; but we are not so ignorant as you believe us. Next, you say you don't like the crew. Are they not good seamen?'

'I don't like them, sir,' returned Captain Smollett. 'And I think I should have had the choosing of my own hands, if you go to that.'

'Perhaps you should,' replied the doctor. 'My friend should, perhaps, have taken you along with him; but the slight, if there be one, was unintentional. And you don't like Mr Arrow?'

'I don't, sir. I believe he's a good seaman; but he's too free with the crew to be a good officer. A mate should keep himself to himself—shouldn't drink with the men before the mast!'

'Do you mean he drinks?' cried the squire.

'No, sir,' replied the captain; 'only that he's too familiar.'

'Well, now, and the short and long of it, captain?' asked the doctor. 'Tell us what you want.'

'Well, gentlemen, are you determined to go on this cruise?'

'Like iron,' answered the squire.

'Very good,' said the captain. 'Then, as you've heard me very patiently, saying things that I could not prove, hear me a few words more. They are putting the powder and the arms in the fore hold. Now, you have a good place under the cabin; why not put them there?—first point. Then you are bringing four of your own people with you, and they tell me some of them are to be berthed forward. Why not give them the berths here beside the cabin?—second point.'

'Any more?' asked Mr Trelawney.

'One more,' said the captain. 'There's been too much blabbing already.'

'Far too much,' agreed the doctor.

'I'll tell you what I've heard myself,' continued Captain Smollett: 'that you have a map of an island; that there's crosses on the map to show where treasure is; and that the island lies—' And then he named the latitude and longitude exactly.

'I never told that,' cried the squire, 'to a soul!'

'The hands know it, sir,' returned the captain.

'Livesey, that must have been you or Hawkins,' cried the squire.

'It doesn't much matter who it was,' replied the doctor. And I could see that neither he nor the captain paid much regard to Mr Trelawney's protestations. Neither did I, to be sure, he was so loose a talker; yet in this case I believe he was really right, and that nobody had told the situation of the island.

'Well, gentlemen,' continued the captain, 'I don't know who has this map; but I make it a point, it shall be kept secret even from me and Mr Arrow. Otherwise I would ask you to let me resign.'

'I see,' said the doctor. 'You wish us to keep this matter dark, and to make a garrison of the stern part of the ship, manned with my friend's own people, and provided with all the arms and powder on board. In other words, you fear a mutiny.'

'Sir,' said Captain Smollett, 'with no intention to take offence, I deny your right to put words into my mouth. No captain, sir, would be justified in going to sea at all if he had ground enough to say that. As for Mr Arrow, I believe him thoroughly honest; some of the men are the same; all may be for what I know. But I am responsible for the ship's safety and the life of every man Jack aboard of her. I see things going, as I think, not quite right. And I ask you to take certain precautions, or let me resign my berth. And that's all.'

'Captain Smollett,' began the doctor, with a smile, 'did ever you hear the fable of the mountain and the mouse?* You'll excuse me, I daresay, but you remind me of that fable. When you came in here I'll stake my wig you meant more than this.'

'Doctor,' said the captain, 'you are smart. When I came in here I meant to get discharged. I had no thought that Mr Trelawncy would hear a word.'

'No more I would,' cried the squire. 'Had Livesey not been here I should have seen you to the deuce. As it is, I have heard you. I will do as you desire; but I think the worse of you.'

'That's as you please, sir,' said the captain. 'You'll find I do my duty.'

And with that he took his leave.

'Trelawney,' said the doctor, 'contrary to all my notions, I believe you have managed to get two honest men on board with you—that man and John Silver.'

'Silver, if you like,' cried the squire; 'but as for that intolerable humbug, I declare I think his conduct unmanly, unsailorly, and downright un-English.'

'Well,' says the doctor, 'we shall see.'

When we came on deck, the men had begun already to take out the arms and powder, yo-ho-ing at their work, while the captain and Mr Arrow stood by superintending.

The new arrangement was quite to my liking. The whole schooner had been overhauled; six berths had been made astern, out of what had been the after-part of the main hold; and this set of cabins was only joined to the galley and forecastle by a sparred passage* on the port side. It had been originally meant that the captain, Mr Arrow, Hunter, Joyce, the doctor, and the squire, were to occupy these six berths. Now, Redruth and I were to get two of them, and Mr Arrow and the captain were to sleep on deck in the companion, which had been enlarged on each side till you might almost have called it a round-house. Very low it was still, of course; but there was room to swing two hammocks, and even the mate seemed pleased with the arrangement. Even he, perhaps, had been doubtful as to the crew, but that is only guess; for, as you shall hear, we had not long the benefit of his opinion.

We were all hard at work, changing the powder and the berths, when the last man or two, and Long John along with them, came off in a shore-boat.

The cook came up the side like a monkey for cleverness, and, as soon as he saw what was doing, 'So ho, mates!' says he, 'what's this?'

'We're a-changing of the powder, Jack,' answers one.

'Why, by the powers,' cried Long John, 'if we do, we'll miss the morning tide!'

'My orders!' said the captain shortly. 'You may go below, my man. Hands will want supper.'

'Ay, ay, sir,' answered the cook; and, touching his forelock, he disappeared at once in the direction of his galley.

'That's a good man, captain,' said the doctor.

'Very likely sir,' replied Captain Smollett. 'Easy with that, men—easy,' he ran on, to the fellows who were shifting the powder; and then suddenly observing me examining the swivel we carried amidships, a long brass nine*—'Here, you ship's boy,' he cried, 'out o' that! Off with you to the cook and get some work.'

And then as I was hurrying off I heard him say, quite loudly, to the doctor:—

'I'll have no favourites on my ship.'

I assure you I was quite of the squire's way of thinking, and hated the captain deeply.

CHAPTER X
THE VOYAGE

ALL that night we were in a great bustle getting things stowed in their place, and boatfuls of the squire's friends, Mr Blandly and the like, coming off to wish him a good voyage and a safe return. We never had a night at the 'Admiral Benbow' when I had half the work; and I was dog-tired when, a little before dawn, the boatswain sounded his pipe, and the crew began to man the capstan-bars. I might have been twice as weary, yet I would not have left the deck; all was so new and interesting to me—the brief commands, the shrill note of the whistle, the men bustling to their places in the glimmer of the ship's lanterns.

'Now, Barbecue, tip us a stave,'* cried one voice.

'The old one,' cried another.

'Ay, ay, mates,' said Long John, who was standing by, with his crutch under his arm, and at once broke out in the air and words I knew so well—

'Fifteen men on the dead man's chest—'

And then the whole crew bore chorus:—

'Yo-ho-ho, and a bottle of rum!'

And at the third 'ho!' drove the bars before them with a will.

Even at that exciting moment it carried me back to the old 'Admiral Benbow' in a second; and I seemed to hear the voice of the captain piping in the chorus. But soon the anchor was short up; soon it was hanging dripping at the bows; soon the sails began to draw, and the land and shipping to flit by on either side; and before I could lie down to snatch an hour of slumber the *Hispaniola* had begun her voyage to the Isle of Treasure.

I am not going to relate that voyage in detail. It was fairly prosperous. The ship proved to be a good ship, the crew were capable seamen, and the captain thoroughly understood his business. But before we came the length of Treasure Island, two or three things had happened which require to be known.

Mr Arrow, first of all, turned out even worse than the captain had feared. He had no command among the men, and people did what they pleased with him. But that was by no means the worst of it; for after a day or two at sea he began to appear on deck with hazy eye, red cheeks, stuttering tongue, and other marks of drunkenness. Time after time he was ordered below in disgrace. Sometimes he fell and cut himself; sometimes he lay all day long in his little bunk at one side of the companion; sometimes for a day or two he would be almost sober and attend to his work at least passably.

In the meantime, we could never make out where he got the drink. That was the ship's mystery. Watch him as we pleased, we could do nothing to solve it; and when we asked him to his face, he would only laugh, if he were drunk, and if he were sober, deny solemnly that he ever tasted anything but water.

He was not only useless as an officer, and a bad influence amongst the men, but it was plain that at this rate he must soon kill himself outright; so nobody was much surprised, nor very sorry, when one dark night, with a head sea, he disappeared entirely and was seen no more.

'Overboard!' said the captain. 'Well, gentlemen, that saves the trouble of putting him in irons.'

But there we were, without a mate; and it was necessary, of course, to advance one of the men. The boatswain, Job Anderson, was the likeliest man aboard, and, though he kept his old title, he served in a way as mate. Mr Trelawney had followed the sea, and his knowledge made him very useful, for he often took a watch himself in easy weather. And the coxswain, Israel Hands,* was a careful, wily, old, experienced seaman, who could be trusted at a pinch with almost anything.

He was a great confidant of Long John Silver, and so the mention of his name leads me on to speak of our ship's cook, Barbecue, as the men called him.

Aboard ship he carried his crutch by a lanyard round his neck, to have both hands as free as possible. It was something to see him wedge the foot of the crutch against a bulkhead, and, propped against it, yielding to every movement of the ship, get on with his cooking like someone safe ashore. Still more strange was it to see him in the heaviest of weather cross the deck. He had a line or two rigged up to help him across the widest spaces—Long John's earrings, they were called; and he would hand himself from one place to another, now using the crutch, now trailing it alongside by the lanyard, as quickly as another man could walk. Yet some of the men who had sailed with him before expressed their pity to see him so reduced.

'He's no common man, Barbecue,' said the coxswain to me. 'He had good schooling in his young days, and can speak like a book when so minded; and brave—a lion's nothing alongside of Long John! I seen him grapple four, and knock their heads together—him unarmed.'

All the crew respected and even obeyed him. He had a way of talking to each, and doing everybody some particular service. To me he was unweariedly kind; and always glad to see me in the galley, which he kept as clean as a new pin; the dishes hanging up burnished, and his parrot in a cage in one corner.

'Come away, Hawkins,' he would say; 'come and have a yarn with John. Nobody more welcome than yourself, my son. Sit you down and hear the news. Here's Cap'n Flint—I calls my parrot Cap'n Flint, after the famous buccaneer—here's Cap'n Flint predicting success to our v'yage. Wasn't you, cap'n?'

And the parrot would say, with great rapidity, 'Pieces of eight! pieces of eight! pieces of eight!' till you wondered that it was not out of breath, or till John threw his handkerchief over the cage.

'Now, that bird,' he would say, 'is, may be, two hundred years old, Hawkins—they lives for ever mostly; and if anybody's seen more wickedness, it must be the devil himself. She's sailed with England, the great Cap'n England,* the pirate. She's been at Madagascar, and at Malabar, and Surinam, and Providence, and Portobello.* She was at the fishing up of the wrecked plate ships. It's there she learned "Pieces of eight," and little wonder; three hundred and fifty thousand of 'em,* Hawkins! She was at the boarding of the Viceroy of the Indies out of Goa,* she was; and to look at her you would think she was a babby. But you smelt powder—didn't you, cap'n?'

'Stand by to go about,' the parrot would scream.

'Ah, she's a handsome craft, she is,' the cook would say, and give her sugar from his pocket, and then the bird would peck at the bars and swear straight on, passing belief for wickedness. 'There,' John would add, 'you can't touch pitch and not be mucked,* lad. Here's this poor old innocent bird o' mine swearing blue fire, and none the wiser, you may lay to that. She would swear the same, in a manner of speaking, before chaplain.' And John would touch his forelock with a solemn way he had, that made me think he was the best of men.

In the meantime, the squire and Captain Smollett were still on pretty distant terms with one another. The squire made no bones about the matter; he despised the captain. The captain, on his part, never spoke but when he was spoken to, and then sharp and short and dry, and not a word wasted. He owned, when driven into a corner, that he seemed to have been wrong about the crew, that some of them were as brisk as he wanted to see, and all had behaved fairly well. As for the ship, he had taken a downright fancy to her. 'She'll lie a point nearer the wind than a man has a right to expect of his own married wife, sir. But,' he would add, 'all I say is we're not home again, and I don't like the cruise.'

The squire, at this, would turn away and march up and down the deck, chin in air.

'A trifle more of that man,' he would say, 'and I shall explode.'

We had some heavy weather, which only proved the qualities of the *Hispaniola*. Every man on board seemed well content, and they must have been hard to please if they had been otherwise; for it is my belief there was never a ship's company so spoiled since Noah put to sea. Double grog was going on the least excuse; there was duff* on odd days, as, for instance, if the squire heard it was any man's birthday; and always a barrel of apples standing broached in the waist, for anyone to help himself that had a fancy.

'Never knew good come of it yet,' the captain said to Dr Livesey. 'Spoil foc's'le hands, make devils. That's my belief.'

But good did come of the apple barrel, as you shall hear; for if it had not been for that, we should have had no note of warning, and might all have perished by the hand of treachery.

This was how it came about.

We had run up the trades to get the wind of the island we were after—I am not allowed to be more plain—and now we were running down for it with a bright look-out day and night. It was about the last day of our outward voyage, by the largest computation; some time that night, or, at latest, before noon of the morrow, we should sight the Treasure Island. We were heading S.S.W., and had a steady breeze abeam and a quiet sea. The *Hispaniola* rolled steadily, dipping her bowsprit now and then with a whiff of spray. All was drawing alow and aloft; everyone was in the bravest spirits, because we were now so near an end of the first part of our adventure.

Now, just after sundown, when all my work was over, and I was on my way to my berth, it occurred to me that I should like an apple.

I ran on deck. The watch was all forward looking out for the island. The man at the helm was watching the luff of the sail, and whistling away gently to himself; and that was the only sound excepting the swish of the sea against the bows and around the sides of the ship.

In I got bodily into the apple barrel, and found there was scarce an apple left; but, sitting down there in the dark, what with the sound of the waters and the rocking movement of the ship, I had either fallen asleep, or was on the point of doing so, when a heavy man sat down with rather a clash close by. The barrel shook as he leaned his shoulders against it, and I was just about to jump up when the man began to speak. It was Silver's voice, and, before I had heard a dozen words, I would not have shown myself for all the world, but lay there, trembling and listening, in the extreme of fear and curiosity: for from these dozen words I understood that the lives of all the honest men aboard depended upon me alone.*

CHAPTER XI

WHAT I HEARD IN THE APPLE BARREL

'No, not I,' said Silver. 'Flint was cap'n; I was quartermaster,* along of my timber leg. The same broadside I lost my leg, old Pew lost his deadlights. It was a master surgeon, him that ampytated me—out of college and all—Latin by the bucket, and what not; but he was hanged like a dog, and sun-dried like the rest, at Corso Castle. That was Roberts' men, that was, and comed of changing names to their ships—*Royal Fortune* and so on.* Now, what a ship was christened, so let her stay, I says. So it was with the *Cassandra*,* as brought us all safe home from Malabar, after England took the Viceroy of the Indies; so it was with the old *Walrus*, Flint's old ship, as I've seen a-muck with the red blood and fit to sink with gold.'

'Ah!' cried another voice, that of the youngest hand on board, and evidently full of admiration, 'he was the flower of the flock, was Flint!'

'Davis* was a man, too, by all accounts,' said Silver. 'I never sailed along of him; first with England, then with Flint, that's my story; and now here on my own account, in a manner of speaking. I laid by nine hundred safe, from England, and two thousand after Flint. That aint bad for a man before the mast—all safe in bank. 'Tain't earning now, it's saving does it, you may lay to that. Where's all England's men now? I dunno. Where's Flint's? Why, most on 'em aboard here, and glad to get the duff—been begging before that, some on 'em. Old Pew, as had lost his sight, and might have thought shame, spends twelve hundred pound in a year, like a lord in Parliament. Where is he now? Well, he's dead now and under hatches; but for two year before that, shiver my timbers! the man was starving. He begged, and he stole, and he cut throats, and starved at that, by the powers!'

'Well, it aint much use, after all,' said the young seaman.

''Tain't much use for fools, you may lay to it—that, nor nothing,' cried Silver. 'But now, you look here: you're young, you are, but you're as smart as paint. I see that when I set my eyes on you, and I'll talk to you like a man.'

You may imagine how I felt when I heard this abominable old rogue addressing another in the very same words of flattery as he had used to myself. I think, if I had been able, that I would have killed him through the barrel. Meantime, he ran on, little supposing he was overheard.

'Here it is about gentlemen of fortune. They lives rough, and they risk swinging, but they eat and drink like fighting-cocks, and when a cruise is done, why, it's hundreds of pounds instead of hundreds of farthings in their pockets. Now, the most goes for rum and a good fling, and to sea again in their shirts. But that's not the course I lay. I puts it all away, some here, some there, and none too much anywheres, by reason of suspicion. I'm fifty, mark you; once back from this cruise, I set up gentleman in earnest. Time enough, too, says you. Ah, but I've lived easy in the meantime; never denied myself o' nothing heart desires, and slep' soft and ate dainty all my days, but when at sea. And how did I begin? Before the mast, like you!'

'Well,' said the other, 'but all the other money's gone now, aint it? You daren't show face in Bristol after this.'

'Why, where might you suppose it was?' asked Silver, derisively.

'At Bristol, in banks and places,' answered his companion.

'It were,' said the cook; 'it were when we weighed anchor. But my old missis has it all by now. And the "Spy-glass" is sold, lease and good-will and rigging; and the old girl's off to meet me. I would tell you where, for I trust you; but it 'ud make jealousy among the mates.'

'And can you trust your missis?' asked the other.

'Gentlemen of fortune,' returned the cook, 'usually trusts little among themselves, and right they are, you may lay to it. But I have a way with me, I have. When a mate brings a slip on his cable—one as knows me, I mean—it won't be in the same world with old John. There was some that was feared of Pew, and some that was feared of Flint; but Flint his own self was feared of me.* Feared he was, and proud. They was the roughest crew afloat, was Flint's; the devil himself would have been feared to go to sea with them. Well, now, I tell you, I'm not a boasting man, and you seen yourself how easy I keep company; but when I was quartermaster, *lambs* wasn't the word for Flint's old buccaneers. Ah, you may be sure of yourself in old John's ship.'

'Well, I tell you now,' replied the lad, 'I didn't half a quarter like the job till I had this talk with you, John; but there's my hand on it now.'

'And a brave lad you were, and smart, too,' answered Silver, shaking hands so heartily that all the barrel shook, 'and a finer figure-head for a gentleman of fortune I never clapped my eyes on.'

By this time I had begun to understand the meaning of their terms. By a 'gentleman of fortune' they plainly meant neither more nor less than a common pirate, and the little scene that I had overheard was the last act in the corruption of one of the honest hands—perhaps of the last one left aboard. But on this point I was soon to be relieved, for Silver giving a little whistle, a third man strolled up and sat down by the party.

'Dick's square,' said Silver.

'Oh, I know'd Dick was square,' returned the voice of the coxswain, Israel Hands. 'He's no fool, is Dick.' And he turned his quid and spat. 'But, look here,' he went on, 'here's what I want to know, Barbecue: how long are we a-going to stand off and on like a blessed bumboat? I've had a'most enough o' Cap'n Smollett; he's hazed me long enough, by thunder! I want to go into that cabin, I do. I want their pickles and wines, and that.'

'Israel,' said Silver, 'your head aint much account, nor ever was. But you're able to hear, I reckon; leastways, your ears is big enough. Now, here's what I say: you'll berth forward, and you'll live hard, and you'll speak soft, and you'll keep sober, till I give the word; and you may lay to that, my son.'

'Well, I don't say no, do I?' growled the coxswain. 'What I say is, when? That's what I say.'

'When! by the powers!' cried Silver. 'Well, now, if you want to know, I'll tell you when. The last moment I can manage; and that's when. Here's a first-rate seaman, Cap'n Smollett, sails the blessed ship for us. Here's this squire and doctor with a map and such—I don't know where it is, do I? No more do you, says you. Well, then, I mean this squire and doctor shall find the stuff, and help us to get it aboard, by the powers. Then we'll see. If I was sure of you all, sons of double Dutchmen,* I'd have Cap'n Smollett navigate us half-way back again before I struck.'

'Why, we're all seamen aboard here, I should think,' said the lad Dick.

'We're all foc's'le hands, you mean,' snapped Silver. 'We can steer a course, but who's to set one? That's what all you gentlemen split on, first and last. If I had my way, I'd have Cap'n Smollett work us back into the trades at least; then we'd have no blessed miscalculations and a spoonful of water a day. But I know the sort you are. I'll finish with 'em at the island, as soon's the blunt's* on board, and a pity it is. But you're never happy till you're drunk. Split my sides, I've a sick heart to sail with the likes of you!'

'Easy all, Long John,' cried Israel. 'Who's a-crossin' of you?'

'Why, how many tall ships, think ye, now, have I seen laid aboard? and how many brisk lads drying in the sun at Execution Dock?' cried Silver, 'and all for this same hurry and hurry and hurry. You hear me? I seen a thing or two at sea, I have. If you would on'y lay your course, and a p'int to windward, you would ride in carriages, you would. But not you! I know you. You'll have your mouthful of rum to-morrow, and go hang.'

'Everybody know'd you was a kind of a chapling, John; but there's others as could hand and steer as well as you,' said Israel. 'They liked a bit o' fun, they did. They wasn't so high and dry, nohow, but took their fling, like jolly companions every one.'

'So?' says Silver. 'Well, and where are they now? Pew was that sort, and he died a beggar-man. Flint was, and he died of rum at Savannah. Ah, they was a sweet crew, they was! on'y, where are they?'

'But,' asked Dick, 'when we do lay 'em athwart, what are we to do with 'em, anyhow?'

'There's the man for me!' cried the cook, admiringly. 'That's what I call business. Well, what would you think? Put 'em ashore like maroons? That would have been England's way. Or cut 'em down like that much pork? That would have been Flint's or Billy Bones's.'

'Billy was the man for that,' said Israel. '"Dead men don't bite," says he. Well, he's dead now hisself; he knows the long and short on it now; and if ever a rough hand come to port, it was Billy.'

'Right you are,' said Silver, 'rough and ready. But mark you here: I'm an easy man—I'm quite the gentleman, says you; but this time it's serious. Dooty is dooty, mates. I give my vote—death. When I'm in Parlyment, and riding in my coach, I don't want none of these sea-lawyers in the cabin a-coming home, unlooked for, like the devil at prayers.* Wait is what I say; but when the time comes, why let her rip!'

'John,' cries the coxswain, 'you're a man!'

'You'll say so, Israel, when you see,' said Silver. 'Only one thing I claim—I claim Trelawney. I'll wring his calf's head off his body with these hands. Dick!' he added, breaking off, 'you just jump up, like a sweet lad, and get me an apple, to wet my pipe like.'

You may fancy the terror I was in! I should have leaped out and run for it, if I had found the strength; but my limbs and heart alike misgave me. I heard Dick begin to rise, and then someone seemingly stopped him, and the voice of Hands exclaimed:—

'Oh, stow that! Don't you get sucking of that bilge, John. Let's have a go of the rum.'

'Dick,' said Silver, 'I trust you. I've a gauge on the keg, mind. There's the key; you fill a pannikin* and bring it up.'

Terrified as I was, I could not help thinking to myself that this must have been how Mr Arrow got the strong waters that destroyed him.

Dick was gone but a little while, and during his absence Israel spoke straight on in the cook's ear. It was but a word or two that I could catch, and yet I garnered some important news; for, besides other scraps that tended to the same purpose, this whole clause was audible: 'Not another man of them 'll jine.' Hence there were still faithful men on board.

When Dick returned, one after another of the trio took the pannikin and drank—one 'To luck'; another with a 'Here's to old Flint'; and Silver himself saying, in a kind of song, 'Here's to ourselves, and hold your luff, plenty of prizes and plenty of duff.'

Just then a sort of brightness fell upon me in the barrel, and looking up, I found the moon had risen, and was silvering the mizzen-top and shining white on the luff of the fore-sail; and almost at the same time the voice of the look-out shouted, 'Land ho!'

CHAPTER XII

COUNCIL OF WAR

THERE was a great rush of feet across the deck. I could hear people tumbling up from the cabin and the foc's'le; and, slipping in an instant outside my barrel, I dived behind the fore-sail, made a double towards the stern, and came out upon the open deck in time to join Hunter and Dr Livesey in the rush for the weather bow.

There all hands were already congregated. A belt of fog had lifted almost simultaneously with the appearance of the moon. Away to the south-west of us we saw two low hills, about a couple of miles apart, and rising behind one of them a third and higher hill, whose peak was still buried in the fog. All three seemed sharp and conical in figure.

So much I saw, almost in a dream, for I had not yet recovered from my horrid fear of a minute or two before. And then I heard the voice of Captain Smollett issuing orders. The *Hispaniola* was laid a couple of points nearer the wind, and now sailed a course that would just clear the island on the east.

'And now, men,' said the captain, when all was sheeted home, 'has any one of you ever seen that land ahead?'

'I have, sir,' said Silver. 'I've watered there with a trader I was cook in.'

'The anchorage is on the south, behind an islet, I fancy?' asked the captain.

'Yes, sir; Skeleton Island they calls it. It were a main place for pirates once, and a hand we had on board knowed all their names for it. That hill to the nor'ard they calls the Fore-mast Hill; there are three hills in a row running south'ard—fore, main, and mizzen, sir. But the main—that's the big 'un, with the cloud on it—they usually calls the Spy-glass, by reason of a look-out they kept when they was in the anchorage cleaning; for it's there they cleaned their ships, sir, asking your pardon.'

'I have a chart here,' says Captain Smollett. 'See if that's the place.'

Long John's eyes burned in his head as he took the chart; but, by the fresh look of the paper, I knew he was doomed to disappointment. This was not the map we found in Billy Bones's chest, but an accurate copy, complete in all things—names and heights and soundings—with the single exception of the red crosses and the written notes.

Sharp as must have been his annoyance, Silver had the strength of mind to hide it.

'Yes, sir,' said he, 'this is the spot to be sure; and very prettily drawed out. Who might have done that, I wonder? The pirates were too ignorant, I reckon. Ay, here it is: "Capt. Kidd's Anchorage"*—just the name my shipmate called it. There's a strong current runs along the south, and then away nor'ard up the west coast. Right you was, sir,' says he, 'to haul your wind and keep the weather of the island. Leastways, if such was your intention as to enter and careen, and there ain't no better place for that in these waters.'

'Thank you, my man,' says Captain Smollett. 'I'll ask you, later on, to give us a help. You may go.'

I was surprised at the coolness with which John avowed his knowledge of the island; and I own I was half-frightened when I saw him drawing nearer to myself. He did not know, to be sure, that I had overheard his council from the apple barrel, and yet I had, by this time, taken such a horror of his cruelty, duplicity, and power, that I could scarce conceal a shudder when he laid his hand upon my arm.

'Ah,' says he, 'this here is a sweet spot, this island—a sweet spot for a lad to get ashore on. You'll bathe, and you'll climb trees, and you'll hunt goats, you will; and you'll get aloft on them hills like a goat yourself. Why, it makes me young again. I was going to forget my timber leg, I was. It's a pleasant thing to be young, and have ten toes, and you may lay to that. When you want to go a bit of exploring, you just ask old John, and he'll put up a snack for you to take along.'

And clapping me in the friendliest way upon the shoulder, he hobbled off forward and went below.

Captain Smollett, the squire, and Dr Livesey were talking together on the quarterdeck, and, anxious as I was to tell them my story, I durst not interrupt them openly. While I was still casting about in my thoughts to find some probable excuse, Dr Livesey called me to his side. He had left his pipe below, and being a slave to tobacco, had meant that I should fetch it; but as soon as I was near enough to speak and not to be overheard, I broke out immediately: 'Doctor, let me speak. Get the captain and squire down to the cabin, and then make some pretence to send for me. I have terrible news.'

The doctor changed countenance a little, but next moment he was master of himself.

'Thank you, Jim,' said he, quite loudly, 'that was all I wanted to know,' as if he had asked me a question.

And with that he turned on his heel and rejoined the other two. They spoke together for a little, and though none of them started, or raised his voice, or so much as whistled, it was plain enough that Dr Livesey had communicated my request; for the next thing that I heard was the captain giving an order to Job Anderson, and all hands were piped on deck.

'My lads,' said Captain Smollett, 'I've a word to say to you. This land that we have sighted is the place we have been sailing for. Mr Trelawney, being a very open-handed gentleman, as we all know, has just asked me a word or two, and as I was able to tell him that every man on board had done his duty, alow and aloft, as I never ask to see it done better, why, he and I and the doctor are going below to the cabin to drink *your* health and luck, and you'll have grog served out for you to drink *our* health and luck. I'll tell you what I think of this: I think it handsome. And if you think as I do, you'll give a good sea cheer for the gentleman that does it.'

The cheer followed—that was a matter of course; but it rang out so full and hearty, that I confess I could hardly believe these same men were plotting for our blood.

'One more cheer for Cap'n Smollett,' cried Long John, when the first had subsided.

And this also was given with a will.

On the top of that the three gentlemen went below, and not long after, word was sent forward that Jim Hawkins was wanted in the cabin.

I found them all three seated round the table, a bottle of Spanish wine and some raisins before them, and the doctor smoking away, with his wig on his lap, and that, I knew, was a sign that he was agitated. The stern window was open, for it was a warm night, and you could see the moon shining behind on the ship's wake.

'Now, Hawkins,' said the squire, 'you have something to say. Speak up.'

I did as I was bid, and as short as I could make it, told the whole details of Silver's conversation. Nobody interrupted me till I was done, nor did any one of the three of them make so much as a movement, but they kept their eyes upon my face from first to last.

'Jim,' said Dr Livesey, 'take a seat.'

And they made me sit down at table beside them, poured me out a glass of wine, filled my hands with raisins, and all three, one after the other, and each with a bow, drank my good health, and their service to me, for my luck and courage.

'Now, captain,' said the squire, 'you were right, and I was wrong. I own myself an ass, and I await your orders.'

'No more an ass than I, sir,' returned the captain. 'I never heard of a crew that meant to mutiny but what showed signs before, for any man that had an eye in his head to see the mischief and take steps according. But this crew,' he added, 'beats me.'

'Captain,' said the doctor, 'with your permission, that's Silver. A very remarkable man.'

'He'd look remarkably well from a yard-arm, sir,' returned the captain. 'But this is talk; this don't lead to anything. I see three or four points, and with Mr Trelawney's permission, I'll name them.'

'You, sir, are the captain. It is for you to speak,' says Mr Trelawney, grandly.

'First point,' began Mr Smollett. 'We must go on, because we can't turn back. If I gave the word to go about, they would rise at once. Second point, we have time before us—at least, until this treasure's found. Third point, there are faithful hands. Now, sir, it's got to come to blows sooner or later; and what I propose is, to take time by the forelock, as the saying is, and come to blows some fine day when they least expect it. We can count, I take it, on your own home servants, Mr Trelawney?'

'As upon myself,' declared the squire.

'Three,' reckoned the captain, 'ourselves make seven, counting Hawkins, here. Now, about the honest hands?'

'Most likely Trelawney's own men,' said the doctor; 'those he had picked up for himself, before he lit on Silver.'

'Nay,' replied the squire, 'Hands was one of mine.'

'I did think I could have trusted Hands,' added the captain.

'And to think that they're all Englishmen!' broke out the squire. 'Sir, I could find it in my heart to blow the ship up.'

'Well, gentlemen,' said the captain, 'the best that I can say is not much. We must lay to, if you please, and keep a bright look out. It's trying on a man, I know. It would be pleasanter to come to blows. But there's no help for it till we know our men. Lay to, and whistle for a wind, that's my view.'

'Jim here,' said the doctor, 'can help us more than anyone. The men are not shy with him, and Jim is a noticing lad.'

'Hawkins, I put prodigious faith in you,' added the squire.

I began to feel pretty desperate at this, for I felt altogether helpless; and yet, by an odd train of circumstances, it was indeed through me that safety came. In the meantime, talk as we pleased, there were only seven out of the twenty-six on whom we knew we could rely; and out of these seven one was a boy, so that the grown men on our side were six to their nineteen.

PART III

MY SHORE ADVENTURE

CHAPTER XIII

HOW MY SHORE ADVENTURE BEGAN

THE appearance of the island when I came on deck next morning was altogether changed. Although the breeze had now utterly ceased, we had made a great deal of way during the night, and were now lying becalmed about half a mile to the south-east of the low eastern coast. Grey-coloured woods covered a large part of the surface. This even tint was indeed broken up by streaks of yellow sandbreak in the lower lands, and by many tall trees of the pine family, out-topping the others—some singly, some in clumps; but the general colouring was uniform and sad. The hills ran up clear above the vegetation in spires of naked rock. All were strangely shaped, and the Spy-glass, which was by three or four hundred feet the tallest on the island, was likewise the strangest in configuration, running up sheer from almost every side, then suddenly cut off at the top like a pedestal to put a statue on.

The *Hispaniola* was rolling scuppers under in the ocean swell. The booms were tearing at the blocks, the rudder was banging to and fro, and the whole ship creaking, groaning, and jumping like a manufactory. I had to cling tight to the backstay, and the world turned giddily before my eyes; for though I was a good enough sailor when there was way on, this standing still and being rolled about like a bottle was a thing I never learned to stand without a qualm or so, above all in the morning, on an empty stomach.

Perhaps it was this—perhaps it was the look of the island, with its grey, melancholy woods, and wild stone spires, and the surf that we could both see and hear foaming and thundering on the steep beach—at least, although the sun shone bright and hot, and the shore birds were fishing and crying all around us, and you would have thought anyone would have been glad to get to land after being so long at sea, my heart sank, as the saying is, into my boots; and from that first look onward, I hated the very thought of Treasure Island.

We had a dreary morning's work before us, for there was no sign of any wind, and the boats had to be got out and manned, and the ship warped three or four miles round the corner of the island, and up the narrow passage to the haven behind Skeleton Island. I volunteered for one of the boats, where I had, of course, no business. The heat was sweltering, and the men grumbled fiercely over their work. Anderson was in command of my boat, and instead of keeping the crew in order, he grumbled as loud as the worst.

'Well,' he said, with an oath, 'it's not for ever.'

I thought this was a very bad sign; for, up to that day, the men had gone briskly and willingly about their business; but the very sight of the island had relaxed the cords of discipline.

All the way in, Long John stood by the steersman and conned the ship. He knew the passage like the palm of his hand; and though the man in the chains got everywhere more water than was down in the chart,* John never hesitated once.

'There's a strong scour with the ebb,' he said, 'and this here passage has been dug out, in a manner of speaking, with a spade.'

We brought up just where the anchor was in the chart, about a third of a mile from each shore, the mainland on one side, and Skeleton Island on the other. The bottom was clean sand. The plunge of our anchor sent up clouds of birds wheeling and crying over the woods; but in less than a minute they were down again, and all was once more silent.

The place was entirely land-locked, buried in woods, the trees coming right down to high-water mark, the shores mostly flat, and the hill-tops standing round at a distance in a sort of amphitheatre, one here, one there. Two little rivers, or, rather, two swamps, emptied out into this pond, as you might call it; and the foliage round that part of the shore had a kind of poisonous brightness. From the ship, we could see nothing of the house or stockade, for they were quite buried among trees; and if it had not been for the chart on the companion, we might have been the first that had ever anchored there since the island arose out of the seas.

There was not a breath of air moving, nor a sound but that of the surf booming half a mile away along the beaches and against the rocks outside. A peculiar stagnant smell hung over the anchorage—a smell of sodden leaves and rotting tree trunks. I observed the doctor sniffing and sniffing, like someone tasting a bad egg.

'I don't know about treasure,' he said, 'but I'll stake my wig there's fever here.'

If the conduct of the men had been alarming in the boat, it became truly threatening when they had come aboard. They lay about the deck growling together in talk. The slightest order was received with a black look, and grudgingly and carelessly obeyed. Even the honest hands must have caught the infection, for there was not one man aboard to mend another. Mutiny, it was plain, hung over us like a thundercloud.

And it was not only we of the cabin party who perceived the danger. Long John was hard at work going from group to group, spending himself in good advice, and as for example no man could have shown a better. He fairly outstripped himself in willingness and civility; he was all smiles to everyone. If an order were given, John would be on his crutch in an instant, with the cheeriest 'Ay, ay, sir!' in the world; and when there was nothing else to do, he kept up one song after another, as if to conceal the discontent of the rest.

Of all the gloomy features of that gloomy afternoon, this obvious anxiety on the part of Long John appeared the worst.

We held a council in the cabin.

'Sir,' said the captain, 'if I risk another order, the whole ship'll come about our ears by the run. You see, sir, here it is. I get a rough answer, do I not? Well, if I speak back, pikes will be going in two shakes; if I don't, Silver will see there's something under that, and the game's up. Now, we've only one man to rely on.'

'And who is that?' asked the squire.

'Silver, sir,' returned the captain; 'he's as anxious as you and I to smother things up. This is a tiff; he'd soon talk 'em out of it if he had the chance, and what I propose to do is to give him the chance. Let's allow the men an afternoon ashore. If they all go, why, we'll fight the ship. If they none of them go, well, then, we hold the cabin, and God defend the right. If some go, you mark my words, sir, Silver'll bring 'em aboard again as mild as lambs.'

It was so decided; loaded pistols were served out to all the sure men; Hunter, Joyce, and Redruth were taken into our confidence, and received the news with less surprise and a better spirit than we had looked for, and then the captain went on deck and addressed the crew.

'My lads,' said he, 'we've had a hot day, and are all tired and out of sorts. A turn ashore'll hurt nobody—the boats are still in the water; you can take the gigs, and as many as please may go ashore for the afternoon. I'll fire a gun half an hour before sundown.'

I believe the silly fellows must have thought they would break their shins over treasure as soon as they were landed; for they all came out of their sulks in a moment, and gave a cheer that started the echo in a far-away hill, and sent the birds once more flying and squalling round the anchorage.

The captain was too bright to be in the way. He whipped out of sight in a moment, leaving Silver to arrange the party; and I fancy it was as well he did so. Had he been on deck, he could no longer so much as have pretended not to understand the situation. It was as plain as day. Silver was the captain, and a mighty rebellious crew he had of it. The honest hands—and I was soon to see it proved that there were such on board—must have been stupid fellows. Or, rather I suppose the truth was this, that all hands were disaffected by the example of the ringleaders—only some more, some less: and a few, being good fellows in the main, could neither be led nor driven any further. It is one thing to be idle and skulk, and quite another to take a ship and murder a number of innocent men.

At last, however, the party was made up. Six fellows were to stay on board, and the remaining thirteen, including Silver, began to embark.

Then it was that there came into my head the first of the mad notions that contributed so much to save our lives. If six men were left by Silver, it was plain our party could not take and fight the ship; and since only six were left, it was equally plain that the cabin party had no present need of my assistance. It occurred to me at once to go ashore. In a jiffy I had slipped over the side, and curled up in the fore-sheets of the nearest boat, and almost at the same moment she shoved off.

No one took notice of me, only the bow oar saying, 'Is that you, Jim? Keep your head down.' But Silver, from the other boat, looked sharply over and called out to know if that were me; and from that moment I began to regret what I had done.

The crews raced for the beach; but the boat I was in, having some start, and being at once the lighter and the better manned, shot far ahead of her consort, and the bow had struck among the shoreside trees, and I had caught a branch and swung myself out, and plunged into the nearest thicket, while Silver and the rest were still a hundred yards behind.

'Jim, Jim!' I heard him shouting.

But you may suppose I paid no heed; jumping, ducking, and breaking through, I ran straight before my nose, till I could run no longer.

CHAPTER XIV

THE FIRST BLOW

I WAS so pleased at having given the slip to Long John, that I began to enjoy myself and look around me with some interest on the strange land that I was in.*

I had crossed a marshy tract full of willows, bulrushes, and odd, outlandish, swampy trees; and I had now come out upon the skirts of an open piece of undulating, sandy country, about a mile long, dotted with a few pines, and a great number of contorted trees, not unlike the oak in growth, but pale in the foliage, like willows. On the far side of the open stood one of the hills, with two quaint, craggy peaks, shining vividly in the sun.

I now felt for the first time the joy of exploration. The isle was uninhabited; my shipmates I had left behind, and nothing lived in front of me but dumb brutes and fowls. I turned hither and thither among the trees. Here and there were flowering plants, unknown to me; here and there I saw snakes, and one raised his head from a ledge of rock and hissed at me with a noise not unlike the spinning of a top. Little did I suppose that he was a deadly enemy, and that the noise was the famous rattle.

Then I came to a long thicket of these oak-like trees—live, or evergreen, oaks,* I heard afterwards they should be called—which grew low along the sand like brambles, the boughs curiously twisted, the foliage compact, like thatch. The thicket stretched down from the top of one of the sandy knolls, spreading and growing taller as it went, until it reached the margin of the broad, reedy fen, through which the nearest of the little rivers soaked its way into the anchorage. The marsh was steaming in the strong sun, and the outline of the Spy-glass trembled through the haze.

All at once there began to go a sort of bustle among the bulrushes; a wild duck flew up with a quack, another followed, and soon over the whole surface of the marsh a great cloud of birds hung screaming and circling in the air. I judged at once that some of my shipmates must be drawing near along the borders of the fen. Nor was I deceived; for soon I heard the very distant and low tones of a human voice, which, as I continued to give ear, grew steadily louder and nearer.

This put me in a great fear, and I crawled under cover of the nearest live-oak, and squatted there, hearkening, as silent as a mouse.

Another voice answered; and then the first voice, which I now recognised to be Silver's, once more took up the story, and ran on for a long while in a stream, only now and again interrupted by the other. By the sound they must have been talking earnestly, and almost fiercely; but no distinct word came to my hearing.

At last the speakers seemed to have paused, and perhaps to have sat down; for not only did they cease to draw any nearer, but the birds themselves began to grow more quiet, and to settle again to their places in the swamp.

And now I began to feel that I was neglecting my business; that since I had been so foolhardy as to come ashore with these desperadoes, the least I could do was to overhear them at their councils; and that my plain and obvious duty was to draw as close as I could manage, under the favourable ambush of the crouching trees.

I could tell the direction of the speakers pretty exactly, not only by the sound of their voices, but by the behaviour of the few birds that still hung in alarm above the heads of the intruders.

Crawling on all-fours, I made steadily but slowly towards them; till at last, raising my head to an aperture among the leaves, I could see clear down into a little green dell beside the marsh, and closely set about with trees, where Long John Silver and another of the crew stood face to face in conversation.

The sun beat full upon them. Silver had thrown his hat beside him on the ground, and his great, smooth, blond face, all shining with heat, was lifted to the other man's in a kind of appeal.

'Mate,' he was saying, 'it's because I thinks gold dust of you—gold dust, and you may lay to that! If I hadn't took to you like pitch, do you think I'd have been here a-warning of you? All's up—you can't make nor mend; it's to save your neck that I'm a-speaking, and if one of the wild 'uns knew it, where 'ud I be, Tom—now, tell me, where 'ud I be?'

'Silver,' said the other man—and I observed he was not only red in the face, but spoke as hoarse as a crow, and his voice shook, too, like a taut rope—'Silver,' says he, 'you're old, and you're honest, or has the name for it; and you've money, too, which lots of poor sailors hasn't; and you're brave, or I'm mistook. And will you tell me you'll let yourself be led away with that kind of a mess of swabs? not you! As sure as God sees me, I'd sooner lose my hand. If I turn agin my dooty—'

And then all of a sudden he was interrupted by a noise. I had found one of the honest hands—well, here, at that same moment, came news of another. Far away out in the marsh there arose, all of a sudden, a sound like the cry of anger, then another on the back of it; and then one horrid, long-drawn scream. The rocks of the Spy-glass re-echoed it a score of times; the whole troop of marsh-birds rose again, darkening heaven, with a simultaneous whirr; and long after that death yell was still ringing in my brain, silence had re-established its empire, and only the rustle of the redescending birds and the boom of the distant surges disturbed the languor of the afternoon.

Tom had leaped at the sound, like a horse at the spur; but Silver had not winked an eye. He stood where he was, resting lightly on his crutch, watching his companion like a snake about to spring.

'John!' said the sailor, stretching out his hand.

'Hands off!' cried Silver, leaping back a yard, as it seemed to me, with the speed and security of a trained gymnast.

'Hands off, if you like, John Silver,' said the other. 'It's a black conscience that can make you feared of me. But, in heaven's name, tell me what was that?'

'That?' returned Silver, smiling away, but warier than ever, his eye a mere pin-point in his big face, but gleaming like a crumb of glass.* 'That? Oh, I reckon that'll be Alan.'

And at this poor Tom flashed out like a hero.

'Alan!' he cried. 'Then rest his soul for a true seaman! And as for you, John Silver, long you've been a mate of mine, but you're mate of mine no more. If I die like a dog, I'll die in my dooty. You've killed Alan, have you? Kill me, too, if you can. But I defies you.'

And with that, this brave fellow turned his back directly on the cook, and set off walking for the beach. But he was not destined to go far. With a cry, John seized the branch of a tree, whipped the crutch out of his armpit, and sent that uncouth missile hurtling through the air. It struck poor Tom, point foremost, and with stunning violence, right between the shoulders in the middle of his back. His hands flew up, he gave a sort of gasp, and fell.

Whether he were injured much or little, none could ever tell. Like enough, to judge from the sound, his back was broken on the spot. But he had no time given him to recover. Silver, agile as a monkey, even without leg or crutch, was on the top of him next moment, and had twice buried his knife up to the hilt in that defenceless body. From my place of ambush, I could hear him pant aloud as he struck the blows.

I do not know what it rightly is to faint, but I do know that for the next little while the whole world swam away from before me in a whirling mist; Silver and the birds, and the tall Spy-glass hill-top, going round and round and topsy-turvy before my eyes, and all manner of bells ringing and distant voices shouting in my ear.

When I came again to myself, the monster had pulled himself together, his crutch under his arm, his hat upon his head. Just before him Tom lay motionless upon the sward; but the murderer minded him not a whit, cleansing his bloodstained knife the while upon a wisp of grass. Everything else was unchanged, the sun still shining mercilessly on the steaming marsh and the tall pinnacle of the mountain, and I could scarce persuade myself that murder had been actually done, and a human life cruelly cut short a moment since, before my eyes.

But now John put his hand into his pocket, brought out a whistle, and blew upon it several modulated blasts, that rang far across the heated air. I could not tell, of course, the meaning of the signal; but it instantly awoke my fears. More men would be coming. I might be discovered. They had already slain two of the honest people; after Tom and Alan, might not I come next?

Instantly I began to extricate myself and crawl back again, with what speed and silence I could manage, to the more open portion of the wood. As I did so, I could hear hails coming and going between the old buccaneer and his comrades, and this sound of danger lent me wings. As soon as I was clear of the thicket, I ran as I never ran before, scarce minding the direction of my flight, so long as it led me from the murderers; and as I ran, fear grew and grew upon me, until it turned into a kind of frenzy.

Indeed, could anyone be more entirely lost than I? When the gun fired, how should I dare to go down to the boats among those fiends, still smoking from their crime? Would not the first of them who saw me wring my neck like a snipe's? Would not my absence itself be an evidence to them of my alarm, and therefore of my fatal knowledge? It was all over, I thought. Good-bye to the *Hispaniola*; good-bye to the squire, the doctor, and the captain! There was nothing left for me but death by starvation, or death by the hands of the mutineers.

All this while, as I say, I was still running, and, without taking any notice, I had drawn near to the foot of the little hill with the two peaks, and had got into a part of the island where the live-oaks grew more widely apart, and seemed more like forest trees in their bearing and dimensions. Mingled with these were a few scattered pines, some fifty, some nearer seventy, feet high. The air, too, smelt more freshly than down beside the marsh.

And here a fresh alarm brought me to a standstill with a thumping heart.

CHAPTER XV

THE MAN OF THE ISLAND

FROM the side of the hill, which was here steep and stony, a spout of gravel was dislodged, and fell rattling and bounding through the trees. My eyes turned instinctively in that direction, and I saw a figure leap with great rapidity behind the trunk of a pine. What it was, whether bear or man or monkey, I could in no wise tell. It seemed dark and shaggy; more I knew not. But the terror of this new apparition brought me to a stand.

I was now, it seemed, cut off upon both sides; behind me the murderers, before me this lurking nondescript.* And immediately I began to prefer the dangers that I knew to those I knew not. Silver himself appeared less terrible in contrast with this creature of the woods, and I turned on my heel, and, looking sharply behind me over my shoulder, began to retrace my steps in the direction of the boats.

Instantly the figure reappeared, and, making a wide circuit, began to head me off. I was tired, at any rate; but had I been as fresh as when I rose, I could see it was in vain for me to contend in speed with such an adversary. From trunk to trunk the creature flitted like a deer, running manlike on two legs, but unlike any man that I had ever seen, stooping almost double as it ran. Yet a man it was, I could no longer be in doubt about that.

I began to recall what I had heard of cannibals. I was within an ace of calling for help. But the mere fact that he was a man, however wild, had somewhat reassured me, and my fear of Silver began to revive in proportion. I stood still, therefore, and cast about for some method of escape; and as I was so thinking, the recollection of my pistol flashed into my mind. As soon as I remembered I was not defenceless, courage glowed again in my heart; and I set my face resolutely for this man of the island, and walked briskly towards him.

He was concealed by this time, behind another tree trunk; but he must have been watching me closely, for as soon as I began to move in his direction he reappeared and took a step to meet me. Then he hesitated, drew back, came forward again, and at last, to my wonder and confusion, threw himself on his knees and held out his clasped hands in supplication.

At that I once more stopped.

'Who are you?' I asked.

'Ben Gunn,' he answered, and his voice sounded hoarse and awkward, like a rusty lock. 'I'm poor Ben Gunn,* I am; and I haven't spoke with a Christian these three years.'

I could now see that he was a white man like myself, and that his features were even pleasing. His skin, wherever it was exposed, was burnt by the sun; even his lips were black; and his fair eyes looked quite startling in so dark a face. Of all the beggar-men that I had seen or fancied, he was the chief for raggedness. He was clothed with tatters of old ship's canvas and old sea cloth; and this extraordinary patchwork was all held together by a system of the most various and incongruous fastenings, brass buttons, bits of stick, and loops of tarry gaskin.* About his waist he wore an old brass-buckled leather belt, which was the one thing solid in his whole accoutrement.

'Three years!' I cried. 'Were you shipwrecked?'

'Nay, mate,' said he—'marooned.'

I had heard the word, and I knew it stood for a horrible kind of punishment common enough among the buccaneers, in which the offender is put ashore with a little powder and shot, and left behind on some desolate and distant island.*

'Marooned three years agone,' he continued, 'and lived on goats since then, and berries, and oysters.* Wherever a man is, says I, a man can do for himself. But, mate, my heart is sore for Christian diet. You mightn't happen to have a piece of cheese about you, now? No? Well, many's the long night I've dreamed of cheese—toasted, mostly—and woke up again, and here I were.'

'If ever I can get aboard again,' said I, 'you shall have cheese by the stone.'*

All this time he had been feeling the stuff of my jacket, smoothing my hands, looking at my boots, and generally, in the intervals of his speech, showing a childish pleasure in the presence of a fellow-creature. But at my last words he perked up into a kind of startled slyness.

'If ever you can get aboard again, says you?' he repeated. 'Why, now, who's to hinder you?'

'Not you, I know,' was my reply.

'And right you was,' he cried. 'Now you—what do you call yourself, mate?'

'Jim,' I told him.

'Jim, Jim,' says he, quite pleased apparently. 'Well, now, Jim, I've lived that rough as you'd be ashamed to hear of. Now, for instance, you wouldn't think I had had a pious mother—to look at me?' he asked.

'Why, no, not in particular,' I answered.

'Ah, well,' said he, 'but I had—remarkable pious. And I was a civil, pious boy, and could rattle off my catechism that fast, as you couldn't tell one word from another. And here's what it come to, Jim, and it begun with chuck-farthen* on the blessed grave-stones! That's what it begun with, but it went further'n that; and so my mother told me, and predicked the whole, she did, the pious woman! But it were Providence that put me here. I've thought it all out in this here lonely island, and I'm back on piety. You don't catch me tasting rum so much; but just a thimbleful for luck, of course, the first chance I have. I'm bound I'll be good, and I see the way to. And, Jim'—looking all round him, and lowering his voice to a whisper—'I'm rich.'

I now felt sure that the poor fellow had gone crazy in his solitude, and I suppose I must have shown the feeling in my face, for he repeated the statement hotly:—

'Rich! rich! I says. And I'll tell you what: I'll make a man of you, Jim. Ah, Jim, you'll bless your stars, you will, you was the first that found me!'

And at this there came suddenly a lowering shadow over his face; and he tightened his grasp upon my hand, and raised a forefinger threateningly before my eyes.

'Now, Jim, you tell me true: that ain't Flint's ship?' he asked.

At this I had a happy inspiration. I began to believe that I had found an ally, and I answered him at once.

'It's not Flint's ship, and Flint is dead; but I'll tell you true, as you ask me—there are some of Flint's hands aboard; worse luck for the rest of us.'

'Not a man—with one—leg?' he gasped.

'Silver?' I asked.

'Ah, Silver!' says he; 'that were his name.'

'He's the cook; and the ringleader, too.'

He was still holding me by the wrist, and at that he gave it quite a wring.

'If you was sent by Long John,' he said, 'I'm as good as pork, and I know it. But where was you, do you suppose?'

I had made my mind up in a moment, and by way of answer told him the whole story of our voyage, and the predicament in which we found ourselves. He heard me with the keenest interest, and when I had done he patted me on the head.

'You're a good lad, Jim,' he said; 'and you're all in a clove hitch, ain't you? Well, you just put your trust in Ben Gunn—Ben Gunn's the man to do it. Would you think it likely, now, that your squire would prove a liberal-minded one in case of help—him being in a clove hitch, as you remark?'

I told him the squire was the most liberal of men.

'Ay, but you see,' returned Ben Gunn, 'I didn't mean giving me a gate to keep, and a shuit of livery clothes, and such; that's not my mark, Jim. What I mean is, would he be likely to come down to the toon of, say one thousand pounds out of money that's as good as a man's own already?'

'I am sure he would,' said I. 'As it was, all hands were to share.'

'*And* a passage home?' he added, with a look of great shrewdness.

'Why,' I cried, 'the squire's a gentleman. And, besides, if we got rid of the others, we should want you to help work the vessel home.'

'Ah,' said he, 'so you would.' And he seemed very much relieved.

'Now, I'll tell you what,' he went on. 'So much I'll tell you, and no more. I were in Flint's ship when he buried the treasure; he and six along—six strong seamen. They were ashore nigh on a week, and us standing off and on in the old *Walrus*. One fine day up went the signal, and here come Flint by himself in a little boat, and his head done up in a blue scarf. The sun was getting up, and mortal white he looked about the cut-water. But, there he was, you mind, and the six all dead—dead and buried. How he done it, not a man aboard us could make out. It was battle, murder, and sudden death, leastways—him against six. Billy Bones was the mate; Long John, he was quartermaster; and they asked him where the treasure was. "Ah," says he, "you can go ashore, if you like, and stay," he says; "but as for the ship, she'll beat up for more, by thunder!" That's what he said.

'Well, I was in another ship three years back, and we sighted this island. "Boys," said I, "here's Flint's treasure; let's land and find it." The cap'n was displeased at that; but my messmates were all of a mind, and landed. Twelve days they looked for it, and every day they had the worse word for me, until one fine morning all hands went aboard. "As for you, Benjamin Gunn," says they, "here's a musket," they says, "and a spade, and pick-axe. You can stay here, and find Flint's money for yourself," they says.

'Well, Jim, three years have I been here, and not a bite of Christian diet from that day to this. But now, you look here; look at me. Do I look like a man before the mast? No, says you. Nor I weren't, neither, I says.'

And with that he winked and pinched me hard.

'Just you mention them words to your squire, Jim'—he went on: 'Nor he weren't, neither—that's the words. Three years he were the man of this island, light and dark, fair and rain; and sometimes he would, maybe, think upon a prayer (says you), and sometimes he would, maybe, think of his old mother, so be as she's alive (you'll say); but the most part of Gunn's time (this is what you'll say)—the most part of his time was took up with another matter. And then you'll give him a nip, like I do.'

And he pinched me again in the most confidential manner.

'Then,' he continued—'then you'll up, and you'll say this:—Gunn is a good man (you'll say), and he puts a precious sight more confidence—a precious sight, mind that—in a gen'leman born than in these gen'lemen of fortune, having been one hisself.'

'Well,' I said. 'I don't understand one word that you've been saying. But that's neither here nor there; for how am I to get on board?'

'Ah,' said he, 'that's the hitch, for sure. Well, there's my boat, that I made with my two hands. I keep her under the white rock. If the worst come to the worst, we might try that after dark. Hi!' he broke out, 'what's that?'

For just then, although the sun had still an hour or two to run, all the echoes of the island awoke and bellowed to the thunder of a cannon.

'They have begun to fight!' I cried. 'Follow me.'

And I began to run towards the anchorage, my terrors all forgotten; while, close at my side, the marooned man in his goatskins* trotted easily and lightly.

'Left, left,' says he; 'keep to your left hand, mate Jim! Under the trees with you! Theer's where I killed my first goat. They don't come down here now; they're all mast-headed on them mountings for the fear of Benjamin Gunn.* Ah! And there's the cetemery'—cemetery, he must have meant. 'You see the mounds? I come here and prayed, nows and thens, when I thought maybe a Sunday would be about doo.

It weren't quite a chapel, but it seemed more solemn like; and then, says you, Ben Gunn was short-handed—no chapling, nor so much as a Bible and a flag, you says.'

So he kept talking as I ran, neither expecting nor receiving any answer.

The cannon-shot was followed, after a considerable interval, by a volley of small arms.

Another pause, and then, not a quarter of a mile in front of me, I beheld the Union Jack flutter in the air above a wood.

PART IV

THE STOCKADE

CHAPTER XVI

NARRATIVE CONTINUED BY THE DOCTOR: HOW THE SHIP WAS ABANDONED

It was about half-past one—three bells in the sea phrase—that the two boats went ashore from the *Hispaniola*. The captain, the squire, and I were talking matters over in the cabin. Had there been a breath of wind we should have fallen on the six mutineers who were left aboard with us, slipped our cable, and away to sea. But the wind was wanting; and, to complete our helplessness, down came Hunter with the news that Jim Hawkins had slipped into a boat and gone ashore with the rest.

It never occurred to us to doubt Jim Hawkins; but we were alarmed for his safety. With the men in the temper they were in, it seemed an even chance if we should see the lad again. We ran on deck. The pitch was bubbling in the seams; the nasty stench of the place turned me sick; if ever a man smelt fever and dysentery, it was in that abominable anchorage. The six scoundrels were sitting grumbling under a sail in the forecastle; ashore we could see the gigs made fast, and a man sitting in each, hard by where the river runs in. One of them was whistling 'Lillibullero.'*

Waiting was a strain; and it was decided that Hunter and I should go ashore with the jolly-boat, in quest of information. The gigs had leaned to their right; but Hunter and I pulled straight in, in the direction of the stockade upon the chart. The two who were left guarding their boats seemed in a bustle at our appearance; 'Lillibullero' stopped off, and I could see the pair discussing what they ought to do. Had they gone and told Silver, all might have turned out differently; but they had their orders, I suppose, and decided to sit quietly where they were and hark back again to 'Lillibullero.'

There was a slight bend in the coast, and I steered so as to put it between us; even before we landed we had thus lost sight of the gigs.

I jumped out, and came as near running as I durst, with a big silk handkerchief under my hat for coolness' sake, and a brace of pistols ready primed* for safety.

I had not gone a hundred yards when I reached the stockade.

This was how it was: a spring of clear water rose almost at the top of a knoll. Well, on the knoll, and enclosing the spring, they had clapped a stout log-house, fit to hold two score of people on a pinch, and loop-holed for musketry* on every side. All round this they had cleared a wide space, and then the thing was completed by a paling six feet high, without door or opening, too strong to pull down without time and labour, and too open to shelter the besiegers. The people in the log-house had them in every way; they stood quiet in shelter and shot the others like partridges. All they wanted was a good watch and food; for, short of a complete surprise, they might have held the place against a regiment.

What particularly took my fancy was the spring. For, though we had a good enough place of it in the cabin of the *Hispaniola*, with plenty of arms and ammunition, and things to eat, and excellent wines, there had been one thing overlooked—we had no water. I was thinking this over, when there came ringing over the island the cry of a man at the point of death. I was not new to violent death—I have served his Royal Highness the Duke of Cumberland, and got a wound myself at Fontenoy*—but I know my pulse went dot and carry one. 'Jim Hawkins is gone' was my first thought.

It is something to have been an old soldier, but more still to have been a doctor. There is no time to dilly-dally in our work. And so now I made up my mind instantly, and with no time lost returned to the shore, and jumped on board the jolly-boat.

By good fortune Hunter pulled a good oar. We made the water fly; and the boat was soon alongside, and I aboard the schooner.

I found them all shaken, as was natural. The squire was sitting down, as white as a sheet, thinking of the harm he had led us to, the good soul! and one of the six forecastle hands was little better.

'There's a man,' says Captain Smollett, nodding towards him, 'new to this work. He came nigh-hand* fainting, doctor, when he heard the cry. Another touch of the rudder and that man would join us.'

I told my plan to the captain, and between us we settled on the details of its accomplishment.

We put old Redruth in the gallery between the cabin and the forecastle, with three or four loaded muskets and a mattress for protection.

Hunter brought the boat round under the stern-port, and Joyce and I set to work loading her with powder tins, muskets, bags of biscuits, kegs of pork, a cask of cognac, and my invaluable medicine chest.

In the meantime, the squire and the captain stayed on deck, and the latter hailed the coxswain, who was the principal man aboard.

'Mr Hands,' he said, 'here are two of us with a brace of pistols each. If any one of you six make a signal of any description, that man's dead.'

They were a good deal taken aback; and, after a little consultation, one and all tumbled down the fore companion, thinking, no doubt, to take us on the rear. But when they saw Redruth waiting for them in the sparred gallery, they went about ship at once, and a head popped out again on deck.

'Down, dog!' cries the captain.

And the head popped back again; and we heard no more, for the time, of these six very faint-hearted seamen.

By this time, tumbling things in as they came, we had the jolly-boat loaded as much as we dared. Joyce and I got out through the stern-port, and we made for shore again, as fast as oars could take us.

This second trip fairly aroused the watchers along shore. 'Lillibullero' was dropped again; and just before we lost sight of them behind the little point, one of them whipped ashore and disappeared. I had half a mind to change my plan and destroy their boats, but I feared that Silver and the others might be close at hand, and all might very well be lost by trying for too much.

We had soon touched land in the same place as before, and set to provision the block house. All three made the first journey, heavily laden, and tossed our stores over the palisade. Then, leaving Joyce to guard them—one man, to be sure, but with half a dozen muskets—Hunter and I returned to the jolly-boat, and loaded ourselves once more. So we proceeded without pausing to take breath, till the whole cargo was bestowed, when the two servants took up their position in the block house, and I, with all my power, sculled back to the *Hispaniola*.

That we should have risked a second boat load seems more daring than it really was. They had the advantage of numbers, of course, but we had the advantage of arms. Not one of the men ashore had a musket, and before they could get within range for pistol shooting, we flattered ourselves we should be able to give a good account of a half-dozen at least.

The squire was waiting for me at the stern window, all his faintness gone from him. He caught the painter and made it fast, and we fell to loading the boat for our very lives. Pork, powder, and biscuit was the cargo, with only a musket and a cutlass apiece for the squire and me and Redruth and the captain. The rest of the arms and powder we dropped overboard in two fathoms and a half of water, so that we could see the bright steel shining far below us in the sun, on the clean, sandy bottom.

By this time the tide was beginning to ebb, and the ship was swinging round to her anchor. Voices were heard faintly halloaing in the direction of the two gigs; and though this reassured us for Joyce and Hunter, who were well to the eastward, it warned our party to be off.

Redruth retreated from his place in the gallery, and dropped into the boat, which we then brought round to the ship's counter, to be handier for Captain Smollett.

'Now men,' said he, 'do you hear me?'

There was no answer from the forecastle.

'It's to you, Abraham Gray—it's to you, I am speaking.'

Still no reply.

'Gray,' resumed Mr Smollett, a little louder, 'I am leaving this ship, and I order you to follow your captain. I know you are a good man at bottom, and I daresay not one of the lot of you's as bad as he makes out. I have my watch here in my hand; I give you thirty seconds to join me in.'

There was a pause.

'Come, my fine fellow,' continued the captain, 'don't hang so long in stays. I'm risking my life, and the lives of these good gentlemen every second.'

There was a sudden scuffle, a sound of blows, and out burst Abraham Gray with a knife-cut on the side of the cheek, and came running to the captain, like a dog to the whistle.

'I'm with you, sir,' said he.

And the next moment he and the captain had dropped aboard of us, and we had shoved off and given way.

We were clear out of the ship; but not yet ashore in our stockade.

CHAPTER XVII

NARRATIVE CONTINUED BY THE DOCTOR: THE JOLLY-BOAT'S LAST TRIP

THIS fifth trip was quite different from any of the others. In the first place, the little gallipot* of a boat that we were in was gravely overloaded. Five grown men, and three of them—Trelawney, Redruth, and the captain—over six feet high, was already more than she was meant to carry. Add to that the powder, pork, and bread-bags. The gunwale was lipping astern. Several times we shipped a little water, and my breeches and the tails of my coat were all soaking wet before we had gone a hundred yards.

The captain made us trim the boat, and we got her to lie a little more evenly. All the same, we were afraid to breathe.

In the second place, the ebb was now making—a strong rippling current running westward through the basin, and then south'ard and seaward down the straits by which we had entered in the morning. Even the ripples were a danger to our overloaded craft; but the worst of it was that we were swept out of our true course, and away from our proper landing-place behind the point. If we let the current have its way we should come ashore beside the gigs, where the pirates might appear at any moment.

'I cannot keep her head for the stockade, sir,' said I to the captain. I was steering, while he and Redruth, two fresh men, were at the oars. 'The tide keeps washing her down. Could you pull a little stronger?'

'Not without swamping the boat,' said he. 'You must bear up, sir, if you please—bear up until you see you're gaining.'

I tried, and found by experiment that the tide kept sweeping us westward until I had laid her head due east, or just about right angles to the way we ought to go.

'We'll never get ashore at this rate,' said I.

'If it's the only course that we can lie, sir, we must even lie it,' returned the captain. 'We must keep up-stream. You see, sir,' he went on, 'if once we dropped to leeward of the landing-place, it's hard to say where we should get ashore, besides the chance of being boarded by the gigs; whereas, the way we go the current must slacken, and then we can dodge back along the shore.'

'The current's less a'ready, sir,' said the man Gray, who was sitting in the fore-sheets; 'you can ease her off a bit.'

'Thank you, my man,' said I, quite as if nothing had happened; for we had all quietly made up our minds to treat him like one of ourselves.

Suddenly the captain spoke up again, and I thought his voice was a little changed.

'The gun!' said he.

'I have thought of that,' said I, for I made sure he was thinking of a bombardment of the fort. 'They could never get the gun ashore, and if they did, they could never haul it through the woods.'

'Look astern, doctor,' replied the captain.

We had entirely forgotten the long nine; and there, to our horror, were the five rogues busy about her, getting off her jacket, as they called the stout tarpaulin cover under which she sailed. Not only that, but it flashed into my mind at the same moment that the round-shot and the powder for the gun had been left behind, and a stroke with an axe would put it all into the possession of the evil ones aboard.

'Israel was Flint's gunner,' said Gray, hoarsely.

At any risk, we put the boat's head direct for the landing-place. By this time we had got so far out of the run of the current that we kept steerage way even at our necessarily gentle rate of rowing, and I could keep her steady for the goal. But the worst of it was, that with the course I now held, we turned our broadside instead of our stern to the *Hispaniola*, and offered a target like a barn door.

I could hear, as well as see, that brandy-faced rascal, Israel Hands, plumping down a round-shot on the deck.

'Who's the best shot?' asked the captain.

'Mr Trelawney, out and away,' said I.

'Mr Trelawney, will you please pick me off one of these men, sir? Hands, if possible,' said the captain.

Trelawney was as cool as steel. He looked to the priming of his gun.

'Now,' cried the captain, 'easy with that gun, sir, or you'll swamp the boat. All hands stand by to trim her when he aims.'

The squire raised his gun, the rowing ceased, and we leaned over to the other side to keep the balance, and all was so nicely contrived that we did not ship a drop.

They had the gun, by this time, slewed round upon the swivel, and Hands, who was at the muzzle with the rammer, was, in consequence, the most exposed. However, we had no luck; for just as Trelawney fired, down he stooped, the ball whistled over him, and it was one of the other four who fell.

The cry he gave was echoed, not only by his companions on board, but by a great number of voices from the shore, and looking in that direction I saw the other pirates trooping out from among the trees and tumbling into their places in the boats.

'Here come the gigs, sir,' said I.

'Give way then,' cried the captain. 'We mustn't mind if we swamp her now. If we can't get ashore, all's up.'

'Only one of the gigs is being manned, sir,' I added, 'the crew of the other most likely going round by shore to cut us off.'

'They'll have a hot run, sir,' returned the captain. 'Jack ashore,* you know. It's not them I mind; it's the round-shot. Carpet-bowls! My lady's maid couldn't miss. Tell us, squire, when you see the match, and we'll hold water.'

In the meanwhile we had been making headway at a good pace for a boat so overloaded, and we had shipped but little water in the process. We were now close in; thirty or forty strokes and we should beach her; for the ebb had already disclosed a narrow belt of sand below the clustering trees. The gig was no longer to be feared; the little point had already concealed it from our eyes. The ebb-tide, which had so cruelly delayed us, was now making reparation, and delaying our assailants. The one source of danger was the gun.

'If I durst,' said the captain, 'I'd stop and pick off another man.'

But it was plain that they meant nothing should delay their shot. They had never so much as looked at their fallen comrade, though he was not dead, and I could see him trying to crawl away.

'Ready!' cried the squire.

'Hold!' cried the captain, quick as an echo.

And he and Redruth backed with a great heave that sent her stern bodily under water. The report fell in at the same instant of time. This was the first that Jim heard, the sound of the squire's shot not having reached him. Where the ball passed, not one of us precisely knew; but I fancy it must have been over our heads, and that the wind of it may have contributed to our disaster.

At any rate, the boat sank by the stern, quite gently, in three feet of water, leaving the captain and myself, facing each other, on our feet. The other three took complete headers, and came up again, drenched and bubbling.

So far there was no great harm. No lives were lost, and we could wade ashore in safety. But there were all our stores at the bottom, and, to make things worse, only two guns out of five remained in a state for service. Mine I had snatched from my knees and held over my head, by a sort of instinct. As for the captain, he had carried his over his shoulder by a bandoleer, and, like a wise man, lock uppermost. The other three had gone down with the boat.

To add to our concern, we heard voices already drawing near us in the woods along shore; and we had not only the danger of being cut off from the stockade in our half-crippled state, but the fear before us whether, if Hunter and Joyce were attacked by half a dozen, they would have the sense and conduct to stand firm. Hunter was steady, that we knew; Joyce was a doubtful case—a pleasant, polite man for a valet, and to brush one's clothes, but not entirely fitted for a man of war.

With all this in our minds, we waded ashore as fast as we could, leaving behind us the poor jolly-boat, and a good half of all our powder and provisions.

CHAPTER XVIII

NARRATIVE CONTINUED BY THE DOCTOR: END OF THE FIRST DAY'S FIGHTING

WE made our best speed across the strip of wood that now divided us from the stockade; and at every step we took, the voices of the buccaneers rang nearer. Soon we could hear their footfalls as they ran, and the cracking of the branches as they breasted across a bit of thicket.

I began to see we should have a brush for it in earnest, and looked to my priming.

'Captain,' said I, 'Trelawney is the dead shot. Give him your gun; his own is useless.'

They exchanged guns, and Trelawney, silent and cool as he had been since the beginning of the bustle, hung a moment on his heel to see that all was fit for service. At the same time, observing Gray to be unarmed, I handed him my cutlass. It did all our hearts good to see him spit in his hand, knit his brows, and make the blade sing through the air. It was plain from every line of his body that our new hand was worth his salt.

Forty paces farther we came to the edge of the wood and saw the stockade in front of us. We struck the enclosure about the middle of the south side, and, almost at the same time, seven mutineers—Job Anderson, the boatswain, at their head—appeared in full cry at the south-western corner.

They paused, as if taken aback; and before they recovered, not only the squire and I, but Hunter and Joyce from the block house, had time to fire. The four shots came in rather a scattering volley; but they did the business: one of the enemy actually fell, and the rest, without hesitation, turned and plunged into the trees.

After reloading, we walked down the outside of the palisade to see the fallen enemy. He was stone dead—shot through the heart.

We began to rejoice over our good success, when just at that moment a pistol cracked in the bush, a ball whistled close past my ear, and poor Tom Redruth stumbled and fell his length on the ground. Both the squire and I returned the shot; but as we had nothing to aim at, it is probable we only wasted powder. Then we reloaded, and turned our attention to poor Tom.

The captain and Gray were already examining him; and I saw with half an eye that all was over.

I believe the readiness of our return volley had scattered the mutineers once more, for we were suffered without further molestation to get the poor old gamekeeper hoisted over the stockade, and carried, groaning and bleeding, into the log-house.

Poor old fellow, he had not uttered one word of surprise, complaint, fear, or even acquiescence, from the very beginning of our troubles till now, when we had laid him down in the log-house to die. He had lain like a Trojan behind his mattress in the gallery; he had followed every order silently, doggedly, and well; he was the oldest of our party by a score of years; and now, sullen, old, serviceable servant, it was he that was to die.

The squire dropped down beside him on his knees and kissed his hand, crying like a child.

'Be I going, doctor?' he asked.

'Tom, my man,' said I, 'you're going home.'

'I wish I had had a lick at them with the gun first,' he replied.

'Tom,' said the squire, 'say you forgive me, won't you?'

'Would that be respectful like, from me to you, squire?' was the answer. 'Howsoever, so be it, amen!'

After a little while of silence, he said he thought somebody might read a prayer. 'It's the custom, sir,' he added, apologetically. And not long after, without another word, he passed away.

In the meantime the captain, whom I had observed to be wonderfully swollen about the chest and pockets, had turned out a great many various stores—the British colours, a Bible, a coil of stoutish rope, pen, ink, the log-book, and pounds of tobacco. He had found a longish fir-tree lying felled and trimmed in the enclosure, and, with the help of Hunter, he had set it up at the corner of the log-house where the trunks crossed and made an angle. Then, climbing on the roof, he had with his own hand bent and run up the colours.

This seemed mightily to relieve him. He re-entered the log-house, and set about counting up the stores, as if nothing else existed. But he had an eye on Tom's passage for all that; and as soon as all was over, came forward with another flag, and reverently spread it on the body.

'Don't you take on, sir,' he said, shaking the squire's hand. 'All's well with him; no fear for a hand that's been shot down in his duty to captain and owner. It mayn't be good divinity, but it's a fact.'

Then he pulled me aside.

'Dr Livesey,' he said, 'in how many weeks do you and squire expect the consort?'

I told him it was a question, not of weeks, but of months; that if we were not back by the end of August, Blandly was to send to find us; but neither sooner nor later. 'You can calculate for yourself,' I said.

'Why, yes,' returned the captain, scratching his head, 'and making a large allowance, sir, for all the gifts of Providence, I should say we were pretty close hauled.'

'How do you mean?' I asked.

'It's a pity, sir, we lost that second load. That's what I mean,' replied the captain. 'As for powder and shot, we'll do. But the rations are short, very short—so short, Dr Livesey, that we're, perhaps, as well without that extra mouth.'

And he pointed to the dead body under the flag.

Just then, with a roar and a whistle, a round-shot passed high above the roof of the log-house and plumped far beyond us in the wood.

'Oho!' said the captain. 'Blaze away! You've little enough powder already my lads.'

At the second trial, the aim was better, and the ball descended inside the stockade, scattering a cloud of sand, but doing no further damage.

'Captain,' said the squire, 'the house is quite invisible from the ship. It must be the flag they are aiming at. Would it not be wiser to take it in?'

'Strike my colours!' cried the captain. 'No, sir, not I;' and, as soon as he had said the words, I think we all agreed with him. For it was not only a piece of stout, seamanly, good feeling; it was good policy besides, and showed our enemies that we despised their cannonade.

All through the evening they kept thundering away. Ball after ball flew over or fell short, or kicked up the sand in the enclosure; but they had to fire so high that the shot fell dead and buried itself in the soft sand. We had no ricochet to fear; and though one popped in through the roof of the log-house and out again through the floor, we soon got used to that sort of horse-play, and minded it no more than cricket.

'There is one thing good about all this,' observed the captain; 'the wood in front of us is likely clear. The ebb has made a good while; our stores should be uncovered. Volunteers to go and bring in pork.'

Gray and Hunter were the first to come forward. Well armed, they stole out of the stockade; but it proved a useless mission. The mutineers were bolder than we fancied, or they put more trust in Israel's gunnery. For four or five of them were busy carrying off our stores, and wading out with them to one of the gigs that lay close by, pulling an oar or so to hold her steady against the current. Silver was in the stern-sheets in command; and every man of them was now provided with a musket from some secret magazine of their own.

The captain sat down to his log, and here is the beginning of the entry:—

'Alexander Smollett, master; David Livesey, ship's doctor; Abraham Gray, carpenter's mate; John Trelawney, owner; John Hunter and Richard Joyce, owner's servants, landsmen—being all that is left faithful of the ship's company—with stores for ten days at short rations, came ashore this day, and flew British colours on the log-house in Treasure Island. Thomas Redruth, owner's servant, landsman, shot by the mutineers; James Hawkins, cabin-boy—'

And at the same time I was wondering over poor Jim Hawkins's fate.

A hail on the land side.

'Somebody hailing us,' said Hunter, who was on guard.

'Doctor! squire! captain! Hullo, Hunter, is that you?' came the cries.

And I ran to the door in time to see Jim Hawkins, safe and sound, come climbing over the stockade.

CHAPTER XIX

NARRATIVE RESUMED BY JIM HAWKINS: THE GARRISON IN THE STOCKADE

As soon as Benn Gunn saw the colours he came to a halt, stopped me by the arm, and sat down.

'Now,' said he, 'there's your friends, sure enough.'

'Far more likely it's the mutineers,' I answered.

'That!' he cried. 'Why, in a place like this, where nobody puts in but gen'lemen of fortune, Silver would fly the Jolly Roger, you don't make no doubt of that. No; that's your friends. There's been blows, too, and I reckon your friends has had the best of it; and here they are ashore in the old stockade, as was made years and years ago by Flint. Ah, he was the man to have a headpiece, was Flint! Barring rum, his match were never seen. He were afraid of none, not he; on'y Silver—Silver was that genteel.'

'Well,' said I, 'that may be so, and so be it; all the more reason that I should hurry on and join my friends.'

'Nay, mate,' returned Ben, 'not you. You're a good boy, or I'm mistook; but you're on'y a boy, all told. Now, Ben Gunn is fly. Rum wouldn't bring me there, where you're going—not rum wouldn't, till I see your born gen'leman, and gets it on his word of honour. And you won't forget my words: "A precious sight (that's what you'll say), a precious sight more confidence"—and then nips him.'

And he pinched me the third time with the same air of cleverness.

'And when Ben Gunn is wanted, you know where to find him, Jim. Just wheer you found him to-day. And him that comes is to have a white thing in his hand: and he's to come alone. Oh! and you'll say this: "Ben Gunn," says you, "has reasons of his own."'

'Well,' said I, 'I believe I understand. You have something to propose, and you wish to see the squire or the doctor; and you're to be found where I found you. Is that all?'

'And when? says you,' he added. 'Why, from about noon observation to about six bells.'*

'Good,' said I, 'and now may I go?'

'You won't forget?' he inquired, anxiously. 'Precious sight, and reasons of his own, says you. Reasons of his own; that's the mainstay;

as between man and man. Well, then'—still holding me—'I reckon you can go, Jim. And, Jim, if you was to see Silver, you wouldn't go for to sell Ben Gunn? wild horses wouldn't draw it from you? No, says you. And if them pirates camp ashore, Jim, what would you say but there'd be widders in the morning?'

Here he was interrupted by a loud report, and a cannonball came tearing through the trees and pitched in the sand, not a hundred yards from where we two were talking. The next moment each of us had taken to his heels in a different direction.

For a good hour to come frequent reports shook the island, and balls kept crashing through the woods. I moved from hiding-place to hiding-place, always pursued, or so it seemed to me, by these terrifying missiles. But towards the end of the bombardment, though still I durst not venture in the direction of the stockade, where the balls fell oftenest, I had begun, in a manner, to pluck up my heart again; and after a long detour to the east, crept down among the shore-side trees.

The sun had just set, the sea breeze was rustling and tumbling in the woods, and ruffling the grey surface of the anchorage; the tide, too, was far out, and great tracts of sand lay uncovered; the air, after the heat of the day, chilled me through my jacket.

The *Hispaniola* still lay where she had anchored; but, sure enough, there was the Jolly Roger*—the black flag of piracy—flying from her peak. Even as I looked, there came another red flash and another report, that sent the echoes clattering, and one more round-shot whistled through the air. It was the last of the cannonade.

I lay for some time, watching the bustle which succeeded the attack. Men were demolishing something with axes on the beach near the stockade; the poor jolly-boat, I afterwards discovered. Away, near the mouth of the river, a great fire was glowing among the trees, and between that point and the ship one of the gigs kept coming and going, the men, whom I had seen so gloomy, shouting at the oars like children. But there was a sound in their voices which suggested rum.

At length I thought I might return towards the stockade. I was pretty far down on the low, sandy spit that encloses the anchorage to the east, and is joined at half-water to Skeleton Island; and now, as I rose to my feet, I saw, some distance further down the spit, and rising from among low bushes, an isolated rock, pretty high, and peculiarly white in colour. It occurred to me that this might be the white rock of which Ben Gunn had spoken, and that some day or other a boat might be wanted, and I should know where to look for one.

Then I skirted among the woods until I had regained the rear, or shoreward side, of the stockade, and was soon warmly welcomed by the faithful party.

I had soon told my story, and began to look about me. The log-house was made of unsquared trunks of pine—roof, walls, and floor. The latter stood in several places as much as a foot or a foot and a half above the surface of the sand. There was a porch at the door, and under this porch the little spring welled up into an artificial basin of a rather odd kind—no other than a great ship's kettle of iron, with the bottom knocked out, and sunk 'to her bearings,' as the captain said, among the sand.

Little had been left beside the framework of the house; but in one corner there was a stone slab laid down by way of hearth, and an old rusty iron basket to contain the fire.

The slopes of the knoll and all the inside of the stockade had been cleared of timber to build the house, and we could see by the stumps what a fine and lofty grove had been destroyed. Most of the soil had been washed away or buried in drift after the removal of the trees; only where the streamlet ran down from the kettle a thick bed of moss and some ferns and little creeping bushes were still green among the sand. Very close around the stockade—too close for defence, they said—the wood still flourished high and dense, all of fir on the land side, but towards the sea with a large admixture of live-oaks.

The cold evening breeze, of which I have spoken, whistled through every chink of the rude building, and sprinkled the floor with a continual rain of fine sand. There was sand in our eyes, sand in our teeth, sand in our suppers, sand dancing in the spring at the bottom of the kettle, for all the world like porridge beginning to boil. Our chimney was a square hole in the roof; it was but a little part of the smoke that found its way out, and the rest eddied about the house, and kept us coughing and piping the eye.*

Add to this that Gray, the new man, had his face tied up in a bandage for a cut he had got in breaking away from the mutineers; and that poor old Tom Redruth, still unburied, lay along the wall, stiff and stark, under the Union Jack.

If we had been allowed to sit idle, we should all have fallen in the blues but Captain Smollett was never the man for that. All hands were called up before him, and he divided us into watches. The doctor, and Gray, and I, for one; the squire, Hunter, and Joyce, upon the other. Tired though we all were, two were sent out for firewood; two more were set to dig a grave for Redruth; the doctor was named cook; I was put sentry at the door; and the captain himself went from one to another, keeping up our spirits and lending a hand wherever it was wanted.

From time to time the doctor came to the door for a little air and to rest his eyes, which were almost smoked out of his head; and whenever he did so, he had a word for me.

'That man Smollett,' he said once, 'is a better man than I am. And when I say that it means a deal, Jim.'

Another time he came and was silent for a while. Then he put his head on one side, and looked at me.

'Is this Ben Gunn a man?' he asked.

'I do not know, sir,' said I. 'I am not very sure whether he's sane.'

'If there's any doubt about the matter, he is,' returned the doctor. 'A man who has been three years biting his nails on a desert island, Jim, can't expect to appear as sane as you or me. It doesn't lie in human nature. Was it cheese you said he had a fancy for?'

'Yes, sir, cheese,' I answered.

'Well, Jim,' says he, 'just see the good that comes of being dainty in your food. You've seen my snuff-box, haven't you? And you never saw me take snuff; the reason being that in my snuff-box I carry a piece of Parmesan cheese—a cheese made in Italy, very nutritious. Well, that's for Ben Gunn!'

Before supper was eaten we buried old Tom in the sand, and stood round him for a while bareheaded in the breeze. A good deal of firewood had been got in, but not enough for the captain's fancy; and he shook his head over it, and told us we 'must get back to this tomorrow rather livelier.' Then, when we had eaten our pork, and each had a good stiff glass of brandy grog, the three chiefs got together in a corner to discuss our prospects.

It appears they were at their wits' end what to do, the stores being so low that we must have been starved into surrender long before help came. But our best hope, it was decided, was to kill off the buccaneers until they either hauled down their flag or ran away with the *Hispaniola*. From nineteen they were already reduced to fifteen, two others were wounded, and one, at least—the man shot beside the gun—severely wounded, if he were not dead. Every time we had a crack at them, we were to take it, saving our own lives, with the extremest care. And, besides that, we had two able allies—rum and the climate.

As for the first, though we were about half a mile away, we could hear them roaring and singing late into the night; and as for the second, the doctor staked his wig that, camped where they were in the marsh, and unprovided with remedies, the half of them would be on their backs before a week.

'So,' he added, 'if we are not all shot down first they'll be glad to be packing in the schooner. It's always a ship, and they can get to buccaneering again, I suppose.'

'First ship that ever I lost,' said Captain Smollett.

I was dead tired, as you may fancy; and when I got to sleep, which was not till after a great deal of tossing, I slept like a log of wood.

The rest had long been up, and had already breakfasted and increased the pile of firewood by about half as much again, when I was wakened by a bustle and the sound of voices.

'Flag of truce!' I heard someone say; and then, immediately after, with a cry of surprise, 'Silver himself!'

And, at that, up I jumped, and, rubbing my eyes, ran to a loophole in the wall.

CHAPTER XX

SILVER'S EMBASSY

SURE enough, there were two men just outside the stockade, one of them waving a white cloth; the other, no less a person than Silver himself, standing placidly by.

It was still quite early, and the coldest morning that I think I ever was abroad in; a chill that pierced into the marrow. The sky was bright and cloudless overhead, and the tops of the trees shone rosily in the sun. But where Silver stood with his lieutenant all was still in shadow, and they waded knee deep in a low, white vapour, that had crawled during the night out of the morass. The chill and the vapour taken together told a poor tale of the island. It was plainly a damp, feverish, unhealthy spot.

'Keep indoors, men,' said the captain. 'Ten to one this is a trick.'

Then he hailed the buccaneer.

'Who goes? Stand, or we fire.'

'Flag of truce,' cried Silver.

The captain was in the porch, keeping himself carefully out of the way of a treacherous shot should any be intended. He turned and spoke to us:—

'Doctor's watch on the look out. Dr Livesey take the north side, if you please; Jim, the east; Gray, west. The watch below, all hands to load muskets. Lively, men, and careful.'

And then he turned again to the mutineers.

'And what do you want with your flag of truce?' he cried.

This time it was the other man who replied.

'Cap'n Silver, sir, to come on board and make terms,' he shouted.

'Cap'n Silver! Don't know him. Who's he?' cried the captain. And we could hear him adding to himself: 'Cap'n, is it? My heart, and here's promotion!'

Long John answered for himself.

'Me, sir. These poor lads have chosen me cap'n, after your desertion, sir'—laying a particular emphasis upon the word 'desertion.' 'We're willing to submit, if we can come to terms, and no bones about it. All I ask is your word, Cap'n Smollett, to let me safe and sound out of this here stockade, and one minute to get out o' shot before a gun is fired.'

'My man,' said Captain Smollett, 'I have not the slightest desire to talk to you. If you wish to talk to me, you can come, that's all. If there's any treachery, it'll be on your side, and the Lord help you.'

'That's enough, cap'n,' shouted Long John, cheerily. 'A word from you's enough. I know a gentleman, and you may lay to that.'

We could see the man who carried the flag of truce attempting to hold Silver back. Nor was that wonderful, seeing how cavalier had been the captain's answer. But Silver laughed at him aloud, and slapped him on the back, as if the idea of alarm had been absurd. Then he advanced to the stockade, threw over his crutch, got a leg up, and with great vigour and skill succeeded in surmounting the fence and dropping safely to the other side.

I will confess that I was far too much taken up with what was going on to be of the slightest use as sentry; indeed, I had already deserted my eastern loophole, and crept up behind the captain, who had now seated himself on the threshold, with his elbows on his knees, his head in his hands, and his eyes fixed on the water, as it bubbled out of the old iron kettle in the sand. He was whistling to himself, 'Come, Lasses and Lads.'*

Silver had terrible hard work getting up the knoll. What with the steepness of the incline, the thick tree stumps, and the soft sand, he and his crutch were as helpless as a ship in stays. But he stuck to it like a man in silence, and at last arrived before the captain, whom he saluted in the handsomest style. He was tricked out in his best; an immense blue coat, thick with brass buttons, hung as low as to his knees, and a fine laced hat was set on the back of his head.

'Here you are, my man,' said the captain, raising his head. 'You had better sit down.'

'You aint a-going to let me inside, cap'n?' complained Long John. 'It's a main cold morning, to be sure, sir, to sit outside upon the sand.'

'Why, Silver,' said the captain, 'if you had pleased to be an honest man, you might have been sitting in your galley. It's your own doing. You're either my ship's cook—and then you were treated handsome—or Cap'n Silver, a common mutineer and pirate, and then you can go hang!'

'Well, well, cap'n,' returned the sea-cook, sitting down as he was bidden on the sand, 'you'll have to give me a hand up again, that's all. A sweet pretty place you have of it here. Ah, there's Jim! The top of the morning to you, Jim. Doctor, here's my service. Why, there you all are together like a happy family, in a manner of speaking.'

'If you have anything to say, my man, better say it,' said the captain.

'Right you were, Cap'n Smollett,' replied Silver. 'Dooty is dooty, to be sure. Well, now, you look here, that was a good lay of yours last night. I don't deny it was a good lay. Some of you pretty handy with a handspike-end. And I'll not deny neither but what some of my people was shook—maybe all was shook; maybe I was shook myself; maybe that's why I'm here for terms. But you mark me, cap'n, it won't do twice, by thunder! We'll have to do sentry-go, and ease off a point or so on the rum. Maybe you think we were all a sheet in the wind's eye.* But I'll tell you I was sober; I was on'y dog tired; and if I'd awoke a second sooner I'd a' caught you at the act, I would. He wasn't dead when I got round to him, not he.'

'Well?' says Captain Smollett, as cool as can be.

All that Silver said was a riddle to him, but you would never have guessed it from his tone. As for me, I began to have an inkling. Ben Gunn's last words came back to my mind. I began to suppose that he had paid the buccaneers a visit while they all lay drunk together round their fire, and I reckoned up with glee that we had only fourteen enemies to deal with.

'Well, here it is,' said Silver. 'We want that treasure, and we'll have it—that's our point! You would just as soon save your lives, I reckon; and that's yours. You have a chart, haven't you?'

'That's as may be,' replied the captain.

'Oh, well, you have, I know that,' returned Long John. 'You needn't be so husky with a man; there aint a particle of service in that, and you may lay to it. What I mean is, we want your chart. Now, I never meant you no harm, myself.'

'That won't do with me, my man,' interrupted the captain. 'We know exactly what you meant to do, and we don't care; for now, you see, you can't do it.'

And the captain looked at him calmly, and proceeded to fill a pipe.

'If Abe Gray—' Silver broke out.

'Avast there!' cried Mr Smollett. 'Gray told me nothing, and I asked him nothing; and what's more I would see you and him and this whole island blown clean out of the water into blazes first. So there's my mind for you, my man, on that.'

This little whiff of temper seemed to cool Silver down. He had been growing nettled before, but now he pulled himself together.

'Like enough,' said he. 'I would set no limits to what gentlemen might consider shipshape, or might not, as the case were. And, seein' as how you are about to take a pipe, cap'n, I'll make so free as do likewise.'

And he filled a pipe and lighted it; and the two men sat silently smoking for quite a while, now looking each other in the face, now stopping their tobacco, now leaning forward to spit. It was as good as the play to see them.

'Now,' resumed Silver, 'here it is. You give us the chart to get the treasure by, and drop shooting poor seamen, and stoving of their heads in while asleep. You do that, and we'll offer you a choice. Either you come aboard along of us, once the treasure shipped, and then I'll give you my affy-davy, upon my word of honour, to clap you somewhere safe ashore. Or, if that aint to your fancy, some of my hands being rough, and having old scores, on account of hazing, then you can stay here, you can. We'll divide stores with you, man for man; and I'll give my affy-davy, as before, to speak the first ship I sight, and send 'em here to pick you up. Now you'll own that's talking. Handsomer you couldn't look to get, not you. And I hope'—raising his voice—'that all hands in this here block-house will overhaul my words, for what is spoke to one is spoke to all.'

Captain Smollett rose from his seat, and knocked out the ashes of his pipe in the palm of his left hand.

'Is that all?' he asked.

'Every last word, by thunder!' answered John. 'Refuse that, and you've seen the last of me but musket-balls.'

'Very good,' said the captain. 'Now you'll hear me. If you'll come up one by one, unarmed, I'll engage to clap you all in irons, and take you home to a fair trial in England. If you won't, my name is Alexander Smollett, I've flown my sovereign's colours, and I'll see you all to Davy Jones.* You can't find the treasure. You can't sail the ship—there's not a man among you fit to sail the ship. You can't fight us—Gray, there, got away from five of you. Your ship's in irons, Master Silver; you're on a lee shore, and so you'll find. I stand here and tell you so; and they're the last good words you'll get from me; for, in the name of heaven, I'll put a bullet in your back when next I meet you. Tramp, my lad. Bundle out of this, please, hand over hand, and double quick.'

Silver's face was a picture; his eyes started in his head with wrath. He shook the fire out of his pipe.

'Give me a hand up!' he cried.

'Not I,' returned the captain.

'Who'll give me a hand up?' he roared.

Not a man among us moved. Growling the foulest imprecations, he crawled along the sand till he got hold of the porch and could hoist himself again upon his crutch. Then he spat into the spring.

'There!' he cried, 'that's what I think of ye. Before an hour's out, I'll stove in your old block-house like a rum puncheon. Laugh, by thunder, laugh! Before an hour's out, ye'll laugh upon the other side. Them that die'll be the lucky ones.'

And with a dreadful oath he stumbled off, ploughed down the sand, was helped across the stockade, after four or five failures, by the man with the flag of truce, and disappeared in an instant afterwards among the trees.

CHAPTER XXI

THE ATTACK

As soon as Silver disappeared, the captain, who had been closely watching him, turned towards the interior of the house, and found not a man of us at his post but Gray. It was the first time we had ever seen him angry.

'Quarters!' he roared. And then, as we all slunk back to our places, 'Gray,' he said, 'I'll put your name in the log; you've stood by your duty like a seaman. Mr Trelawney, I'm surprised at you, sir. Doctor, I thought you had worn the king's coat! If that was how you served at Fontenoy, sir, you'd have been better in your berth.'

The doctor's watch were all back at their loopholes, the rest were busy loading the spare muskets, and every one with a red face, you may be certain, and a flea in his ear, as the saying is.

The captain looked on for a while in silence. Then he spoke.

'My lads,' said he, 'I've given Silver a broadside. I pitched it in red-hot on purpose; and before the hour's out, as he said, we shall be boarded. We're outnumbered, I needn't tell you that, but we fight in shelter: and, a minute ago, I should have said we fought with discipline. I've no manner of doubt that we can drub them, if you choose.'

Then he went the rounds, and saw, as he said, that all was clear.

On the two short sides of the house, east and west, there were only two loopholes; on the south side where the porch was, two again; and on the north side, five. There was a round score of muskets for the seven of us; the firewood had been built into four piles—tables, you might say—one about the middle of each side, and on each of these tables some ammunition and four loaded muskets were laid ready to the hand of the defenders. In the middle, the cutlasses lay ranged.

'Toss out the fire,' said the captain; 'the chill is past, and we mustn't have smoke in our eyes.'

The iron fire-basket was carried bodily out by Mr Trelawney, and the embers smothered among sand.

'Hawkins hasn't had his breakfast. Hawkins, help yourself, and back to your post to eat it,' continued Captain Smollett. 'Lively, now, my lad; you'll want it before you've done. Hunter, serve out a round of brandy to all hands.'

And while this was going on, the captain completed, in his own mind, the plan of the defence.

'Doctor, you will take the door,' he resumed. 'See, and don't expose yourself; keep within, and fire through the porch. Hunter, take the east side, there. Joyce, you stand by the west, my man. Mr Trelawney, you are the best shot—you and Gray will take this long north side, with the five loopholes; it's there the danger is. If they can get up to it, and fire in upon us through our own ports, things would begin to look dirty. Hawkins, neither you nor I are much account at the shooting; we'll stand by to load and bear a hand.'

As the captain had said, the chill was past. As soon as the sun had climbed above our girdle of trees, it fell with all its force upon the clearing, and drank up the vapours at a draught. Soon the sand was baking, and the resin melting in the logs of the block-house. Jackets and coats were flung aside; shirts thrown open at the neck, and rolled up to the shoulders; and we stood there, each at his post, in a fever of heat and anxiety.

An hour passed away.

'Hang them!' said the captain. 'This is as dull as the doldrums. Gray, whistle for a wind.'

And just at that moment came the first news of the attack.

'If you please, sir,' said Joyce, 'if I see anyone am I to fire?'

'I told you so!' cried the captain.

'Thank you, sir,' returned Joyce, with the same quiet civility.

Nothing followed for a time; but the remark had set us all on the alert, straining ears and eyes—the musketeers with their pieces balanced in their hands, the captain out in the middle of the block-house, with his mouth very tight and a frown on his face.

So some seconds passed, till suddenly Joyce whipped up his musket and fired. The report had scarcely died away ere it was repeated and repeated from without in a scattering volley, shot behind shot, like a string of geese, from every side of the enclosure. Several bullets struck the log-house, but not one entered; and, as the smoke cleared away and vanished, the stockade and the woods around it looked as quiet and empty as before. Not a bough waved, not the gleam of a musket-barrel betrayed the presence of our foes.

'Did you hit your man?' asked the captain.

'No, sir,' replied Joyce. 'I believe not, sir.'

'Next best thing to tell the truth,' muttered Captain Smollett.

'Load his gun, Hawkins. How many should you say there were on your side, doctor?'

'I know precisely,' said Dr Livesey. 'Three shots were fired on this side. I saw the three flashes—two close together—one farther to the west.'

'Three!' repeated the captain. 'And how many on yours, Mr Trelawney?'

But this was not so easily answered. There had come many from the north—seven, by the squire's computation; eight or nine, according to Gray. From the east and west only a single shot had been fired. It was plain, therefore, that the attack would be developed from the north, and that on the other three sides we were only to be annoyed by a show of hostilities. But Captain Smollett made no change in his arrangements. If the mutineers succeeded in crossing the stockade, he argued, they would take possession of any unprotected loophole, and shoot us down like rats in our own stronghold.

Nor had we much time left to us for thought. Suddenly, with a loud huzza, a little cloud of pirates leaped from the woods on the north side, and ran straight on the stockade. At the same moment, the fire was once more opened from the woods, and a rifle-ball* sang through the doorway, and knocked the doctor's musket into bits.

The boarders swarmed over the fence like monkeys. Squire and Gray fired again and yet again; three men fell, one forwards into the enclosure, two back on the outside. But of these, one was evidently more frightened than hurt, for he was on his feet again in a crack, and instantly disappeared among the trees.

Two had bit the dust,* one had fled, four had made good their footing inside our defences; while from the shelter of the woods seven or eight men, each evidently supplied with several muskets, kept up a hot though useless fire on the log-house.

The four who had boarded made straight before them for the building, shouting as they ran, and the men among the trees shouted back to encourage them. Several shots were fired; but, such was the hurry of the marksmen, that not one appeared to have taken effect. In a moment, the four pirates had swarmed up the mound and were upon us.

The head of Job Anderson, the boatswain, appeared at the middle loophole.

'At 'em, all hands—all hands!' he roared, in a voice of thunder.

At the same moment, another pirate grasped Hunter's musket by the muzzle, wrenched it from his hands, plucked it through the loop-hole, and, with one stunning blow, laid the poor fellow senseless on the floor. Meanwhile a third, running unharmed all round the house, appeared suddenly in the doorway, and fell with his cutlass on the doctor.

Our position was utterly reversed. A moment since we were firing, under cover, at an exposed enemy; now it was we who lay uncovered, and could not return a blow.

The log-house was full of smoke, to which we owed our comparative safety. Cries and confusion, the flashes and reports of pistol-shots, and one loud groan, rang in my ears.

'Out, lads, out, and fight 'em in the open! Cutlasses!' cried the captain.

I snatched a cutlass from the pile, and someone, at the same time snatching another, gave me a cut across the knuckles which I hardly felt. I dashed out of the door into the clear sunlight. Someone was close behind, I knew not whom. Right in front, the doctor was pursuing his assailant down the hill, and, just as my eyes fell upon him, beat down his guard, and sent him sprawling on his back, with a great slash across the face.

'Round the house, lads! round the house!' cried the captain; and even in the hurly-burly I perceived a change in his voice.

Mechanically I obeyed, turned eastwards, and with my cutlass raised, ran round the corner of the house. Next moment I was face to face with Anderson. He roared aloud, and his hanger* went up above his head, flashing in the sunlight. I had not time to be afraid, but, as the blow still hung impending, leaped in a trice upon one side, and missing my foot in the soft sand, rolled headlong down the slope.

When I had first sallied from the door, the other mutineers had been already swarming up the palisade to make an end of us. One man, in a red night-cap, with his cutlass in his mouth, had even got upon the top and thrown a leg across. Well, so short had been the interval, that when I found my feet again all was in the same posture, the fellow with the red night-cap still half-way over, another still just showing his head above the top of the stockade. And yet, in this breath of time, the fight was over, and the victory was ours.

Gray, following close behind me, had cut down the big boatswain ere he had time to recover from his lost blow. Another had been shot at a loophole in the very act of firing into the house, and now lay in agony, the pistol still smoking in his hand. A third, as I had seen, the doctor had disposed of at a blow. Of the four who had scaled the palisade, one only remained unaccounted for, and he, having left his cutlass on the field, was now clambering out again with the fear of death upon him.

'Fire—fire from the house!' cried the doctor. 'And you, lads, back into cover.'

But his words were unheeded, no shot was fired, and the last boarder made good his escape, and disappeared with the rest into the wood. In three seconds nothing remained of the attacking party but the five who had fallen, four on the inside, and one on the outside, of the palisade.

The doctor and Gray and I ran full speed for shelter. The survivors would soon be back where they had left their muskets, and at any moment the fire might recommence.

The house was by this time somewhat cleared of smoke, and we saw at a glance the price we had paid for victory. Hunter lay beside his loophole, stunned; Joyce by his, shot through the head, never to move again; while right in the centre, the squire was supporting the captain, one as pale as the other.

'The captain's wounded,' said Mr Trelawney.

'Have they run?' asked Mr Smollett.

'All that could, you may be bound,' returned the doctor; 'but there's five of them will never run again.'

'Five!' cried the captain. 'Come, that's better. Five against three leaves us four to nine. That's better odds than we had at starting. We were seven to nineteen then, or thought we were, and that's as bad to bear.'[1]

[1] The mutineers were soon only eight in number, for the man shot by Mr Trelawney on board the schooner died that same evening of his wound. But this was, of course, not known till after by the faithful party.

PART V

MY SEA ADVENTURE

CHAPTER XXII

HOW MY SEA ADVENTURE BEGAN

THERE was no return of the mutineers—not so much as another shot out of the woods. They had 'got their rations for that day,' as the captain put it, and we had the place to ourselves and a quiet time to overhaul the wounded and get dinner. Squire and I cooked outside in spite of the danger, and even outside we could hardly tell what we were at, for horror of the loud groans that reached us from the doctor's patients.

Out of the eight men who had fallen in the action, only three still breathed—that one of the pirates who had been shot at the loophole, Hunter, and Captain Smollett; and of these the first two were as good as dead; the mutineer, indeed, died under the doctor's knife, and Hunter, do what we could, never recovered consciousness in this world. He lingered all day, breathing loudly like the old buccaneer at home in his apoplectic fit; but the bones of his chest had been crushed by the blow and his skull fractured in falling, and some time in the following night, without sign or sound, he went to his Maker.

As for the captain, his wounds were grievous indeed, but not dangerous. No organ was fatally injured. Anderson's ball—for it was Job that shot him first—had broken his shoulder-blade and touched the lung, not badly; the second had only torn and displaced some muscles in the calf. He was sure to recover, the doctor said, but, in the meantime and for weeks to come, he must not walk nor move his arm, nor so much as speak when he could help it.

My own accidental cut across the knuckles was a flea-bite. Dr Livesey patched it up with plaster, and pulled my ears for me into the bargain.

After dinner the squire and the doctor sat by the captain's side a while in consultation; and when they had talked to their heart's content, it being then a little past noon, the doctor took up his hat and pistols, girt on a cutlass, put the chart in his pocket, and with a musket over his shoulder, crossed the palisade on the north side, and set off briskly through the trees.

Gray and I were sitting together at the far end of the block-house, to be out of earshot of our officers consulting; and Gray took his pipe out of his mouth and fairly forgot to put it back again, so thunder-struck he was at this occurrence.

'Why, in the name of Davy Jones,' said he, 'is Dr Livesey mad?'

'Why, no,' says I. 'He's about the last of this crew for that, I take it.'

'Well, shipmate,' said Gray, 'mad he may not be; but if *he's* not, you mark my words, *I* am.'

'I take it,' replied I, 'the doctor has his idea; and if I am right, he's going now to see Ben Gunn.'

I was right, as appeared later; but, in the meantime, the house being stifling hot, and the little patch of sand inside the palisade ablaze with midday sun, I began to get another thought into my head, which was not by any means so right. What I began to do was to envy the doctor, walking in the cool shadow of the woods, with the birds about him, and the pleasant smell of the pines, while I sat grilling, with my clothes stuck to the hot resin, and so much blood about me, and so many poor dead bodies lying all around, that I took a disgust of the place that was almost as strong as fear.

All the time I was washing out the block-house, and then washing up the things from dinner, this disgust and envy kept growing stronger and stronger, till at last, being near a bread-bag, and no one then observing me, I took the first step towards my escapade, and filled both pockets of my coat with biscuit.

I was a fool, if you like, and certainly I was going to do a foolish, over-bold act; but I was determined to do it with all the precautions in my power. These biscuits, should anything befall me, would keep me, at least, from starving till far on in the next day.

The next thing I laid hold of was a brace of pistols, and as I already had a powder-horn and bullets, I felt myself well supplied with arms.

As for the scheme I had in my head, it was not a bad one in itself. I was to go down the sandy spit that divides the anchorage on the east from the open sea, find the white rock I had observed last evening, and ascertain whether it was there or not that Ben Gunn had hidden his boat; a thing quite worth doing, as I still believe. But as I was certain I should not be allowed to leave the enclosure, my only plan was to take French leave,* and slip out when nobody was watching; and that was so bad a way of doing it as made the thing itself wrong. But I was only a boy, and I had made my mind up.

Well, as things at last fell out, I found an admirable opportunity. The squire and Gray were busy helping the captain with his bandages; the coast was clear; I made a bolt for it over the stockade and into the thickest of the trees, and before my absence was observed I was out of cry of my companions.

This was my second folly, far worse than the first, as I left but two sound men to guard the house; but like the first, it was a help towards saving all of us.

I took my way straight for the east coast of the island, for I was determined to go down the sea side of the spit to avoid all chance of observation from the anchorage. It was already late in the afternoon, although still warm and sunny. As I continued to thread the tall woods I could hear from far before me not only the continuous thunder of the surf, but a certain tossing of foliage and grinding of boughs which showed me the sea breeze had set in higher than usual. Soon cool draughts of air began to reach me; and a few steps farther I came forth into the open borders of the grove, and saw the sea lying blue and sunny to the horizon, and the surf tumbling and tossing its foam along the beach.

I have never seen the sea quiet round Treasure Island. The sun might blaze overhead, the air be without a breath, the surface smooth and blue, but still these great rollers would be running along all the external coast, thundering and thundering by day and night; and I scarce believe there is one spot in the island where a man would be out of earshot of their noise.

I walked along beside the surf with great enjoyment, till, thinking I was now got far enough to the south, I took the cover of some thick bushes, and crept warily up to the ridge of the spit.

Behind me was the sea, in front the anchorage. The sea breeze, as though it had the sooner blown itself out by its unusual violence, was already at an end; it had been succeeded by light, variable airs from the south and south-east, carrying great banks of fog; and the anchorage, under lee of Skeleton Island, lay still and leaden as when first we entered it. The *Hispaniola*, in that unbroken mirror, was exactly portrayed from the truck to the water line, the Jolly Roger hanging from her peak.

Alongside lay one of the gigs, Silver in the stern-sheets—him I could always recognise—while a couple of men were leaning over the stern bulwarks, one of them with a red cap—the very rogue that I had seen some hours before stride-legs upon the palisade. Apparently they were talking and laughing, though at that distance—upwards of a mile—I could, of course, hear no word of what was said. All at once, there began the most horrid, unearthly screaming, which at first startled me badly, though I had soon remembered the voice of Captain Flint, and even thought I could make out the bird by her bright plumage as she sat perched upon her master's wrist.

Soon after the jolly-boat* shoved off and pulled for shore, and the man with the red cap and his comrade went below by the cabin companion.

Just about the same time the sun had gone down behind the Spy-glass, and as the fog was collecting rapidly, it began to grow dark in earnest. I saw I must lose no time if I were to find the boat that evening.

The white rock, visible enough above the brush, was still some eighth of a mile further down the spit, and it took me a goodish while to get up with it, crawling, often on all-fours, among the scrub. Night had almost come when I laid my hand on its rough sides. Right below it there was an exceedingly small hollow of green turf, hidden by banks and a thick underwood about knee-deep, that grew there very plentifully; and in the centre of the dell, sure enough, a little tent of goat-skins, like what the gipsies carry about with them in England.

I dropped into the hollow, lifted the side of the tent, and there was Ben Gunn's boat—home-made if ever anything was home-made: a rude, lop-sided framework of tough wood, and stretched upon that a covering of goat-skin, with the hair inside. The thing was extremely small, even for me, and I can hardly imagine that it could have floated with a full-sized man. There was one thwart set as low as possible, a kind of stretcher in the bows, and a double paddle for propulsion.

I had not then seen a coracle,* such as the ancient Britons made, but I have seen one since, and I can give you no fairer idea of Ben Gunn's boat than by saying it was like the first and the worst coracle ever made by man. But the great advantage of the coracle it certainly possessed, for it was exceedingly light and portable.

Well, now that I had found the boat, you would have thought I had had enough of truantry for once; but, in the meantime, I had taken another notion, and became so obstinately fond of it, that I would have carried it out, I believe, in the teeth of Captain Smollett himself. This was to slip out under cover of the night, cut the *Hispaniola* adrift, and let her go ashore where she fancied. I had quite made up my mind that the mutineers, after their repulse of the morning, had nothing nearer their hearts than to up anchor and away to sea; this, I thought, it would be a fine thing to prevent, and now that I had seen how they left their watchmen unprovided with a boat, I thought it might be done with little risk.

Down I sat to wait for darkness, and made a hearty meal of biscuit. It was a night out of ten thousand for my purpose. The fog had now buried all heaven. As the last rays of daylight dwindled and disappeared, absolute blackness settled down on Treasure Island. And when, at last, I shouldered the coracle, and groped my way stumblingly out of the hollow where I had supped, there were but two points visible on the whole anchorage.

One was the great fire on shore, by which the defeated pirates lay carousing in the swamp. The other, a mere blur of light upon the darkness, indicated the position of the anchored ship. She had swung round to the ebb—her bow was now towards me—the only lights on board were in the cabin; and what I saw was merely a reflection on the fog of the strong rays that flowed from the stern window.

The ebb had already run some time, and I had to wade through a long belt of swampy sand, where I sank several times above the ankle, before I came to the edge of the retreating water, and wading a little way in, with some strength and dexterity, set my coracle, keel downwards, on the surface.

CHAPTER XXIII

THE EBB-TIDE RUNS

THE coracle—as I had ample reason to know before I was done with her—was a very safe boat for a person of my height and weight, both buoyant and clever in a seaway; but she was the most cross-grained lop-sided craft to manage. Do as you please, she always made more leeway than anything else, and turning round and round was the manœuvre she was best at. Even Ben Gunn himself has admitted that she was 'queer to handle till you knew her way.'

Certainly I did not know her way. She turned in every direction but the one I was bound to go; the most part of the time we were broadside on, and I am very sure I never should have made the ship at all but for the tide. By good fortune, paddle as I pleased, the tide was still sweeping me down; and there lay the *Hispaniola* right in the fairway, hardly to be missed.

First she loomed before me like a blot of something yet blacker than darkness, then her spars and hull began to take shape, and the next moment, as it seemed (for, the further I went, the brisker grew the current of the ebb), I was alongside of her hawser, and had laid hold.

The hawser was as taut as a bowstring, and the current so strong she pulled upon her anchor. All round the hull, in the blackness, the rippling current bubbled and chattered like a little mountain stream. One cut with my sea-gully, and the *Hispaniola* would go humming down the tide.

So far so good; but it next occurred to my recollection that a taut hawser, suddenly cut, is a thing as dangerous as a kicking horse. Ten to one, if I were so foolhardy as to cut the *Hispaniola* from her anchor, I and the coracle would be knocked clean out of the water.

This brought me to a full stop, and if fortune had not again particularly favoured me, I should have had to abandon my design. But the light airs which had begun blowing from the south-east and south had hauled round after nightfall into the south-west. Just while I was meditating, a puff came, caught the *Hispaniola*, and forced her up into the current; and to my great joy, I felt the hawser slacken in my grasp, and the hand by which I held it dip for a second under water.

With that I made my mind up, took out my gully, opened it with my teeth, and cut one strand after another, till the vessel swung only by two. Then I lay quiet, waiting to sever these last when the strain should be once more lightened by a breath of wind.

All this time I had heard the sound of loud voices from the cabin; but, to say truth, my mind had been so entirely taken up with other thoughts that I had scarcely given ear. Now, however, when I had nothing else to do, I began to pay more heed.

One I recognised for the coxswain's, Israel Hands, that had been Flint's gunner in former days. The other was, of course, my friend of the red night-cap. Both men were plainly the worse of drink, and they were still drinking; for, even while I was listening, one of them, with a drunken cry, opened the stern window and threw out something, which I divined to be an empty bottle. But they were not only tipsy; it was plain that they were furiously angry. Oaths flew like hailstones, and every now and then there came forth such an explosion as I thought was sure to end in blows. But each time the quarrel passed off, and the voices grumbled lower for a while, until the next crisis came, and, in its turn, passed away without result.

On shore, I could see the glow of the great camp fire burning warmly through the shore-side trees. Someone was singing, a dull, old, droning sailor's song, with a droop and a quaver at the end of every verse, and seemingly no end to it at all but the patience of the singer. I had heard it on the voyage more than once, and remembered these words:—

> 'But one man of her crew alive,
> What put to sea with seventy-five.'*

And I thought it was a ditty rather too dolefully appropriate for a company that had met such cruel losses in the morning. But, indeed, from what I saw, all these buccaneers were as callous as the sea they sailed on.

At last the breeze came; the schooner sidled and drew nearer in the dark; I felt the hawser slacken once more, and with a good, tough effort, cut the last fibres through.

The breeze had but little action on the coracle, and I was almost instantly swept against the bows of the *Hispaniola*. At the same time the schooner began to turn upon her heel, spinning slowly, end for end, across the current.

I wrought like a fiend, for I expected every moment to be swamped; and since I found I could not push the coracle directly off, I now shoved straight astern. At length I was clear of my dangerous neighbour; and just as I gave the last impulsion, my hands came across a light cord that was trailing overboard across the stern bulwarks. Instantly I grasped it.

Why I should have done so I can hardly say. It was at first mere instinct; but once I had it in my hands and found it fast, curiosity began to get the upper hand, and I determined I should have one look through the cabin window.

I pulled in hand over hand on the cord, and, when I judged myself near enough, rose at infinite risk to about half my height, and thus commanded the roof and a slice of the interior of the cabin.

By this time the schooner and her little consort were gliding pretty swiftly through the water; indeed, we had already fetched up level with the camp fire. The ship was talking, as sailors say, loudly, treading the innumerable ripples with an incessant weltering splash; and until I got my eye above the window-sill I could not comprehend why the watchmen had taken no alarm. One glance, however, was sufficient; and it was only one glance that I durst take from that unsteady skiff. It showed me Hands and his companion locked together in deadly wrestle, each with a hand upon the other's throat.

I dropped upon the thwart again, none too soon, for I was near overboard. I could see nothing for the moment but these two furious, encrimsoned faces, swaying together under the smoky lamp; and I shut my eyes to let them grow once more familiar with the darkness.

The endless ballad had come to an end at last, and the whole diminished company about the camp fire had broken into the chorus I had heard so often:—

> 'Fifteen men on the dead man's chest—
> Yo-ho-ho, and a bottle of rum!
> Drink and the devil had done for the rest—
> Yo-ho-ho, and a bottle of rum!'

I was just thinking how busy drink and the devil were at that very moment in the cabin of the *Hispaniola*, when I was surprised by a sudden lurch of the coracle. At the same moment she yawed sharply and seemed to change her course. The speed in the meantime had strangely increased.

I opened my eyes at once. All round me were little ripples, combing over with a sharp, bristling sound and slightly phosphorescent. The *Hispaniola* herself, a few yards in whose wake I was still being whirled along, seemed to stagger in her course, and I saw her spars toss a little against the blackness of the night; nay, as I looked longer, I made sure she also was wheeling to the southward.

I glanced over my shoulder, and my heart jumped against my ribs. There, right behind me, was the glow of the camp fire. The current had turned at right angles, sweeping round along with it the tall schooner and the little dancing coracle; ever quickening, ever bubbling higher, ever muttering louder, it went spinning through the narrows for the open sea.

Suddenly the schooner in front of me gave a violent yaw, turning, perhaps, through twenty degrees; and almost at the same moment one shout followed another from on board; I could hear feet pounding on the companion ladder; and I knew that the two drunkards had at last been interrupted in their quarrel and awakened to a sense of their disaster.

I lay down flat in the bottom of that wretched skiff, and devoutly recommended my spirit to its Maker. At the end of the straits, I made sure we must fall into some bar of raging breakers, where all my troubles would be ended speedily; and though I could, perhaps, bear to die, I could not bear to look upon my fate as it approached.

So I must have lain for hours, continually beaten to and fro upon the billows, now and again wetted with flying sprays, and never ceasing to expect death at the next plunge. Gradually weariness grew upon me; a numbness, an occasional stupor, fell upon my mind even in the midst of my terrors; until sleep at last supervened, and in my sea-tossed coracle I lay and dreamed of home and the old 'Admiral Benbow.'

CHAPTER XXIV

THE CRUISE OF THE CORACLE

IT was broad day when I awoke, and found myself tossing at the south-west end of Treasure Island. The sun was up, but was still hid from me behind the great bulk of the Spy-glass, which on this side descended almost to the sea in formidable cliffs.

Haulbowline Head and Mizzen-mast Hill were at my elbow; the hill bare and dark, the head bound with cliffs forty or fifty feet high, and fringed with great masses of fallen rock. I was scarce a quarter of a mile to seaward, and it was my first thought to paddle in and land.

That notion was soon given over. Among the fallen rocks the breakers spouted and bellowed; loud reverberations, heavy sprays flying and falling, succeeded one another from second to second; and I saw myself, if I ventured nearer, dashed to death upon the rough shore, or spending my strength in vain to scale the beetling crags.

Nor was that all; for crawling together on flat tables of rock, or letting themselves drop into the sea with loud reports, I beheld huge slimy monsters—soft snails as it were, of incredible bigness—two or three score of them together, making the rocks to echo with their barkings.

I have understood since that they were sea lions,* and entirely harmless. But the look of them, added to the difficulty of the shore and the high running of the surf, was more than enough to disgust me of that landing-place. I felt willing rather to starve at sea than to confront such perils.

In the meantime I had a better chance, as I supposed, before me. North of Haulbowline Head, the land runs in a long way, leaving, at low tide, a long stretch of yellow sand. To the north of that, again, there comes another cape—Cape of the Woods, as it was marked upon the chart—buried in tall green pines, which descended to the margin of the sea.

I remembered what Silver had said about the current that sets northward along the whole west coast of Treasure Island; and seeing from my position that I was already under its influence, I preferred to leave Haulbowline Head behind me, and reserve my strength for an attempt to land upon the kindlier-looking Cape of the Woods.

There was a great, smooth swell upon the sea. The wind blowing steady and gentle from the south, there was no contrariety between that and the current, and the billows rose and fell unbroken.

Had it been otherwise, I must long ago have perished; but as it was, it is surprising how easily and securely my little and light boat could ride. Often, as I still lay at the bottom, and kept no more than an eye above the gunwale, I would see a big blue summit heaving close above me; yet the coracle would but bounce a little, dance as if on springs, and subside on the other side into the trough as lightly as a bird.

I began after a little to grow very bold, and sat up to try my skill at paddling. But even a small change in the disposition of the weight will produce violent changes in the behaviour of a coracle. And I had hardly moved before the boat, giving up at once her gentle dancing movement, ran straight down a slope of water so steep that it made me giddy, and struck her nose, with a spout of spray, deep into the side of the next wave.

I was drenched and terrified, and fell instantly back into my old position, whereupon the coracle seemed to find her head again, and led me as softly as before among the billows. It was plain she was not to be interfered with, and at that rate, since I could in no way influence her course, what hope had I left of reaching land?

I began to be horribly frightened, but I kept my head, for all that. First, moving with all care, I gradually baled out the coracle with my sea-cap; then getting my eye once more above the gunwale, I set myself to study how it was she managed to slip so quietly through the rollers.

I found each wave, instead of the big, smooth glossy mountain it looks from shore, or from a vessel's deck, was for all the world like any range of hills on the dry land, full of peaks and smooth places and valleys. The coracle, left to herself, turning from side to side, threaded, so to speak, her way through these lower parts, and avoided the steep slopes and higher, toppling summits of the wave.

'Well, now,' thought I to myself, 'it is plain I must lie where I am, and not disturb the balance; but it is plain, also, that I can put the paddle over the side, and from time to time, in smooth places, give her a shove or two towards land.' No sooner thought upon than done. There I lay on my elbows, in the most trying attitude, and every now and again gave a weak stroke or two to turn her head to shore.

It was very tiring, and slow work, yet I did visibly gain ground; and, as we drew near the Cape of the Woods, though I saw I must infallibly miss that point, I had still made some hundred yards of easting. I was, indeed, close in. I could see the cool, green tree-tops swaying together in the breeze, and I felt sure I should make the next promontory without fail.

It was high time, for I now began to be tortured with thirst. The glow of the sun from above, its thousandfold reflection from the waves, the seawater that fell and dried upon me, caking my very lips with salt, combined to make my throat burn and my brain ache. The sight of the trees so near at hand had almost made me sick with longing; but the current had soon carried me past the point; and, as the next reach of sea opened out, I beheld a sight that changed the nature of my thoughts.

Right in front of me, not half a mile away, I beheld the *Hispaniola* under sail. I made sure, of course, that I should be taken; but I was so distressed for want of water, that I scarce knew whether to be glad or sorry at the thought; and, long before I had come to a conclusion, surprise had taken entire possession of my mind, and I could do nothing but stare and wonder.

The *Hispaniola* was under her main-sail and two jibs, and the beautiful white canvas shone in the sun like snow or silver. When I first sighted her, all her sails were drawing; she was lying a course about north-west; and I presumed the men on board were going round the island on their way back to the anchorage. Presently she began to fetch more and more to the westward, so that I thought they had sighted me and were going about in chase. At last, however, she fell right into the wind's eye, was taken dead aback, and stood there a while helpless, with her sails shivering.

'Clumsy fellows,' said I; 'they must still be drunk as owls.' And I thought how Captain Smollett would have set them skipping.

Meanwhile, the schooner gradually fell off, and filled again upon another tack, sailed swiftly for a minute or so, and brought up once more dead in the wind's eye. Again and again was this repeated. To and fro, up and down, north, south, east, and west, the *Hispaniola* sailed by swoops and dashes, and at each repetition ended as she had begun, with idly-flapping canvas. It became plain to me that nobody was steering. And, if so, where were the men? Either they were dead drunk, or had deserted her, I thought, and perhaps if I could get on board, I might return the vessel to her captain.

The current was bearing coracle and schooner southward at an equal rate. As for the latter's sailing, it was so wild and intermittent, and she hung each time so long in irons, that she certainly gained nothing, if she did not even lose. If only I dared to sit up and paddle, I made sure that I could overhaul her. The scheme had an air of adventure that inspired me, and the thought of the water-breaker* beside the fore companion doubled my growing courage.

Up I got, was welcomed almost instantly by another cloud of spray, but this time stuck to my purpose; and set myself, with all my strength and caution, to paddle after the unsteered *Hispaniola*. Once I shipped a sea so heavy that I had to stop and bale, with my heart fluttering like a bird; but gradually I got into the way of the thing, and guided my coracle among the waves, with only now and then a blow upon her bows and a dash of foam in my face.

I was now gaining rapidly on the schooner; I could see the brass glisten on the tiller as it banged about; and still no soul appeared upon her decks. I could not choose but suppose she was deserted. If not, the men were lying drunk below, where I might batten them down, perhaps, and do what I chose with the ship.

For some time she had been doing the worst thing possible for me—standing still. She headed nearly due south, yawing, of course, all the time. Each time she fell off her sails partly filled, and these brought her, in a moment, right to the wind again. I have said this was the worst thing possible for me; for helpless as she looked in this situation, with the canvas cracking like cannon, and the blocks trundling and banging on the deck, she still continued to run away from me, not only with the speed of the current, but by the whole amount of her leeway, which was naturally great.

But now, at last, I had my chance. The breeze fell, for some seconds, very low, and the current gradually turning her, the *Hispaniola* revolved slowly round her centre, and at last presented me her stern, with the cabin window still gaping open, and the lamp over the table still burning on into the day. The main-sail hung drooped like a banner. She was stock-still, but for the current.

For the last little while I had even lost; but now, redoubling my efforts, I began once more to overhaul the chase.

I was not a hundred yards from her when the wind came again in a clap; she filled on the port tack, and was off again, stooping and skimming like a swallow.

My first impulse was one of despair, but my second was towards joy. Round she came, till she was broadside on to me—round still till she had covered a half, and then two-thirds, and then three-quarters of the distance that separated us. I could see the waves boiling white under her forefoot. Immensely tall she looked to me from my low station in the coracle.

And then, of a sudden, I began to comprehend. I had scarce time to think—scarce time to act and save myself. I was on the summit of one swell when the schooner came stooping over the next. The bowsprit was over my head. I sprang to my feet, and leaped, stamping the coracle under water. With one hand I caught the jib-boom, while my foot was lodged between the stay and the brace; and as I still clung there panting, a dull blow told me that the schooner had charged down upon and struck the coracle, and that I was left without retreat on the *Hispaniola*.

CHAPTER XXV

I STRIKE THE JOLLY ROGER

I HAD scarce gained a position on the bowsprit, when the flying jib flapped and filled upon the other tack, with a report like a gun. The schooner trembled to her keel under the reverse; but next moment, the other sails still drawing, the jib flapped back again, and hung idle.

This had nearly tossed me off into the sea; and now I lost no time, crawled back along the bowsprit, and tumbled head foremost on the deck.

I was on the lee-side of the forecastle, and the main-sail, which was still drawing, concealed from me a certain portion of the after-deck. Not a soul was to be seen. The planks, which had not been swabbed since the mutiny, bore the print of many feet; and an empty bottle, broken by the neck, tumbled to and fro like a live thing in the scuppers.

Suddenly the *Hispaniola* came right into the wind. The jibs behind me cracked aloud; the rudder slammed to; the whole ship gave a sickening heave and shudder, and at the same moment the main-boom swung inboard, the sheet groaning in the blocks, and showed me the lee after-deck.

There were the two watchmen, sure enough: red-cap on his back, as stiff as a handspike, with his arms stretched out like those of a crucifix, and his teeth showing through his open lips; Israel Hands propped against the bulwarks, his chin on his chest, his hands lying open before him on the deck, his face as white, under its tan, as a tallow candle.

For a while the ship kept bucking and sidling like a vicious horse, the sails filling, now on one tack, now on another, and the boom swinging to and fro till the mast groaned aloud under the strain. Now and again, too, there would come a cloud of light sprays over the bulwark, and a heavy blow of the ship's bows against the swell: so much heavier weather was made of it by this great rigged ship than by my home-made, lop-sided coracle, now gone to the bottom of the sea.

At every jump of the schooner, red-cap slipped to and fro; but—what was ghastly to behold—neither his attitude nor his fixed teeth-disclosing grin was anyway disturbed by this rough usage. At every jump, too, Hands appeared still more to sink into himself and settle down upon the deck, his feet sliding ever the farther out, and the whole body canting towards the stern, so that his face became, little by little, hid from me; and at last I could see nothing beyond his ear and the frayed ringlet of one whisker.

At the same time, I observed around both of them, splashes of dark blood upon the planks, and began to feel sure that they had killed each other in their drunken wrath.

While I was thus looking and wondering, in a calm moment, when the ship was still, Israel Hands turned partly round, and, with a low moan, writhed himself back to the position in which I had seen him first. The moan, which told of pain and deadly weakness, and the way in which his jaw hung open, went right to my heart. But when I remembered the talk I had overheard from the apple barrel, all pity left me.

I walked aft until I reached the mainmast.

'Come aboard, Mr Hands,' I said ironically.

He rolled his eyes round heavily; but he was too far gone to express surprise. All he could do was to utter one word, 'Brandy.'

It occurred to me there was no time to lose; and, dodging the boom as it once more lurched across the deck, I slipped aft, and down the companion-stairs into the cabin.

It was such a scene of confusion as you can hardly fancy. All the lock-fast places had been broken open in quest of the chart. The floor was thick with mud, where ruffians had sat down to drink or consult after wading in the marshes round their camp. The bulkheads, all painted in clear white, and beaded round with gilt, bore a pattern of dirty hands. Dozens of empty bottles clinked together in corners to the rolling of the ship. One of the doctor's medical books lay open on the table, half of the leaves gutted out, I suppose, for pipelights. In the midst of all this the lamp still cast a smoky glow, obscure and brown as umber.

I went into the cellar; all the barrels were gone, and of the bottles a most surprising number had been drunk out and thrown away. Certainly, since the mutiny began, not a man of them could ever have been sober.

Foraging about, I found a bottle with some brandy left, for Hands; and for myself I routed out some biscuits, some pickled fruits, a great bunch of raisins, and a piece of cheese. With these I came on deck, put down my own stock behind the rudder-head, and well out of the coxswain's reach, went forward to the water-breaker, and had a good, deep drink of water, and then, and not till then, gave Hands the brandy.

He must have drunk a gill before he took the bottle from his mouth.

'Aye,' said he, 'by thunder, but I wanted some o' that!'

I had sat down already in my own corner and begun to eat.

'Much hurt?' I asked him.

He grunted, or, rather I might say, he barked.

'If that doctor was aboard,' he said, 'I'd be right enough in a couple of turns; but I don't have no manner of luck, you see, and that's what's the matter with me. As for that swab, he's good and dead, he is,' he added, indicating the man with the red cap. 'He warn't no seaman, anyhow. And where mought you have come from?'

'Well,' said I, 'I've come aboard to take possession of this ship, Mr Hands; and you'll please regard me as your captain until further notice.'

He looked at me sourly enough, but said nothing. Some of the colour had come back into his cheeks, though he still looked very sick, and still continued to slip out and settle down as the ship banged about.

'By-the-bye,' I continued, 'I can't have these colours, Mr Hands; and, by your leave, I'll strike 'em. Better none than these.'

And, again dodging the boom, I ran to the colour lines, handed down their cursed black flag, and chucked it overboard.

'God save the king!' said I, waving my cap; 'and there's an end to Captain Silver!'

He watched me keenly and slyly, his chin all the while on his breast.

'I reckon,' he said at last—'I reckon, Cap'n Hawkins, you'll kind of want to get ashore, now. S'pose we talks.'

'Why, yes,' says I, 'with all my heart, Mr Hands. Say on.' And I went back to my meal with a good appetite.

'This man,' he began, nodding feebly at the corpse—'O'Brien were his name—a rank Irelander—this man and me got the canvas on her, meaning for to sail her back. Well, *he's* dead now, he is—as dead as bilge; and who's to sail this ship, I don't see. Without I gives you a hint, you aint that man, as far's I can tell. Now, look here, you gives me food and drink, and a old scarf or ankecher to tie my wound up, you do; and I'll tell you how to sail her; and that's about square all round, I take it.'

'I'll tell you one thing,' says I: 'I'm not going back to Captain Kidd's anchorage. I mean to get into North Inlet, and beach her quietly there.'

'To be sure you did,' he cried. 'Why, I aint sich an infernal lubber, after all. I can see, can't I? I've tried my fling, I have, and I've lost, and it's you has the wind of me. North Inlet? Why, I haven't no ch'ice, not I! I'd help you sail her up to Execution Dock,* by thunder! so I would.'

Well, as it seemed to me, there was some sense in this. We struck our bargain on the spot. In three minutes I had the *Hispaniola* sailing easily before the wind along the coast of Treasure Island, with good hopes of turning the northern point ere noon, and beating down again as far as North Inlet before high water, when we might beach her safely, and wait till the subsiding tide permitted us to land.

Then I lashed the tiller and went below to my own chest, where I got a soft silk handkerchief of my mother's. With this, and with my aid, Hands bound up the great bleeding stab he had received in the thigh, and after he had eaten a little and had a swallow or two more of the brandy, he began to pick up visibly, sat straighter up, spoke louder and clearer, and looked in every way another man.

The breeze served us admirably. We skimmed before it like a bird, the coast of the island flashing by, and the view changing every minute. Soon we were past the high lands and bowling beside low, sandy country, sparsely dotted with dwarf pines, and soon we were beyond that again, and had turned the corner of the rocky hill that ends the island on the north.

I was greatly elated with my new command, and pleased with the bright, sunshiny weather and these different prospects of the coast. I had now plenty of water and good things to eat, and my conscience, which had smitten me hard for my desertion, was quieted by the great conquest I had made. I should, I think, have had nothing left me to desire but for the eyes of the coxswain as they followed me derisively about the deck, and the odd smile that appeared continually on his face. It was a smile that had in it something both of pain and weakness—a haggard, old man's smile; but there was, besides that, a grain of derision, a shadow of treachery, in his expression as he craftily watched, and watched, and watched me at my work.

CHAPTER XXVI

ISRAEL HANDS

THE wind, serving us to a desire, now hauled into the west. We could run so much the easier from the north-east corner of the island to the mouth of the North Inlet. Only, as we had no power to anchor, and dared not beach her till the tide had flowed a good deal farther, time hung on our hands. The coxswain told me how to lay the ship to; after a good many trials I succeeded, and we both sat in silence, over another meal.

'Cap'n,' said he, at length, with that same uncomfortable smile, 'here's my old shipmate, O'Brien; s'pose you was to heave him overboard. I ain't partic'lar as a rule, and I don't take no blame for settling his hash; but I don't reckon him ornamental, now, do you?'

'I'm not strong enough, and I don't like the job; and there he lies, for me,' said I.

'This here's an unlucky ship—this *Hispaniola,* Jim,' he went on, blinking. 'There's a power of men been killed in this *Hispaniola*—a sight o' poor seamen dead and gone since you and me took ship to Bristol. I never seen sich dirty luck, not I. There was this here O'Brien, now—he's dead, aint he? Well, now, I'm no scholar, and you're a lad as can read and figure; and, to put it straight, do you take it as a dead man is dead for good, or do he come alive again?'

'You can kill the body, Mr Hands, but not the spirit; you must know that already,' I replied. 'O'Brien there is in another world, and maybe watching us.'

'Ah!' says he. 'Well, that's unfort'nate—appears as if killing parties was a waste of time. Howsomever, sperrits don't reckon for much, by what I've seen. I'll chance it with the sperrits, Jim. And now, you've spoke up free, and I'll take it kind if you'd step down into that there cabin and get me a—well, a—shiver my timbers! I can't hit the name on't; well, you get me a bottle of wine, Jim—this here brandy's too strong for my head.'

Now, the coxswain's hesitation seemed to be unnatural; and as for the notion of his preferring wine to brandy, I entirely disbelieved it. The whole story was a pretext. He wanted me to leave the deck—so much was plain; but with what purpose I could in no way imagine.

His eyes never met mine; they kept wandering to and fro, up and down, now with a look to the sky, now with a flitting glance upon the dead O'Brien. All the time he kept smiling, and putting his tongue out in the most guilty, embarrassed manner, so that a child could have told that he was bent on some deception. I was prompt with my answer, however, for I saw where my advantage lay; and that with a fellow so densely stupid I could easily conceal my suspicions to the end.

'Some wine?' I said. 'Far better. Will you have white or red?'

'Well, I reckon it's about the blessed same to me, shipmate,' he replied; 'so it's strong, and plenty of it, what's the odds?'

'All right,' I answered. 'I'll bring you port, Mr Hands. But I'll have to dig for it.'

With that I scuttled down the companion with all the noise I could, slipped off my shoes, ran quietly along the sparred gallery, mounted the forecastle ladder, and popped my head out of the fore companion. I knew he would not expect to see me there; yet I took every precaution possible; and certainly the worst of my suspicions proved too true.

He had risen from his position to his hands and knees; and, though his leg obviously hurt him pretty sharply when he moved—for I could hear him stifle a groan—yet it was at a good, rattling rate that he trailed himself across the deck. In half a minute he had reached the port scuppers, and picked, out of a coil of rope, a long knife, or rather a short dirk, discoloured to the hilt with blood. He looked upon it for a moment, thrusting forth his under jaw, tried the point upon his hand, and then, hastily concealing it in the bosom of his jacket, trundled back again into his old place against the bulwark.

This was all that I required to know. Israel could move about; he was now armed; and if he had been at so much trouble to get rid of me, it was plain that I was meant to be the victim. What he would do afterwards—whether he would try to crawl right across the island from North Inlet to the camp among the swamps, or whether he would fire Long Tom, trusting that his own comrades might come first to help him, was, of course, more than I could say.

Yet I felt sure that I could trust him in one point, since in that our interests jumped together, and that was in the disposition of the schooner. We both desired to have her stranded safe enough, in a sheltered place, and so that, when the time came, she could be got off again with as little labour and danger as might be; and until that was done I considered that my life would certainly be spared.

While I was thus turning the business over in my mind, I had not been idle with my body. I had stolen back to the cabin, slipped once more into my shoes, and laid my hand at random on a bottle of wine, and now, with this for an excuse, I made my reappearance on the deck.

Hands lay as I had left him, all fallen together in a bundle, and with his eyelids lowered, as though he were too weak to bear the light. He looked up, however, at my coming, knocked the neck off the bottle, like a man who had done the same thing often, and took a good swig, with his favourite toast of 'Here's luck!' Then he lay quiet for a little, and then, pulling out a stick of tobacco, begged me to cut him a quid.

'Cut me a junk o' that,' says he, 'for I haven't no knife, and hardly strength enough, so be as I had. Ah, Jim, Jim, I reckon I've missed stays! Cut me a quid, as 'll likely be the last, lad; for I'm for my long home, and no mistake.'

'Well,' said I, 'I'll cut you some tobacco; but if I was you and thought myself so badly, I would go to my prayers, like a Christian man.'

'Why?' said he. 'Now, you tell me why.'

'Why?' I cried. 'You were asking me just now about the dead. You've broken your trust; you've lived in sin and lies and blood; there's a man you killed lying at your feet this moment; and you ask me why! For God's mercy, Mr Hands, that's why.'

I spoke with a little heat, thinking of the bloody dirk he had hidden in his pocket, and designed, in his ill thoughts, to end me with. He, for his part, took a great draught of the wine, and spoke with the most unusual solemnity.

'For thirty years,' he said, 'I've sailed the seas, and seen good and bad, better and worse, fair weather and foul, provisions running out, knives going, and what not. Well, now I tell you, I never seen good come o' goodness yet. Him as strikes first is my fancy; dead men don't bite; them's my views—amen, so be it. And now, you look here,' he added, suddenly changing his tone, 'we've had about enough of this foolery. The tide's made good enough by now. You just take my orders, Cap'n Hawkins, and we'll sail slap in and be done with it.'

All told, we had scarce two miles to run; but the navigation was delicate, the entrance to this northern anchorage was not only narrow and shoal, but lay east and west, so that the schooner must be nicely handled to be got in. I think I was a good, prompt subaltern, and I am very sure that Hands was an excellent pilot; for we went about and about, and dodged in, shaving the banks, with a certainty and a neatness that were a pleasure to behold.

Scarcely had we passed the heads before the land closed around us. The shores of North Inlet were as thickly wooded as those of the southern anchorage; but the space was longer and narrower, and more like, what in truth it was, the estuary of a river. Right before us, at the southern end, we saw the wreck of a ship in the last stages of dilapidation. It had been a great vessel of three masts, but had lain so long exposed to the injuries of the weather, that it was hung about with great webs of dripping seaweed, and on the deck of it shore bushes had taken root, and now flourished thick with flowers. It was a sad sight, but it showed us that the anchorage was calm.

'Now,' said Hands, 'look there; there's a pet bit for to beach a ship in. Fine flat sand, never a catspaw, trees all around of it, and flowers a-blowing like a garding on that old ship.'

'And once beached,' I inquired, 'how shall we get her off again?'

'Why, so,' he replied: 'you take a line ashore there on the other side at low water: take a turn about one o' them big pines; bring it back, take a turn round the capstan, and lie-to for the tide. Come high water, all hands take a pull upon the line, and off she comes as sweet as natur'. And now, boy, you stand by. We're near the bit now, and she's too much way on her. Starboard a little—so—steady—starboard—larboard a little—steady—steady!'

So he issued his commands, which I breathlessly obeyed; till, all of a sudden, he cried, 'Now, my hearty, luff!' And I put the helm hard up, and the *Hispaniola* swung round rapidly, and ran stem on for the low wooded shore.

The excitement of these last manœuvres had somewhat interfered with the watch I had kept hitherto, sharply enough, upon the coxswain. Even then I was still so much interested, waiting for the ship to touch, that I had quite forgot the peril that hung over my head, and stood craning over the starboard bulwarks and watching the ripples spreading wide before the bows. I might have fallen without a struggle for my life, had not a sudden disquietude seized upon me, and made me turn my head. Perhaps I had heard a creak, or seen his shadow moving with the tail of my eye; perhaps it was an instinct like a cat's; but, sure enough, when I looked round, there was Hands, already half-way towards me, with the dirk in his right hand.

We must both have cried out aloud when our eyes met; but while mine was the shrill cry of terror, his was a roar of fury like a charging bull's. At the same instant he threw himself forward, and I leapt sideways towards the bows. As I did so, I let go of the tiller, which sprang sharp to leeward; and I think this saved my life, for it struck Hands across the chest, and stopped him, for the moment, dead.

Before he could recover, I was safe out of the corner where he had me trapped, with all the deck to dodge about. Just forward of the mainmast I stopped, drew a pistol from my pocket, took a cool aim, though he had already turned and was once more coming directly after me, and drew the trigger. The hammer fell, but there followed neither flash nor sound; the priming was useless with sea water. I cursed myself for my neglect. Why had not I, long before, reprimed and reloaded my only weapons? Then I should not have been as now, a mere fleeing sheep before this butcher.

Wounded as he was, it was wonderful how fast he could move, his grizzled hair tumbling over his face, and his face itself as red as a red ensign with his haste and fury. I had no time to try my other pistol, nor, indeed, much inclination, for I was sure it would be useless. One thing I saw plainly: I must not simply retreat before him, or he would speedily hold me boxed into the bows, as a moment since he had so nearly boxed me in the stern. Once so caught, and nine or ten inches of the bloodstained dirk would be my last experience on this side of eternity. I placed my palms against the mainmast, which was of a goodish bigness, and waited, every nerve upon the stretch.

Seeing that I meant to dodge, he also paused; and a moment or two passed in feints on his part, and corresponding movements upon mine. It was such a game as I had often played at home about the rocks of Black Hill Cove; but never before, you may be sure, with such a wildly beating heart as now. Still, as I say, it was a boy's game, and I thought I could hold my own at it, against an elderly seaman with a wounded thigh. Indeed, my courage had begun to rise so high, that I allowed myself a few darting thoughts on what would be the end of the affair; and while I saw certainly that I could spin it out for long, I saw no hope of any ultimate escape.

Well, while things stood thus, suddenly the *Hispaniola* struck, staggered, ground for an instant in the sand, and then, swift as a blow, canted over to the port side, till the deck stood at an angle of forty-five degrees, and about a puncheon of water splashed into the scupper holes, and lay, in a pool, between the deck and bulwark.

We were both of us capsized in a second, and both of us rolled, almost together, into the scuppers; the dead red-cap, with his arms still spread out, tumbling stiffly after us. So near were we, indeed, that my head came against the coxswain's foot with a crack that made my teeth rattle. Blow and all, I was the first afoot again; for Hands had got involved with the dead body. The sudden canting of the ship had made the deck no place for running on; I had to find some new way of escape, and that upon the instant, for my foe was almost touching me. Quick as thought, I sprang into the mizzen shrouds, rattled up hand over hand, and did not draw a breath till I was seated on the cross-trees.

I had been saved by being prompt; the dirk had struck not half a foot below me, as I pursued my upward flight; and there stood Israel Hands with his mouth open and his face upturned to mine, a perfect statue of surprise and disappointment.

Now that I had a moment to myself, I lost no time in changing the priming of my pistol, and then, having one ready for service, and to make assurance doubly sure, I proceeded to draw the load of the other, and recharge it afresh from the beginning.

My new employment struck Hands all of a heap; he began to see the dice going against him; and after an obvious hesitation, he also hauled himself heavily into the shrouds, and, with the dirk in his teeth, began slowly and painfully to mount. It cost him no end of time and groans to haul his wounded leg behind him; and I had quietly finished my arrangements before he was much more than a third of the way up. Then, with a pistol in either hand, I addressed him.

'One more step, Mr Hands,' said I, 'and I'll blow your brains out! Dead men don't bite, you know,' I added, with a chuckle.

He stopped instantly. I could see by the working of his face that he was trying to think, and the process was so slow and laborious that, in my new-found security, I laughed aloud. At last, with a swallow or two, he spoke, his face still wearing the same expression of extreme perplexity. In order to speak he had to take the dagger from his mouth, but, in all else, he remained unmoved.

'Jim,' says he, 'I reckon we're fouled,* you and me, and we'll have to sign articles. I'd have had you but for that there lurch: but I don't have no luck, not I; and I reckon I'll have to strike, which comes hard, you see, for a master mariner to a ship's younker* like you, Jim.'

I was drinking in his words and smiling away, as conceited as a cock upon a wall, when, all in a breath, back went his right hand over his shoulder. Something sang like an arrow through the air; I felt a blow and then a sharp pang, and there I was pinned by the shoulder to the mast. In the horrid pain and surprise of the moment—I scarce can say it was by my own volition, and I am sure it was without a conscious aim—both my pistols went off, and both escaped out of my hands. They did not fall alone; with a choked cry, the coxswain loosed his grasp upon the shrouds, and plunged head first into the water.

CHAPTER XXVII

'PIECES OF EIGHT'

OWING to the cant of the vessel, the masts hung far out over the water, and from my perch on the cross-trees I had nothing below me but the surface of the bay. Hands, who was not so far up, was, in consequence, nearer to the ship, and fell between me and the bulwarks. He rose once to the surface in a lather of foam and blood, and then sank again for good. As the water settled, I could see him lying huddled together on the clean, bright sand in the shadow of the vessel's sides. A fish or two whipped past his body. Sometimes, by the quivering of the water, he appeared to move a little, as if he were trying to rise. But he was dead enough, for all that, being both shot and drowned, and was food for fish in the very place where he had designed my slaughter.

I was no sooner certain of this than I began to feel sick, faint, and terrified. The hot blood was running over my back and chest. The dirk, where it had pinned my shoulder to the mast, seemed to burn like a hot iron; yet it was not so much these real sufferings that distressed me, for these, it seemed to me, I could bear without a murmur; it was the horror I had upon my mind of falling from the cross-trees into that still green water, beside the body of the coxswain.

I clung with both hands till my nails ached, and I shut my eyes as if to cover up the peril. Gradually my mind came back again, my pulses quieted down to a more natural time, and I was once more in possession of myself.

It was my first thought to pluck forth the dirk; but either it stuck too hard or my nerve failed me; and I desisted with a violent shudder. Oddly enough, that very shudder did the business. The knife, in fact, had come the nearest in the world to missing me altogether; it held me by a mere pinch of skin, and this the shudder tore away. The blood ran down the faster, to be sure; but I was my own master again, and only tacked to the mast by my coat and shirt.

These last I broke through with a sudden jerk, and then regained the deck by the starboard shrouds. For nothing in the world would I have again ventured, shaken as I was, upon the overhanging port shrouds, from which Israel had so lately fallen.

I went below, and did what I could for my wound; it pained me a good deal, and still bled freely; but it was neither deep nor dangerous, nor did it greatly gall me when I used my arm. Then I looked around me, and as the ship was now, in a sense, my own, I began to think of clearing it from its last passenger—the dead man, O'Brien.

He had pitched, as I have said, against the bulwarks, where he lay like some horrible, ungainly sort of puppet; life-sized, indeed, but how different from life's colour or life's comeliness! In that position, I could easily have my way with him; and as the habit of tragical adventures had worn off almost all my terror for the dead, I took him by the waist as if he had been a sack of bran, and, with one good heave, tumbled him overboard. He went in with a sounding plunge; the red cap came off, and remained floating on the surface; and as soon as the splash subsided, I could see him and Israel lying side by side, both wavering with the tremulous movement of the water. O'Brien, though still quite a young man, was very bald. There he lay, with that bald head across the knees of the man who had killed him, and the quick fishes steering to and fro over both.

I was now alone upon the ship; the tide had just turned. The sun was within so few degrees of setting that already the shadow of the pines upon the western shore began to reach right across the anchorage, and fall in patterns on the deck. The evening breeze had sprung up, and though it was well warded off by the hill with the two peaks upon the east, the cordage had begun to sing a little softly to itself and the idle sails to rattle to and fro.

I began to see a danger to the ship. The jibs I speedily doused and brought tumbling to the deck; but the mainsail was a harder matter. Of course, when the schooner canted over, the boom had swung out-board, and the cap of it and a foot or two of sail hung even under water. I thought this made it still more dangerous; yet the strain was so heavy that I half feared to meddle. At last, I got my knife and cut the halyards. The peak dropped instantly, a great belly of loose canvas floated broad upon the water; and since, pull as I liked, I could not budge the downhaul, that was the extent of what I could accomplish. For the rest, the *Hispaniola* must trust to luck, like myself.

By this time the whole anchorage had fallen into shadow—the last rays, I remember, falling through a glade of the wood, and shining bright as jewels, on the flowery mantle of the wreck. It began to be chill; the tide was rapidly fleeting seaward, the schooner settling more and more on her beam-ends.

I scrambled forward and looked over. It seemed shallow enough, and holding the cut hawser in both hands for a last security, I let myself drop softly overboard. The water scarcely reached my waist; the sand was firm and covered with ripple marks, and I waded ashore in great spirits, leaving the *Hispaniola* on her side, with her mainsail trailing wide upon the surface of the bay. About the same time the sun went fairly down, and the breeze whistled low in the dusk among the tossing pines.

At least, and at last, I was off the sea, nor had I returned thence empty-handed. There lay the schooner, clear at last from buccaneers and ready for our own men to board and get to sea again. I had nothing nearer my fancy than to get home to the stockade and boast of my achievements. Possibly I might be blamed a bit for my truantry, but the recapture of the *Hispaniola* was a clenching answer, and I hoped that even Captain Smollett would confess I had not lost my time.

So thinking, and in famous spirits, I began to set my face homeward for the block-house and my companions. I remembered that the most easterly of the rivers which drain into Captain Kidd's anchorage ran from the two-peaked hill upon my left; and I bent my course in that direction that I might pass the stream while it was small. The wood was pretty open, and keeping along the lower spurs, I had soon turned the corner of that hill, and not long after waded to the mid-calf across the water-course.

This brought me near to where I had encountered Ben Gunn, the maroon; and I walked more circumspectly, keeping an eye on every side. The dusk had come nigh hand completely, and, as I opened out the cleft between the two peaks, I became aware of a wavering glow against the sky, where, as I judged, the man of the island was cooking his supper before a roaring fire. And yet I wondered, in my heart, that he should show himself so careless. For if I could see this radiance, might it not reach the eyes of Silver himself where he camped upon the shore among the marshes?

Gradually the night fell blacker; it was all I could do to guide myself even roughly towards my destination; the double hill behind me and the Spy-glass on my right hand loomed faint and fainter; the stars were few and pale; and in the low ground where I wandered I kept tripping among bushes and rolling into sandy pits.

Suddenly a kind of brightness fell about me. I looked up; a pale glimmer of moonbeams had alighted on the summit of the Spy-glass, and soon after I saw something broad and silvery moving low down behind the trees, and knew the moon had risen.

With this to help me, I passed rapidly over what remained to me of my journey; and, sometimes walking, sometimes running, impatiently drew near to the stockade. Yet, as I began to thread the grove that lies before it, I was not so thoughtless but that I slacked my pace and went a trifle warily. It would have been a poor end of my adventures to get shot down by my own party in mistake.

The moon was climbing higher and higher; its light began to fall here and there in masses through the more open districts of the wood; and right in front of me a glow of a different colour appeared among the trees. It was red and hot, and now and again it was a little darkened—as it were the embers of a bonfire smouldering.

For the life of me, I could not think what it might be.

At last I came right down upon the borders of the clearing. The western end was already steeped in moonshine; the rest, and the block-house itself, still lay in a black shadow, chequered with long, silvery streaks of light. On the other side of the house an immense fire had burned itself into clear embers and shed a steady, red reverberation, contrasted strongly with the mellow paleness of the moon. There was not a soul stirring, nor a sound beside the noises of the breeze.

I stopped, with much wonder in my heart, and perhaps a little terror also. It had not been our way to build great fires; we were, indeed, by the captain's orders, somewhat niggardly of firewood; and I began to fear that something had gone wrong while I was absent.

I stole round by the eastern end, keeping close in shadow, and at a convenient place, where the darkness was thickest, crossed the palisade.

To make assurance surer, I got upon my hands and knees, and crawled, without a sound, towards the corner of the house. As I drew nearer, my heart was suddenly and greatly lightened. It is not a pleasant noise in itself, and I have often complained of it at other times; but just then it was like music to hear my friends snoring together so loud and peaceful in their sleep. The sea cry of the watch, that beautiful 'All's well,' never fell more reassuringly on my ear.

In the meantime, there was no doubt of one thing; they kept an infamous bad watch. If it had been Silver and his lads that were now creeping in on them, not a soul would have seen daybreak. That was what it was thought I, to have the captain wounded; and again I blamed myself sharply for leaving them in that danger with so few to mount guard.

By this time I had got to the door and stood up. All was dark within, so that I could distinguish nothing by the eye. As for sounds, there was the steady drone of the snorers, and a small occasional noise, a flickering or pecking that I could in no way account for.

With my arms before me I walked steadily in. I should lie down in my own place (I thought, with a silent chuckle) and enjoy their faces when they found me in the morning.

My foot struck something yielding—it was a sleeper's leg; and he turned and groaned, but without awaking.

And then, all of a sudden, a shrill voice broke forth out of the darkness:

'Pieces of eight! pieces of eight! pieces of eight! pieces of eight! pieces of eight!' and so forth, without pause or change, like the clacking of a tiny mill.

Silver's green parrot. Captain Flint! It was she whom I had heard pecking at a piece of bark; it was she, keeping better watch than any human being, who thus announced my arrival with her wearisome refrain.

I had no time left me to recover. At the sharp, clipping tone of the parrot, the sleepers awoke and sprang up; and with a mighty oath, the voice of Silver cried:—

'Who goes?'

I turned to run, struck violently against one person, recoiled, and ran full into the arms of a second, who, for his part, closed upon and held me tight.

'Bring a torch, Dick,' said Silver, when my capture was thus assured.

And one of the men left the log-house, and presently returned with a lighted brand.

PART VI

CAPTAIN SILVER

CHAPTER XXVIII

IN THE ENEMY'S CAMP

THE red glare of the torch, lighting up the interior of the block-house, showed me the worst of my apprehensions realised. The pirates were in possession of the house and stores: there was the cask of cognac, there were the pork and bread, as before; and, what tenfold increased my horror, not a sign of any prisoner. I could only judge that all had perished, and my heart smote me sorely that I had not been there to perish with them.

There were six of the buccaneers, all told; not another man was left alive. Five of them were on their feet, flushed and swollen, suddenly called out of the first sleep of drunkenness. The sixth had only risen upon his elbow: he was deadly pale, and the blood-stained bandage round his head told that he had recently been wounded, and still more recently dressed. I remembered the man who had been shot and had run back among the woods in the great attack, and doubted not that this was he.

The parrot sat, preening her plumage, on Long John's shoulder. He himself, I thought, looked somewhat paler and more stern than I was used to. He still wore the fine broadcloth* suit in which he had fulfilled his mission, but it was bitterly the worse for wear, daubed with clay and torn with the sharp briers of the wood.

'So,' said he, 'here's Jim Hawkins, shiver my timbers! dropped in, like, eh? Well, come, I take that friendly.'

And thereupon he sat down across the brandy cask, and began to fill a pipe.

'Give me a loan of the link,* Dick,' said he; and then, when he had a good light, 'that'll do, lad,' he added; 'stick the glim in the wood heap; and you, gentlemen, bring yourselves to!—you needn't stand up for Mr Hawkins; *he'll* excuse you, you may lay to that. And so, Jim'—stopping the tobacco—'here you were, and quite a pleasant surprise for poor old John. I see you were smart when first I set my eyes on you; but this here gets away from me clean, it do.'

To all this, as may be well supposed, I made no answer. They had set me with my back against the wall; and I stood there, looking Silver in the face, pluckily enough, I hope, to all outward appearance, but with black despair in my heart.

Silver took a whiff or two of his pipe with great composure, and then ran on again.

'Now, you see, Jim, so be as you *are* here,' says he, 'I'll give you a piece of my mind. I've always liked you, I have, for a lad of spirit, and the picter of my own self when I was young and handsome. I always wanted you to jine and take your share, and die a gentleman, and now, my cock, you've got to. Cap'n Smollett's a fine seaman, as I'll own up to any day, but stiff on discipline. "Dooty is dooty," says he, and right he is. Just you keep clear of the cap'n. The doctor himself is gone dead again you—"ungrateful scamp" was what he said; and the short and the long of the whole story is about here: you can't go back to your own lot, for they won't have you; and, without you start a third ship's company all by yourself, which might be lonely, you'll have to jine with Cap'n Silver.'

So far so good. My friends, then, were still alive, and though I partly believed the truth of Silver's statement, that the cabin party were incensed at me for my desertion, I was more relieved than distressed by what I heard.

'I don't say nothing as to your being in our hands,' continued Silver, 'though there you are, and you may lay to it. I'm all for argyment; I never seen good come out o' threatening. If you like the service, well, you'll jine; and if you don't, Jim, why, you're free to answer no—free and welcome, shipmate; and if fairer can be said by mortal seaman, shiver my sides!'

'Am I to answer, then?' I asked, with a very tremulous voice. Through all this sneering talk, I was made to feel the threat of death that overhung me, and my cheeks burned and my heart beat painfully in my breast.

'Lad,' said Silver, 'no one's a-pressing of you. Take your bearings. None of us won't hurry you, mate; time goes so pleasant in your company, you see.'

'Well,' says I, growing a bit bolder, 'if I'm to choose, I declare I have a right to know what's what, and why you're here, and where my friends are.'

'Wot's wot?' repeated one of the buccaneers, in a deep growl. 'Ah, he'd be a lucky one as knowed that!'

'You'll, perhaps, batten down your hatches till you're spoke to, my friend,' cried Silver truculently to this speaker. And then, in his first gracious tones, he replied to me: 'Yesterday morning, Mr Hawkins,' said he, 'in the dog-watch,* down came Doctor Livesey with a flag of truce. Says he, "Cap'n Silver, you're sold out. Ship's gone." Well, maybe we'd been taking a glass, and a song to help it round. I won't say no. Leastways, none of us had looked out. We looked out, and, by thunder! the old ship was gone. I never seen a pack o' fools look fishier; and you may lay to that, if I tells you that looked the fishiest. "Well," says the doctor, "let's bargain." We bargained, him and I, and here we are: stores, brandy, block-house, the firewood you was thoughtful enough to cut, and, in a manner of speaking, the whole blessed boat, from cross-trees to kelson.* As for them, they've tramped; I don't know where's they are.'

He drew again quietly at his pipe.

'And lest you should take it into that head of yours,' he went on, 'that you was included in the treaty, here's the last word that was said: "How many are you," says I, "to leave?" "Four," says he—"four, and one of us wounded. As for that boy, I don't know where he is, confound him," says he, "nor I don't much care. We're about sick of him." These was his words.'

'Is that all?' I asked.

'Well, it's all that you're to hear, my son,' returned Silver.

'And now I am to choose?'

'And now you are to choose, and you may lay to that,' said Silver.

'Well,' said I, 'I am not such a fool but I know pretty well what I have to look for. Let the worst come to the worst, it's little I care. I've seen too many die since I fell in with you. But there's a thing or two I have to tell you,' I said, and by this time I was quite excited; 'and the first is this: here you are, in a bad way: ship lost, treasure lost, men lost; your whole business gone to wreck; and if you want to know who did it—it was I! I was in the apple barrel the night we sighted land, and I heard you, John, and you, Dick Johnson, and Hands, who is now at the bottom of the sea, and told every word you said before the hour was out. And as for the schooner, it was I who cut her cable, and it was I that killed the men you had aboard of her, and it was I who brought her where you'll never see her more, not one of you.

The laugh's on my side; I've had the top of this business from the first; I no more fear you than I fear a fly. Kill me, if you please, or spare me. But one thing I'll say, and no more; if you spare me, bygones are bygones, and when you fellows are in court for piracy, I'll save you all I can. It is for you to choose. Kill another and do yourselves no good, or spare me and keep a witness to save you from the gallows.'

I stopped, for, I tell you, I was out of breath, and, to my wonder, not a man of them moved, but all sat staring at me like as many sheep. And while they were still staring, I broke out again:—

'And now, Mr Silver,' I said, 'I believe you're the best man here, and if things go to the worst, I'll take it kind of you to let the doctor know the way I took it.'

'I'll bear it in mind,' said Silver, with an accent so curious that I could not, for the life of me, decide whether he were laughing at my request, or had been favourably affected by my courage.

'I'll put one to that,' cried the old mahogany-faced seaman—Morgan by name—whom I had seen in Long John's public-house upon the quays of Bristol. 'It was him that knowed Black Dog.'

'Well, and see here,' added the sea-cook. 'I'll put another again to that, by thunder! for it was this same boy that faked* the chart from Billy Bones. First and last, we've split upon Jim Hawkins!'

'Then here goes!' said Morgan, with an oath.

And he sprang up, drawing his knife as if he had been twenty.

'Avast, there!' cried Silver. 'Who are you, Tom Morgan? Maybe you thought you was cap'n here, perhaps. By the powers, but I'll teach you better! Cross me, and you'll go where many a good man's gone before you, first and last, these thirty year back—some to the yard-arm, shiver my timbers! and some by the board, and all to feed the fishes. There's never a man looked me between the eyes and seen a good day a'terwards, Tom Morgan, you may lay to that.'

Morgan paused; but a hoarse murmur rose from the others.

'Tom's right,' said one.

'I stood hazing long enough from one,' added another. 'I'll be hanged if I'll be hazed by you, John Silver.'

'Did any of you gentlemen want to have it out with *me*?' roared Silver, bending far forward from his position on the keg, with his pipe still glowing in his right hand. 'Put a name on what you're at; you aint dumb, I reckon. Him that wants shall get it. Have I lived this many years, and a son of a rum puncheon cock his hat athwart my hawse* at the latter end of it? You know the way; you're all gentlemen o' fortune, by your account. Well, I'm ready. Take a cutlass, him that dares, and I'll see the colour of his inside, crutch and all, before that pipe's empty.'

Not a man stirred; not a man answered.

'That's your sort, is it?' he added, returning his pipe to his mouth. 'Well, you're a gay lot to look at, anyway. Not much worth to fight, you aint. P'r'aps you can understand King George's English. I'm cap'n here by 'lection. I'm cap'n here because I'm the best man by a long sea-mile. You won't fight, as gentlemen o' fortune should; then, by thunder, you'll obey, and you may lay to it! I like that boy, now; I never seen a better boy than that. He's more a man than any pair of rats of you in this here house, and what I say is this: let me see him that'll lay a hand on him—that's what I say, and you may lay to it.'

There was a long pause after this. I stood straight up against the wall, my heart still going like a sledge-hammer, but with a ray of hope now shining in my bosom. Silver leant back against the wall, his arms crossed, his pipe in the corner of his mouth, as calm as though he had been in church; yet his eye kept wandering furtively, and he kept the tail of it on his unruly followers. They, on their part, drew gradually together towards the far end of the block-house, and the low hiss of their whispering sounded in my ear continuously, like a stream. One after another, they would look up, and the red light of the torch would fall for a second on their nervous faces; but it was not towards me, it was towards Silver that they turned their eyes.

'You seem to have a lot to say,' remarked Silver, spitting far into the air. 'Pipe up and let me hear it, or lay to.'

'Ax your pardon, sir,' returned one of the men, 'you're pretty free with some of the rules; maybe you'll kindly keep an eye upon the rest. This crew's dissatisfied; this crew don't vally bullying a marlin-spike; this crew has its rights like other crews, I'll make so free as that; and by your own rules, I take it we can talk together. I ax your pardon, sir, acknowledging you for to be capting at this present; but I claim my right, and steps outside for a council.'

And with an elaborate sea-salute, this fellow, a long, ill-looking, yellow-eyed man of five-and-thirty, stepped coolly towards the door and disappeared out of the house. One after another, the rest followed his example; each making a salute as he passed; each adding some apology. 'According to rules,' said one. 'Fo'c's'le council,' said Morgan.

And so with one remark or another, all marched out,* and left Silver and me alone with the torch.

The sea-cook instantly removed his pipe.

'Now, look you here, Jim Hawkins,' he said, in a steady whisper, that was no more than audible, 'you're within half a plank of death, and, what's a long sight worse, of torture. They're going to throw me off. But, you mark, I stand by you through thick and thin. I didn't mean to; no, not till you spoke up. I was about desperate to lose that much blunt, and be hanged into the bargain. But I see you was the right sort. I says to myself: You stand by Hawkins, John, and Hawkins 'll stand by you. You're his last card, and, by the living thunder, John, he's yours! Back to back, says I. You save your witness, and he'll save your neck!'

I began dimly to understand.

'You mean all's lost?' I asked.

'Ay, by gum, I do!' he answered. 'Ship gone, neck gone—that's the size of it. Once I looked into that bay, Jim Hawkins, and seen no schooner—well, I'm tough, but I gave out. As for that lot and their council, mark me, they're outright fools and cowards. I'll save your life—if so be as I can—from them. But, see here, Jim—tit for tat—you save Long John from swinging.'

I was bewildered; it seemed a thing so hopeless he was asking—he, the old buccaneer, the ringleader throughout.

'What I can do, that I'll do,' I said.

'It's a bargain!' cried Long John. 'You speak up plucky, and, by thunder! I've a chance.'

He hobbled to the torch, where it stood propped among the fire-wood, and took a fresh light to his pipe.

'Understand me, Jim,' he said, returning. 'I've a head on my shoulders, I have. I'm on squire's side now. I know you've got that ship safe somewheres. How you done it, I don't know, but safe it is. I guess Hands and O'Brien turned soft. I never much believed in neither of *them*. Now you mark me. I ask no questions, nor I won't let others. I know when a game's up, I do; and I know a lad that's staunch. Ah, you that's young—you and me might have done a power of good together!'

He drew some cognac from the cask into a tin cannikin.

'Will you taste, messmate?' he asked; and when I had refused: 'Well, I'll take a drain myself, Jim,' said he. 'I need a caulker,* for there's trouble on hand. And, talking o' trouble, why did that doctor give me the chart, Jim?'

My face expressed a wonder so unaffected that he saw the needlessness of further questions.

'Ah, well, he did, though,' said he. 'And there's something under that, no doubt—something, surely, under that, Jim—bad or good.'

And he took another swallow of the brandy, shaking his great fair head like a man who looks forward to the worst.

CHAPTER XXIX

THE BLACK SPOT AGAIN

THE council of the buccaneers had lasted some time, when one of them re-entered the house, and with a repetition of the same salute, which had in my eyes an ironical air, begged for a moment's loan of the torch. Silver briefly agreed; and this emissary retired again, leaving us together in the dark.

'There's a breeze coming, Jim,' said Silver, who had, by this time, adopted quite a friendly and familiar tone.

I turned to the loophole nearest me and looked out. The embers of the great fire had so far burned themselves out, and now glowed so low and duskily, that I understood why these conspirators desired a torch. About halfway down the slope to the stockade, they were collected in a group; one held the light; another was on his knees in their midst, and I saw the blade of an open knife shine in his hand with varying colours, in the moon and torchlight. The rest were all somewhat stooping, as though watching the manœuvres of this last. I could just make out that he had a book as well as a knife in his hand; and was still wondering how anything so incongruous had come in their possession, when the kneeling figure rose once more to his feet, and the whole party began to move together towards the house.

'Here they come,' said I; and I returned to my former position, for it seemed beneath my dignity that they should find me watching them.

'Well, let 'em come, lad—let 'em come,' said Silver, cheerily. 'I've still a shot in my locker.'

The door opened, and the five men, standing huddled together just inside, pushed one of their number forward. In any other circumstances it would have been comical to see his slow advance, hesitating as he set down each foot, but holding his closed right hand in front of him.

'Step up, lad,' cried Silver. 'I won't eat you. Hand it over, lubber. I know the rules, I do; I won't hurt a depytation.'

Thus encouraged, the buccaneer stepped forth more briskly, and having passed something to Silver, from hand to hand, slipped yet more smartly back again to his companions.

The sea-cook looked at what had been given him.

'The black spot! I thought so,' he observed. 'Where might you have got the paper? Why, hillo! look here, now: this aint lucky! You've gone and cut this out of a Bible. What fool's cut a Bible?'

'Ah, there!' said Morgan—'there! Wot did I say? No good'll come o' that, I said.'

'Well, you've about fixed it now, among you,' continued Silver. 'You'll all swing now, I reckon. What soft-headed lubber had a Bible?'

'It was Dick,' said one.

'Dick, was it? Then Dick can get to prayers,' said Silver. 'He's seen his slice of luck, has Dick, and you may lay to that.'

But here the long man with the yellow eyes struck in.

'Belay that talk, John Silver,' he said. 'This crew has tipped you the black spot in full council, as in dooty bound; just you turn it over, as in dooty bound, and see what's wrote there. Then you can talk.'

'Thanky, George,' replied the sea-cook. 'You always was brisk for business, and has the rules by heart, George, as I'm pleased to see. Well, what is it, anyway? Ah! "Deposed"—that's it, is it? Very pretty wrote, to be sure; like print, I swear. Your hand o' write, George? Why, you was gettin' quite a leadin' man in this here crew. You'll be cap'n next, I shouldn't wonder. Just oblige me with that torch again, will you? this pipe don't draw.'

'Come, now,' said George, 'you don't fool this crew no more. You're a funny man, by your account; but you're over now, and you'll maybe step down off that barrel, and help vote.'

'I thought you said you knowed the rules,' returned Silver, contemptuously. 'Leastways, if you don't, I do; and I wait here—and I'm still your cap'n, mind—till you outs with your grievances, and I reply, in the meantime, your black spot aint worth a biscuit. After that, we'll see.'

'Oh,' replied George, 'you don't be under no kind of apprehension; *we're* all square, we are. First, you've made a hash of this cruise—you'll be a bold man to say no to that. Second, you let the enemy out o' this here trap for nothing. Why did they want out? I dunno; but it's pretty plain they wanted it. Third, you wouldn't let us go at them upon the march. Oh, we see through you, John Silver; you want to play booty, that's what's wrong with you. And then, fourth, there's this here boy.'

'Is that all?' asked Silver quietly.

'Enough, too,' retorted George. 'We'll all swing and sundry for your bungling.'

'Well, now, look here, I'll answer these four p'ints; one after another I'll answer 'em. I made a hash o' this cruise, did I? Well, now, you all know what I wanted; and you all know, if that had been done, that we'd 'a' been aboard the *Hispaniola* this night as ever was, every man of us alive, and fit, and full of good plum-duff, and the treasure in the hold of her, by thunder! Well, who crossed me? Who forced my hand, as was the lawful cap'n? Who tipped me the black spot the day we landed, and began this dance? Ah, it's a fine dance—I'm with you there—and looks mighty like a hornpipe in a rope's end at Execution Dock by London town, it does. But who done it? Why, it was Anderson, and Hands, and you, George Merry! And you're the last above board of that same meddling crew; and you have the Davy Jones's insolence to up and stand for cap'n over me—you, that sank the lot of us! By the powers! but this tops the stiffest yarn to nothing.'

Silver paused, and I could see by the faces of George and his late comrades that these words had not been said in vain.

'That's for number one,' cried the accused, wiping the sweat from his brow, for he had been talking with a vehemence that shook the house. 'Why, I give you my word, I'm sick to speak to you. You've neither sense nor memory, and I leave it to fancy where your mothers was that let you come to sea. Sea! Gentlemen o' fortune! I reckon tailors is your trade.'

'Go on, John,' said Morgan. 'Speak up to the others.'

'Ah, the others!' returned John. 'They're a nice lot, aint they? You say this cruise is bungled. Ah! by gum, if you could understand how bad it's bungled, you would see! We're that near the gibbet that my neck's stiff with thinking on it. You've seen 'em, maybe, hanged in chains, birds about 'em, seamen p'inting 'em out as they go down with the tide. "Who's that?" says one. "That! Why, that's John Silver. I knowed him well," says another. And you can hear the chains a-jangle as you go about and reach for the other buoy. Now, that's about where we are, every mother's son of us, thanks to him, and Hands, and Anderson, and other ruination fools of you. And if you want to know about number four, and that boy, why, shiver my timbers! isn't he a hostage? Are we a-going to waste a hostage? No, not us; he might be our last chance, and I shouldn't wonder. Kill that boy? not me, mates!

And number three? Ah, well, there's a deal to say to number three. Maybe you don't count it nothing to have a real college doctor come to see you every day—you, John, with your head broke—or you, George Merry, that had the ague shakes upon you not six hours agone, and has your eyes the colour of lemon peel to this same moment on the clock? And maybe, perhaps, you didn't know there was a consort coming, either? But there is; and not so long till then: and we'll see who'll be glad to have a hostage when it comes to that. And as for number two, and why I made a bargain—well, you came crawling on your knees to me to make it—on your knees you came, you was that downhearted—and you'd have starved, too, if I hadn't—but that's a trifle! you look there—that's why!'

And he cast down upon the floor a paper that I instantly recognised—none other than the chart on yellow paper, with the three red crosses, that I had found in the oilcloth at the bottom of the captain's chest. Why the doctor had given it to him was more than I could fancy.

But if it were inexplicable to me, the appearance of the chart was incredible to the surviving mutineers. They leaped upon it like cats upon a mouse. It went from hand to hand, one tearing it from another; and by the oaths and the cries and the childish laughter with which they accompanied their examination, you would have thought, not only they were fingering the very gold, but were at sea with it, besides, in safety.

'Yes,' said one, 'that's Flint, sure enough. J.F., and a score below, with a clove hitch to it; so he done ever.'

'Mighty pretty,' said George. 'But how are we to get away with it, and us no ship?'

Silver suddenly sprang up, and supporting himself with a hand against the wall: 'Now I give you warning, George,' he cried. 'One more word of your sauce, and I'll call you down and fight you. How? Why, how do I know? You had ought to tell me that—you and the rest, that lost me my schooner, with your interference, burn you! But not you, you can't; you hain't got the invention of a cockroach. But civil you can speak, and shall, George Merry, you may lay to that.'

'That's fair enow,' said the old man Morgan.

'Fair! I reckon so,' said the sea-cook. 'You lost the ship; I found the treasure. Who's the better man at that? And now I resign, by thunder! Elect whom you please to be your cap'n now; I'm done with it.'

'Silver!' they cried. 'Barbecue for ever! Barbecue for cap'n!'

'So that's the toon, is it?' cried the cook. 'George, I reckon you'll have to wait another turn, friend; and lucky for you as I'm not a revengeful man. But that was never my way. And now, shipmates, this black spot? 'Tain't much good now, is it? Dick's crossed his luck and spoiled his Bible, and that's about all.'

'It'll do to kiss the book on still, won't it?' growled Dick, who was evidently uneasy at the curse he had brought upon himself.

'A Bible with a bit cut out!' returned Silver, derisively. 'Not it. It don't bind no more'n a ballad-book.'

'Don't it, though?' cried Dick, with a sort of joy. 'Well, I reckon that's worth having, too.'

'Here, Jim—here's a cur'osity for you,' said Silver; and he tossed me the paper.

It was a round about the size of a crown piece. One side was blank, for it had been the last leaf; the other contained a verse or two of Revelation—these words among the rest, which struck sharply home upon my mind: 'Without are dogs and murderers.'* The printed side had been blackened with wood ash, which already began to come off and soil my fingers; on the blank side had been written with the same material the one word 'Depposed.' I have that curiosity beside me at this moment; but not a trace of writing now remains beyond a single scratch, such as a man might make with his thumb-nail.

That was the end of the night's business. Soon after, with a drink all round, we lay down to sleep, and the outside of Silver's vengeance was to put George Merry up for sentinel, and threaten him with death if he should prove unfaithful.

It was long ere I could close an eye, and Heaven knows I had matter enough for thought in the man whom I had slain that afternoon, in my own most perilous position, and, above all, in the remarkable game that I saw Silver now engaged upon—keeping the mutineers together with one hand, and grasping, with the other, after every means, possible and impossible, to make his peace and save his miserable life. He himself slept peacefully, and snored aloud; yet my heart was sore for him, wicked as he was, to think on the dark perils that environed, and the shameful gibbet that awaited him.

CHAPTER XXX

ON PAROLE

I WAS wakened—indeed, we were all wakened, for I could see even the sentinel shake himself together from where he had fallen against the door-post—by a clear, hearty voice hailing us from the margin of the wood:—

'Block-house, ahoy!' it cried. 'Here's the doctor.'

And the doctor it was. Although I was glad to hear the sound, yet my gladness was not without admixture. I remembered with confusion my insubordinate and stealthy conduct; and when I saw where it had brought me—among what companions and surrounded by what dangers—I felt ashamed to look him in the face.

He must have risen in the dark, for the day had hardly come; and when I ran to a loophole and looked out, I saw him standing, like Silver once before, up to the mid-leg in creeping vapour.

'You, doctor! Top o' the morning to you, sir!' cried Silver, broad awake and beaming with good-nature in a moment. 'Bright and early, to be sure: and it's the early bird, as the saying goes, that gets the rations. George, shake up your timbers, son, and help Dr Livesey over the ship's side. All a-doin' well, your patients was—all well and merry.'

So he pattered on, standing on the hill-top, with his crutch under his elbow, and one hand upon the side of the log-house—quite the old John in voice, manner, and expression.

'We've quite a surprise for you, too, sir,' he continued. 'We've a little stranger here—he! he! A noo boarder and lodger, sir, and looking fit and taut as a fiddle; slep' like a supercargo, he did, right alongside of John—stem to stem we was, all night.'

Dr Livesey was by this time across the stockade and pretty near the cook; and I could hear the alteration in his voice as he said:—

'Not Jim?'

'The very same Jim as ever was,' says Silver.

The doctor stopped outright, although he did not speak, and it was some seconds before he seemed able to move on.

'Well, well,' he said, at last, 'duty first and pleasure afterwards, as you might have said yourself, Silver. Let us overhaul these patients of yours.'

A moment afterwards he had entered the block-house, and, with one grim nod to me, proceeded with his work among the sick. He seemed under no apprehension, though he must have known that his life, among these treacherous demons, depended on a hair; and he rattled on to his patients as if he were paying an ordinary professional visit in a quiet English family. His manner, I suppose, reacted on the men; for they behaved to him as if nothing had occurred—as if he were still ship's doctor, and they still faithful hands before the mast.

'You're doing well, my friend,' he said to the fellow with the bandaged head, 'and if ever any person had a close shave, it was you; your head must be as hard as iron. Well, George, how goes it? You're a pretty colour, certainly; why, your liver, man, is upside down. Did you take that medicine? Did he take that medicine, men?'

'Ay, ay, sir, he took it, sure enough,' returned Morgan.

'Because, you see, since I am mutineers' doctor, or prison doctor, as I prefer to call it,' says Dr Livesey, in his pleasantest way, 'I make it a point of honour not to lose a man for King George (God bless him!) and the gallows.'

The rogues looked at each other, but swallowed the home-thrust in silence.

'Dick don't feel well, sir,' said one.

'Don't he?' replied the doctor. 'Well, step up here. Dick, and let me see your tongue. No, I should be surprised if he did! the man's tongue is fit to frighten the French. Another fever.'

'Ah, there,' said Morgan, 'that comed of sp'iling Bibles.'

'That comed—as you call it—of being arrant asses,' retorted the doctor, 'and not having sense enough to know honest air from poison, and the dry land from a vile, pestiferous slough. I think it most probable—though, of course, it's only an opinion—that you'll all have the deuce to pay before you get that malaria out of your systems. Camp in a bog, would you? Silver, I'm surprised at you. You're less of a fool than many, take you all round; but you don't appear to me to have the rudiments of a notion of the rules of health.'

'Well,' he added, after he had dosed them round, and they had taken his prescriptions, with really laughable humility, more like charity school-children than blood-guilty mutineers and pirates—'well, that's done for to-day. And now I should wish to have a talk with that boy, please.'

And he nodded his head in my direction carelessly.

George Merry was at the door, spitting and spluttering over some bad-tasted medicine; but at the first word of the doctor's proposal he swung round with a deep flush, and cried 'No!' and swore.

Silver struck the barrel with his open hand.

'Si-lence!' he roared, and looked about him positively like a lion. 'Doctor,' he went on, in his usual tones, 'I was a-thinking of that, knowing as how you had a fancy for the boy. We're all humbly grateful for your kindness, and, as you see, puts faith in you, and takes the drugs down like that much grog. And I take it I've found a way as'll suit all. Hawkins, will you give me your word of honour as a young gentleman—for a young gentleman you are, although poor born—your word of honour not to slip your cable?'

I readily gave the pledge required.

'Then, doctor,' said Silver, 'you just step outside o' that stockade, and once you're there, I'll bring the boy down on the inside, and I reckon you can yarn through the spars. Good-day to you, sir, and all our dooties to the squire and Cap'n Smollett.'

The explosion of disapproval, which nothing but Silver's black looks had restrained, broke out immediately the doctor had left the house. Silver was roundly accused of playing double—of trying to make a separate peace for himself—of sacrificing the interests of his accomplices and victims; and, in one word, of the identical, exact thing that he was doing. It seemed to me so obvious, in this case, that I could not imagine how he was to turn their anger. But he was twice the man the rest were; and his last night's victory had given him a huge preponderance on their minds. He called them all the fools and dolts you can imagine, said it was necessary I should talk to the doctor, fluttered the chart in their faces, asked them if they could afford to break the treaty the very day they were bound a-treasure-hunting.

'No, by thunder!' he cried, 'it's us must break the treaty when the time comes: and till then I'll gammon* that doctor, if I have to ile his boots with brandy.'

And then he bade them get the fire lit, and stalked out upon his crutch, with his hand on my shoulder, leaving them in a disarray, and silenced by his volubility rather than convinced.

'Slow, lad, slow,' he said. 'They might round upon us in a twinkle of an eye, if we was seen to hurry.'

Very deliberately, then, did we advance across the sand to where the doctor awaited us on the other side of the stockade, and as soon as we were within easy speaking distance, Silver stopped.

'You'll make a note of this here also, doctor,' says he, 'and the boy'll tell you how I saved his life, and were deposed for it, too, and you may lay to that. Doctor, when a man's steering as near the wind as me—playing chuck-farthing with the last breath in his body, like—you wouldn't think it too much, mayhap, to give him one good word? You'll please bear in mind it's not my life only now—it's that boy's into the bargain; and you'll speak me fair, doctor, and give me a bit o' hope to go on, for the sake of mercy.'

Silver was a changed man, once he was out there and had his back to his friends and the block-house; his cheeks seemed to have fallen in, his voice trembled; never was a soul more dead in earnest.

'Why, John, you're not afraid?' asked Dr Livesey.

'Doctor, I'm no coward; no, not I—not *so* much!' and he snapped his fingers. 'If I was I wouldn't say it. But I'll own up fairly, I've the shakes upon me for the gallows. You're a good man and a true; I never seen a better man! And you'll not forget what I done good, not any more than you'll forget the bad, I know. And I step aside—see here—and leave you and Jim alone. And you'll put that down for me, too, for it's a long stretch, is that!'

So saying, he stepped back a little way, till he was out of earshot, and there sat down upon a tree-stump and began to whistle; spinning round now and again upon his seat so as to command a sight, sometimes of me and the doctor, and sometimes of his unruly ruffians as they went to and fro in the sand, between the fire—which they were busy rekindling—and the house, from which they brought forth pork and bread to make the breakfast.

'So, Jim,' said the doctor, sadly, 'here you are. As you have brewed, so shall you drink, my boy. Heaven knows, I cannot find it in my heart to blame you; but this much I will say, be it kind or unkind: when Captain Smollett was well, you dared not have gone off; and when he was ill, and couldn't help it, by George, it was downright cowardly!'

I will own that I here began to weep. 'Doctor,' I said, 'you might spare me. I have blamed myself enough; my life's forfeit anyway, and I should have been dead by now, if Silver hadn't stood for me; and doctor, believe this, I can die—and I daresay I deserve it—but what I fear is torture. If they come to torture me—'

'Jim,' the doctor interrupted, and his voice was quite changed, 'Jim I can't have this. Whip over, and we'll run for it.'

'Doctor,' said I, 'I passed my word.'

'I know, I know,' he cried. 'We can't help that, Jim, now. I'll take it on my shoulders, holus bolus,* blame and shame, my boy; but stay here, I cannot let you. Jump! One jump, and you're out, and we'll run for it like antelopes.'

'No,' I replied, 'you know right well you wouldn't do the thing yourself; neither you, nor squire, nor captain; and no more will I. Silver trusted me; I passed my word, and back I go. But, doctor, you did not let me finish. If they come to torture me, I might let slip a word of where the ship is; for I got the ship, part by luck and part by risking, and she lies in North Inlet, on the southern beach, and just below high water. At half-tide she must be high and dry.'

'The ship!' exclaimed the doctor.

Rapidly I described to him my adventures, and he heard me out in silence.

'There is a kind of fate in this,' he observed, when I had done. 'Every step, it's you that saves our lives; and do you suppose by any chance that we are going to let you lose yours? That would be a poor return, my boy. You found out the plot; you found Ben Gunn—the best deed that ever you did, or will do, though you live to ninety. Oh, by Jupiter, and talking of Ben Gunn! why, this is the mischief in person. Silver!' he cried, 'Silver!—I'll give you a piece of advice,' he continued, as the cook drew near again; 'don't you be in any great hurry after that treasure.'

'Why, sir, I do my possible, which that aint,' said Silver. 'I can only, asking your pardon, save my life and the boy's by seeking for that treasure; and you may lay to that.'

'Well, Silver,' replied the doctor, 'if that is so, I'll go one step further: look out for squalls when you find it.'

'Sir,' said Silver, 'as between man and man, that's too much and too little. What you're after, why you left the block-house, why you given me that there chart, I don't know, now, do I? and yet I done your bidding with my eyes shut and never a word of hope! But no, this here's too much. If you won't tell me what you mean plain out, just say so, and I'll leave the helm.'

'No,' said the doctor, musingly, 'I've no right to say more; it's not my secret, you see, Silver, or, I give you my word, I'd tell it you. But I'll go as far with you as I dare go, and a step beyond; for I'll have my wig sorted by the captain or I'm mistaken! And, first, I'll give you a bit of hope: Silver, if we both get alive out of this wolf-trap, I'll do my best to save you, short of perjury.'

Silver's face was radiant. 'You couldn't say more, I'm sure, sir, not if you was my mother,' he cried.

'Well, that's my first concession,' added the doctor. 'My second is a piece of advice: Keep the boy close beside you, and when you need help, halloo. I'm off to seek it for you, and that itself will show you if I speak at random. Good-bye, Jim.'

And Dr Livesey shook hands with me through the stockade, nodded to Silver, and set off at a brisk pace into the wood.

CHAPTER XXXI

THE TREASURE HUNT—FLINT'S POINTER

'JIM,' said Silver, when we were alone, 'if I saved your life, you saved mine; and I'll not forget it. I seen the doctor waving you to run for it—with the tail of my eye, I did; and I seen you say no, as plain as hearing. Jim, that's one to you. This is the first glint of hope I had since the attack failed, and I owe it you. And now, Jim, we're to go in for this here treasure hunting, with sealed orders, too, and I don't like it; and you and me must stick close, back to back like, and we'll save our necks in spite o' fate and fortune.'

Just then a man hailed us from the fire that breakfast was ready, and we were soon seated here and there about the sand over biscuit and fried junk.* They had lit a fire fit to roast an ox; and it was now grown so hot that they could only approach it from the windward, and even there not without precaution. In the same wasteful spirit, they had cooked, I suppose, three times more than we could eat; and one of them, with an empty laugh, threw what was left into the fire, which blazed and roared again over this unusual fuel. I never in my life saw men so careless of the morrow,* hand to mouth is the only word that can describe their way of doing; and what with wasted food and sleeping sentries, though they were bold enough for a brush and be done with it, I could see their entire unfitness for anything like a prolonged campaign.

Even Silver, eating away, with Captain Flint upon his shoulder, had not a word of blame for their recklessness. And this the more surprised me, for I thought he had never shown himself so cunning as he did then.

'Ay, mates,' said he, 'it's lucky you have Barbecue to think for you with this here head. I got what I wanted, I did. Sure enough, they have the ship. Where they have it, I don't know yet; but once we hit the treasure, we'll have to jump about and find out. And then, mates, us that has the boats, I reckon, has the upper hand.'

Thus he kept running on, with his mouth full of the hot bacon: thus he restored their hope and confidence, and, I more than suspect, repaired his own at the same time.

'As for hostage,' he continued, 'that's his last talk, I guess, with them he loves so dear. I've got my piece o' news, and thanky to him for that; but it's over and done. I'll take him in a line when we go treasure-hunting, for we'll keep him like so much gold, in case of accidents, you mark, and in the meantime. Once we got the ship and treasure both, and off to sea like jolly companions, why, men, we'll talk Mr Hawkins over, we will, and we'll give him his share, to be sure, for all his kindness.'

It was no wonder the men were in a good humour now. For my part, I was horribly cast down. Should the scheme he had now sketched prove feasible, Silver, already doubly a traitor, would not hesitate to adopt it. He had still a foot in either camp, and there was no doubt he would prefer wealth and freedom with the pirates to a bare escape from hanging, which was the best he had to hope on our side.

Nay, and even if things so fell out that he was forced to keep his faith with Dr Livesey, even then what danger lay before us! What a moment that would be when the suspicions of his followers turned to certainty, and he and I should have to fight for dear life—he, a cripple, and I, a boy—against five strong and active seamen!

Add to this double apprehension, the mystery that still hung over the behaviour of my friends; their unexplained desertion of the stockade; their inexplicable cession of the chart; or, harder still to understand, the doctor's last warning to Silver, 'Look out for squalls when you find it;' and you will readily believe how little taste I found in my breakfast, and with how uneasy a heart I set forth behind my captors on the quest for treasure.

We made a curious figure, had anyone been there to see us; all in soiled sailor clothes, and all but me armed to the teeth. Silver had two guns slung about him—one before and one behind—besides the great cutlass at his waist, and a pistol in each pocket of his square-tailed coat. To complete his strange appearance, Captain Flint sat perched upon his shoulder and gabbling odds and ends of purposeless sea-talk. I had a line about my waist, and followed obediently after the sea-cook, who held the loose end of the rope, now in his free hand, now between his powerful teeth. For all the world, I was led like a dancing bear.

The other men were variously burthened; some carrying picks and shovels—for that had been the very first necessary they brought ashore from the *Hispaniola*—others laden with pork, bread, and brandy for the midday meal. All the stores, I observed, came from our stock; and I could see the truth of Silver's words the night before.

Had he not struck a bargain with the doctor, he and his mutineers, deserted by the ship, must have been driven to subsist on clear water and the proceeds of their hunting. Water would have been little to their taste; a sailor is not usually a good shot; and, besides all that, when they were so short of eatables, it was not likely they would be very flush of powder.

Well, thus equipped, we all set out—even the fellow with the broken head, who should certainly have kept in shadow—and straggled, one after another, to the beach, where the two gigs awaited us. Even these bore trace of the drunken folly of the pirates, one in a broken thwart, and both in their muddy and unbailed condition. Both were to be carried along with us, for the sake of safety; and so, with our numbers divided between them, we set forth upon the bosom of the anchorage.

As we pulled over, there was some discussion on the chart. The red cross was, of course, far too large to be a guide; and the terms of the note on the back, as you will hear, admitted of some ambiguity. They ran, the reader may remember, thus:—

'Tall tree, Spy-glass shoulder, bearing a point to the N. of N.N.E.
'Skeleton Island E.S.E. and by E.
'Ten feet.'

A tall tree was thus the principal mark. Now, right before us, the anchorage was bounded by a plateau from two to three hundred feet high, adjoining on the north the sloping southern shoulder of the Spy-glass, and rising again towards the south into the rough, cliffy eminence called the Mizzen-mast Hill. The top of the plateau was dotted thickly with pine trees of varying height. Every here and there, one of a different species rose forty or fifty feet clear above its neighbours,* and which of these was the particular 'tall tree' of Captain Flint could only be decided on the spot, and by the readings of the compass.

Yet, although that was the case, every man on board the boats had picked a favourite of his own ere we were halfway over, Long John alone shrugging his shoulders and bidding them wait till they were there.

We pulled easily, by Silver's directions, not to weary the hands prematurely; and, after quite a long passage, landed at the mouth of the second river—that which runs down a woody cleft of the Spy-glass.

Thence, bending to our left, we began to ascend the slope towards the plateau.

At the first outset, heavy, miry ground and a matted, marish vegetation, greatly delayed our progress; but by little and little the hill began to steepen and become stony under foot, and the wood to change its character and to grow in a more open order. It was, indeed, a most pleasant portion of the island that we were now approaching. A heavy-scented broom and many flowering shrubs had almost taken the place of grass. Thickets of green nutmeg trees* were dotted here and there with the red columns and the broad shadow of the pines; and the first mingled their spice with the aroma of the others. The air, besides, was fresh and stirring, and this, under the sheer sunbeams, was a wonderful refreshment to our senses.

The party spread itself abroad, in a fan shape, shouting and leaping to and fro. About the centre, and a good way behind the rest, Silver and I followed—I tethered by my rope, he ploughing, with deep pants, among the sliding gravel. From time to time, indeed, I had to lend him a hand, or he must have missed his footing and fallen backward down the hill.

We had thus proceeded for about half a mile, and were approaching the brow of the plateau, when the man upon the farthest left began to cry aloud, as if in terror. Shout after shout came from him, and the others began to run in his direction.

'He can't 'a' found the treasure,' said old Morgan, hurrying past us from the right, 'for that's clean a-top.'

Indeed, as we found when we also reached the spot, it was something very different. At the foot of a pretty big pine, and involved in a green creeper, which had even partly lifted some of the smaller bones, a human skeleton* lay, with a few shreds of clothing, on the ground. I believe a chill struck for a moment to every heart.

'He was a seaman,' said George Merry, who, bolder than the rest, had gone up close, and was examining the rags of clothing. 'Leastways, this is good sea-cloth.'

'Ay, ay,' said Silver, 'like enough; you wouldn't look to find a bishop here, I reckon. But what sort of a way is that for bones to lie? 'Tain't in natur'.'

Indeed, on a second glance, it seemed impossible to fancy that the body was in a natural position. But for some disarray (the work, perhaps, of the birds that had fed upon him, or of the slow-growing creeper that had gradually enveloped his remains) the man lay perfectly straight—his feet pointing in one direction, his hands, raised above his head like a diver's, pointing directly in the opposite.

'I've taken a notion into my old numskull,'* observed Silver. 'Here's the compass; there's the tip-top p'int o' Skeleton Island, stickin' out like a tooth. Just take a bearing, will you, along the line of them bones.'

It was done. The body pointed straight in the direction of the island, and the compass read duly E.S.E. and by E.

'I thought so,' cried the cook; 'this here is a p'inter. Right up there is our line for the Pole Star and the jolly dollars. But, by thunder! if it don't make me cold inside to think of Flint. This is one of *his* jokes, and no mistake. Him and these six was alone here; he killed 'em, every man; and this one he hauled here and laid down by compass, shiver my timbers! They're long bones, and the hair's been yellow. Ay, that would be Allardyce. You mind Allardyce, Tom Morgan?'

'Ay, ay,' returned Morgan, 'I mind him; he owed me money, he did, and took my knife ashore with him.'

'Speaking of knives,' said another, 'why don't we find his'n lying round? Flint warn't the man to pick a seaman's pocket; and the birds, I guess, would leave it be.'

'By the powers, and that's true!' cried Silver.

'There aint a thing left here,' said Merry, still feeling round among the bones, 'not a copper doit* nor a baccy box. It don't look nat'ral to me.'

'No, by gum, it don't,' agreed Silver; 'not nat'ral, nor not nice, says you. Great guns! messmates, but if Flint was living, this would be a hot spot for you and me. Six they were, and six are we; and bones is what they are now.'

'I saw him dead with these here deadlights,' said Morgan. 'Billy took me in. There he laid, with penny-pieces on his eyes.'

'Dead—ay, sure enough he's dead and gone below,' said the fellow with the bandage; 'but if ever sperrit walked, it would be Flint's. Dear heart, but he died bad, did Flint!'

'Ay, that he did,' observed another; 'now he raged, and now he hollered for the rum, and now he sang. "Fifteen Men" were his only song, mates; and I tell you true, I never rightly liked to hear it since. It was main hot, and the windy was open, and I hear that old song comin' out as clear as clear—and the death-haul on the man already.'

'Come, come,' said Silver, 'stow this talk. He's dead, and he don't walk, that I know; leastways, he won't walk by day, and you may lay to that. Care killed a cat. Fetch ahead for the doubloons.'

We started, certainly; but in spite of the hot sun and the staring daylight, the pirates no longer ran separate and shouting through the wood, but kept side by side and spoke with bated breath. The terror of the dead buccaneer had fallen on their spirits.

CHAPTER XXXII

THE TREASURE HUNT—THE VOICE AMONG THE TREES

PARTLY from the damping influence of this alarm, partly to rest Silver and the sick folk, the whole party sat down as soon as they had gained the brow of the ascent.

The plateau being somewhat tilted towards the west, this spot on which we had paused commanded a wide prospect on either hand. Before us, over the tree-tops, we beheld the Cape of the Woods fringed with surf; behind, we not only looked down upon the anchorage and Skeleton Island, but saw—clear across the spit and the eastern low-lands—a great field of open sea upon the east. Sheer above us rose the Spy-glass, here dotted with single pines, there black with precipices. There was no sound but that of the distant breakers, mounting from all round, and the chirp of countless insects in the brush. Not a man, not a sail upon the sea; the very largeness of the view increased the sense of solitude.

Silver, as he sat, took certain bearings with his compass.

'There are three "tall trees,"' said he, 'about in the right line from Skeleton Island. "Spy-glass Shoulder," I take it, means that lower p'int there. It's child's play to find the stuff now. I've half a mind to dine first.'

'I don't feel sharp,' growled Morgan. 'Thinkin' o' Flint—I think it were—as done me.'

'Ah, well, my son, you praise your stars he's dead,' said Silver.

'He were an ugly devil,' cried a third pirate, with a shudder; 'that blue in the face, too!'

'That was how the rum took him,' added Merry. 'Blue! well, I reckon he was blue. That's a true word.'

Ever since they had found the skeleton and got upon this train of thought, they had spoken lower and lower, and they had almost got to whispering by now, so that the sound of their talk hardly interrupted the silence of the wood. All of a sudden, out of the middle of the trees in front of us, a thin, high, trembling voice struck up the well-known air and words:—

> 'Fifteen men on the dead man's chest—
> Yo-ho-ho, and a bottle of rum!'

I never have seen men more dreadfully affected than the pirates. The colour went from their six faces like enchantment; some leaped to their feet, some clawed hold of others; Morgan grovelled on the ground.

'It's Flint, by—!' cried Merry.

The song had stopped as suddenly as it began—broken off, you would have said, in the middle of a note, as though someone had laid his hand upon the singer's mouth. Coming so far through the clear, sunny atmosphere among the green tree-tops, I thought it had sounded airily and sweetly;* and the effect on my companions was the stranger.

'Come,' said Silver, struggling with his ashen lips to get the word out, 'this won't do. Stand by to go about. This is a rum start, and I can't name the voice: but it's someone skylarking—someone that's flesh and blood, and you may lay to that.'

His courage had come back as he spoke, and some of the colour to his face along with it. Already the others had begun to lend an ear to this encouragement, and were coming a little to themselves, when the same voice broke out again—not this time singing, but in a faint distant hail, that echoed yet fainter among the clefts of the Spy-glass.

'Darby M'Graw,'* it wailed—for that is the word that best describes the sound—'Darby M'Graw! Darby M'Graw!' again and again and again; and then rising a little higher, and with an oath that I leave out, 'Fetch aft the rum, Darby!'

The buccaneers remained rooted to the ground, their eyes starting from their heads. Long after the voice had died away they still stared in silence, dreadfully, before them.

'That fixes it!' gasped one. 'Let's go.'

'They was his last words,' moaned Morgan, 'his last words above board.'

Dick had his Bible out, and was praying volubly. He had been well brought up, had Dick, before he came to sea and fell among bad companions.

Still, Silver was unconquered. I could hear his teeth rattle in his head; but he had not yet surrendered.

'Nobody in this here island ever heard of Darby,' he muttered; 'not one but us that's here.' And then, making a great effort, 'Shipmates,' he cried, 'I'm here to get that stuff, and I'll not be beat by man nor devil. I never was feared of Flint in his life, and, by the powers, I'll face him dead. There's seven hundred thousand pound not a quarter of a mile from here. When did ever a gentleman o' fortune show his stern to that much dollars, for a boosy old seaman with a blue mug—and him dead, too?'

But there was no sign of re-awakening courage in his followers; rather, indeed, of growing terror at the irreverence of his words.

'Belay there, John!' said Merry. 'Don't you cross a sperrit.'

And the rest were all too terrified to reply. They would have run away severally had they dared; but fear kept them together, and kept them close by John, as if his daring helped them. He, on his part, had pretty well fought his weakness down.

'Sperrit? Well, maybe,' he said. 'But there's one thing not clear to me. There was an echo. Now, no man ever seen a sperrit with a shadow; well, then, what's he doing with an echo to him, I should like to know? That aint in natur', surely?'

This argument seemed weak enough to me. But you can never tell what will affect the superstitious, and, to my wonder, George Merry was greatly relieved.

'Well, that's so,' he said. 'You've a head upon your shoulders, John, and no mistake. 'Bout ship, mates! This here crew is on a wrong tack, I do believe. And come to think on it, it was like Flint's voice, I grant you, but not just so clear-away like it, after all. It was liker somebody else's voice now—it was liker—'

'By the powers, Ben Gunn!' roared Silver.

'Ay, and so it were,' cried Morgan, springing on his knees. 'Ben Gunn it were!'

'It don't make much odds, do it, now?' asked Dick. 'Ben Gunn's not here in the body, any more'n Flint.'

But the older hands greeted this remark with scorn.

'Why nobody minds Ben Gunn,' cried Merry; 'dead or alive, nobody minds him.'

It was extraordinary how their spirits had returned, and how the natural colour had revived in their faces. Soon they were chatting together, with intervals of listening; and not long after, hearing no further sound, they shouldered the tools and set forth again, Merry walking first with Silver's compass to keep them on the right line with Skeleton Island. He had said the truth: dead or alive, nobody minded Ben Gunn.

Dick alone still held his Bible, and looked around him as he went, with fearful glances; but he found no sympathy, and Silver even joked him on his precautions.

'I told you,' said he—'I told you, you had sp'iled your Bible. If it aint no good to swear by, what do you suppose a sperrit would give for it? Not that!' and he snapped his big fingers, halting a moment on his crutch.

But Dick was not to be comforted; indeed, it was soon plain to me that the lad was falling sick; hastened by heat, exhaustion, and the shock of his alarm, the fever, predicted by Doctor Livesey, was evidently growing swiftly higher.

It was fine open walking here, upon the summit; our way lay a little downhill, for, as I have said, the plateau tilted towards the west. The pines, great and small, grew wide apart; and even between the clumps of nutmeg and azalea, wide open spaces baked in the hot sunshine. Striking, as we did, pretty near north-west across the island, we drew, on the one hand ever nearer under the shoulders of the Spy-glass, and on the other, looked ever wider over that western bay where I had once tossed and trembled in the coracle.

The first of the tall trees was reached, and by the bearing, proved the wrong one. So with the second. The third rose nearly two hundred feet into the air above a clump of underwood; a giant of a vegetable, with a red column as big as a cottage, and a wide shadow around in which a company could have manœuvred. It was conspicuous far to sea both on the east and west, and might have been entered as a sailing mark upon the chart.

But it was not its size that now impressed my companions; it was the knowledge that seven hundred thousand pounds in gold lay somewhere buried below its spreading shadow. The thought of the money, as they drew nearer, swallowed up their previous terrors. Their eyes burned in their heads; their feet grew speedier and lighter; their whole soul was bound up in that fortune, that whole lifetime of extravagance and pleasure, that lay waiting there for each of them.

Silver hobbled, grunting, on his crutch; his nostrils stood out and quivered; he cursed like a madman when the flies settled on his hot and shiny countenance; he plucked furiously at the line that held me to him, and, from time to time, turned his eyes upon me with a deadly look. Certainly he took no pains to hide his thoughts; and certainly I read them like print. In the immediate nearness of the gold, all else had been forgotten; his promise and the doctor's warning were both things of the past; and I could not doubt that he hoped to seize upon the treasure, find and board the *Hispaniola* under cover of night, cut every honest throat about that island, and sail away as he had at first intended, laden with crimes and riches.

Shaken as I was with these alarms, it was hard for me to keep up with the rapid pace of the treasure-hunters. Now and again I stumbled; and it was then that Silver plucked so roughly at the rope and launched at me his murderous glances. Dick, who had dropped behind us, and now brought up the rear, was babbling to himself both prayers and curses, as his fever kept rising. This also added to my wretchedness, and, to crown all, I was haunted by the thought of the tragedy that had once been acted on that plateau, when that ungodly buccaneer with the blue face—he who died at Savannah, singing and shouting for drink—had there, with his own hand, cut down his six accomplices. This grove, that was now so peaceful, must then have rung with cries, I thought; and even with the thought I could believe I heard it ringing still.

We were now at the margin of the thicket.

'Huzza, mates, altogether!' shouted Merry; and the foremost broke into a run.

And suddenly, not ten yards further, we beheld them stop. A low cry arose. Silver doubled his pace, digging away with the foot of his crutch like one possessed; and next moment he and I had come also to a dead halt.

Before us was a great excavation, not very recent, for the sides had fallen in and grass had sprouted on the bottom. In this were the shaft of a pick broken in two and the boards of several packing-cases strewn around. On one of these boards I saw, branded with a hot iron, the name *Walrus*—the name of Flint's ship.

All was clear to probation.* The *cache* had been found and rifled: the seven hundred thousand pounds were gone!

CHAPTER XXXIII

THE FALL OF A CHIEFTAIN

THERE never was such an overturn in this world. Each of these six men was as though he had been struck. But with Silver the blow passed almost instantly. Every thought of his soul had been set full-stretch, like a racer, on that money; well, he was brought up in a single second, dead; and he kept his head, found his temper, and changed his plan before the others had had time to realise the disappointment.

'Jim,' he whispered, 'take that, and stand by for trouble.'

And he passed me a double-barrelled pistol.

At the same time he began quietly moving northward, and in a few steps had put the hollow between us two and the other five. Then he looked at me and nodded, as much as to say, 'Here is a narrow corner,' as, indeed, I thought it was. His looks were now quite friendly; and I was so revolted at these constant changes, that I could not forbear whispering, 'So you've changed sides again.'

There was no time left for him to answer in. The buccaneers, with oaths and cries, began to leap, one after another, into the pit, and to dig with their fingers, throwing the boards aside as they did so. Morgan found a piece of gold. He held it up with a perfect spout of oaths. It was a two-guinea piece, and it went from hand to hand among them for a quarter of a minute.

'Two guineas!' roared Merry, shaking it at Silver. 'That's your seven hundred thousand pounds, is it? You're the man for bargains, aint you? You're him that never bungled nothing, you wooden-headed lubber!'

'Dig away, boys,' said Silver, with the coolest insolence; 'you'll find some pig-nuts and I shouldn't wonder.'

'Pig-nuts!' repeated Merry, in a scream. 'Mates, do you hear that? I tell you, now, that man there knew it all along. Look in the face of him, and you'll see it wrote there.'

'Ah, Merry,' remarked Silver, 'standing for cap'n again? You're a pushing lad, to be sure.'

But this time everyone was entirely in Merry's favour. They began to scramble out of the excavation, darting furious glances behind them. One thing I observed, which looked well for us: they all got out upon the opposite side from Silver.

Well, there we stood, two on one side, five on the other, the pit between us, and nobody screwed up high enough to offer the first blow. Silver never moved; he watched them, very upright on his crutch, and looked as cool as ever I saw him. He was brave, and no mistake.

At last, Merry seemed to think a speech might help matters.

'Mates,' says he, 'there's two of them alone there; one's the old cripple that brought us all here and blundered us down to this; the other's that cub that I mean to have the heart of. Now, mates—'

He was raising his arm and his voice, and plainly meant to lead a charge. But just then—crack! crack! crack!—three musket-shots flashed out of the thicket. Merry tumbled head foremost into the excavation; the man with the bandage spun round like a teetotum,* and fell all his length upon his side, where he lay dead, but still twitching; and the other three turned and ran for it with all their might.

Before you could wink, Long John had fired two barrels of a pistol into the struggling Merry; and as the man rolled up his eyes at him in the last agony, 'George,' said he, 'I reckon I settled you.'

At the same moment the doctor, Gray, and Ben Gunn joined us, with smoking muskets, from among the nutmeg trees.

'Forward!' cried the doctor. 'Double quick, my lads. We must head 'em off the boats.'

And we set off at a great pace, sometimes plunging through the bushes to the chest.

I tell you, but Silver was anxious to keep up with us. The work that man went through, leaping on his crutch till the muscles of his chest were fit to burst, was work no sound man ever equalled; and so thinks the doctor. As it was, he was already thirty yards behind us, and on the verge of strangling,* when we reached the brow of the slope.

'Doctor,' he hailed, 'see there! no hurry!'

Sure enough there was no hurry. In a more open part of the plateau, we could see the three survivors still running in the same direction as they had started, right for Mizzen-mast Hill. We were already between them and the boats; and so we four sat down to breathe, while Long John, mopping his face, came slowly up with us.

'Thank ye kindly, doctor,' says he. 'You came in in about the nick, I guess, for me and Hawkins. And so it's you, Ben Gunn!' he added. 'Well, you're a nice one to be sure.'

'I'm Ben Gunn, I am,' replied the maroon, wriggling like an eel in his embarrassment. 'And,' he added, after a long pause, 'how do, Mr Silver? Pretty well, I thank ye, says you.'

'Ben, Ben,' murmured Silver, 'to think as you've done me!'

The doctor sent back Gray for one of the pickaxes, deserted, in their flight, by the mutineers; and then as we proceeded leisurely down hill to where the boats were lying, related, in a few words, what had taken place. It was a story that profoundly interested Silver; and Ben Gunn, the half-idiot maroon, was the hero from beginning to end.

Ben, in his long, lonely wanderings about the island, had found the skeleton—it was he that had rifled it; he had found the treasure; he had dug it up (it was the haft of his pickaxe that lay broken in the excavation); he had carried it on his back, in many weary journeys, from the foot of the tall pine to a cave he had on the two-pointed hill at the north-east angle of the island, and there it had lain stored in safety since two months before the arrival of the *Hispaniola*.

When the doctor had wormed this secret from him, on the afternoon of the attack, and when, next morning he saw the anchorage deserted, he had gone to Silver, given him the chart, which was now useless—given him the stores, for Ben Gunn's cave was well supplied with goats' meat salted by himself—given anything and everything to get a chance of moving in safety from the stockade to the two-pointed hill, there to be clear of malaria and keep a guard upon the money.

'As for you, Jim,' he said, 'it went against my heart, but I did what I thought best for those who had stood by their duty; and if you were not one of these, whose fault was it?'

That morning, finding that I was to be involved in the horrid disappointment he had prepared for the mutineers, he had run all the way to the cave, and, leaving the squire to guard the captain, had taken Gray and the maroon, and started, making the diagonal across the island, to be at hand beside the pine. Soon, however, he saw that our party had the start of him; and Ben Gunn, being fleet of foot, had been despatched in front to do his best alone. Then it had occurred to him to work upon the superstitions of his former shipmates; and he was so far successful that Gray and the doctor had come up and were already ambushed* before the arrival of the treasure-hunters.

'Ah', said Silver, 'it were fortunate for me that I had Hawkins here. You would have let old John be cut to bits, and never given it a thought, doctor.'

'Not a thought,' replied Doctor Livesey, cheerily.

And by this time we had reached the gigs. The doctor, with the pick-axe, demolished one of them, and then we all got aboard the other, and set out to go round by sea for North Inlet.

This was a run of eight or nine miles. Silver, though he was almost killed already with fatigue, was set to an oar, like the rest of us, and we were soon skimming swiftly over a smooth sea. Soon we passed out of the straits and doubled the south-east corner of the island, round which, four days ago, we had towed the *Hispaniola*. As we passed the two-pointed hill, we could see the black mouth of Ben Gunn's cave, and a figure standing by it, leaning on a musket. It was the squire; and we waved a handkerchief and gave him three cheers, in which the voice of Silver joined as heartily as any.

Three miles, farther, just inside the mouth of North Inlet, what should we meet but the *Hispaniola*, cruising by herself? The last flood had lifted her; and had there been much wind, or a strong tide current, as in the southern anchorage, we should never have found her more, or found her stranded beyond help. As it was, there was little amiss, beyond the wreck of the mainsail. Another anchor was got ready, and dropped in a fathom and a half of water. We all pulled round again to Rum Cove, the nearest point for Ben Gunn's treasure-house; and then Gray, single-handed, returned with the gig to the *Hispaniola*, where he was to pass the night on guard.

A gentle slope ran up from the beach to the entrance of the cave. At the top, the squire met us. To me he was cordial and kind, saying nothing of my escapade, either in the way of blame or praise. At Silver's polite salute he somewhat flushed.

'John Silver,' he said, 'you're a prodigious villain and impostor—a monstrous impostor, sir. I am told I am not to prosecute you. Well, then, I will not. But the dead men, sir, hang about your neck like millstones.'

'Thank you kindly, sir,' replied Long John, again saluting.

'I dare you to thank me!' cried the squire. 'It is a gross dereliction of my duty. Stand back.'

And thereupon we all entered the cave. It was a large, airy place, with a little spring and a pool of clear water, overhung with ferns. The floor was sand. Before a big fire lay Captain Smollett; and in a far corner, only duskily flickered over by the blaze, I beheld great heaps of coin and quadrilaterals built of bars of gold. That was Flint's treasure that we had come so far to seek, and that had cost already the lives of seventeen men from the *Hispaniola*. How many it had cost in the amassing, what blood and sorrow, what good ships scuttled on the deep, what brave men walking the plank blindfold, what shot of cannon, what shame and lies and cruelty, perhaps no man alive could tell. Yet there were still three upon that island—Silver, and old Morgan, and Ben Gunn—who had each taken his share in these crimes, as each had hoped in vain to share in the reward.

'Come in, Jim,' said the captain. 'You're a good boy in your line, Jim; but I don't think you and me'll go to sea again. You're too much of the born favourite for me. Is that you, John Silver? What brings you here, man?'

'Come back to my dooty, sir,' returned Silver.

'Ah!' said the captain; and that was all he said.

What a supper I had of it that night, with all my friends around me; and what a meal it was, with Ben Gunn's salted goat, and some delicacies and a bottle of old wine from the *Hispaniola*. Never, I am sure, were people gayer or happier. And there was Silver, sitting back almost out of the firelight, but eating heartily, prompt to spring forward when anything was wanted, even joining quietly in our laughter—the same bland, polite, obsequious seaman of the voyage out.

CHAPTER XXXIV

AND LAST

THE next morning we fell early to work, for the transportation of this great mass of gold near a mile by land to the beach, and thence three miles by boat to the *Hispaniola*, was a considerable task for so small a number of workmen. The three fellows still abroad upon the island did not greatly trouble us; a single sentry on the shoulder of the hill was sufficient to insure us against any sudden onslaught, and we thought, besides, they had had more than enough of fighting.

Therefore the work was pushed on briskly. Gray and Ben Gunn came and went with the boat, while the rest during their absences, piled treasure on the beach. Two of the bars, slung in a rope's-end, made a good load for a grown man—one that he was glad to walk slowly with. For my part, as I was not much use at carrying, I was kept busy all day in the cave, packing the minted money into bread-bags.

It was a strange collection, like Billy Bones's hoard for the diversity of coinage, but so much larger and so much more varied that I think I never had more pleasure than in sorting them. English, French, Spanish, Portuguese, Georges, and Louises, doubloons and double guineas and moidores and sequins,* the pictures of all the kings of Europe for the last hundred years, strange Oriental pieces stamped with what looked like wisps of string or bits of spider's web, round pieces and square pieces, and pieces bored through the middle, as if to wear them round your neck—nearly every variety of money in the world must, I think, have found a place in that collection; and for number, I am sure they were like autumn leaves, so that my back ached with stooping and my fingers with sorting them out.

Day after day this work went on; by every evening a fortune had been stowed aboard, but there was another fortune waiting for the morrow; and all this time we heard nothing of the three surviving mutineers.

At last—I think it was on the third night—the doctor and I were strolling on the shoulder of the hill where it overlooks the lowlands of the isle, when, from out the thick darkness below, the wind brought us a noise between shrieking and singing. It was only a snatch that reached our ears, followed by the former silence.

'Heaven forgive them,' said the doctor; ' 'tis the mutineers!'

'All drunk, sir,' struck in the voice of Silver from behind us.

Silver, I should say, was allowed his entire liberty, and, in spite of daily rebuffs, seemed to regard himself once more as quite a privileged and friendly dependant. Indeed, it was remarkable how well he bore these slights, and with what unwearying politeness he kept on trying to ingratiate himself with all. Yet, I think, none treated him better than a dog; unless it was Ben Gunn, who was still terribly afraid of his old quartermaster, or myself, who had really something to thank him for; although for that matter, I suppose, I had reason to think even worse of him than anybody else, for I had seen him meditating a fresh treachery upon the plateau. Accordingly, it was pretty gruffly that the doctor answered him.

'Drunk or raving,' said he.

'Right you were, sir,' replied Silver; 'and precious little odds which, to you and me.'

'I suppose you would hardly ask me to call you a humane man,' returned the doctor, with a sneer, 'and so my feelings may surprise you, Master Silver. But if I were sure they were raving—as I am morally certain one, at least, of them is down with fever—I should leave this camp, and, at whatever risk to my own carcase, take them the assistance of my skill.'

'Ask your pardon, sir, you would be very wrong,' quoth Silver. 'You would lose your precious life, and you may lay to that. I'm on your side now, hand and glove; and I shouldn't wish for to see the party weakened, let alone yourself, seeing as I know what I owes you. But these men down there, they couldn't keep their word—no, not supposing they wished to; and what's more, they couldn't believe as you could.'

'No,' said the doctor. 'You're the man to keep your word, we know that.'

Well, that was about the last news we had of the three pirates. Only once we heard a gunshot a great way off, and supposed them to be hunting. A council was held, and it was decided that we must desert them on the island—to the huge glee, I must say, of Ben Gunn, and with the strong approval of Gray. We left a good stock of powder and shot, the bulk of the salt goat, a few medicines, and some other necessaries, tools, clothing, a spare sail, a fathom or two of rope, and, by the particular desire of the doctor, a handsome present of tobacco.

That was about our last doing on the island. Before that, we had got the treasure stowed, and had shipped enough water and the remainder of the goat meat, in case of any distress; and at last, one fine morning, we weighed anchor, which was about all that we could manage, and stood out of North Inlet, the same colours flying that the captain had flown and fought under at the palisade.

The three fellows must have been watching us closer than we thought for, as we soon had proved. For, coming through the narrows, we had to lie very near the southern point, and there we saw all three of them kneeling together on a spit of sand, with their arms raised in supplication. It went to all our hearts, I think, to leave them in that wretched state; but we could not risk another mutiny; and to take them home for the gibbet would have been a cruel sort of kindness. The doctor hailed them and told them of the stores we had left, and where they were to find them. But they continued to call us by name, and appeal to us, for God's sake, to be merciful, and not leave them to die in such a place.

At last, seeing the ship still bore on her course, and was now swiftly drawing out of earshot, one of them—I know not which it was—leapt to his feet with a hoarse cry, whipped his musket to his shoulder, and sent a shot whistling over Silver's head and through the mainsail.

After that, we kept under cover of the bulwarks, and when next I looked out they had disappeared from the spit, and the spit itself had almost melted out of sight in the growing distance. That was, at least, the end of that; and before noon, to my inexpressible joy, the highest rock of Treasure Island had sunk into the blue round of sea.

We were so short of men, that everyone on board had to bear a hand—only the captain lying on a mattress in the stern and giving his orders; for, though greatly recovered he was still in want of quiet. We laid her head for the nearest port in Spanish America, for we could not risk the voyage home without fresh hands; and as it was, what with baffling winds and a couple of fresh gales, we were all worn out before we reached it.

It was just at sundown when we cast anchor in a most beautiful land-locked gulf, and were immediately surrounded by shore boats full of negroes, and Mexican Indians, and half-bloods, selling fruits and vegetables, and offering to dive for bits of money. The sight of so many good-humoured faces (especially the blacks), the taste of the tropical fruits, and above all, the lights that began to shine in the town, made a most charming contrast to our dark and bloody sojourn on the island; and the doctor and the squire, taking me along with them, went ashore to pass the early part of the night. Here they met the captain of an English man-of-war, fell in talk with him, went on board his ship, and, in short, had so agreeable a time, that day was breaking when we came alongside the *Hispaniola*.

Ben Gunn was on deck alone, and, as soon as we came on board, he began, with wonderful contortions, to make us a confession. Silver was gone. The maroon had connived at his escape in a shore boat some hours ago, and he now assured us he had only done so to preserve our lives, which would certainly have been forfeit if 'that man with the one leg had stayed aboard.' But this was not all. The sea-cook had not gone empty handed. He had cut through a bulkhead unobserved, and had removed one of the sacks of coin, worth, perhaps, three or four hundred guineas, to help him on his further wanderings.

I think we were all pleased to be so cheaply quit of him.*

Well, to make a long story short, we got a few hands on board, made a good cruise home, and the *Hispaniola* reached Bristol just as Mr Blandly was beginning to think of fitting out her consort. Five men only of those who had sailed returned with her. 'Drink and the devil had done for the rest,' with a vengeance; although, to be sure, we were not quite in so bad a case as that other ship they sang about:

'With one man of her crew alive,
What put to sea with seventy-five.'

All of us had an ample share of the treasure, and used it wisely or foolishly, according to our natures. Captain Smollett is now retired from the sea. Gray not only saved his money, but, being suddenly smit with the desire to rise, also studied his profession; and he is now mate and part owner of a fine full-rigged ship; married besides, and the father of a family. As for Ben Gunn, he got a thousand pounds, which he spent or lost in three weeks, or, to be more exact, in nineteen days, for he was back begging on the twentieth. Then he was given a lodge to keep, exactly as he had feared upon the island; and he still lives, a great favourite, though something of a butt, with the country boys, and a notable singer in church on Sundays and saints' days.

Of Silver we have heard no more. That formidable seafaring man with one leg has at last gone clean out of my life; but I daresay he met his old negress, and perhaps still lives in comfort with her and

Captain Flint. It is to be hoped so, I suppose, for his chances of comfort in another world are very small.

The bar silver and the arms still lie, for all that I know, where Flint buried them; and certainly they shall lie there for me. Oxen and wain-ropes* would not bring me back again to that accursed island; and the worst dreams that ever I have are when I hear the surf booming about its coasts, or start upright in bed, with the sharp voice of Captain Flint still ringing in my ears: 'Pieces of eight! pieces of eight!'

APPENDIX 1

MY FIRST BOOK

TREASURE ISLAND

[Probably written in 1893, this essay was first printed in *The Idler*, 4 (August 1894, 2–11), the humorous journal founded by Robert Barr and Jerome K. Jerome; in *McClure's Magazine,* 3 in the USA (September 1894, 283–93); and then in Jerome's *My First Book* (London: Chatto and Windus, 1894), 297–309—a volume that also contained essays by 'Q' (on *Dead Man's Cove*), Conan Doyle, and R. M. Ballantyne (who died in 1894).]

It was far indeed from being my first book, for I am not a novelist alone. But I am well aware that my paymaster, the Great Public, regards what else I have written with indifference, if not aversion; if it call upon me at all, it calls on me in the familiar and indelible character; and when I am asked to talk of my first book, no question in the world but what is meant is my first novel.

Sooner or later, somehow, anyhow, I was bound to write a novel. It seems vain to ask why. Men are born with various manias: from my earliest childhood, it was mine to make a plaything of imaginary series of events; and as soon as I was able to write, I became a good friend to the paper-makers. Reams upon reams must have gone to the making of 'Rathillet,' 'The Pentland Rising,'[1] 'The King's Pardon' (otherwise 'Park Whitehead'), 'Edward Daven,' 'A Country Dance,' and 'A Vendetta in the West'; and it is consolatory to remember that these reams are now all ashes, and have been received again into the soil. I have named but a few of my ill-fated efforts, only such indeed as came to a fair bulk ere they were desisted from; and even so they cover a long vista of years. 'Rathillet' was attempted before fifteen, 'The Vendetta' at twenty-nine, and the succession of defeats lasted unbroken till I was thirty-one. By that time, I had written little books and little essays and short stories; and had got patted on the back and paid for them—though not enough to live upon. I had quite a reputation, I was the successful man; I passed my days in toil, the futility of which would sometimes make my cheek to burn—that I should spend a man's energy upon this business, and yet could not earn a livelihood: and still there

[1] *Ne pas confondre.* Not the slim green pamphlet with the imprint of Andrew Elliot, for which (as I see with amazement from the book-lists) the gentlemen of England are willing to pay fancy prices; but its predecessor, a bulky historical romance without a spark of merit, and now deleted from the world.

shone ahead of me an unattained ideal: although I had attempted the thing with vigour not less than ten or twelve times, I had not yet written a novel. All—all my pretty ones—had gone for a little, and then stopped inexorably like a schoolboy's watch. I might be compared to a cricketer of many years' standing who should never have made a run. Anybody can write a short story—a bad one, I mean—who has industry and paper and time enough; but not everyone may hope to write even a bad novel. It is the length that kills. The accepted novelist may take his novel up and put it down, spend days upon it in vain, and write not any more than he makes haste to blot. Not so the beginner. Human nature has certain rights; instinct—the instinct of self-preservation—forbids that any man (cheered and supported by the consciousness of no previous victory) should endure the miseries of unsuccessful literary toil beyond a period to be measured in weeks. There must be something for hope to feed upon. The beginner must have a slant of wind, a lucky vein must be running, he must be in one of those hours when the words come and the phrases balance of themselves—*even to begin.* And having begun, what a dread looking forward is that until the book shall be accomplished! For so long a time, the slant is to continue unchanged, the vein to keep running, for so long a time you must keep at command the same quality of style: for so long a time your puppets are to be always vital, always consistent, always vigorous! I remember I used to look, in those days, upon every three-volume novel with a sort of veneration, as a feat—not possibly of literature—but at least of physical and moral endurance and the courage of Ajax.

In the fated year I came to live with my father and mother at Kinnaird, above Pitlochry. Then I walked on the red moors and by the side of the golden burn; the rude, pure air of our mountains inspirited, if it did not inspire us, and my wife and I projected a joint volume of bogey stories, for which she wrote 'The Shadow on the Bed,' and I turned out 'Thrawn Janet' and a first draft of 'The Merry Men.' I love my native air, but it does not love me; and the end of this delightful period was a cold, a fly-blister, and a migration by Strathairdle and Glenshee to the Castelton of Braemar. There it blew a good deal and rained in a proportion; my native air was more unkind than man's ingratitude,* and I must consent to pass a good deal of my time between four walls in a house lugubriously known as the Late Miss McGregor's Cottage. And now admire the finger of predestination. There was a schoolboy in the Late Miss McGregor's Cottage, home for the holidays, and much in want of 'something craggy to break his mind upon.' He had no thought of literature; it was the art of Raphael that received his fleeting suffrages; and with the aid of pen and ink and a shilling box of water colours, he had soon turned one of the rooms into a picture gallery. My more immediate duty towards the gallery was to be showman; but I would sometimes unbend a little, join the artist (so to speak) at the easel, and pass the afternoon with him in a generous emulation, making coloured drawings. On one of these occasions, I made the map of an island;* it was elaborately and (I thought) beautifully coloured; the shape of it took my fancy beyond expression; it contained harbours that pleased me like sonnets; and with the unconsciousness of the predestined, I ticketed my performance 'Treasure Island.' I am told there are people who do not care for maps, and find it hard to believe. The names, the shapes of the woodlands, the courses of the roads and rivers, the prehistoric footsteps of man still distinctly traceable up hill and down dale, the mills and the ruins, the ponds and the ferries, perhaps the *Standing Stone* or the *Druidic Circle* on the heath; here is an inexhaustible fund of interest for any man with eyes to see or twopenceworth of imagination to understand with! No child but must remember laying his head in the grass, staring into the infinitesimal forest and seeing it grow populous with fairy armies. Somewhat in this way, as I paused upon my map of 'Treasure Island,' the future character of the book began to appear there visibly among imaginary woods; and their brown faces and bright weapons peeped out upon me from unexpected quarters, as they passed to and fro, fighting and hunting treasure, on these few square inches of a flat projection. The next thing I knew I had some papers before me and was writing out a list of chapters. How often have I done so, and the thing gone no further! But there seemed elements of success about this enterprise. It was to be a story for boys; no need of psychology or fine writing; and I had a boy at hand to be a touchstone. Women were excluded. I was unable to handle a brig (which the *Hispaniola* should have been), but I thought I could make shift to sail her as a schooner without public shame. And then I had an idea for John Silver from which I promised myself funds of entertainment; to take an admired friend of mine (whom the reader very likely knows and admires as much as I do), to deprive him of all his finer qualities and higher graces of temperament, to leave him with nothing but his strength, his courage, his quickness, and his magnificent geniality, and to try to express these in terms of the culture of a raw tarpaulin. Such psychical surgery is, I think, a common way of 'making character'; perhaps it is, indeed, the only way. We can put in the quaint figure that spoke a hundred words with us yesterday by the wayside; but do we know him? Our friend, with his infinite variety and flexibility, we know—but can we put him in? Upon the first, we must engraft secondary and imaginary qualities, possibly all wrong; from the second, knife in hand, we must cut away and deduct the needless arborescence of his nature, but the trunk and the few branches that remain we may at least be fairly sure of.

On a chill September morning, by the cheek of a brisk fire, and the rain drumming on the window, I began *The Sea Cook,* for that was the original title. I have begun (and finished) a number of other books, but I cannot remember to have sat down to one of them with more complacency. It is not to be wondered at, for stolen waters are proverbially sweet. I am now upon a painful chapter. No doubt the parrot once belonged to Robinson Crusoe. No doubt the skeleton is conveyed from Poe. I think little of these, they are trifles and details; and no man can hope to have a monopoly of skeletons or make a corner in talking birds. The stockade, I am told, is from *Masterman Ready.* It may be I care not a jot. These useful writers had fulfilled the poet's saying: departing, they had left behind them

'Footprints on the sands of time;
Footprints that perhaps another*—'

and I was the other! It is my debt to Washington Irving that exercises my conscience, and justly so, for I believe plagiarism was rarely carried farther. I chanced to pick up the *Tales of a Traveller* some years ago with a view to an anthology of prose narrative, and the book flew up and struck me: Billy Bones, his chest, the company in the parlour, the whole inner spirit, and a good deal of the material detail of my first chapters—all were there, all were the property of Washington Irving. But I had no guess of it then as I sat writing by the fireside, in what seemed the spring-tides of a somewhat pedestrian inspiration; nor yet day by day, after lunch, as I read aloud my morning's work to the family. It seemed to me original as sin; it seemed to belong to me like my right eye. I had counted on one boy, I found I had two in my audience. My father caught fire at once with all the romance and childishness of his original nature. His own stories, that every night of his life he put himself to sleep with, dealt perpetually with ships, roadside inns, robbers, old sailors, and commercial travellers before the era of steam. He never finished one of these romances; the lucky man did not require to! But in *Treasure Island* he recognized something kindred to his own imagination; it was *his* kind of picturesque; and he not only heard with delight the daily chapter, but set himself acting to collaborate. When the time came for Billy Bones's chest to be ransacked, he must have passed the better part of a day preparing, on the back of a legal envelope, an inventory of its contents, which I exactly followed; and the name of 'Flint's old ship'—the *Walrus*—was given at his particular request. And now who should come dropping in, *ex machina*, but Dr Japp,* like the disguised prince who is to bring down the curtain upon peace and happiness in the last act; for he carried in his pocket, not a horn or a talisman, but a publisher—had, in fact, been charged by my old friend, Mr Henderson, to unearth new writers for *Young Folks.* Even the ruthlessness of a united family recoiled before the extreme measure of inflicting on our guest the mutilated members of *The Sea Cook*; at the same time, we would by no means stop our readings; and accordingly the tale was begun again at the beginning, and solemnly re-delivered for the benefit of Dr Japp. From that moment on, I have thought highly of his critical faculty; for when he left us, he carried away the manu-script in his portmanteau.

Here, then, was everything to keep me up, sympathy, help, and now a positive engagement. I had chosen besides a very easy style. Compare it with the almost contemporary *Merry Men*; one reader may prefer the one style, one the other—'tis an affair of character, perhaps of mood; but no expert can fail to see that the one is much more difficult, and the other much easier to maintain. It seems as though a full-grown experienced man of letters might engage to turn out *Treasure Island* at so many pages a day, and keep his pipe alight. But alas! this was not my case. Fifteen days I stuck to it, and turned out fifteen chapters; and then, in the early para-graphs of the sixteenth, ignominiously lost hold. My mouth was empty; there was not one word of *Treasure Island* in my bosom; and here were the proofs of the beginning already waiting me at the 'Hand and Spear'!* Then I corrected them, living for the most part alone, walking on the heath at Weybridge in dewy autumn mornings, a good deal pleased with what I had done, and more appalled than I can depict to you in words at what remained for me to do. I was thirty-one; I was the head of a family; I had lost my health; I had never yet paid my way, never yet made £200 a year; my father had quite recently bought back and cancelled a book that was judged a failure:* was this to be another and last fiasco? I was indeed very close on despair; but I shut my mouth hard, and during the journey to Davos, where I was to pass the winter, had the resolution to think of other things and bury myself in the novels of M. de Boisgobey.* Arrived at my destination, down I sat one morning to the unfinished tale; and behold! it flowed from me like small talk; and in a second tide of delighted industry, and again at a rate of a chapter a day, I finished *Treasure Island*. It had to be transcribed almost exactly; my wife was ill; the schoolboy remained alone of the faithful; and John Addington Symonds* (to whom I timidly men-tioned what I was engaged on) looked on me askance. He was at that time very eager I should write on the characters of Theophrastus: so far out may be the judgments of the wisest men. But Symonds (to be sure) was scarce the confidant to go to for sympathy on a boy's story. He was large-minded; 'a full man,' if there was one; but the very name of my enterprise would suggest to him only capitulations of sincerity and solecisms of style. Well! he was not far wrong.

Treasure Island—it was Mr Henderson who deleted the first title, *The Sea Cook*—appeared duly in the story paper, where it figured in the ignoble midst, without woodcuts,* and attracted not the least attention. I did not care. I liked the tale myself, for much the same reason as my father liked the beginning: it was my kind of picturesque. I was not a little proud of John Silver, also; and to this day rather admire that smooth and formidable adventurer. What was infinitely more exhilarating, I had passed a landmark; I had finished a tale, and written 'The End' upon my manuscript, as I had not done since 'The Pentland Rising,' when I was a boy of sixteen not yet at college. In truth it was so by a set of lucky accidents; had not Dr Japp come on his visit, had not the tale flowed from me with singular ease, it must have been laid aside like its predecessors, and found a circuitous and unlamented way to the fire. Purists may suggest it would have been better so. I am not of that mind. The tale seems to have given much pleasure, and it brought (or was the means of bringing) fire and food and wine to a deserving family in which I took an interest. I need scarcely say I mean my own.

But the adventures of *Treasure Island* are not yet quite at an end. I had written it up to the map. The map was the chief part of my plot. For instance, I had called an islet 'Skeleton Island,' not knowing what I meant, seeking only for the immediate picturesque, and it was to justify this name that I broke into the gallery of Mr Poe and stole Flint's pointer. And in the same way, it was because I had made two harbours that the *Hispaniola* was sent on her wanderings with Israel Hands. The time came when it was decided to republish, and I sent in my manuscript, and the map along with it, to Messrs. Cassell. The proofs came, they were corrected, but I heard nothing of the map. I wrote and asked; was told it had never been received, and sat aghast. It is one thing to draw a map at random, set a scale in one corner of it at a venture, and write up a story to the measurements. It is quite another to have to examine a whole book, make an inventory of all the allusions contained in it, and, with a pair of compasses, painfully design a map to suit the data. I did it; and the map was drawn again in my father's office, with embellishments of blowing whales and sailing ships, and my father himself brought into service a knack he had of various writing, and elaborately *forged* the signature of Captain Flint, and the sailing directions of Billy Bones. But somehow it was never *Treasure Island* to me.

I have said the map was the most of the plot. I might almost say it was the whole. A few reminiscences of Poe, Defoe, and Washington Irving, a copy of Johnson's *Buccaneers*, the name of the Dead Man's Chest from Kingsley's *At Last*, some recollections of canoeing on the high seas, and the map itself, with its infinite, eloquent suggestion, made up the whole of my materials. It is, perhaps, not often that a map figures so largely in a tale, yet it is always important. The author must know his countryside, whether real or imaginary, like his hand; the distances, the points of the compass, the place of the sun's rising, the behaviour of the moon, should all be beyond cavil. And how troublesome the moon is! I have come to grief over the moon in *Prince Otto*, and so soon as that was pointed out to me, adopted a precaution which I recommend to other men—I never write now without an almanack. With an almanack, and the map of the country, and the plan of every house, either actually plotted on paper or already and immediately apprehended in the mind, a man may hope to avoid some of the grossest possible blunders. With the map before him, he will scarce allow the sun to set in the east, as it does in *The Antiquary.* With the almanack at hand, he will scarce allow two horsemen, journeying on the most urgent affair, to employ six days, from three of the Monday morning till late in the Saturday night, upon a journey of, say, ninety or a hundred miles, and before the week is out, and still on the same nags, to cover fifty in one day, as may be read at length in the inimitable novel of *Rob Roy.* And it is certainly well, though far from necessary, to avoid such 'croppers.' But it is my contention—my superstition, if you like—that who is faithful to his map, and consults it, and draws from it his inspiration, daily and hourly, gains positive support, and not mere negative immunity from accident. The tale has a root there; it grows in that soil; it has a spine of its own behind the words. Better if the country be real, and he has walked every foot of it and knows every milestone. But even with imaginary places, he will do well in the beginning to provide a map; as he studies it, relations will appear that he had not thought upon; he will discover obvious, though unsuspected, short-cuts and footprints for his messengers; and even when a map is not all the plot, as it was in *Treasure Island*, it will be found to be a mine of suggestion.

APPENDIX 2

A FABLE

THE PERSONS OF THE TALE

[Written between 1881 and 1894, and published in *Longmans Magazine* (1895), and in *Strange Case of Dr Jekyll and Mr Hyde. With Other Fables* (London: Longmans Green, 1896). Reprinted from the Tusitala Edition (1923), ii. 223–6.]

AFTER the 32nd chapter of *Treasure Island*, two of the puppets strolled out to have a pipe before business should begin again, and met in an open place not far from the story.

'Good morning, Cap'n,' said the first, with a man-o'-war salute and a beaming countenance.

'Ah, Silver!' grunted the other. 'You're in a bad way, Silver.'

'Now, Cap'n Smollett,' remonstrated Silver, 'dooty is dooty, as I knows, and none better; but we're off dooty now; and I can't see no call to keep up the morality business.'

'You're a damned rogue, my man,' said the Captain.

'Come, come, Cap'n, be just,' returned the other. 'There's no call to be angry with me in earnest. I'm on'y a chara'ter in a sea story. I don't really exist.'

'Well, I don't really exist either,' says the Captain, 'which seems to meet that.'

'I wouldn't set no limits to what a virtuous chara'ter might consider argument,' responded Silver. 'But I'm the villain of this tale, I am; and speaking as one seafaring man to another, what I want to know is, what's the odds?'

'Were you never taught your catechism?' said the Captain. 'Don't you know there's such a thing as an Author?'

'Such a thing as a Author?' returned John, derisively. 'And who better'n me? And the p'int is, if the Author made you, he made Long John, and he made Hands, and Pew, and George Merry—not that George is up to much, for he's little more'n a name; and he made Flint, what there is of him; and he made this here mutiny, you keep such a work about; and he had Tom Redruth shot; and—well, if that's a Author, give me Pew!'

'Don't you believe in a future state?' said Smollett. 'Do you think there's nothing but the present story-paper?'

'I don't rightly know for that,' said Silver; 'and I don't see what it's got to do with it anyway. What I know is this: if there is sich a thing as a

Author, I'm his favourite chara'ter. He does me fathoms better'n he does you—fathoms, he does. And he likes doing me. He keeps me on deck mostly all the time, crutch and all; and he leaves you measling in the hold, where nobody can't see you, nor wants to, and you may lay to that! If there is a Author, by thunder, but he's on my side, and you may lay to it!'

'I see he's giving you a long rope,' said the Captain. 'But that can't change a man's convictions. I know the Author respects me; I feel it in my bones; when you and I had that talk at the blockhouse door, who do you think he was for, my man?'

'And don't he respect me?' cried Silver. 'Ah, you should 'a' heard me putting down my mutiny, George Merry and Morgan and that lot, no longer ago'n last chapter; you'd 'a' heard something then! You'd 'a' seen what the Author thinks o' me! But come now, do you consider yourself a virtuous chara'ter clean through?'

'God forbid!' said Captain Smollett solemnly. 'I am a man that tries to do his duty, and makes a mess of it as often as not. I'm not a very popular man at home, Silver, I'm afraid,' and the Captain sighed.

'Ah,' says Silver. 'Then how about this sequel of yours? Are you to be Cap'n Smollett just the same as ever, and not very popular at home, says you! And if so, why it's *Treasure Island* over again, by thunder; and I'll be Long John, and Pew'll be Pew; and we'll have another mutiny, as like as not. Or are you to be somebody else? And if so, why, what the better are you? and what the worse am I?'

'Why, look here, my man,' returned the Captain, 'I can't understand how this story comes about at all, can I? I can't see how you and I, who don't exist, should get to speaking here, and smoke our pipes for all the world like reality? Very well, then, who am I to pipe up with my opinions? I know the Author's on the side of good; he tells me so, it runs out of his pen as he writes. Well, that's all I need to know; I'll take my chance upon the rest.'

'It's a fact he seemed to be against George Merry,' Silver admitted musingly. 'But George is little more'n a name at the best of it,' he added brightening. 'And to get into soundings for once. What is this good? I made a mutiny, and I been a gentleman o' fortune; well, but by all stories, you ain't no such saint. I'm a man that keeps company very easy; even by your own account, you ain't, and to my certain knowledge, you're a devil to haze. Which is which? Which is good, and which bad? Ah, you tell me that! Here we are in stays, and you may lay to it!'

'We're none of us perfect,' replied the Captain. 'That's a fact of religion, my man. All I can say is, I try to do my duty; and if you try to do yours, I can't compliment you on your success.'

'And so you was the judge, was you?' said Silver, derisively.

'I would be both judge and hangman for you, my man, and never turn a hair,' returned the Captain. 'But I get beyond that: it mayn't be sound theology, but it's common sense, that what is good is useful too—or there and thereabout, for I don't set up to be a thinker. Now, where would a story go to, if there were no virtuous characters?'

'If you go to that,' replied Silver, 'where would a story begin, if there wasn't no villains?'

'Well, that's pretty much my thought,' said Captain Smollett. 'The author has to get a story; that's what he wants; and to get a story, and to have a man like the doctor (say) given a proper chance, he has to put in men like you and Hands. But he's on the right side; and you mind your eye! You're not through this story yet; there's trouble coming for you.'

'What'll you bet?' asked John.

'Much I care if there ain't,' returned the Captain. 'I'm glad enough to be Alexander Smollett, bad as he is; and I thank my stars upon my knees that I'm not Silver. But there's the ink-bottle opening. To quarters!'

And indeed the author was just then beginning to write the words:

CHAPTER XXXIII

APPENDIX 3
SOURCES AND ANALOGUES

In 'My First Book', Stevenson 'confessed' to borrowing from Defoe's *Robinson Crusoe*, Edgar Allan Poe, Captain Marryat's *Masterman Ready*, and plagiarizing Washington Irving. He was drawing on a rich heritage of sea stories, and some of the more striking parallels are reprinted here.

In Washington Irving's 'Wolfert Webber; or Golden Dreams' in *Tales of a Traveller* [by Geoffrey Crayon, Gent, 1824] an old seaman at the village inn is described thus:

> The inn had been aroused several months before, on a dark stormy night, by repeated long shouts, that seemed like the howlings of a wolf. They came from the water-side; and at length were distinguished to be hailing the house in the seafaring manner. 'House-a-hoy!' . . . On approaching the place from whence the voice proceeded, they found this amphibious-looking personage at the water's edge, quite alone, and seated on a great oaken sea-chest. How he came there, whether he had been set on shore from some boat, or had floated to land on his chest, nobody could tell, for he did not seem disposed to answer questions, and there was something in his looks and manners that put a stop to all questioning. Suffice it to say, he took possession of a corner room of the inn, to which his chest was removed with great difficulty. Here he had remained ever since, keeping about the inn and its vicinity. . . . He always appeared to have plenty of money, though often of very strange, outlandish coinage; and he regularly paid his bill every evening before turning in.
>
> He had fitted up his room to his own fancy, having slung a hammock from the ceiling instead of a bed, and decorated the walls with rusty pistols and cutlasses of foreign workmanship. A great part of his time was passed in this room, seated by the window, which commanded a wide view of the Sound, a short old-fashioned pipe in his mouth, a glass of rum toddy at his elbow, and a pocket telescope in his hand, with which he reconnoitred every boat that moved upon the water. Large square-rigged vessels seemed to excite but little attention; but the moment he descried any thing with a shoulder-of-mutton sail, or that a barge, or yawl, or jolly boat hove in sight, up went the telescope, and he examined it with the most scrupulous attention.
>
> All this might have passed without much notice, for in those times the province was so much the resort of adventurers of all characters and

climes that any oddity in dress or behavior attracted but little attention. But in a little while this strange sea monster, thus strangely cast up on dry land, began to encroach upon the long-established customs and customers of the place; to interfere in a dictatorial manner in the affairs of the ninepin alley and the bar-room, until in the end he usurped an absolute command over the little inn. It was in vain to attempt to withstand his authority. He was not exactly quarrelsome, but boisterous and peremptory, like one accustomed to tyrannize on a quarter deck; and there was a dare-devil air about every thing he said and did, that inspired a wariness in all bystanders. Even the half-pay officer, so long the hero of the club, was soon silenced by him; and the quiet burghers stared with wonder at seeing their inflammable man of war so readily and quietly extinguished.

And then the tales that he would tell were enough to make a peaceable man's hair stand on end. There was not a sea fight, or marauding or free-booting adventure that had happened within the last twenty years but he seemed perfectly versed in it. He delighted to talk of the exploits of the buccaneers in the West-Indies and on the Spanish Main . . . If any one, however, pretended to contradict him in any of his stories he was on fire in an instant. His very cocked hat assumed a momentary fierceness, and seemed to resent the contradiction.—'How the devil should you know as well as I! I tell you it was as I say!' and he would at the same time let slip a broadside of thundering oaths and tremendous sea phrases, such as had never been heard before within those peaceful walls . . .

The landlord was almost in despair, but he knew not how to get rid of this sea monster and his sea-chest, which seemed to have grown like fixtures, or excrescences on his establishment.

James Fenimore Cooper's *The Sea Lions* (1849) hinges upon the treasure map owned by a dying seaman, Thomas Daggett, who is interviewed by the greedy deacon Pratt:

'I wish you would show me, yourself, the precise places on the chart, where them islands are to be found. There is nothing like seeing a thing with one's own eyes.'

'You forget my oath, deacon Pratt. Every man on us took his bible oath not to point out the position of the islands, until a'ter the year 1820. Then, each and all on us is at liberty to do as he pleases. But, the chart is in my chest, and not only the islands, but the key, is so plainly laid down, that any mariner could find 'em. With that chest, however, I cannot part so long as I live. Get me well, and I will sail in the *Sea Lion*, and tell your captain Gar'ner all he will have occasion to know. The man's fortune will be made who first gets to either of them places.' . . .

'You think there was no mistake in the pirate's account of that key, and of the buried treasure?' asked the deacon, anxiously.

'I would swear to the truth of what he said, as freely as if I had seen the box myself. They was necessitated, as you may suppose, or they never would have left so much gold, in sich an uninhabited place; but leave it they did, on the word of a dying man.' . . .

'I see but one thing needful just now, and that is that you should give me the chart at once, in order that I may study it well, before the schooner sails.'

'Do you mean to make the v'y'ge yourself, deacon?' asked Daggett, in some surprise. (chapter 3)

Later, when Daggett dies, Pratt opens his sea chest:

Certainly, nothing like treasure presented itself to his eyes, when all that Daggett had left behind him lay exposed to view. The chest of a common sailor is usually but ill-furnished unless it may be just after his return from a long and well-paid voyage, and before he has had time to fall back on his purchases of clothes, as a fund to supply his cravings for personal gratification. This of Daggett's formed no exception to the rule. The few clothes it contained were of the lightest sort, having been procured in warm climates, and were well worn, in addition. The palms, needles, and shells, and carving in whale-bone, had all been sold, to meet their owner's wants, and nothing of that sort remained. There were two old, dirty, and ragged charts, and on these the deacon laid his hands, much as the hawk, in its swoop, descends on its prey. As it did, however, a tremor came over him, that actually compelled him to throw himself into a chair, and to rest for a moment.

The first of the charts opened, the deacon saw at a glance, was that of the Antarctic circle. There, sure enough, was laid down in ink, three or four specks for islands, with lat. —°, —″, and long. —°., —″, written out at its side. We are under obligations not to give the figures that stand on the chart, for the discovery is deemed to be important, by those who possess the secret, even to the present hour. We are at liberty to tell the whole story, with this one exception; and we shall proceed to do so, with a proper regard to the pledges made in the premises.

The deacon scarcely breathed as he assured himself of the important fact just mentioned, and his hands trembled to such a degree as to fairly cause the paper of the chart to rattle. Then he had recourse to an expedient that was strictly characteristic of the man. He wrote the latitude and longitude in a memorandum-book that he carried on his person; after which he again sat down, and with great care erased the island and the writing from the chart, with the point of a penknife. (chapter 4)

The sea jargon that Stevenson uses gives an authentic flavour to *Treasure Island* but may also be a private joke. Captain Marryat, in *Peter Simple* (1834), had taken a similar pleasure in sailors' language, but that was at the expense of the character:

> I went on the quarter-deck. All the sailors were busy at work, and the first lieutenant cried out to the gunner, 'Now, Mr Dispart, if you're ready, we'll breech these guns.'
>
> 'Now, my lads,' said the first lieutenant, 'we must slue (the part the breeches cover) more forward.' As I never heard of a gun having breeches, I was very anxious to see what was going on, and went up close to the first lieutenant, who said to me, 'Youngster, hand me that *monkey's tail.*' I saw nothing like a *monkey's tail*; but I was so frightened that I snatched up the first thing that I saw, which was a short bar of iron, and it so happened that it was the very article which he wanted. When I gave it to him, the first lieutenant looked at me, and said, 'So you know what a monkey's tail is already, do you? Now don't you ever sham stupid after that.'
>
> Thought I to myself, I'm very lucky, but if that's a monkey's tail it's a very stiff one!
>
> I resolved to learn the names of every thing as fast as I could, that I might be prepared, so I listened attentively to what was said; but I soon became quite confused, and despaired of remembering anything.
>
> 'Mr Chucks,' said the first lieutenant to the boatswain, 'what blocks have we below—not on charge?'
>
> 'Let me see, sir, I've one *sister*, t'other we split in half the other day, and I think I have a couple of *monkeys* down in the store-room.—I say, you Smith, pass that brace through the *bull's eye*, and take the *sheepshank* out before you come down.'
>
> 'And, Mr Chucks, recollect this afternoon that you *bleed* all the *buoys.*'
>
> Bleed the boys! thought I, what can that be for? at all events, the surgeon appears to be the proper person to perform that operation.
>
> This last incomprehensible remark drove me off the deck. (chapter 6)

Long John Silver's attempt to keep his crew sober may be an echo from Captain Marryat's *The Pirate* (1836). During a storm, the crew want to break into the spirit room, and they're stopped by Oswald, the mate, who says: 'Do you call yourselves men, when, for the sake of a little liquor now, you would lose your only chance of getting drunk every day as soon as we get on shore again? There's a time for all things; and I've a notion this is a time to be sober.' (chapter 4)

In Captain Marryat's *Masterman Ready* (1841, chapters 42–5) the Seagraves' stockade is attacked by savages. There are protracted fights, and the defenders suffer from thirst, as their spring is not inside the stockade. Masterman Ready is fatally wounded while fetching water. A similar battle is described in W. H. Kingston's *The Early Life of Old Jack* (1859), when Captain Helfrich and his party hold a planter's house against runaway slaves (maroons):

> The maroons did not leave us long in suspense . . . Loopholes had been left in all the windows, and every now and then I peeped through one of them, to try and discover what was taking place . . . Captain Helfrich was watching [the maroons] . . . 'Now, my lads, give it to them! Don't throw your shots away on the bushes!'
>
> Obedient to the order, every man in the house fired, and continued firing as fast as he could load his musket. I dropped on my knee alongside the arms the captain had appropriated, and as I handed a loaded musket to him, he gave me back the one he had fired, which I reloaded as fast as I could . . . As yet none of our people had been killed, though some of the enemy's shot had found their way through the loopholes in the windows and doors. Growing, however, more desperate at the loss of their companions . . . they rushed up closer to the house, pouring in their fire, which searched out every hole and cranny . . . A poor fellow was standing at the window next to me. A bullet struck him in the breast . . . down he fell, crying out piteously . . . I tried to place him in a sitting posture, but he fell back again.
>
> 'Let him alone, Jack,' cried the captain, 'his work is done; he is no longer a slave.' . . .
>
> . . . 'So my men, let us sally out, and sell our lives dearly . . .' As he said this, he seized a cutlass that lay on the ground . . . and rushed through the back door . . . (i.5)

Jim Hawkins's voyage in the coracle has some similarities to another of Washington Irving's *Tales of a Traveller* (1824), the story 'Hell Gate'.

> About six miles from the renowned city of the Manhattoes, and in that Sound, or arm of the sea, which passes between the main land and Nassau or Long Island, there is a narrow strait, where the current is violently compressed between shouldering promontories, and horribly irritated and perplexed by rocks and shoals. Being at the best of times a very violent, hasty current, it takes these impediments in mighty dudgeon; boiling in whirlpools; brawling and fretting in ripples and breakers; and, in short, indulging in all kinds of wrong-headed paroxysms. At such times, woe to any unlucky vessel that ventures within its clutches.
>
> This termagant humor is said to prevail only at half tides. At low water it is as pacific as any other stream. As the tide rises, it begins to

> fret; at half tide it rages and roars as if bellowing for more water; but when the tide is full it relapses again into quiet . . . This mighty, blustering, bullying little strait was a place of great difficulty and danger to the Dutch navigators of ancient days; hectoring their tub-built barks in a most unruly style; whirling them about, in a manner to make any but a Dutchman giddy, and not unfrequently stranding them upon rocks and reefs.

The discussion between Israel Hands and Jim Hawkins aboard the *Hispaniola* can be read as a parody of a scene in R. M. Ballantyne's *The Coral Island* (1857). The young Ralph Rover is alone on a schooner (which has a brass swivel-mounted cannon) with the wounded pirate Bloody Bill, for whom he gets brandy and biscuit from below decks. He then lashes the helm:

> 'And what will you do [Bill said] if it comes on to blow a storm?'
>
> This question silenced me, while I considered what I should do in such a case. At length I laid my hand on his arm, and said, 'Bill, when a man has done all that he can do, he ought to leave the rest to God.'
>
> 'O Ralph,' said my companion in a faint voice, looking anxiously into my face. 'I wish that I had the feelin's about God that you seem to have, at this hour. I'm dyin', Ralph; yet I, who have braved death a hundred times, am afraid to die. I'm afraid to enter the next world. Something within tells me there will be a reckoning when I go there. But it's all over with me, Ralph. I feel that there's no chance o' my bein' saved.'
>
> 'Don't say that, Bill,' said I in deep compassion; 'don't say that. I'm quite sure there's hope even for you, but I can't remember the words of the Bible that make me think so. Is there not a Bible on board, Bill?'
>
> 'No; the last that was in the ship belonged to a poor boy that was taken aboard against his will. He died, poor lad—I think through ill-treatment and fear. After he was gone the captain found his Bible and flung it overboard.'
>
> I now reflected, with great sadness and self-reproach, on the way in which I had neglected my Bible; and it flashed across me that I was actually in the sight of God a greater sinner than this blood-stained pirate; for, thought I, he tells me that he never read the Bible, and was never brought up to care for it; whereas I was carefully taught to read it by my own mother, and had read it daily as long as I possessed one, yet to so little purpose that I could not now call to mind a single text that would meet this poor man's case, and afford him the consolation he so much required. I was much distressed, and taxed my memory for a long time. At last a text did flash into my mind, and I wondered much that I had not thought of it before.

'Bill,' said I in a low voice, '"Believe on the Lord Jesus Christ, and thou shalt be saved."'

'Ay, Ralph, I've heard the missionaries say that before now, but what good can it do me? It's not for me, that; it's not for the likes o' me . . .'

'Bill,' said I, '"Though your sins be red like crimson, they shall be white as snow." Only believe.'

'Only believe!' cried Bill, starting up on his elbow. 'I've heard men talk o' believing as if it was easy. Ha! 'tis easy enough for a man to point to a rope and say, "I believe that would bear my weight;" but 'tis another thing for a man to catch hold o' that rope and swing himself by it over the edge of a precipice!'

The energy with which he said this, and the action with which it was accompanied, were too much for Bill. He sank back with a deep groan. As if the very elements sympathised with this man's sufferings, a low moan came sweeping over the sea.

'Hist, Ralph!' said Bill, opening his eyes; 'there's a squall coming, lad. Look alive, boy! Clew up the fore-sail. Drop the main-sail peak. Them squalls come quick sometimes.' (chapter 27)

In James F. Bowman's *The Island Home* (1852), a source for *The Coral Island*, one of the crew of the *Washington* takes refuge from mutineers at the ship's foretop, but is persuaded to descend when threatened with a fowling-piece (chapter 3).

Jim Hawkins's encounter with Long John Silver when he returns to the stockade has some similarities to the behaviour of Ambrose in 'Alone in the Pirate's Lair', in *Boys of England,* 1 (1866), while in Ballantyne's *The Coral Island*, Ralph Rover, captured by pirates, throws a keg of gunpowder overboard so that it will be washed ashore to his friends, and confronts the captain:

'I don't know what stuff I'm made of—I never thought much about that subject—but I'm quite certain of this, that I am made of such stuff as the like of you shall never tame, though you should do your worst.'

To my surprise the captain, instead of flying into a rage, smiled, and thrusting his hand into the voluminous shawl that encircled his waist, turned on his heel and walked aft, while I went below.

Here, instead of being rudely handled, as I had expected, the men received me with a shout of laughter, and one of them, patting me on the back, said, 'Well done, lad! you're a brick, and I have no doubt will turn out a rare cove. Bloody Bill there was just such a fellow as you are, and he's now the biggest cut-throat of us all.' (chapter 22)

'No doubt,' Stevenson wrote in 'My First Book', 'the skeleton is conveyed from Poe.' He may have been thinking of the way in which Captain Flint disposed of his helpers; in 'The Gold Bug' (1843), Poe wrote:

> '. . . and now there is only one point which puzzles me. What are we to make of the skeletons found in the hole?'
>
> 'That is a question I am no more able to answer than yourself. There seems, however, only one plausible way of accounting for them—and yet it is dreadful to believe in such atrocity as my suggestion would imply. It is clear that Kidd—if Kidd indeed secreted this treasure, which I doubt not—it is clear that he must have had assistance in the labor. But this labor concluded, he may have thought it expedient to remove all participants in his secret. Perhaps a couple of blows with a mattock were sufficient, while his coadjutors were busy in the pit; perhaps it required a dozen—who shall tell?'

'The Gold Bug', like *Treasure Island*, ends with the treasure being counted:

> Having assorted all with care, we found ourselves possessed of even vaster wealth than we had at first supposed. In coin there was rather more than four hundred and fifty thousand dollars—estimating the value of the pieces, as accurately as we could, by the tables of the period. There was not a particle of silver. All was gold of antique date and of great variety—French, Spanish, and German money, with a few English guineas, and some counters, of which we had never seen specimens before. There were several very large and heavy coins, so worn that we could make nothing of their inscriptions. There was no American money. The value of the jewels we found more difficulty in estimating. There were diamonds—some of them exceedingly large and fine—a hundred and ten in all, and not one of them small; eighteen rubies of remarkable brilliancy;—three hundred and ten emeralds, all very beautiful; and twenty-one sapphires, with an opal. These stones had all been broken from their settings and thrown loose in the chest.

EXPLANATORY NOTES

ABBREVIATIONS

Dear and Kemp	I. C. B. Dear and Peter Kemp, *The Oxford Companion to Ships and the Sea*, 2nd edn. (Oxford: Oxford University Press, 2005)
Letters	*The Letters of Robert Louis Stevenson*, 8 vols., ed. Bradford A. Booth and Ernest Mehew (New Haven: Yale University Press, 1994–5)
Pyrates	[Daniel Defoe], *A General History of the Pyrates*, ed. Manuel Schonhorn (Mineola, NY: Dover, 1999)
SOED	*Shorter Oxford English Dictionary*
Tusitala Edition	*The Works of Robert Louis Stevenson*, Tusitala Edition (London: William Heinemann in association with Chatto and Windus, Cassell, and Longmans, Green, 1923–4)

TO THE HESITATING PURCHASER

3 *maroons*: people cast ashore by buccaneers as a punishment; originally, runaway slaves in the West Indies.

Buccaneers: in the late sixteenth century, the Carib Indians' name in the Arawak language for dried meat was 'boucan'; this was applied by French adventurers to the English 'freebooters' on Hispaniola, whose target was Spanish treasure ships. Stevenson makes no distinction between 'buccaneers' and 'pirates' who were, technically, the historical successors of the buccaneers, preying on ships of any country.

Kingston . . . Cooper: W. H. G. Kingston (1814–80), whose first boys' book was *Peter the Whaler* (1851). He wrote more than 130 books, and the first serial in the *Boy's Own Paper* (1879). R. M. Ballantyne's (1825–94) seventy-two carefully researched adventure stories included *The Coral Island* (1858), *Martin Rattler* (1858), and *The Dog Crusoe* (1861) (see W. O. G. Lofts and D. J. Adley, *The Men Behind Boys' Fiction* (London: Howard Barker, 1970), 46–7). Stevenson met Ballantyne briefly in the mid-1860s, probably when Ballantyne was visiting David Stevenson for his research for *The Lighthouse* (1865). Eric Quayle recounts how Stephenson, at the age of 15, invited Ballantyne to dinner at his uncle's house, Colington Manse in Leith, and told him that he had read *The Coral Island* twice 'and hoped to read it twice more'. Stevenson, however, claimed to have been tongue-tied. On Ballantyne's death, Stevenson subscribed to a memorial fund, suggesting that the bulk of the money go to Ballantyne's family. He also commented that Ballantyne's works 'scarce seem to me designed for immortality' (Eric Quayle, *Ballantyne the Brave* (London: Hart-Davis,

1967), 217, 298–9; Robert Louis Stevenson, 'Memoirs of Himself', Tusitala Edition (1924), xxix. 161).

James Fenimore Cooper (1789–1851) was perhaps most famous for his five 'Leatherstocking' novels, from *The Pioneers* (1823) to *The Deerslayer* (1841). He also wrote eleven novels of the sea, including *The Pilot* (1824), which has some claim to be the originator of 'sea-fiction', and *The Sea-Lions* (1849), which hinges upon a treasure map owned by a dying seaman.

4 [*dedication*] *S. L. O.*: Samuel Lloyd Osbourne, Stevenson's stepson, known as Sam until 1886. In later editions the dedication reads 'To Lloyd Osbourne'.

TREASURE ISLAND

9 *Trelawney*: in a letter to W. E. Henley (24/25 Aug., 1881) Stevenson wrote that the book has 'a fine old Squire Trelawney (the real Tre, purged of literature and sin, to shuit [*sic*] the infant mind) . . . My Trelawney has a strong dash of Landor, as I see him from here' (*Letters*, iii. 225). He was referring to Edward John Trelawny (1792–1881), author of *Adventures of a Younger Son* (1831) and *Records of Shelley, Byron and the Author* (1878). He is the subject of a popular picture by John Everett Millais, *The Northwest Passage* (1874). Walter Savage Landor (1775–1864) was quick-tempered but well liked; Dickens caricatured him as Boythorn in *Bleak House*.

'Admiral Benbow': the inn is appropriately named after John Benbow (1653–1702) who was commander of the King's ships in the West Indies in pursuit of pirates (1698, 1701). The second act of *Admiral Guinea*, the play written in collaboration with W. E. Henley, is set here. There was an inn with the same name in Captain Lyons's *The Boy Sailor* (Newsagents' Publishing Company, 1865; repr. in Brett's Boy's Library as *Harry Halliard*, 1879) (see Kevin Carpenter, *Desert Isles and Pirate Islands: The Island Theme in Nineteenth-Century English Juvenile Fiction, A Survey and Bibliography* (Frankfurt am Main: Peter Lang, 1984), 83).

under our roof: in his essay 'A Gossip on Romance' (*Longman's Magazine*, 1882, collected in *Memories and Portraits*, 1887), Stevenson wrote: 'For my part, I liked a story to begin with an old wayside inn where, "toward the close of the year 17—," several gentlemen in three-cocked hats were playing bowls . . . I can still hear that merry clatter of the hoofs along the midnight lane . . . and the words "post-chaise," the "great North road," "ostler," and "nag" still sound in my ears like poetry' (Tusitala Edition (1924), xxix. 119–20).

tarry pigtail: sailors frequently braided their hair and kept it in place with Stockholm tar, used to treat rigging. This is a possible root of the word 'tar' meaning sailor. 'Jack Tar' was first used in William Congreve's *Love for Love* (1695).

livid white: in Washington Irving's story, 'Wolfert Webber; or Golden Dreams', from *Tales of a Traveller* [by Geoffrey Crayon, Gent, 1824] there is a stranger at the inn

> who seemed . . . completely at home in the chair and the tavern. He was rather under-size, but deep-chested, square, and muscular. His broad shoulders, double joints, and bow-knees, gave tokens of prodigious strength. His face was dark and weather-beaten; a deep scar, as if from the slash of a cutlass, had almost divided his nose, and made a gash in his upper lip, through which his teeth shone like a bull-dog's. A mass of iron gray hair gave a grizzly finish to his hard-favored visage. His dress was of an amphibious character. He wore an old hat edged with tarnished lace, and cocked in martial style, on one side of his head; a rusty blue military coat with brass buttons, and a wide pair of short petticoat trousers, or rather breeches, for they were gathered up at the knees. He ordered every body about him with an authoritative air; talked in a brattling voice, that sounded like the crackling of thorns under a pot; damned the landlord and servants with perfect impunity.

Stevenson wrote in 'My First Book' (see Appendix 1): 'Billy Bones, his chest, the company in the parlour, the whole inner spirit, and a good deal of the material detail of my first chapters—all were there, all were the property of Washington Irving.' J. C. Furnas noted that 'anyone needing example of the difference between fuzzy and hard-twist writing should read the original Irving and then what Louis did with the same materials filtered through discipline' (*Voyage to Windward: The Life of Robert Louis Stevenson* (London: Faber and Faber, 1952), 182).

the dead man's chest: in mid-November 1887, Stevenson wrote to John Paul Bocock: 'The shanty in *Treasure Island* is my own invention entirely; founded on one of the Buccaneer islets' (*Letters*, vi. 56). Dead Chest Island is in what are now the British Virgin Islands between Peter Island and Tortola Island. The pirate Blackbeard (Edward Teach) is said to have marooned mutineers there *c.*1717; fifteen survived. Stevenson wrote to his friend Sidney Colvin (late May 1884) '*Treasure Island* came out of Kingsley's *At Last*; where I got the 'Dead Man's Chest'—that was the seed' (*Letters*, iv. 300). Kingsley's text reads:

> We were crawling slowly along . . . and were away in a gray shoreless world of waters, were looking out for Virgin Gorda; the first of those numberless isles which Columbus, so goes the tale, discovered on St. Ursula's day, and named them after the Saint and her eleven thousand mystical virgins. Unfortunately, English buccaneers have since then given to most of them less poetic names. The Dutchman's Cap, Broken Jerusalem, The Dead Man's Chest, Rum Island, and so forth, mark a time and a race more prosaic, but still more terrible . . . than the Spanish Conquistadores. (*At Last: a Christmas in the West Indies* (1871: chapter 1, 'Outward Bound')

Darton points out that the capital letters of the name were lost in the printing: 'by a typographical error [the name] has become more gruesome than it should be' (F. J. Harvey Darton, *Children's Books in England*, 3rd edn. rev. Brian Alderson (Cambridge: Cambridge University Press, 1982), 295 n.).

9 *grog-shop*: grog is a mixture of one part rum to three parts water. Vice Admiral Edward Vernon issued the first grog on 21 August 1740; prior to this the daily ration of rum was one pint of rum for men and a half-pint for boys. The name comes from the fact that Vernon was known as 'Old Grog' because he wore a grogram coat made of silk and wool/mohair and gum. (This is also the derivation of *groggy*.)

10 *silver fourpenny*: a groat, issued from *c.*1300 to 1561, and then irregularly until the mid-nineteenth century.

11 *Dry Tortugas*: a group of atolls 70 miles west of Key West in Florida. Tortuga is an island off the north coast of Haiti.

Spanish Main: the shores of the Caribbean Sea, from Florida to Venezuela (and by extension, the sea).

12 *having fallen down*: on the tricorn hat, the brim was pinned to the crown at each side and at the back.

powder: powdered wig. Wigs were fashionable from the reign (1610–43) of Louis XIII through to the end of the eighteenth century, when, in 1795, the British Government imposed a tax on the powder. The powder was made of starch, lavender, and orris root.

13 *low oath*: Stevenson wrote to Henley (24/25 Aug. 1881) 'the trouble is to work it off without oaths. Buccaneers without oaths—bricks without straw. But youth and the fond parent have to be consulted' (*Letters*, iii. 225).

clasp-knife: a folding knife with a locking blade.

assizes: judges from the King's Bench Division of the High Court travelled the country, setting up courts to try crimes more serious than those dealt with by the local Magistrates' Courts. Assizes were abolished in 1972.

14 *cutlass*: a short, heavy backsword, often with a curved blade, widely used by navies (and pirates).

17 *chine*: spine or backbone.

18 *Billy Bones*: Robert Leighton, an editor at *Young Folks* (said to be responsible for changing the title of the novel from *The Sea-Cook* to *Treasure Island*), claimed that this is an echo of the name 'Billy Bo'son' which Stevenson had read in a serial that overlapped with *Treasure Island*. The story was refuted by Dr Japp on the grounds that Stevenson had not seen a copy of *Young Folks* before beginning to write (Glenda Norquay, 'Trading Texts: Negotiations of the Professional and the Popular in the Case of *Treasure Island*', in Richard Ambrosini and Richard Dury (eds.), *R.L. Stevenson: Writer of Boundaries* (Madison: University of Wisconsin

Press, 2006), 61–2). Stevenson's letters show that he had read a copy of *Young Folks* by early September. 1881 (*Letters*, iii. 228).

opened a vein: bloodletting was a regular medical procedure until well into the nineteenth century. It had been practised for over three thousand years, on the basis of various theories of bodily humours and astrology, and was a treatment for apoplexy because it supposedly reduced blood pressure. The median basilic vein in the crook of the elbow was commonly used (hence Dr Livesey ripping the sleeve). Mrs Isabella Beeton, in her *The Book of Household Management* (1861), gives instructions for bleeding (para. 2605): 'In cases of great emergency, such as the strong kind of apoplexy, and when a surgeon cannot possibly be obtained for some considerable time, the life of the patient depends almost entirely on the fact of his being bled or not.'

Black Dog: 'black dog' was a supposed form of the devil, and is an idiomatic phrase for depression. It was also 'an early 18th-century name for a counterfeit shilling or other "silver" coin made of pewter' (*Brewer's Dictionary of Phrase and Fable* (London: Cassell, 1999), 134–5).

like the man in the Bible: Judas. The Revd Dr Andrew Bishop suggests that the Doctor is quoting Acts 1: 25, when a new apostle is being sought 'that he may take part of this ministry and apostleship, from which Judas by transgression fell, that he might go to his own place' (King James Bible, 1611). Modern versions read 'to go where he belonged' or variants. (This line was added in the revision of the text of *Treasure Island*.)

20 *Yellow Jack*: yellow fever.

hulk on a lee shore: like a derelict ship stranded by an onshore wind (and see Glossary).

the horrors: delirium tremens, characterized by hallucinations.

noggin: a small cup, usually a quarter-pint.

21 *the black spot*: this appears to be an original idea of Stevenson's; it may echo the (alleged) practice of pirates accusing a man of treachery by showing him the Ace of Spades. It has moved into common parlance: in Arthur Ransome's *Swallows and Amazons* (1930, chapters 24–5) the children tip their Uncle Jim, alias Captain Flint, the Black Spot, but at no point does the author feel it necessary to explain the reference.

going about to get the wind of me: turning their ship so as to take the wind out of his sails (*not* to get the scent of).

Savannah: Flint dies at Key West in *Young Folks*. In a letter to W. E. Henley (24/25 Aug. 1881) Stevenson refers to the sea shanty, 'Yo-ho-ho and a bottle of rum' as 'a real buccaneer's song, only known to the crew of the late Captain Flint (died of rum at Key West, much regretted, friends will please accept this intimation)' (*Letters*, iii. 225).

peach: betray, inform on.

23 *dreadful looking figure*: Stevenson made an attempt to reuse Blind Pew and the searching of the sea chest in a play written in collaboration with W. E. Henley, *Admiral Guinea*, in 1884. He later rejected the play, describing it as 'a low, black, dirty, blackguard, ragged piece: vomitable in many parts—simply vomitable. Pew is in places, a reproach of both art and man' (*Letters*, v. 101). In that play, Captain Gaunt elaborates on Pew's career: 'I know your life; and first and last, it is one broadside of wickedness. You were a porter in a school, and beat a boy to death; you ran for it, turned slaver . . . In five years' time you made yourself the terror and abhorrence of your messmates. The worst hands detested you . . . Who was it stabbed the Portuguese and made off inland with his miserable wife? Who, raging drunk on rum, clapped fire to the baracoons [wooden slave-pens] and burned the poor soul-less creatures in their chains? Ay, you were a scandal to the Guinea coast . . . and when at last I sent you ashore, a marooned man—your shipmates, devils as they were, cheering and rejoicing to be quit of you' (i. 1).

24 *thundering apoplexy*: a severe stroke or brain haemorrhage.

27 *pigtail tobacco*: [black] chewing or smoking tobacco, perique, twisted into a pigtail shape and sometimes soaked with rum.

gully: sheath-knife.

canikin: small drinking vessel.

28 *doubloons . . . pieces of eight*: the doubloon was a Spanish gold coin, originally worth 32 reales; louis d'ors were first struck in the reign of Louis XIII, 1640; an 'eight' was a Spanish coin stamped '8R' (8 reales). Dear and Kemp note that 'such vast numbers of [pieces of eight] were minted in Spain during the 17th and 18th centuries that they were accepted almost as a world currency during that time' (427).

31 *Flint's fist*: handwriting.

glim: candle or taper.

hang a leg: to hold back, to be reluctant or tardy (*SOED*).

32 *Georges*: slang for coins in general; originally a coin with the image of St George, the 'George noble', introduced by Henry VIII: a half-crown.

36 *Jim Hawkins*: possibly named (ironically) after Sir John Hawkins (1532–95) by turns slave-trader in the Caribbean, treasurer of the Royal Navy (1571–95), and one of the three vice admirals who defeated the Spanish Armada. A Captain Hawkins was captured by the pirate Captain Francis Spriggs (*Pyrates*, 353).

Blackbeard: Edward Teach or Thatch (d. 1718) is described in *The History of the Pyrates*: 'He . . . had sailed some Time out of Jamaica in Privateers . . . [His] beard was black, which he suffered to grow of an extravagant Length; as to Breadth, it came up to his Eyes; he was accustomed to twist it with Ribbons, in small Tails . . . and turn them about his ears.' On one occasion he fired pistols at random into his crew, wounding the Master of his ship, Israel Hands, on the grounds that 'if he did not now and then kill one of them, they would forget who he was'; on another he decided to make his own hell below decks, confined his crew there, and burned brimstone 'and other combustible Matter' to see who could survive longest (71, 84, 85). Stevenson featured him in *The Master of Ballantrae* (chapter 3):

> Their leader was a horrible villain, with his face blacked and his whiskers curled in ringlets; Teach, his name; a most notorious pirate. He stamped about the deck, raving and crying out that his name was Satan, and his ship was called Hell. There was something about him like a wicked child or a half-witted person, that daunted me beyond expression. . . . Early next day we smelled him burning sulphur in his cabin and crying out of "Hell, hell!" which was well understood among the crew, and filled their minds with apprehension. Presently he comes on deck, a perfect figure of fun, his face blacked, his hair and whiskers curled, his belt stuck full of pistols; chewing bits of glass so that the blood ran down his chin, and brandishing a dirk.

rum-puncheon: a cask.

Port of Spain: capital of what is now Trinidad and Tobago.

38 *account-book*: perhaps an echo of Blackbeard's journal: 'in Black-beard's Journal, which was taken, there were several Memorandums of the following Nature, found writ with his own Hand.—*Such a Day, Rum all out:—Our Company somewhat sober:—A damn'd Confusion amongst us!—Rogues a plotting;—great Talk of Separation.—So I look'd sharp for a Prize; such a Day took one, with a great deal of Liquor on board, so kept The Company hot, damn'd hot, then all things went well again* (*Pyrates*, 86).

a fat dragon standing up: the shape of the island may resemble Haiti; Norman Island in the British Virgin Islands claims to be the model for Treasure Island (complete with Pirates' Bar) (Harold F. Watson, *Coasts of Treasure Island: A Study of The Backgrounds And Sources for Robert Louis Stevenson's Romance of The Sea* (San Antonio, Tex.: Naylor, 1969), 126–7).

39 *play duck and drake with*: from the game of skimming flat stones over water.

41 *schooner . . . Hispaniola*: a schooner is generally a two-masted, fore-and-aft rigged ship. The first illustrated edition of *Treasure Island* (the 5th, 1885) used pictures by George Roux from the 1885 French edition, in which the artist corrected Stevenson's 'deliberate anachronism'. Stevenson wrote: 'It was a blow to me . . . to find the *Hispaniola* figured as a full-rigged brig [a two-masted, square-rigged ship]; for in the days of John Silver, there was no such vessel as a schooner known upon the seas. But how could Jim manoeuvre a brig around the island? And how could the author have superintended him? A schooner it had to be; for it was in a schooner that this very fresh-water nautical novelist had acquired his shallow knowledge' (Kevin Carpenter, 'R. L. Stevenson on the *Treasure Island* Illustrations', *Notes and Queries*, 277 (NS 294) (Aug. 1982), 325). Stevenson may have

been mistaken here: two-masted boats with this rigging have been built since the sixteenth century. Dear and Kemp cite the launch of the first specific craft of this type at Gloucester, Mass., in 1713 (495); William Falconer's *Dictionary of the Marine* (1769) shows a two-masted schooner (*Pyrates*, xlviii). The *Hispaniola* has two masts, the main, and, in front of it, the mizzen. Presumably, by the mizzen-mast, Stevenson meant the fore-mast, as the *Hispaniola* has a fore-sail and a bowsprit (to carry foresails), and a jib-boom (for jibs flown from the fore-mast stays), while the waist (where the apple-barrel sits) is customarily between the fore-mast and the mainmast. Silver's description of the three hills on Treasure Island, with the mizzen astern of, and smaller than, the mainmast, shows that Stevenson was aware of the customary terminology.

Hispaniola was the name of a Caribbean Island (now Haiti and the Dominican Republic), which was the centre of English and French privateering in the late sixteenth century.

42 *odious French*: Britain was at war with France on at least six occasions in the eighteenth century. The date of the *Hispaniola*'s voyage must be around 1750, as it is after the battle of Fontenoy (1745), while Silver, who is 50, sailed with Captain England, who died in 1720.

Long John Silver: Stevenson wrote to W. E. Henley in May 1883: 'It was the sight of your maimed strength and masterfulness that begot John Silver in *Treasure Island*. Of course, he is not in any other quality or feature the least like you' (*Letters*, iv. 129). Harman suggests that Silver's character might owe a debt to Stevenson's experience at a restaurant in the USA in 1879: 'for who is [Jules] Simoneau like so much as the "sea-cook" Silver, with his rough kindness and his rattling among the pans, and who more like the pirates of the Spy-Glass inn or the Admiral Benbow than the scruffy male clientele of Simoneau's restaurant, Monterey?' (Claire Harman, *Robert Louis Stevenson: A Biography* (London: HarperCollins, 2005), 184–5). In R. M. Ballantyne's *The Coral Island*, the boy heroes find evidence of previous occupation of the island in the form of a stump of a tree, with the initials 'J.S.' carved upon it (chapter 6). In the eighteenth century, silver (as opposed to gold) connoted debasement, and 'silver-beggar' or 'silver-lurker' was 'a tramp with forged papers showing he had suffered great losses through shipwreck' (Naomi J. Wood, 'Gold Standards and Silver Subversions: Treasure Island and the Romance of Money', *Children's Literature*, 26 (1998), 66). In Thomas Rowlandson's (1756–1827) 'Ranks in Nelson's Navy' (1799), presently in the National Maritime Museum, the Sea-Cook is shown as having one wooden leg (the left). Captain Edward England once encountered 'a fellow with a terrible Pair of Whiskers and a Wooden Leg, being stuck around with pistols' (*Pyrates*, 121).

the immortal Hawke: Edward, first Baron Hawke (1705–81), First Lord of the Admiralty 1766–71; notable for his victory over the French fleet at the battle of Quiberon Bay, near St Nazaire, in November in 1759. This was one of the military victories that inspired the Royal Navy's official march, 'Hearts of Oak' by William Boyce and David Garrick. The action in which Silver is supposed to have lost his leg would have been either the battle of Toulon in 1744 or the second battle of Cape Finisterre in 1747.

43 *come post*: post-haste, as quickly as possible.

47 *Morgan*: reminiscent of the Welsh pirate Sir Henry Morgan (*c*.1635–88), who was described on the title page of Esquemeling's *The Buccaneers of America* (trans. 1684–5) as 'our Jamaican hero, who sacked Porto Bello, burnt Panama, etc.'. Morgan ended his life prosperously, and took Esquemeling's English printers to court for libel.

rolling his quid: moving his piece of chewing tobacco in his mouth. 'Quid' is a form of 'cud'.

48 *son of a Dutchman*: the derogatory references to the Dutch derive from the Anglo-Dutch wars of the seventeenth century. 'Dutchman' is also sailors' jargon for Scandinavian and German sailors.

49 *shiver my timbers*: a shock, as when a ship strikes an obstacle. Dear and Kemp note that 'although the saying has an obviously nautical origin, and is widely attributed to seamen by many writers of sea stories, it is unlikely that it was used much, if at all, by seamen afloat or ashore' (529).

take my davy: affidavit.

quart of ale with a toast in it: a spiced slice of toast was used to flavour wine or ale. By extension, 'any person . . . to whom a company is requested to drink', from the idea that the toast (the name) flavoured the drink: hence '*to toast someone*' (*SOED*).

51 *Captain Smollett*: perhaps named after Tobias Smollett (1721–71) the sardonic author of *The Adventures of Roderick Random* (1748) which contains early elements of the sea story. Smollett was a surgeon's mate at the unsuccessful attempt to take the Spanish-held Caribbean port of Cartagena in 1741, led by Admiral Edward Vernon ('Old Grog').

53 *the mountain and the mouse*: a great effort for a small result, from Aesop's *Fables*, and Horace's *Ars Poetica* (first century BC): 'mountains will go into labour, and a silly little mouse will be born'.

54 *sparred passage*: made from planks with spaces between them.

55 *long brass nine*: a bronze gun (polished to look like brass) firing a 9 lb. ball. In Captain Marryat's *The Pirate* (1836) the pirate schooner has a 'brass' swivel-mounted gun: 'indeed, no schooner could carry a long iron gun of that calibre' (chapter 8). Writing to W. E. Henley in September 1881, Stevenson suggested that he shouldn't read 'noble old Fred's *Pirate* anyhow; it is written in sand with a salt spoon . . . It's *damnable*, Henley. I don't go much on *The Sea Cook*; but it's a little fruitier than the *Pirate* by Cap'n Mary-at' (*Letters*, iii. 231).

56 *Now, Barbecue, tip us a stave*: give us a song. The term 'barbecue', meaning a cooking-frame, originated in the Caribbean, possibly in Haiti or Hispaniola,

from Carib, Arawak, or Taíno languages. Its earliest use in English prose may be when the eponymous slave-hero of Aphra Behn's *Oroonoko* (1688) is killed by being barbecued and dismembered. William Dampier uses 'barbecue' in *New Voyage Around the World* (1699) in the sense of a raised sleeping platform.

57 *Israel Hands*: Stevenson may have taken the name from the Master of Blackbeard's ship. He was about to be executed, when a ship arrived at Virginia with a pardon for pirates; Captain Johnson concludes that he 'was alive some Time ago in *London*, begging his bread' (*Pyrates*, 72, 84).

58 *Cap'n England*: Edward England (originally Seeger), a pirate who was deposed by his crew in 1720 and marooned on the island of Mauritius, for the lenient treatment of a prisoner: 'Captain *England* having sided too much to Captain *Macka's* Interest, was a means of making him many Enemies among the Crew; they thinking such good usage inconsistent with their Polity' (*Pyrates*, 122). He escaped from the island on a makeshift boat, and died in poverty in 1720.

Madagascar . . . Portobello: all these ports were refuges for pirates associated with Captain England.

three hundred and fifty thousand of 'em: Stevenson takes this episode from *Pyrates*: 'Spanish Galleons—or the Plate Fleet, had been cast away in the Gulf of *Florida* . . . The *Spaniards* had recovered some Millions of Pieces of Eight and had carry'd it all to the *Havana*; but they had at present about 350000 Pieces of Eight in Silver [which was] deposited in a Store-House.' This was looted by a small fleet led by Captain Henry Jennings, who later accepted an amnesty, and died a rich plantation owner (35–6).

boarding of the Viceroy of the Indies out of Goa: England's crew, having captured a damaged Portuguese ship, in April 1721, ransomed the viceroy of Goa, who was on board, for 2,000 dollars (*Pyrates*, 130).

and not be mucked: a quotation from the King James Bible Apocrypha: Sirah (or Ecclesiasticus) 13: 1: 'He that toucheth pitch shall be defiled therewith; and he that hath fellowship with a proud man shall be like unto him.' On p. 77, Silver takes to Tom 'like pitch'.

59 *duff*: flour boiled in water, sometimes with added suet, molasses, raisins (plums), or egg. 'Duff is a former northern pronunciation of 'dough' (John Ayto, *A Gourmet's Guide: Food and Drink from A to Z* (Oxford: Oxford University Press, 1994), 269). It is first recorded in R. H. Dana's *Two Years Before the Mast* (1840): 'To enhance the value of the Sabbath to the crew, they are allowed on that day a pudding, or, as it is called, a "n." This is nothing more than flour boiled with water, and eaten with molasses. It is very heavy, dark, and clammy, yet it is looked upon as a luxury, and really forms an agreeable variety with salt beef and pork. Many a rascally captain has made friends of his crew by allowing them duff twice a week on the passage home' (chapter 3).

60 *upon me alone*: this incident reflects a story told by Stevenson about his

grandfather in his *Records of a Family of Engineers* (1893). The captain of one of the ships that Robert Stevenson used, Soutar, had 'a stronghold in my grandfather's estimation . . . My father and uncles, with the devilish penetration of the boy, were far from being deceived; and my father, indeed, was favoured with an object-lesson not to be mistaken. He had crept one rainy night into an apple-barrel on deck, and from this place of ambush overheard Soutar and a comrade conversing in their oilskins. The smooth sycophant of the cabin had wholly disappeared, and the boy listened with wonder to a vulgar and truculent ruffian' (Tusitala Edition (1924), xix. 194). Carpenter identifies a similar incident in chapter 2 of *Rob the Rover* (1871) (Kevin Carpenter, *Desert Isles and Pirate Islands, The Island Theme in Nineteenth-Century English Juvenile Fiction: A Survey and Bibliography* (Frankfurt am Main: Peter Lang, 1984), 83).

61 *quartermaster*: officially in charge of steering and stowage; in pirate ships, he was elected, and was second only to the captain, and responsible for discipline. If men could not resolve a quarrel aboard, the quartermaster would take them ashore for a duel (*Pyrates*, 212).

a master surgeon . . . Royal Fortune and so on: Captain Bartholomew [John] Roberts (1662–1722) ('Barti Ddu') began his career with Howel Davis, and was a notorious pirate in Surinam and the West Indies. He captured a frigate, *Onslow*, at Sestos and renamed it *Royal Fortune* (*Pyrates*, 218); he was killed in a battle with the English man-of-war *Swallow*. The 'articles' of Roberts's pirate code have survived; they included: 'IX: No man to talk of breaking up their Way of Living, till each had shared a 1000*l*. If in order to do this, any Man should lose a Limb, or become a Cripple in their Service, he was to have 800 Dollars, out of the publick Stock, and for lesser Hurts, proportionably' (*Pyrates*, 212). Roberts's crew were tried (March–April 1722), at Corso Castle, a British fort on the Gold Coast of the Gulf of Guinea: fifty-two were hanged. The ship's surgeon was one Peter Scudamore, who, it was claimed, signed the pirate 'articles' voluntarily (*Pyrates*, 272). He tried to persuade the pirates to continue: 'It was better venturing to . . . run down the Coast, and raise a new Company, than to proceed to Cape *Corso*, and be hang'd like Dogs, and Sun dry'd' (*Pyrates*, 247).

Cassandra: a ship captured by Captain England off Madagascar, August 1720.

Davis: Howel Davis (*c.*1690–1719) was the mate of Captain England, and had a brief independent career. Davis was notable for his stratagems, such as pretending that a captured crew was his own, and may have suggested Long John Silver's plans (*Pyrates*, 166–78, 191–3).

62 *feared of me*: in J. M. Barrie's *Peter and Wendy* (1911), Captain Hook is described as 'Blackbeard's bo'sun . . . He is the worst of them all. He is the only man of whom Barbecue was afraid' (chapter 4). Also in Hook's crew

is Bill Jukes 'who got six dozen on the *Walrus* from Flint before he would drop the bag of miodores [coins]' (chapter 5).

63 *double Dutchmen*: 'double Dutch' = gibberish.

64 *blunt*: *SOED* records blunt as 'ready money' from 1812.

64 *like the devil at prayers*: this reference (which was not in *Young Folks*) may derive from Stevenson's religious upbringing by Alison Cunningham. Geoff Fox suggests that it may refer to the idea that Satan is always present when believers are at prayer, and can undermine their thoughts. The Revd Canon Guy Wilkinson detects a reference to the temptations of Christ, and the Lord's Prayer. It may (also) refer to Robert Burns's poem 'Address to the Deil' (1785):

> When twilight did my graunie summon,
> To say her pray'rs, douse, honest woman!
> Aft'yont the dyke she's heard you bummin,
> Wi' eerie drone . . .

65 *pannikin*: a small metal drinking vessel, usually tinned iron (*SOED*).

67 *"Capt. Kidd's Anchorage"*: William Kidd (*c.*1645–1701), British captain turned pirate. He is reputed to have buried treasure at Gardiner's Island, between the western arms of Long Island, New York State.

72 *though the man . . . than was down in the chart*: the man judging the depth of the water by means of a lead-weighted line found it was always deeper than the chart indicated.

76 *strange land that I was in*: the appearance of Treasure Island may have been suggested either by Edinburgh as seen from the Pentland Hills, or by the island of Unst in the Shetlands, the most northerly populated island in the UK (which has similar tides and anchorages) (David Barnett, *A Stevenson Study: Treasure Island* (1924), 10–16 (quoted in Roger G. Swearingen, *The Prose Writings of Robert Louis Stevenson: A Guide* (London: Macmillan, 1980), 68)). The Muckle Flugga lighthouse on Unst was built by Thomas and David Stevenson in 1858. Stevenson said that Treasure Island was 'not in the Pacific. I only wish myself that I knew where it was . . . However, it is generally supposed to be in the West Indies' (*Sydney Morning Herald*, 14 February 1893).

Little did I suppose . . . live, or evergreen, oaks: rattlesnakes are confined to the American mainland, and live oaks are characteristic of the Monterey coastline.

78 *gleaming like a crumb of glass*: Fanny Stevenson noted that this phrase 'which has often been quoted with approbation, always made my husband wince when he read it. "A crumb," he would repeat with scorn: "why a *crumb* of glass? better a piece—a bit, anything of glass but a crumb!" ' ('Prefatory Note' [to *Treasure Island*] (Tusitala Edition (1923), vol. ii, p. xxii)).

81 *nondescript*: a species that had not hitherto been described (early nineteenth century) (*SOED*).

82 *Ben Gunn*: the name Benjamin Gunn occurs in Johnson's *Pyrates*, and Gunn is a Caithness family name. The idea of the castaway may derive from Alexander Selkirk, the original of Robinson Crusoe; a copy of *A Cruising Voyage Around the World* by Woodes Rogers, who rescued Selkirk from his island, was owned by Stevenson's father.

tarry gaskin: trousers or stockings. In a letter in early March 1882, Thomas Stevenson objected to part of the novel as it had appeared in *Young Folks*: 'I object to the goatskin dress which is merely R. Crusoe . . . He ought to have some tattered naval uniform, for a coat and ragged canvas.' (*Letters*, iii. 242 n.) Stevenson changed Gunn's appearance. Defoe describes Robinson Crusoe's clothes, thus:

> I have mentioned that I saved the skins of all the creatures that I killed . . . The first thing I made of these was a great cap for my head, with the hair on the outside, to shoot off the rain; and this I performed so well, that after this I made me a suit of clothes wholly of these skins, that is to say, a waistcoat, and breeches open at knees . . . I must not omit to acknowledge that they were wretchedly made; for if I was a bad carpenter, I was a worse tailor.

distant island: the 'Articles' signed by the crew of the pirate Captain John Phillips, of the *Revenge*, included the provision that 'If any Man offer to run away, or keep any Secret from the Company, he shall be maroon'd, with one Bottle of Powder, one Bottle of Water, one small Arm and Shot' (*Pyrates*, 342).

and oysters: *Young Folks* added, 'I can run the goats down upon my naked feet.' Stevenson's father objected (26 February 1882, *Letters*, iii. 242 n.) that this was from *Robinson Crusoe*, and Stevenson removed it. Thomas Stevenson, however, misremembered Defoe's novel: Crusoe shoots and traps the goats, and on one occasion runs to save a kid from his dog, but does not run them down.

cheese by the stone: a stone of cheese would have weighed 16 lb.

83 *chuck-farthen*: William Hogarth's *Industry and Idleness*, plate 3, 'The Idle 'Prentice at Play in the Church Yard During Divine Service' (30 September 1747), shows a game that could be 'chuck-farthen'. Players toss coins towards a hole; the one whose coin lands nearest to the hole gathers all the coins, throws them together at the hole, and keeps those that fall into it. The second most accurate player then repeats the process until all the coins are gone. It is the first game described in one of the earliest of all children's books, John Newbery's *A Little Pretty Pocket Book* (1744), as 'The *great* A play': 'As you value your pence. | At the *hole* take your Aim; | Chuck all safely in. | And you'll win the game. MORAL. *Chuck-Farthing*, like Trade | Requires great Care; | The more you observe. | The better you'll fare.'

85 *in his goatskins*: Stevenson clearly forgot to alter this to match Gunn's change of clothes from *Young Folks*, described earlier.

for the fear of Benjamin Gunn: Stevenson's father suggested (26 February 1882) that the goats were too reminiscent of *Robinson Crusoe*; Stevenson replied (early March 1882): 'I cannot give up the goats: the phrase amuses me so much' (*Letters*, iii. 292). 'Mast-heading' was a punishment for midshipmen, who were sent to the top of a mast.

87 '*Lillibullero*': song in support of William of Orange during the deposition of James II in the Glorious Revolution of 1688. The words are said to derive from the Irish supporters of William. The implication may be that some of the pirates (like O'Brien, killed by Israel Hands) were Irish. It is said that some pirate captains disliked Irish sailors, to the extent that landsmen would pretend to be Irish to avoid being recruited.

88 *primed*: flintlock weapons were loaded (or recharged) by pouring powder into the barrel, followed by a ball wrapped in paper or cloth, and ramming this down. The gun was then 'primed' by pouring a small quantity of powder into the pan, which was connected to the closed end of the barrel by a small hole, and closing the cover, or 'frizzen' over it. The gun was then cocked, and when the trigger was pulled, the flint struck a steel, simultaneously opening the frizzen and exposing the powder in the pan; the spark ignited this powder, which ignited the main charge, via the small hole.

musketry: the musket was the predecessor of the rifle, a long-barrelled flintlock muzzle-loader, fired from the shoulder, accurate (for human-sized targets) up to about 100 metres, and potentially lethal up to 200 metres.

Duke of Cumberland . . . Fontenoy: William Augustus (1721–65), youngest son of George II, was defeated by the French at the battle of Fontenoy, May 1745. After defeating the forces of 'the Young Pretender', Charles Edward Stuart ('Bonnie Prince Charlie') at the battle of Culloden in 1746, he was nicknamed 'Butcher' Cumberland for his actions against Jacobite soldiers and civilians. Critics have suggested that Stevenson's choice of an anti-Scottish general reflected his own rebellious nature.

nigh-hand: close to; nearly.

91 *gallipot*: a small, earthenware glazed pot.

93 *Jack ashore*: drunk, hence unsteady; an expression recorded from the late nineteenth century. There is a sea song, 'Get Up Jack, John Sit Down' or 'Jolly Rovin' Tar' which refers to this:

> When Jack's ashore he'll make his way to some old boarding house
> He's welcomed in with rum and gin, likewise with fork and scouse
> And he'll spend and he'll spend and never offend, 'til he lies drunk
> on the ground . . .

99 *six bells*: 3 p.m.

100 *Jolly Roger*: pirate ships often flew black or red flags. Captain Edward

England's flag featured a skull and crossbones. Dear and Kemp, however, claim that 'there is no evidence that such a flag was ever flown by a pirate ship at sea' (292). 'Roger' was slang for a thief or rogue.

101 *piping the eye*: to shed tears (originally nautical slang) from 1779 or 1789 (*SOED*).

105 *'Come, Lasses and Lads'*: traditional English song (c.1670). A shortened version formed the words for one of Randolph Caldecott's *Picture Books* (1884). It begins:

> Come lasses and lads, get leave of your dads
> And away to the maypole hie
> For every fair has a sweetheart there
> And the fiddler's standing by.

106 *sheet in the wind's eye*: the first stage of drunkenness, equivalent to a rope used to trim the sails (a sheet), flapping loose, directly away from the wind. The third stage of drunkenness is 'three sheets in [or to] the wind'.

107 *Davy Jones*: Tobias Smollett in *The Adventures of Peregrine Pickle* (1751) describes him thus: 'This same Davy Jones, according to the mythology of sailors, is the fiend that presides over all the evil spirits of the deep, and is often seen in various shapes, perching among the rigging on the eve of hurricanes, shipwrecks, and other disasters, to which a seafaring life is exposed; warning the devoted wretch of death and woe' (chapter 13).

111 *rifle-ball*: probably an anachronism. Rifled muskets were not commonly used until the nineteenth century.

bit the dust: an expression first recorded in Tobias Smollett's translation of Le Sage's *The Adventures of Gil Blas of Santillane* (1748, iii. 2).

112 *hanger*: a short sword hung from a belt.

117 *French leave*: to leave without permission; from an eighteenth-century French custom of leaving without saying goodbye to the host.

118 *jolly-boat*: possibly a mistake by Stevenson, as the jolly-boat was destroyed earlier (p. 93).

coracle: Welsh *corwgl* or Irish *curach*; a boat made of animal skins and wicker work.

121 *What put to sea with seventy-five*: an original couplet by Stevenson.

124 *sea lions*: these animals are found off California, but *not* in the Atlantic Ocean.

127 *water-breaker*: a small keg.

132 *Execution Dock*: located below the low-tide mark at Wapping, between Wapping New Stairs and King Edward's Stairs. The bodies were left until three tides had washed over them, and those of notorious pirates

were preserved in tar and hung in chains at the mouth of the Thames. Executions continued into the nineteenth century.

138 *fouled*: entangled; in a difficult situation. When an object gets between the target and the firing ship (and 'Hands was Flint's gunner').

139 *younker*: youngster, young gentleman.

145 *broadcloth*: high-quality, double-width, plain-woven cloth.

link: a torch made of tow and pitch, etc. (*SOED*).

147 *dog-watch*: a mistake by Stevenson. The 'dog watches' are from 4 p.m. to 6 p.m., and 6 p.m. to 8 p.m.

cross-trees to kelson: from the highest to the lowest parts of a ship.

148 *faked*: stole (*SOED* 1812).

149 *cock his hat athwart my hawse*: insult or challenge me to my face.

150 *all marched out*: the principles of the pirates' codes of behaviour here reflect the 'Articles' found in *Pyrates*: Captain Roberts' (11–12), Captain Lowther's (307–8), and Captain John Phillips' (342–3). For example, the procedure of Phillips and his crew was as follows: 'The first thing they now had to do, was to choose officers, draw up Articles, and settle their little Commonwealth, to prevent Disputes and Ranglings afterwards . . . One of them writ out the following Articles and all swore to 'em upon a Hatchet for want of a Bible' (342).

caulker: a strong drink (*SOED*, 1808); to caulk is to prevent leaks in a ship.

156 '*Without are dogs and murderers*': King James Bible, Revelation 22:

> 13: I am Alpha and Omega, the beginning and the end, the first and the last.
> 14: Blessed are they that do his commandments, that they may have right to the tree of life, and may enter in through the gates into the city.
> 15: For without are dogs, and sorcerers, and whoremongers, and murderers, and idolaters, and whosoever loveth and maketh a lie.

159 *gammon*: to cheat or hoax.

161 *holus bolus*: all in a lump, all at once.

163 *fried junk*: salt meat used on long voyages (junk also means pieces of old cable or rope).

so careless of the morrow: perhaps an ironic echo of King James Bible, Matthew 6: 34: 'Take therefore no thought for the morrow: for the morrow shall take thought for the things of itself. Sufficient unto the day is the evil thereof.'

165 *clear above its neighbours*: Stevenson seems to have had Californian Redwood trees in mind.

166 *nutmeg trees*: an anachronism. Nutmeg trees, natives of Molucca in Indonesia, were first introduced into the Caribbean by the British in the

early nineteenth century. Nutmeg and mace are now major exports from Grenada.

a human skeleton: despite Stevenson's recollection in 'My First Book', the skull which acts as a pointer to Captain Kidd's buried treasure in Edgar Allan Poe's story 'The Gold Bug' (1843) is only incidental to the crux of the story—the deciphering of a cipher. However, two skeletons are found when the searchers are digging for the treasure.

167 *numskull*: head of a dull person.

copper doit: a small Dutch coin (hence a very small sum).

170 *airily and sweetly*: possibly an echo of Ferdinand in *The Tempest*, I. ii:

> Where should this music be? I' the air or the earth?
> It sounds no more . . .
> This music crept by me upon the waters,
> Allaying both their fury and my passion
> With its sweet air.

Darby M'Graw: compare Darby Mullins in Captain Kidd's crew. With Kidd and five others, he was 'executed at *Execution-dock*, and afterwards hung up in Chains . . . down the River, where their Bodies hung exposed for many Years' (*Pyrates*, 451).

173 *to probation*: examination, proof.

175 *teetotum*: a spinning-top.

strangling: choking or suffocating.

176 *ambushed*: prepared to ambush; lying in wait.

179 *moidores and sequins*: moidores were Portuguese coins minted between 1640 and 1742; sequins were Italian and Turkish coins, *c.* thirteenth century.

182 *quit of him*: in an unsigned review of *Treasure Island* in *The Athenaeum* (2927 (1 Dec. 1885), 700) Arthur John Butler wrote: 'Boys . . . will demur to [Stevenson's] philosophic rejection of poetical justice in allowing the arch-scoundrel to escape the fate which overtakes all his accomplices. In real life John Silver would hardly have got off; he certainly ought not to do so in fiction' (Paul Maixner (ed.), *Robert Louis Stevenson: The Critical Heritage* (London: Routlcdge and Kegan Paul, 1981), 130–1).

183 *wain-ropes*: wagon-ropes.

APPENDIX 1

186 *ingratitude*: Shakespeare, 'Song' from *As You Like It* (II. ii. 7):

> Blow, blow, thou winter wind,
> Thou art not so unkind
> As man's ingratitude.

187 *map of an island*: Lloyd Osbourne gives a different account in his 'Note' to *Treasure Island* in the Tusitala Edition (1923, vol. ii, p. xviii):

> one rainy morning, busy with a box of paints, I happened to be tinting the map of an island I had drawn. Stevenson came in as I was finishing it, and with his affectionate interest in everything I was doing, leaned over my shoulder, and was soon elaborating the map, and naming it. . . . My stepfather took it away, and the next day at noon I was called mysteriously up to his bedroom (he always spent his mornings writing in bed), and the first thing I saw was my beloved map lying on the coverlet . . . I was told to sit down while my step-father took up some sheets of manuscript, and began to read aloud the first chapter of *Treasure Island*.

188 *Footprints which perhaps another*: cf. Henry Wadsworth Longfellow, 'A Psalm on Life':

> Lives of great men all remind us
> We can make our lives sublime,
> And, departing, leave behind us
> Footprints on the sands of time.

Dr Japp: Alexander Japp (1836–1905), biographer of Thomas de Quincey. He denied having been 'charged . . . to unearth new writers'.

189 *'Hand and Spear!'*: an inn at Weybridge where the Stevensons stayed between Braemar and Davos (*Letters*, iii. 231).

judged a failure: *The Amateur Emigrant*, which Thomas Stevenson thought 'the worst thing you have done' and 'entirely unworthy' (Harman, *Robert Louis Stevenson*: *A Biography*, 215–16).

M. du Boisgobey: 'Fortuné de Boisgobey' (1824–91), writer for the feuilleton section of French newspapers. He wrote detective novels, and took over the character of Lecoq, one of the first detectives, from Émile Gaboriau. Julian Symons noted that, 'although *The Times* praised his facility in creating incidents and unravelling plots, he is almost purely a sensational writer' (*Bloody Murder* (London: Faber and Faber, 1972), 62).

John Addington Symonds: (1840–93), author of works on Renaissance Italy, and long-time resident at Davos.

190 *without woodcuts*: the serial in *Young Folks* had one picture of Billy Bones and Black Dog, and seven ornamental letters at the beginning of chapters.

GLOSSARY OF NAUTICAL TERMS

Sources of definitions include:

I. C. B. Dear and Peter Kemp, *The Oxford Companion to Ships and the Sea*, 2nd edn. (Oxford: Oxford University Press, 2005).

Wilfred Granville, *A Dictionary of Sailors' Slang* (London: André Deutsch, 1962).

W. Clark Russell, *Sailors' Language: A Collection of Sea-Terms and their Definitions* (London: Sampson Low, Marston, Seare and Rivington, 1883).

Treasure Island, ed. F. W. C. Hersey (Boston: Ginn, 1911).

aback [dead aback] ship being driven backwards or to leeward.

abeam at right angles to the keel.

A B master mariner able seaman; Master Mariner—a courtesy title until 1845, when the Board of Trade introduced examinations.

about ship on the opposite tack.

alow and aloft on or near the deck (sometimes or rarely meaning below deck); and anywhere in the rigging or on the masts.

astern behind the ship.

athwart across the course of a ship.

athwart-hawse across or crossing the bow of a ship, or across its anchor-cable.

avast [there] stop, hold.

backstay supporting rope (stay) leading from a mast down behind it to the side of the vessel.

batten down cover with hatches and tarpaulins (secured with battens).

beam-ends when a ship is heeled over so that its deck beams are nearly vertical, or the lee rail is submerged.

bearings [sunk to her bearings] the widest part of the ship below deck-level (or below where the deck joins the hull, the plank-shear).

beat to sail into the wind (to windward).

before the mast living quarters for seamen (not officers) in the forecastle.

bells the maritime day is divided into four-hour segments (watches) marked by the ringing of a bell, two for each hour, and one for the half-hour.

bilge [water] water that collects in lowest part of the inside of a ship, on either side of the keel.

blocks pulley wheels (sheaves) in wooden casings.
board [gone by the board] overboard.
boatswain [bo'sun] in charge of sails, rigging, and deck-work; his orders were sometimes given by whistle-signals (piping).
boom spar to which the bottom edge of a sail is attached.
bows front of a vessel, on each side of the central timber (stem).
bowse to tighten by pulling a rope.
bowsprit a spar projecting from the top of the bows to which the stays (ropes) to support the fore-topmast (an extension above the fore-mast, to carry higher sails) are connected.
brace part of the rigging under the bowsprit, with the forestay.
brace of [old] shakes a short time: when a sail shakes briefly when a ship comes into the wind (is turned to face the wind).
broach tendency of a ship sailing with the wind directly behind it to turn into the wind. To break open a barrel.
bulkhead partitions (sometimes watertight) between cabins, holds, etc.
bulwarks protective planking on stanchions along and above the sides of the upper deck.
bumboat a scavenger's boat, originally used to remove filth from ships lying in the Thames, and/or to carry provisions to ships; a floating stall. (From boom-boat—boats that moored under ships' booms in harbour.)
by the run naval equivalent of 'at the double'; quickly.

cap wooden block on top of a mast, or end of a boom.
capstan a vertical cylinder, often on the fore-deck for winding up the anchor or other heavy lifting: a large windlass.
capstan bars the bars or beams that the sailors push on to rotate the capstan; they fit into pigeonholes on the drumhead at the top of the capstan.
careen clean the bottom of a ship.
catspaw pattern on water caused by a slight breeze; or, a slight breeze.
caulker large dose of rum; to caulk is to prevent leaks in a ship.
chains platforms where a sailor stands to swing the lead—to judge the depth of the water by means of a lead-weighted line. Also the place where the shrouds are connected to the side of a ship, by dead-eyes and chain plates.
clever [craft] nimble, agreeable.
close-hauled sailing as close to the wind as possible (that is, as directly into the wind as the sails will allow).
clove hitch a knot used for tying ropes to spars, or tying up the painter (mooring rope) of a boat.
colour lines flag halyards.

colours national flag (ensign) flown at sea.
companion the framework and windows or skylights covering the steps to the cabin at the stern (rear) of a ship.
companion steps/stairs steps that lead into a cabin.
compasses [pair of] drawing implements for navigation.
con [the ship] give orders to the steersman.
coxswain helmsman of a ship's boat.
cross-trees wooden struts on masts to spread the shrouds or supporting ropes.
cutter [revenue cutter] a fast, single-masted ship with up to five sails, rigged like a sloop, carrying up to ten guns, usually long-barrelled nine-pounders for extra range. Later, any fast vessel.
cut-water the stem of a ship (the centre of the bows). Hence 'face'.

dead-eye 'dead man's eyes', blocks without moving pulley wheels that connect the shrouds (that support the masts, laterally) to the chain-plates on the side of the ship.
deadlights solid coverings for portholes.
death-haul final change of direction or adjustment of sails.
dirk naval dagger.
dog-watches two half-watches (periods of duty) (first dog and last dog) of two hours each, between 4 p.m. and 8 p.m.
double [the corner] to sail around or to the other side of a cape or point.
douse to lower or slacken in haste.
downhaul any rope for lowering a sail, especially for jib or staysail.
drawing when sails are full of wind; moving.

easting progress made towards the east.
ease off/ease off a point pay out a rope so that the ship sails less towards the wind.
easy-all instruction to oarsmen to stop rowing; relax.

fairway navigable channel.
fall off [the wind] to drift away to leeward.
fathom measurement of depth, and of ropes: about 6 feet.
fetch/fetch ahead to take/lay a course; the distance a vessel must sail to reach the open sea.
flying jib a sail set ahead of the jib, supported by a stay from the upward extension of the fore-mast (fore-topgallant) to an extension of the bow-sprit called the flying-jib boom.
foc's'le hands [forecastle hands] the crew.

forecastle/foc's'le space between the fore-decks; the crew's quarters.
fore-companion steps into forecastle.
fore-foot where the stem of the ship meets the keel.
fore-mast in a two-masted schooner, the smaller mast, nearer the bows.
fore-sail sail set in front of the fore-mast.
fore-sheets space between the forward thwart (rowing bench) and the bow of a boat.
fore-stay supporting rope (stay) leading from a mast down in front of it.

galley a ship's kitchen.
get the wind of/have the wind of get between a ship and the wind.
gig light, narrow clinker-built ship's boat, built for speed, with four or six oars.
go about to change tack, alter direction.
grog mixture of rum (or brandy) and water.
gunwale piece of timber running around the edge of the deck; projecting planking above the upper-deck level.

halyards ropes used to lower or raise sails or flags.
handed down lowered, hand over hand.
hand over hand as in climbing a rope or hauling in: rapidly.
handspike/handspike-end wooden bar, used as a lever for windlass (a small capstan used for raising the anchor).
harbour bar a bank of sand or silt across the mouth of a harbour that impedes ships.
haul trim sails so as to sail closer to (more directly into) the wind; **haul your wind** turn into the wind; **the wind hauled** shifted; **death-haul** final change of direction or adjustment of sails.
hawse distance, or space, between the bows of a ship and the anchor on the bottom of the sea.
hawser heavy rope used for towing or mooring ships.
haze punishing by forcing crew to do excessive, disagreeable, or unnecessary work.
head front of boat; direction of boat.
head sea waves moving towards the bow of a ship.
heel after end of a ship's keel.
helm the wood or metal bar (also *tiller*) that moves the rudder and steers the ship; all steering arrangements.
hold water stop the boat by holding the blades of the oars still in the water.

hold your luff keep the ship sailing as close to the wind (as directly into the wind) as possible: continue as you are.

hulk old, condemned or derelict ship.

in stays when a ship comes head to wind while tacking and hangs (or pauses) there.

irons [your ship's in irons] when a ship has stopped, head to wind; when it is caught in the wind and will not 'cast' or move onto the required tack.

jib-boom an extension to the bowsprit, to support the jibs.

jibs triangular sails attached to the stays (supporting ropes) of the fore-mast.

jolly-boat small, clinker-built, ship's boat.

keel-hauling punishment by attaching victim to a rope and pulling him from one side of a ship to another, under the keel.

keep the weather of stay out of the lee of.

kelson internal keel that supports the floors of a ship.

larboard left-hand side of the boat as viewed from the back or stern (lading or loading side); officially changed to 'port' side in 1844.

lash the tiller to tie the tiller into one position.

lay 'as a verb, much used by seamen' (Dear and Kemp): used in *Treasure Island* to mean the following:

- **a good lay** trick, action
- **lay 'em aboard** find them
- **lay 'em athwart** attack them
- **lay the ship to** heave to, stop
- **lay to** work hard, wait
- **lay to that** guarantee that, assure you of
- **lay your course [a p'int to windward]** set your course [closer to the wind]
- **laid a couple of points nearer the wind** sailed more effectively
- **laid her head** steered.

lee/lee side the sheltered side of a ship, island, etc.

lee shore a coast onto which the wind is blowing, therefore dangerous to ships, or difficult to escape from; **on a lee shore** stranded.

leeward away from the wind.

leeway/make leeway drifting while sailing close to the wind (towards the wind).

lubber clumsy person; as in *land-lubber*, sailors' derisory term for lands-person.

luff the leading edge of a sail; the weather side of a sail. As an order, to turn the ship's head closer to the wind; **hold your luff** keep the ship sailing as close to the wind (as directly into the wind) as possible: continue as you are.
lugger ship carrying a four-cornered sail, used for fishing and coastal trading.

master [sailing master] specialist navigator and ship handler whose function was to manoeuvre his ship into a position required by the captain.
mate responsible to the Captain for navigating and handling the ship.
mizzen [mast] rear mast of three of three-masted schooner.
mizzen-top platform at the top of the mizzen-mast.

nor'ard northward.

peak highest part of a sail.
p'int [point] to windward a compass point closer to the wind.
pipe all hands/piped on deck boatswain's signal for all sailors to come on deck.
port side left-hand side of the boat as viewed from the back or stern; previously 'larboard' or lading (loading) side.
put the helm hard up to turn a ship into the wind.

quadrant instrument for making measurements of altitude in navigation.
quarterdeck the deck around the mainmast, from which the captain and officers commanded the ship.
quartermaster assistant to master of the ship, dealing with steering and stowage.

reef/shake out another reef a reef is a part of a sail, that is tied in to reduce the size of the sail, or 'shaken out' to increase the size.
round-house square or rectangular cabin built on the quarterdeck (so called because one could walk round it).
rudder the blade operated by the tiller, that steers a ship.

sailing master [master] specialist navigator and ship handler whose function was to manoeuvre his ship into a position required by the captain.
schooner ship with fore-and-aft rig, usually two or three masts, first launched in 1713. Schooners required fewer crew than an equivalently sized brig.

scuppers/scupper holes drain holes cut through the bulwarks.
sea-calf common seal.
sheeted home sheet is a rope used to trim the sails; 'sheet in' means to 'harden' the sail (make it tauter); to extend sails to their full extent; sails set properly.
shipshape [and Bristol fashion] neat and tidy, normal.
shoal shallow.
short up [of anchor] nearly up.
shrouds fixed rigging that supports the masts from each side.
sidle to move or turn sideways.
slip your cable to allow an anchor cable to run out (attached to a buoy) rather than lifting the anchor. To escape, run away. Also, figuratively, to die.
sparred passage/sparred gallery passage made of planks with spaces between them.
spars wooden supports used in rigging.
split been shipwrecked.
stand by to go about be ready to change tack, so that the wind comes from the other side of the boat.
stay supporting rope.
steerage way having enough speed so that the rudder can steer the boat (or, so she can answer to her helm).
stem the foremost timbers of a ship's bows.
stern rear end of a ship.
stern-port window in stern.
stern sheets the part of an open boat behind the rear thwart (cross-bench).
strike colours lower the national flag or ensign.
swabs mops: from the person who washes the deck with a swab—a swabber; poorly behaved, low ranking.
swivel swivel-mounted gun.

tack the zigzag course taken by a sailing boat sailing towards the wind; change of course; distance sailed with the wind kept on one side of a vessel.
tarpaulins weatherproof canvas for protecting ships' gear, and made into clothes: hence 'tars' meaning sailors.
trades/run up the trades using the trade winds, which blow from the north-east in the northern hemisphere and the south-east in the southern hemisphere, between 25° and 30° North and South.
trim [the boat] balance.

truck the cap at the top of a mast, usually with holes to hold the flag-halyards (thin ropes).

waist the deck between the forecastle and the quarterdeck—between the fore-mast and the mainmast.

warped towed.

watch a four-hour period of duty (except for the two two-hour 'dog-watches'); the sailors on duty.

watch below rest or sleeping period; members of the crew not on active watch.

way forward movement of a ship.

weather bow the side of the bow facing the wind.

wind: get the wind of/have the wind of get between a ship and the wind; **the wind hauled** exchanged direction.

wind's eye where the wind is coming from; **fell into the wind's eye** came head-to-wind; windward towards the wind; into the wind, the way from which the wind blows.

yard-arm the outer end of the spar that crosses the mast horizontally to support the sails on a square-rigged ship, and used for signalling and hanging.

yaw movement away from the desired course produced by a following wind and sea (when the ship is going in the same direction as the wind and the sea).

A SELECTION OF **OXFORD WORLD'S CLASSICS**

Hans Christian Andersen	**Fairy Tales**
J. M. Barrie	**Peter Pan in Kensington Gardens** and **Peter and Wendy**
L. Frank Baum	**The Wonderful Wizard of Oz**
Frances Hodgson Burnett	**The Secret Garden**
Lewis Carroll	**Alice's Adventures in Wonderland** and **Through the Looking-Glass**
Carlo Collodi	**The Adventures of Pinocchio**
Kenneth Grahame	**The Wind in the Willows**
Anthony Hope	**The Prisoner of Zenda**
Thomas Hughes	**Tom Brown's Schooldays**

A SELECTION OF **OXFORD WORLD'S CLASSICS**

JANE AUSTEN	Emma Persuasion Pride and Prejudice Sense and Sensibility
MRS BEETON	Book of Household Management
ANNE BRONTË	The Tenant of Wildfell Hall
CHARLOTTE BRONTË	Jane Eyre
EMILY BRONTË	Wuthering Heights
WILKIE COLLINS	The Moonstone The Woman in White
JOSEPH CONRAD	Heart of Darkness and Other Tales The Secret Agent
CHARLES DARWIN	The Origin of Species
CHARLES DICKENS	Bleak House David Copperfield Great Expectations Hard Times
GEORGE ELIOT	Middlemarch The Mill on the Floss
ELIZABETH GASKELL	North and South
THOMAS HARDY	Jude the Obscure Tess of the d'Urbervilles
WALTER SCOTT	Ivanhoe
MARY SHELLEY	Frankenstein
ROBERT LOUIS STEVENSON	Strange Case of Dr Jekyll and Mr Hyde and Other Tales
BRAM STOKER	Dracula
WILLIAM MAKEPEACE THACKERAY	Vanity Fair
OSCAR WILDE	The Picture of Dorian Gray